Stolen Moments:

Erotic Interludes 2

What Reviewers Say About BOLD STROKES Authors

2

KIM BALDWIN

"Her...crisply written action scenes, juxtaposition of plotlines, and smart dialogue make this a story the reader will absolutely enjoy and long remember."—**Arlene Germain**, book reviewer for the *Lambda Book Report* and the *Midwest Book Review*

Hunter's Pursuit is a "...fierce first novel, an action-packed thriller pitting deadly professional killers against each other. Baldwin's fast-paced plot comes...leavened, as every intelligent adventure novel's excesses ought to be, with some lovin'. Even as she fends off her killers,...the heroine...finds the woman she wants by her side — and in her bed."—**Richard Labonte**, Book Marks, *Q Syndicate*, May 2005

2

ROSE BEECHAM

"...a mystery writer with a delightful sense of humor, as well as an eye for an interesting array of characters..."—*MegaScene*

"...her characters seem fully capable of walking away from the particulars of whodunit and engaging the reader in other aspects of their lives."—*Lambda Book Report*

2

JANE FLETCHER

"...a natural gift for rich storytelling and world-building...one of the best fantasy writers at work today."—**Jean Stewart**, author of the Isis series

"In *The Walls of Westernfort*, Fletcher spins a captivating story about youthful idealism, honor, and courage. The action is fast paced and the characters are compelling in this gripping sci-fi adventure." —**Reader Raves**, BookWoman 2005

2

RADCLY*f*FE

"Powerful characters, engrossing plot, and intelligent writing..." —**Cameron Abbott,** author of *To the Edge* and *An Inexpressible State of Grace*

"...well-honed storytelling skills...solid prose and sure-handedness of the narrative..."—**Elizabeth Flynn**, *Lambda Book Report*

"...well-plotted...lovely romance...I couldn't turn the pages fast enough!"—**Ann Bannon**, author of *The Beebo Brinker Chronicles*

Stolen Moments:

Erotic Interludes 2

edited by

STACIA SEAMAN and

RADCLYƒFE

2005

STOLEN MOMENTS: EROTIC INTERLUDES 2

© 2005 Bold Strokes Books, Inc. All Rights Reserved.

ISBN 1-933110-16-3

This Trade Paperback Original Is Published By
Bold Strokes Books, Inc.,
Pennsylvania, USA

First Printing September 2005

Credits
Editors: Radclyffe and Stacia Seaman
Production Design: Stacia Seaman
Cover Photo: Radclyffe
Cover Design By Sheri (GRAPHICARTIST2020@HOTMAIL.COM)

Contents

INTRODUCTION
RADCLYFFE

By its very nature, an anthology is a study in similarities and contrasts. Despite a common theme, diversity is inherent since the work consists of a collection of pieces by different authors—different styles, different language, different vision of the topic. That's one of the things that makes reading anthologies so much fun—you never quite know what the next page will bring. Adding the element of erotica to the mix creates the potential for even greater surprises. Merely attempting to define the term "erotic" usually leads to considerable debate. What may be erotic to one person may not be to another.

My goal in choosing the selections for this anthology was to have a final work that encompassed a broad interpretation of both the theme, in terms of setting and circumstance, as well as the *sine qua non*, eros. Happily, the task was not difficult. *Erotic Interludes 2* includes works from a talented array of writers from around the world, and whether first-time writers or established authors, they all have one thing in common—they write sizzling erotica with style. With settings as diverse as "love in the stacks" and "mile-high moments," and with flavors ranging from hot stranger-sex to steamy long-term-couple love, these are the stories of women who can't wait a minute longer for their pleasure. Once you start reading, neither will you.

Radclyffe 2005

FOR TWENTY MINUTES OR FOREVER
MARIE LYN

Michelle opens the unlocked door to the Park Slope walk-up and I am immediately assaulted by the piney smoke of incense drifting from someone's first-floor apartment. It's the kind of incense you can buy on the street, the kind that runs pungent through the air outside of the Astor Place K-Mart, a block from my present apartment—a block from the apartment and the life I am leaving.

But it's not my apartment anymore, not really. It's Rebecca's, and it holds the scent of a sadness so salient that living there is something like suffocation.

"This one will be ready by March first," Michelle tells me as I follow her up a flight of stairs. She knocks tentatively at the door, then unlocks it. "Warning knock," she explains, laughing that unbearable giggle that strikes me as artificial as a cartoon.

The apartment is small—a main room with a kitchen and a couch, another door perhaps leading to the bedroom. It's a "glorified closet," as Rebecca would say. She is convinced that by leaving her, not only am I leaving behind the "love of my life" but also the *only* inexpensive apartment in *the entire city* that has enough room for *all of my crap. And I'm not just talking physical crap, Hannah, I'm talking all of your crap, all of your mental crap.*

Those are the kinds of statements that make me want to slam every door of every insufficiently housed couple in the city with a noise that wakes all the neighbors and sends them grabbing for brooms to pound on ceilings and floors. *Shut up, Cut the Noise, Cut the Crap.*

This place is furnished. But it's not the layout I'm staring at now.

The current occupant is on the couch, eating macaroni and cheese from a plastic bowl and watching some makeover show. Everything inside of me rises and turns soft like a hallucination in a movie, like the one-bedroom is an underwater tank and the girl on the couch is the fake mermaid with breasts covered in aqua seashells, and I, in my layers and my sensible slacks and my sensible shoes, feel as sexy as seaweed.

"Hi! I'm so sorry—is this a bad time?" Michelle asks the girl.

"No." She shrugs. "You just called me. I said it was fine."

Michelle giggles again. I am embarrassed to be here with this woman with her nervous laughter and her pink tweed jacket.

"I'm sorry—what's your name again?"

"Vivian."

"Vivian—Vivian—right! Vivian, this is my client Hannah. She's thinking about taking this place off your hands."

Vivian gives a half smile. "It's all yours."

It's all yours. All yours. Speaking of things that could be all mine—

In college, my first (and last) serious boyfriend told me he loved me the most in my sweatpants. He wouldn't say why and so I asked a friend why and she laughed in my face, her eyes wide like gumballs. "Easy access, Hannah! Hello!"

I had blushed then. I blush now because Vivian is wearing sweatpants. I blush because I can see the perfect circles of her nipples under her tank top. I am hoping that she can tell, you know, tell that *I'm into girls,* tell that I am desperate for a fuck, that I've only got half an hour before I have to meet Lenny—a gay friend who makes fun of me all the time (*Did you forget how to read a clock, Hannah? Do you understand how time works, Hannah?*)—at a bar on the corner. And he lives in the neighborhood and wants me to live here too, and so he is buying me a drink as if he is in cahoots with Michelle, presenting promises of the grand life I could have here in the boroughs.

I think Michelle is talking.

Vivian's sweatpants are gray, an athletic seal by her left hip that I can't read. Michelle talks about exposed brick and I am imagining exposing Vivan's pussy lips, parting them like the Red Sea, lowering an eager fingernail over the ticklish sensitivity of her clit.

"Any questions?" Michelle asks me. "This is it for today—so you might want to think about making a decision."

"Um..." I pause. Vivian is looking at me now too, as if she too wants a question. Where do I begin? "How much?"

"Fourteen hundred," Michelle responds, looking at her cell phone.

"Huh."

"It's a good neighborhood," Vivian offers.

"Yeah?" I am pathetic, I am the girl at Girl Scout camp being pushed away by her bunkmate, sloppy and full of hate. "Is it?"

"I like it. It's just so far from work for me—"

"Where are you moving to?" I ask her, trying to be conversational, trying to sound like a woman in a bar, a woman on the street, a woman with my eyes pulled like gravity to her cunt. Vivian is young, brilliant green eyes, short dark hair, and she looks fresh and showered and like something I could lick, without regrets.

"East Village."

"That's where I'm moving from, actually."

"You don't like it?"

"No, it's great—it's just...pricey and—well, I was sharing a one-bedroom with someone—and I can't afford that on my own—you know?"

Vivian nods, and maybe smiles. After three years of reading Rebecca's facial expressions like a practiced translator, the codes of other women are frustrating, baffling, a sort of crippling that makes dating feel like tourism.

Michelle is ready to go, manically looking around the place like an owl.

"You like this one, then?" she asks. "I have to meet another client in Red Hook in a half hour—you want me to draw up the papers?"

Does the girl come with the couch? "I don't know."

And then we are back on the stairs, walking down, and there it is again—the incense from the first floor, a faint smell of marijuana, and I pause by the door. Rebecca. Rebecca with her joints on the fire escape, Rebecca with bath towels that smell like that, sex that smells like that.

I need it. I need sex. I need sex right now. I need my nose nestled in the petals of her pussy, surrounding me with the scent that lingers on my fingers for hours after masturbation.

"Um, I have to make a phone call, so you go ahead," I say to Michelle, hoping she will leave me inside the building while I assess my own courage.

"Um, okay." Michelle hands me her card again, for maybe the tenth time. "Call me."

In the space under the stairs, I catch my breath. I know by the crescendo of my cunt that I can't leave Vivian up there without at least giving it a shot.

For a moment I think perhaps I can forget—forget about Rebecca and her demands, her sadness, about the careful division of things, the inevitable fallout of a relationship that built us together like a house connected to another house with solid material like brick and mortar—of the melancholy thicker than smoke that coats our conversations and makes everything foggy and unbearable.

For a moment I can think, fully, of someone else, someone who can grab me by my cunt and send me elsewhere, leave love dangling in the other room.

And I can't let that moment go.

I walk up the stairs but I am shaking, my knees are weak, I didn't know I could do this, didn't know someone could turn me to jelly without saying anything, by just sitting on a couch in a wifebeater and gray sweatpants eating macaroni and cheese and watching bad television with her dark pageboy hair hanging in her eyes like she needs a haircut and her eyes—God—her eyes—dark green like moss, the kind of dark that I could get lost in forever, forever or for twenty minutes or both or at least twenty minutes that feel, after all, so much like forever.

I knock on the door. Vivian answers it. I can't read her, but this close to her face with its few tentative freckles and skin the color of stationery, I don't even want to try.

"Do you mind if I...look around again?" I ask.

She says nothing but steps back, closes the door behind me. I walk to the window and look out; the view is of another building, of bricks and windows. I nod like I am making mental notes. I walk to the kitchen. I turn one dial, then the other, like a health inspector at a restaurant. Do people do this, I wonder? And then one of the faucets won't turn back off and suddenly I feel Vivian behind me.

She wraps her arms around me slowly and I back up, feeling the bones of her hips against the curve of my ass.

"Let me help you with that." Her voice is husky like a lounge singer's. The feeling of her arms over mine turns the dial of the faucet of my pussy, which is brimming over, and I am wet, wet, so so so wet.

"Got it," she says as the sink's water slurps to a close.

I lean back, taking this uncalculated risk, so my neck is by her lips. She goes for it, kisses me there, sucks, the rim of her teeth grazing the taut skin of my neck. I want her to take a bite out of me, take all of me into her mouth and let me live there, safe and soaked forever, I mean, for twenty minutes, or forever.

I turn to face her, breast to breast, mine covered by a sweater and a scarf and a T-shirt and hers almost there, practically all the way there, the flimsy cotton of her tank top doing little to protect me from the dark nipples I see erect beneath it.

I put both my hands on her neck and take her mouth into mine; our tongues tangle.

"This is..." she pants, separating her lips from mine for moments to speak, "a really...really great apartment."

"I see," I say, and I slip my hand under the elastic band of her sweatpants—*easy access*—to the soft bush of her pussy underneath, no underwear. I am empowered by her brazen sex, by everything about her that is as raw as I am damaged.

My finger slides between the lips of her pussy, my fingertip resting above her opening, and I try not to think of Rebecca, of how she liked it, of when she first told me *I'm sorry, hon, but it's hard to compete with Duracell,* and I am charged when Vivian lights up like new batteries when I touch her, my finger vibrating the base of her clit like the best, most expensive kind of classy sex toy.

My breasts feel full as cantaloupes against hers, and I am ready when, still writhing from my finger, she removes my shirts like a lover discarding old habits, each layer falling neglected and useless to the floor.

This, I remember, is why I love women, the dance of tit against tit, the smell of her like almond soap, of almond hair gel, of anything so sweet and nutty at all.

She pulls my finger from her pussy— "I'm not ready to come yet—let me show you the bed—" and I follow her, my breasts bouncing as I walk. *Yeah, I like your breasts, sure, I love breasts, I guess,* Rebecca would say, *but really I'm an ass girl, I love your ass the most, I'm just not that into breasts,* and I would wilt with neglect, pinching them myself like clothespins while she would eat my cunt with the clinical knowledge lovers have of each other's cunts, the knowledge that gets you every time but that's just it, it gets you every time, in that same dry, educated way.

Her "bedroom" is hardly a glorified closet, just a plain old closet, just room enough for a bed with a dark purple comforter that she throws me on top of.

She takes my nipples into her mouth. At last, the touch of tongue to tit. It's been so long since someone gave them the attention they deserve, and I am relishing it.

I don't feel huge or weird as I usually feel with new lovers, I feel like a pinup girl ripped from a magazine and into a bed, my admirer shifting her hand from her own cunt onto mine.

Then she kisses down my stomach, undoes the belt of my pants and pushes them to the floor. Her teeth grab the rim of my cream-colored underwear and then she teases me, hot breath against the crotch of my panties that makes me so wet I know I could be leaking through onto her lips.

I reach down and take off my own underwear. She stands up and takes off her sweatpants, then her tank top, and I lavish in the presence of her nakedness like a man at a strip club and she bends down to get something from under the bed.

She is beautiful, firm, clean.

She emerges with a dildo, red and rubber and thick, holding it in her hand like a bottle of champagne. "You wanna play?"

"Hmm—let me think about it—" I tease, but she stops me when she shoves the phallus into my cunt like she's popping my goddamn cherry.

She batters me with it until I burst, my climax sending me into convulsions and making time stop.

She crawls up to lie next to me and hold me as I come. It's been a festering orgasm, I know it's been weeks since the last time I had one, and it's brilliant and worth it.

"Damn," she grins. "So you'll take the apartment, then?"

"I'll take you," I whisper, inching down to her cunt and sticking my head between the tight muscles of her thighs. She grips me there, my ears growing hot and red, as I eat her salient cunt like chocolate.

She moans, her voice in a register I haven't heard before. I could lick her pussy like ice cream melting, and I would.

I stick my thumb just inside her pussy, my middle finger clawing her asshole as I lick, and she thrashes around and I can feel her cunt muscles tighten and squeeze my fingertip when she comes. I roll over, my head by her hip, and breathe. Out of the corner of my eye, I see her alarm clock—I have five minutes.

"Fuck," I sigh, "I gotta go."

"Where?"

"Excelsior."

"Fag bar?"

"To meet a friend. He's trying to sell me on the neighborhood."

"That place won't help," she laughs. "I can sell you on the neighborhood, if you're interested—there's a lot of girl bars around here—a lot more than there are boy bars. We should—you should go to Ginger's."

I kiss her thigh. "You've already sold me."

She laughs. "Have I?"

"You had me at 'got it.'"

I get up then, looking for my clothes, and she stays on the bed, naked, her perfect body like a supplicant sculpture beneath my wandering eye. As I dress, she talks about the neighborhood, about her work (she bartends, I make a note to visit her, stare at her, overtip her, sometime soon). My pussy and my panties are wet.

"Can I—I'm sorry—" I blush. "Can I borrow some panties? Mine are—"

"Wet?"

"Yeah—wet."

"No problem. But—then—you might have to return them, you know?"

I smile and blush again as she opens her drawer and sorts through her colorful collection. She pulls out some athletic-looking boy-shorts and tosses them to me. "Will these do?"

"Anything, sweetheart." I smile. "Anything."

She isn't moving, and so I dress while she watches, feeling kind of flushed and too much all over.

"I have to go," I say. "Can I—"

"Your broker has it, right?"

"You're making this hard for me, aren't you?"

She smiles and gets up. "Stop by sometime, if you want another look at the place. Whenever you've got—twenty minutes, or whatever."

"Right."

"Let me see you out."

And, delicately, I follow her to the door, which she opens for me. There is so much I want to say—could say—but instead, I slip quietly out, the fabric that used to house her ass now rubbing softly against mine. It is the feeling that reminds me, as I pass through the scent from the first floor that brings me all the way to the East Village and back here again, as I flee down the block to my date at the fag bar, that there's still a place for me in this city, even if it's farther away on the L train and nothing—nothing like anything I have ever felt before.

FIREWORKS OVER ATLANTA
KAREN L. PERRY

The fast, rhythmic beat of a high-energy song faded into the softer tones of a romantic ballad before I finally took a break and walked up out of the dance pit at Atlanta's hottest lesbian club, Triple Tips. The back of my shirt and the waistband of my pants were soaking wet. Sweat was running down my face, dripping from my short brown hair. I had been dancing for more than an hour.

Rianna, my friend and one of the club's owners, met me at the top of the steps. Placing a cold Budweiser in my hand, she said, "It's about time you took a breather, Nicky. If everyone in here danced as much as you did without buying beer, we'd go out of business."

I knew she was kidding. She and her partner, Claire, were making money hand over fist. Lesbians were lined up outside waiting for a chance to get in. After pushing aside a slew of empty beer bottles and cocktail glasses, I rested my arm on the railing overlooking the dance floor. "Rianna, my friend, I think you're going to do just fine, even if I never pay for another drink. This club was a great idea."

"Maybe too great!" Rianna laughed as she leaned against my side so I could hear her over the music. "We had no idea how popular it would be. We've already gotten two citations for overcrowding, and Claire is talking about expanding. She wants to buy out the bookstore next door and tear down the walls."

We stood in companionable silence as we watched the women in the club. The final notes of the sultry ballad ended and the slow-dancing couples broke apart, many of them leaving the dance floor as the rapid bass beats of a new song began. My body began to move again of its own accord.

As a professional photographer, I prefer to spend most of my time in the wilderness. I love capturing images of the pure, untainted beauty of nature that has not yet been destroyed by the hands of man. I'm lucky enough to make a living from it. I was in Atlanta, far from the small, Tennessee cabin that I call home, only because Rianna had begged me to accept a temporary job for the city's new tourism campaign.

The money was good, and I wanted to see my friends, but the true draw was the music. I could live the rest of my life without a fast food restaurant, a shopping mall, or even a blacktopped road, but I need the music. The console of my truck is crammed with CDs and my stereo at home is always on, but a radio can't duplicate the feel and smell of a dance floor crowded with sexy women.

Rianna nudged my shoulder. "There's someone else who prefers to dance alone."

I searched the crowd, only seeing divisions of two, until she poked me again, pointing to a woman near the back corner. From my vantage point above the dance floor, I could clearly see the lone dancer, and I felt an immediate appreciation. She was beautiful, with long, silky blond hair that cascaded like one of nature's most perfect waterfalls. Her eyes were closed as she allowed the music to fill her, to move her with sounds and tones that were obviously stirring deeply inside her.

I felt a rising, a swelling in my body, as I studied her sleek, trim physique. Black stiletto heels cradled her ankles, and the strongly defined muscles of her calves were flawlessly clear as she moved her long, sexy legs to the rhythm. I followed her thighs upward until they disappeared under the hem of a tiny black leather miniskirt that clung to the curves of her perfect ass.

My eyes were glued to that skirt, mesmerized by the way light reflected from the fabric. Her midriff, bare above the skirt and below a tiny little top that lifted her breasts high, called to me. I wanted my hand on that skin, but I drew back abruptly as another hand, the hand of a stranger, trailed across her flesh.

My girl—that's what I called her because I already thought of her as mine—drew back as well, which pleased me. With the flick of her wrist, she dislodged the unwelcome hand from her body and resumed dancing. I clutched my beer bottle by its neck and watched. Women of all shapes and sizes were moving in on her. There were butches, femmes, and those in between. She was drawing them like flies to honey, but one by one, she shot them down. She continued to dance alone.

I had tuned Rianna out. I might as well have been isolated on top of one of the world's most remote mountains, because all that mattered to me at that moment was watching the blonde. Even though she was in the dance pit and I was high above her at the railing, our bodies were already moving as one. We had the same natural rhythm in our bones.

My beer bottle was empty and I set it down among the others. A waitress would find it later. I had to go to her.

"Where you going?" Rianna shouted as she pulled the sleeve of my shirt. "Ah, Nicky! She just wants to be left alone."

I ignored her as I made my way to the steps and down to the multicolored, flashing squares of the dance floor. Strobe lights bounced off a disco ball that hung from the ceiling, and others played festively over the dancing throng that was brimming with raw sexuality. Hands were clinging boldly to lovers' asses, disappearing under shirts to tweak jutting nipples that begged to be tweaked. The music, along with dark lighting, was the catalyst; it made everything possible.

I skirted along the edge of the dance floor, allowing pulsing music to move me closer to her. I was watchful, hoping that no one else had moved in. She was still alone, her eyes closed, her head tossed back as she danced. I moved cautiously, making no attempts to touch her. I settled in beside her, having no intentions of leaving.

My girl was an island; no one else existed to her. The floor literally shook with the movements of the mass of lesbians that had crammed inside of Triple Tips, but she was oblivious to it all, much like I preferred to be. Before I saw her, I had spent the night on the dance floor in the same kind of solitude. I had shoved aside potential partners as they intruded upon me, not interested in anyone until her.

I no longer wanted to be alone.

When I reached her, I willed her eyes to open. They were indigo blue, the color of the deepest ocean. I watched her gaze at me, appraising me. I wanted her to see the hunger in my eyes, the promise of pleasure on my lips as I smiled rakishly at her. I concealed nothing of the sexual desire I felt just from dancing near her.

When she didn't step away, I bravely lifted a hand and wrapped it in her long, blond tresses. Her eyes closed again. I took a step closer, holding my breath as I pushed my hips into her. I shuddered in pleasure as she welcomed my presence by snaking a hand around my neck, pulling me tighter. Grabbing her hips, I boldly inched her miniskirt higher, sliding my thigh between her legs.

The music was electric, alive with enough voltage to blow the roof from the building, but it was a poor imitation of the current flowing between us. The pulse of the music pounded through the giant speakers and into our bodies. I reveled in the joy of having her in my arms, the overwhelming sexy feel of her skin under my hands and her legs entwined with mine.

Her hand slid down my back and up my rib cage, and I gasped when her thumbs brushed across my hard nipples. Tilting her head sideways, I pushed through her hair with my lips until I captured her mouth. She tasted like honey, and there was no hesitancy in the kiss, no tentative nibbles, as I set about devouring her. I thrust my tongue inside. When she sucked it deeper, a jolt of raw sexual energy tore through my clit. I thought that I was going to come on the dance floor.

It was two a.m. when we finally left the bar. I still didn't know her name, only that I had to have her and that she was sitting beside me in my truck. She played with the short spikes of hair that grew near my ears, occasionally letting her finger dip teasingly inside the ridges, as I struggled to drive us to the guest apartment above Rianna and Claire's garage where I was staying. I had one hand on the wheel; the other was between her thighs, tracing delicate patterns along the smooth skin between her knees and the edge of her skirt.

As I pulled into the driveway, I popped the clutch, allowing the engine to die. Techno dance music continued to play from my radio even as my truck rolled to a stop. I reached below me and threw back the lever, then slid the seat all the way back.

"Come here," I demanded as I wrapped an arm around her waist, lifting and turning her so that she sat facing me.

My mouth was hungry for the taste of her and she seemed just as eager. I held her face, swallowing the deep, sultry moans coming from her throat. Her hands were clinging to my hair, pulling me closer. When our kiss finally broke, she buried my face between her soft breasts.

She sat astride me and I desperately clung to her. We were both breathing frantically as she pulled my shirt over my head. "Take this off," she hissed through clenched teeth.

My nipples were rock hard, straining toward her as she pulled them into her mouth. I was writhing to meet her as she ground down. I wanted to be naked, and I wanted to be inside of her. Reaching behind her, I slid my hands across the smooth leather of her skirt and quivered as I felt her lift slightly so that I could peel it up her hips. Within seconds, I had pushed aside the sexy thong of her underwear and buried my hand inside of her.

"Oh God! Yes!"

She was dripping wet, flowing down my palm and over my wrist as she rode me. Her inner muscles clung, sliding over my fingers like a velvet glove that grew tighter with each thrust. I sucked her tongue into my mouth, mimicking the strokes of my hand, until she lifted even higher, until her head was pressed up against the roof of my truck. She inhaled sharply and stayed that way, seemingly frozen while I triggered her clit with my thumb.

My own body was living vicariously, absorbing the pleasure that was carrying her. When everything finally coalesced into one mind-blowing, body-melting orgasm, she dropped down with a guttural scream that matched my own, impaling herself more firmly onto my hand. With a final shudder, she fell backward against the steering wheel and I eased from within her.

I was breathing heavily, trying to catch my breath. My eyes were riveted to the tiny stream of sweat that coursed down her chest and into the valley between her breasts. Her eyes were closed as I traced its path with my finger, then with my lips. I could taste her nectar that my finger had left behind, and I stroked it hungrily with the flat of my tongue.

Her eyes were midnight blue when she captured my face between her hands. "Take me inside."

I opened the truck door and helped her stand, but my own legs were weak. I held on to her. I had left my shirt wherever she had thrown it, and the cool night air made my nipples grow more erect. The aureoles were puckered, looking like mighty mountain ranges encircling the highest peaks. Her eyes were magnetically drawn to them and I heard her whimper as she drew one into her mouth while her fingers captured the other. My legs gave way at the sensations firing through me. I would have fallen if she had not wrapped a strong arm around me.

The heat of her mouth was causing me to burn. I wanted to force her to her knees, to have that tongue between my thighs, buried in my cunt. I was pressing on her shoulder when a car pulled into the driveway. I could see the lights drawing closer through the trees. I knew it was only Rianna and Claire, but I wasn't interested in putting on a show for my friends. I wanted my girl inside where I could ravish her in the privacy of my own apartment.

It took an infinite amount of willpower, but I finally managed to pull her from the task of bathing my skin with her lips. Her eyes seemed glazed with the same passion I felt in my blood. I stole another kiss, then picked her up. After carrying her up the stairs, I hurriedly closed the apartment door and set her down near the bed.

In the light of the room, I noticed that her skirt was still above her hips. The small underwear did nothing to hide the voluptuous cheeks of her ass. I stepped behind her, felt her shiver as I cupped her behind in my hands. She moaned, pressing backward. I unfastened her top, allowing it to slide down her arms. Her breasts were heaving with pleasure as I held them in my hands for the first time.

She was captivating, and I relished the feel of my own breasts pressed against the bare skin of her back, the satiny softness of her hair. Wrapping my arms around her hips, I gently traced the tops of her thighs until I reached the tiny triangle of fabric that hid her pussy from me. I wanted to take the panties off, but first I ran my fingers between her legs, loving the feel of wetness that I had caused. She moaned urgently as she reached up, trying to capture my head in her hands.

"Not so fast this time, baby," I cooed as I sidestepped, pushing her onto the bed. Lifting her feet, I untied the delicate leather straps of her shoes, massaged her feet. I allowed my fingers to trail up her legs. Her skin was soft, like fine silk, and my mouth soon followed the path upward.

She grew impatient as I teased her. When I reached her panties, she ripped them out of my way. She grunted in frustration when I rose from the bed and stood over her. She was nude with the exception of the skirt.

I caught her eyes with mine and held her captive. I wanted her to wait, and she knew it. I walked around her, watching the way her urgent breathing caused her body to move, the pent-up sexual energy that caused her to writhe with anticipation.

When I'm working with my camera, I often sit with the subject that catches my eye for several minutes before I ever load film. I like to absorb things from all angles until I find the one that captures the full value of my focus. With my girl, it was impossible to find just one perfect viewpoint. They were all perfect; she was perfect.

My hands itched with the desire to take her picture, but they also hungered for so much more. I kicked off my shoes, then held her gaze as I unbuttoned the fly of my jeans, letting them fall to the floor. I stood before her naked. She looked at me, her eyes brushing over my skin, leaving me feeling touched. Her eyes closed again—oh so slowly—as she ran the tip of one finger across her own breast. I held my breath as she took her nipple between two fingers and pinched. Arching her back, she shifted her knees, opening herself to me, like the finest flower revealing its inner petals for me alone.

I lost all restraint. I was on my knees, ravenously engulfing her with my lips, tongue, and hands. Her rich, musky scent caused me to melt into a puddle between her thighs. I ate her until she came again, this time arching so high that the force of it picked us both up from the bed. I tried to hold on, but the next thing I knew, I was lying on my back on the floor.

A number of images that I had enlarged and mounted on matting board had been knocked off the table and lay strewn around us. I was trying to push aside a photo of Atlanta's tallest building, the Bank of America Plaza, when I felt her tug my legs. She was parting them, and I screamed in pleasure as she knelt and drew my extended clit into her mouth without warning. I was so hard, so ready for her, that it was painful.

She knew me without knowing me at all. I still had no clue what her name was, nor she mine, but my body was hers to do with as she willed. When she lifted her chin, slipping one, two, three fingers inside, she filled me with heat that touched a place that had never been touched. Fireworks exploded inside my head, between my thighs as she plunged and sucked my flesh.

When I awoke, early morning light was seeping between the slits of the blinds. My bedroom was in complete disarray. Stacks of photos that I had labored over diligently were tossed about carelessly, like a scattered deck of cards. Rich images of the Atlanta Botanical Gardens, Centennial Park, the Governor's Mansion, Piedmont Park, and the Woodruff Arts Center lay about the room.

One of my favorite photos, the one that I thought would really sell to the committee putting together the new brochure, was lying sideways near the door. It was a time-release image of vibrant red, white, and blue fireworks exploding just above the skyline. I had set my camera on a tripod and left the shutter open, allowing the film to capture one explosion after another in the same frame. The photo captured the fluid movement of colorful sparks as they slowly sank toward the ground.

With my girl still pressed to my side, I knew that I could have stayed in the jumbled clutter all day in spite of the fact the bed was a mess. The covers were on the floor, and the sheets had been pulled from their moorings.

I was completely sated, but I felt a new stirring deep in my center as she shifted, her long hair brushing across my shoulder. At one point during the night, she had knelt above me, caressing my skin with her locks. She had not left an inch of flesh untouched. I wanted to wake her, to have her do it again, but my bladder was bursting. Her arm was across my chest, a leg pressed between my own. Moving slowly, I slid out from under her, smiling when she whimpered and snuggled deeper into my pillow.

I couldn't keep my eyes off her body as I walked to the bathroom. She was so spectacularly gorgeous that I froze. Last night, when I had wanted to so badly that it hurt, I couldn't take her picture. With her sleeping, there were no barriers. Holding my new digital Nikon DX2, I tripped the power switch and read the light settings. After making adjustments, I allowed the flash to power up. I knew that I probably only had one shot because the light would wake her, but I took my chances. There was an oak trunk at the foot of the bed and I cautiously climbed upon it.

Peering down through the lens, I felt cream building between my thighs from just looking at her. Her hair lay around her shoulders and fanned down across her chest. One breast was hidden, but the very tip of the other peeked through blond locks, like a delicate bud about to bloom. Her ribs and tight abdominal muscles were etched with the faintest of shadows, making them appear delicate and exquisitely feminine. Her long legs were bent slightly sideways, and the tiny miniskirt still clung to her hips, hiding all but the finest wisps of curly hair between her legs. Her face was relaxed against the pillow, her lips slightly parted as if welcoming a lover's kiss, my kiss.

I pressed the shutter switch, grateful that I had spent extra money on a camera that promised silence for moments when I wanted to capture shots of shy, elusive creatures. The bright light of the flash abruptly filled the room, and although I was quiet as I got down off my perch and rushed into the bathroom, I heard her shift on the bed behind me.

Although the scent of her upon my skin left me light-headed with desire, I felt sticky. I thought that she would not fully wake until after I showered. I was mistaken. My heart sank, caved in painfully upon itself, when I came out to find that she was gone. I ran outside, mindless of the fact that I was naked and dripping wet from the shower. She was nowhere to be found.

I went back inside and dropped down onto the bed that still smelled of her. I felt a hungry ache eating at me as I stared at the open phone book lying where she had left it. The brightly colored page touted ads for quick taxi services.

I sat for several minutes, feeling dejected beyond belief that I had let her slip away, before I thought of downloading her image from my camera. I hooked up my computer and felt everything inside of me dissolve into warm liquid as the screen filled with the greatest, most unsurpassed photograph that I have ever taken in my life. As I said before, my girl was flawless, a rare creation of feminine perfection.

I sat in front of my monitor for hours, reliving every moment that we were together. When I finally began cleaning up the aftermath of our lovemaking, I eventually found something that cut through the cloak of pain that enshrined me. One of my prints was missing. As badly as I hurt, I smiled, glad that she had something of mine with her.

I also felt a niggling of hope. A small gold label that included my name, address and professional credentials was firmly attached to the back of the image she had taken, an image of fireworks exploding over Atlanta.

ANY MORNING
KARIN KALLMAKER

With your body next to me in our bed, I surrender to sleep every night. My mind goes limp. My dreams wander whichever way they will. You burrow into me some nights and I don't feel you there, not when I am deep in the arms of sleep.

Every morning, when I wake, my mind climbs to a level of bare alertness. Are you there with me? Yes. Are you asleep? Can't tell. My body stays asleep, still in surrender to the warmth of the bed.

It was the very first morning we woke up together that you discovered I could respond to you and yet remain in that sleep-puddle state. That very first morning you whispered in my ear, "You don't have to wake up. At least not much."

You like my body in surrender. Sometimes, when our fire is sizzling hot, you enforce my surrender with soft but effective accessories. But in the morning there is no need for anything more than your voice and the firm command of your hands to transfer me from sleep to your possession.

The sheets rustle and I know you are there. I am not awake when your arm slides across my back and your hair tickles my shoulder blades. Not awake a few minutes later when you stir again and your hand wanders the length of my spine to explore the curve of my ass.

If I weren't asleep I'd purr. Your hands are treated with some kind of magic spell, because wherever you touch me I want to dissolve. My body stays still, relaxed, but I can feel my heartbeat start to increase.

I don't know what time it is. I don't care. It might be Saturday, but it could be any morning. My skin is in rapture as your hand glides over me, and if I weren't asleep, I'd moan when your lips press to the nape of my neck.

Oh, you're naked. I can tell that now. Your arm coils around my ribs and with one fingertip you find my nipple that's barely free of the sheets. Such a gentle touch you have, at least for now. Your fingertip toys lightly and it's a purely physical response for my nipple to harden. I'm not awake and my breathing isn't increasing to match my heartbeat. I'm still in complete surrender to sleep.

Your fingers travel back and forth between my nipples while your naked body presses against my back. Another kiss to the nape of my neck might draw a shiver from me when I'm more alert, but not right now—I'm asleep.

Your hand is abruptly gone. Your body rolls away from mine. I can't help it. I'm awake enough to moan.

"Oh, so you might be not quite asleep?"

"Maybe," I mumble into the pillow.

Your fingers come back and they are no longer gentle. A sharp tug draws a hoarse response from me and I shudder with a wave of arousal as your warm, firm breasts press hard into my back. In that moment I shift from the surrender of sleep to the surrender I have always felt in your arms. I am yours, yours to enjoy, yours to pleasure, yours to love. The transition is lightning-quick and dusts my arms and thighs with gooseflesh.

"Get on your tummy."

I have barely complied when your body is fully atop mine, pressing me down into the bed. You coil my hands around the headboard frame, and I moan. This morning, like many, you want me this way.

"Don't let go." Your voice is husky with want and I hear your breath catch as your hands roam the taut muscles of my shoulders and back. Your hips are moving against my ass and, oh, the sensation brings back so many memories of so many evenings in your arms.

"Up on your knees, spread them wide. Show me—oh yes, show me that beautiful cunt of yours."

I can use my elbows for balance without letting go of the headboard, and the position—my back swayed, hips higher than my head—is vulnerable. I feel cool air between my legs as you settle a towel below me. After a pause, you kneel between my spread knees, then both sets of fingers slip through the folds of my cunt, spreading warm, silky lubricant over every inch of me until I am slippery and moaning hot.

You're quiet for a moment and I slowly draw in my breath. When you want me this way I know what you're going to do, and in that still moment the anticipation of it brings a flood of my own to mingle with the lube.

The heat of your body draping over me draws a moan of pure pleasure from me. Your slick fingers return to my nipples with a sharp squeeze. My moan sharpens, lengthens.

"Awake now?"

"Yes."

"Is this what you want?"

"Yes. Please."

"Please, what?"

"Please make me yours."

"Mine," you whisper softly. Your voice is laden with tenderness and love for me. "Mine."

I close my eyes so I can focus on my body responding to you. I quell the shudder that runs through me as you firmly grasp one nipple while your other hand finds my aching clit. Two fingers close around it and then you squeeze my nipple and clit with the same relentless pressure.

Nerves send equal messages of ecstasy and fire across my body. I gasp and arch as you play with me, reveling in the sensation of your touch.

"Don't come yet," you order. "You know what I want."

Struggling for words, I can only nod frantically. The pressure on my clit with my knees so far apart, my cunt so exposed, creates an empty ache inside me. I want to be filled and yet you're nowhere near my opening. The longer you play with my clit, the more I want you inside.

You play my body until I can think of nothing but you fucking me. You turn me on so you can put out the fire, pleasing us both.

"I love touching you," you admit softly. "I love every inch of you." I feel the hot, wet reality of your cunt on my calf. There is never any doubt in my mind that you are not dispassionately servicing your woman. I am not an object to be used, nor a piece of flesh to be consumed. You are deeply involved in my pleasure and it sparks your own. I could even describe everything we are doing now as prologue, foreplay, because when we are done your need will be as intense as mine is at this moment. "I'm going to enjoy every bit of you. Do *not* let go."

Abruptly the warm weight of you is gone and my hips convulse, trying to find you again. My nipples are sore against the sheets, sending prickles of sensation straight to my clit, which throbs in response.

"Spread your knees more. Yes, oh yes, like that." One finger teases just at my opening. "Wet," you purr. "You're very wet now."

"Yes, please."

"Please?"

"Take what you want," I say between gritted teeth. "What we both wa—oh *yes*."

Four fingers fill me and I am stretched, tight, but I know you won't stop, and we both know what we can do together. You take me, completely, with your thumb tucked tight. I cry out but I can still hear your earthy groan.

I want to let go, wrap my head in my arms and let the feeling of my full cunt overwhelm me to the point of tears. Sometimes you let me do that, let me slip deep into a place of pure feeling. Not today. Today I must hold on and stay with you.

"That is so hot, so unbelievably hot, watching my hand go into you. I can never get enough of it." I feel your other hand on the small of my back, holding me still. "Let's do it again."

"No, stay in me," I plead but you've already removed your hand as I shudder.

Bracing my knees, gripping the headboard, I arch up to meet your thrust and take you inside with a rising cry of need.

"Don't let go or I'll stop," you say sharply, and I realize I was about to.

"I won't. Please don't stop." I want it so badly now. My inner muscles are trying to convulse with pleasure, and my G-spot feels enormous, as if your entire hand can't cover it all.

"Fuck my hand. That's what you want."

Holding tight to the headboard, I shove myself as far down onto your arm as I can go. Mornings I can be so receptive and wild, wet, dripping. This morning is no exception, and the feeling of my wet trickling down my thighs makes me even crazier.

"That's right, that's right," you coo. "So beautiful, the way you grab my hand. That's right…fuck yourself."

"I am," I groan out. I am reaching the point of abandon and I feel again your wet cunt on my leg. I want to ravage you now, want to bury my face between your legs and feast. And I want to fuck you, fuck you until you feel like I do now, free to take it, love it, feel it.

"So beautiful," you say again. Your hand on my back is gentle and steadying now. You love me and you are helping me feel so good. The tenderness in your voice brings tears to my eyes. "Come when you want to. Come when you can't stand it anymore."

It feels so good that I don't want to come, but your hand leaves my back to toy with my clit. Short, gentle pulls, flicks with your fingertips, circles, and direct, firm touches—I am jerking at your every touch, pushing down on your fist. It's too much to hold inside, all the feelings of love and surrender and lust. I scream, at least I think I do, and I am gushing around your fist, squeezing it so tight I would worry that I am going to break it—that is, if I could think beyond the spasms that start high inside me and pour down my entire body. The ecstasy leaves me, drenches the towel, your legs, your arm, and I push your hand out with a cry that leaves me hoarse.

You pull me back onto my haunches, breaking my grip on the headboard. Wrapping my shuddering body tight in your arms, you anchor me hard to your thighs. You squeeze my clit again with your agile, clever fingertips and say fiercely in my ear, "Come again. Right now."

My surrender to your desire washes over me. It's what I revel in, what you crave. I coat your thighs, screaming for breath, giving you what you've asked for, what you've drawn from me with your voice and the firm command of your hands.

Limp, I am falling back to the bed. Falling into your embrace. Falling forever and always under your spell. A half laugh escapes me as the pillows greet me again.

"Not bad," you say, your body as limp as mine as you stretch out next to me.

"Damned good," I murmur, willing to transfer my surrender back to sleep. Sleep wants me, right then, and it is ordering my eyes to close.

You are suddenly close to me, the wonderful smell of you, warm and loving. Gathering me into your arms, you tip my head back for a slow, lazy kiss. "I'm not done with you."

I swallow, hard. Sleep can wait.

Lunch Break
Saskia Walker

W hat can I get you?"
  I glanced up from my pocket mirror, and when I saw the attractive waitress who watched and waited, I was so startled I dropped my lipstick. Her gaze was direct, fearless, and powerfully sexual. My body responded instantly, my pulse rate rising.

"Coffee, please, and a club sandwich." I scrabbled for the lipstick. Her eyes never left mine, but she reached down and shifted the ashtray, nudging the lipstick back in my direction.

"Oh, I just bet you take your coffee sweet and strong," she whispered, low.

"Yes," I replied, mesmerized. "I do."

She gave me a dazzling smile, then turned and walked away, her hips cutting a rhythmic path through the low-slung tables and chairs in the sedate lounge bar. I sat back and watched, my fingers toying idly with the fitted jacket of my business suit, which lay abandoned over the arm of the chair. I had stopped on at Kilpatrick's, the salubrious and rather austere London hotel, after the meeting with my client, the hotel's publicity officer. He was sold on my advertising proposals and I was on a high. I just knew that if I had gotten behind the wheel of my Land Rover in that state, I'd have picked up another speeding ticket, so I stayed on to chill for a while. With the attention I was now getting from the waitress, it looked as if chilling wasn't going to be an option.

When she delivered my order she threw me another look filled with pure, raw sex appeal. She turned my cup in its saucer, facing the handle toward me. Her name badge announced that she was called Martine.

"I'm testing out some new cocktails for the bar. Why don't you drop by before you leave, and I'll give you a taste of something good."

She winked. *Well, that was direct.* I felt the tug of the woman's invitation from the pit of my stomach to the tip of my clit.

"Thanks, I'll do that, Martine."

I mustered a nonchalant smile, my fingers ruffling through my short, cherry-dyed crop, and watched as she walked away, her hips skirting obstacles. She knew that I watched. She stretched her legs back as she bent over the tables, the scalloped edge of her black skirt brushing, so tantalizingly, high against the back of her thighs, offering a glimpse of what appeared to be stocking tops. Her body was lush and curvy, her mouth a ruby pout. She cast sidelong glances back to me, her finger flicking quickly against the corners of her bow tie before smoothing slowly over her fitted waistcoat.

I barely touched the sandwich; my appetite had been redirected toward the waitress. I had never been approached by a woman as forthright and blatant as her before—or as glamorous. It was one of those rare encounters when fizzing chemistry instantly anchors two people together. The situation made me very hot, but could I act on it? I was supposed to be in work mode. *What the hell.* Of course I could act on it!

Martine smiled and her eyes flashed a welcome from under heavy eyelashes when I climbed onto the bar stool in front of her. She was a total sex bomb, with thickly fringed, dark brown eyes and blue-black hair clipped up at the back of the head. The occasional glossy coil escaped to hang tantalizingly over her eyes, giving her subtle cover as she glanced around. There were signs of an alternative edge beneath her smart uniform. She had an electric blue streak in her hair; both her ears were fully studded, and there was evidence of a nose piercing. I liked that. I also had a streak of die-hard glam-punk that refused to conform, despite my career. Through the thin white sleeves of her shirt, I could make out her tattoos flexing as she went about her business behind the bar, rapidly shaking a cocktail mixer in such a physical way that her figure was shown off to perfection. I imagined what it would feel like to be pressed hard against her, to rub against her naked breasts and touch her between those strong thighs. Maybe we would exchange contact details. Maybe we could meet, later on. My sex was heavy with the idea of it, the sensitive flesh crushed inside my G-string plump and swollen.

Martine set up a tall glass in front of me, gave the cocktail mixer a final dramatic shake, and poured me out a long, tall drink over crackling ice, popping in a smart black swizzle stick. She rested two provocatively speared cherries on the edge of the glass at the last moment, then pushed it over.

"A new recipe, please have some…and tell me what you think. Compliments of the bar." She gave me another wink. Her accent was heavy, either French or Italian.

I sipped the vibrant red-orange drink, looking at the waitress over the two plump cherries. Martine watched, her lips slightly open, a devilish look in her eyes. The cocktail hit the back of my throat; it was ice-cold and zappy, exhilarating, instantly making me wow. I could taste cranberry juice and other fruits, grenadine, vodka, and something else, a mystery ingredient I could not identify.

"Mmm…what is it?"

"It is Martine's version of Sex On The Beach," she replied, putting one hand on her hip and the other elbow on the bar, resting her chin on her hand as she looked directly into my eyes. "Shall we call it…Sex In My Bedroom?"

She is definitely coming on to me. I felt a rush of heat traversing my body, from the tips of my toes to the roots of my hair. Was it the effect of the cocktail or the provocative woman who had made it for me?

"Do you think you'd like that—sex in my bedroom?" she added, her voice low.

Wow, direct *wasn't the word!* My heart was racing. I breathed deep, trying to order my thoughts. I had never had such a direct come-on. This was one express lady. What would she be like in bed?

"I think I'd like to try it," I replied.

Martine's mouth slid into another wide grin. "I'm due my lunch break."

I almost dropped the glass on the bar. *She means now?* I glanced at my watch. I was due back at the office in just over an hour. I had promised to catch Jack, my boss, before he left for a board meeting. Martine toyed with a swizzle stick, eyeing my cleavage. My body thundered out its response.

"Okay," I managed. "Let's do it."

She turned to the barman working the other end of the bar and called out some instructions to him in French. He nodded and waved.

She turned back to me, her eyes smoldering. God, she was hot. I wanted to find out exactly how hot.

"Come to room fourteen, lower ground floor, in three minutes." She pulled a key chain from her hip, put a key into the register, and logged herself off. "I have only forty minutes for lunch break, though," she added, lifting her eyebrows suggestively.

Perfect. I could be back at work in time.

The three minutes seemed to drag, but gave me enough time to consider taking flight. I stayed put. Just a few minutes earlier, I had been reflecting on my business meeting. Now, well, now I was on Martine's lunch break with her. I glanced at my watch and swore low under my breath. It was time. I threw back the rest of the drink and stood up.

I clutched my jacket and portfolio against my chest and hurried down the stairs marked "Staff Only." I couldn't quite believe I was doing it, lurking in the hidden corridors of a premier London hotel, heading to an illicit meeting with a sex bomb with whom I had exchanged only a handful of words. A deviant thrill fired my veins.

Perhaps I would wake up.

And then there it was, room fourteen. From inside I could hear the distinct and powerful drum-and-bass sound of industrial dance music. I took a deep breath.

"Come on in," a voice shouted out when I rapped on the door. I turned the handle and pushed open the door. The room was filled with clutter—a metal-framed bed surrounded with stacks of clothes and teetering piles of books; lamps, bric-a-brac, and cushions littering the spaces between. Even the walls were covered with posters, photographs, mirrors, and other paraphernalia. A scarlet sarong was draped across the metal head of the bed, a vivid dash of color in the gloom. Over the bed, a poster of Annie Lennox at her most androgynous grinned cheekily down from the wall. In the center of it all was Martine, sitting on the bed with her legs coiled under her. She chuckled, leapt up, and walked over. She rested one hand on my bare upper arm, stroking me, sending wild threads of electricity between us. I caught a breath of her perfume, something musky and wild.

"What do they call you, Red?" She nodded up to my hair.

"Kim," I replied, smiling.

"Kim, huh? Well, Kim, I like a woman who goes after what she wants." Her tone was admiring. Martine growled in her throat, eyeing my body. The atmosphere positively crackled between us.

"Thank you for your invitation. It made me very…hot."

Martine grinned, proudly, and pulled me into the room by one arm, closing in on my mouth for an urgent kiss as the door slammed shut. Her mouth was lush and hot, damp and inviting. My portfolio clattered to the floor. She backed me toward the bed, her eyes sparkling.

"You have to do it when it happens like this, yes, or you will have a regret, and life, it is too short for regrets, huh?"

She flickered her eyebrows at me. Before I had a chance to reply, she pushed me and I landed on my back on the bed. She moved like lightning, her hands homing in on the heat of my sex, to the wetness that she knew awaited her. I opened my legs, my skirt riding up.

"Take your clothes off, quickly!"

I stripped off my skirt and started to pull my top up and over my head while Martine pulled my silk G-string down my legs. The shelves behind us rattled and something fell; the stereo jumped to the CD's next track. My blood surged with a dangerous, dizzy rush of exhilaration when Martine stroked my legs and moved straight into my heat, taking my clit in her mouth, nursing its fullness and sucking deeply. She moved her mouth over my flesh in deliberate sweeps, ending back on my clitoris, with the tip of her tongue circling it closely, firmly. *Oh, she is good.* I felt as if a bomb was about to go off inside me.

That's when I noticed the mirror that stood close to the bed, and the scene reflected there transfixed me. Martine kneeling between my legs, and as her skirt rode up, I saw she wore stockings but no panties, her pussy naughtily peeping out as she bent between my legs. I could just make out the tip of her tongue, darting out and rolling over my sticky sex folds. It looked so strange, seeing myself like that, with her on me, and it sent me flying toward meltdown.

"Oh fuuuuuck…"

Martine lifted her head. Her fingers replaced her mouth, and she plowed them inside me. Her free hand crept up to my bra, and she bent its cups down, setting my breasts free.

"You want it, don't you?" she asked, as her fingers tweaked at my nipples, bringing it nearer. She kicked off her shoes and slid her body down with her pussy pressed up against my bare thigh.

"Oh fuck," I murmured again when I felt the beautiful wet slide of Martine's heat on my leg. A wave of pleasure rushed up, the first ebbs of my orgasm.

"You're so hot," she said and her eyes were aflame. She began to move her hips, pressing her sex along my thigh, rubbing frantically. "I'm going to come too!"

We exchanged a look of total mutual appreciation, both moving desperately, climbing over the threshold. I let my hands close tightly on Martine's shoulders and pressed my leg up into the hot wet valley of flesh that rode me. Martine's lips parted and her eyes closed. She ground her hips down and pressed home. With a sudden cry, she came. My core pounded with release, my clit a buzz of sensation.

After a few moments of labored breathing, I turned my head to look at the mirror. Did Martine put it there on purpose to entertain her lovers? I suddenly wanted mirrors everywhere; I wanted to see sex from every angle. Turning back, I saw Martine unzip her skirt and quickly drop it on the floor. She threw off her bra as she went over to the wardrobe that stood in the gloomiest corner of the room, and rustled around inside. When she turned back, I didn't know where to look first: at the bright silver barbells that pierced her nipples or at the enormous strap-on cock hanging from one hand.

She walked back and held it out. I took it in my hand, my eyes on stalks as I examined the huge contraption. It was molded with distended veins and the head was huge, engorged, as if it were about to explode. I ran my fingers around the edge of the head, imaging that rubbing against me, inside. My sex clenched.

"Wow," I murmured, looking up at Martine.

"You like it, huh?"

"It's, um, amazing!"

"You must put it on."

"Me?" I blurted.

"Yes, I need more," she demanded impatiently.

The last round was obviously just for openers. I glanced at the clock; there was still time. Martine was already laid out on the bed, her knees pulled up and her legs open. She had two fingers up to the hilt inside her sex, thrusting vigorously. Her breasts had rolled out to the sides. The piercings made her nipples look loaded, like twin torpedoes about to be launched. Between her legs, her fingers were slick with wetness.

I stood over her, filled with a sudden sense of longing and something else: power, raw power ebbing up from deep inside me. I hadn't worn a cock before. What would it be like? I felt a surge of vitality roar up inside me. I was going to fuck this woman, really fuck her. *Hard.* I stepped back and quickly stepped into the harness, pulling it tight against my pussy and between my buttocks. The phallus felt heavy against my intimate parts, and outrageously large. I turned to glance at myself in the mirror, gasping when I saw it in profile. It looked totally strange and perverse in its size, brazen.

"I look obscene," I whispered to myself, a dart of sheer depravity flying around my veins.

Martine moaned from the bed, reaching out for me, her gaze on the cock. Christ, this was so hot! I knelt down between Martine's open legs and took a taste of her. She was so wet, and tasted so good, her nectar creamy and warm. She shuddered against my face when my tongue explored her. I had one hand on the cock, the other over one of her breasts. I captured the knotted skin between thumb and forefinger, rolling the steel barbell between my fingers. I was gratified to hear her moans growing louder. I lifted my head to suck on the other nipple, toying with the barbell with my tongue, moving my hips between hers. Martine looked down when I whispered her name. I guided her hand over the huge head, lubricating it with her wet fingers.

"Oh yes, now," Martine urged. I edged the massive head of the cock into the slippery entrance to her sex, angling my hips to accommodate the movement.

"Oh, mon Dieu," Martine cried out.

I groaned. "Can you take more of it?"

"Yes!" As if to confirm it, she grabbed the cock and hit a switch at its base. I gasped with shock when it started to vibrate, reverberating between us and sending a little jagged riff that went straight up into my clit.

Oh my!

I was wired, hugely aroused, and totally empowered. I looked down at the woman spread in front of me, all wet with sex and wanting. She was like a pool of liquid lust on the bed, bubbling up, ready to be brought off. A sense of sheer and absolute power filled my body. I pulled the base of the cock up against my clit, enjoying the weight and the vibrations there, where I was taut and pounding. The molded thing in my hands felt like a weapon and I jutted my hips forward, reaching and testing the tender succulent flesh of Martine's hole. I worked my hips slowly, edging it inside. Martine's hands flew up to the metal bed frame to brace her. She began to rock in time with my thrusts.

"Oh yes, push hard," she said. I raised up onto my arms, pushing the strap-on firmly against the resistance it met. She suddenly grabbed at my arms. Her hips bucked wildly. I leaned forward watching the reflection of our bodies in the mirror, the line of my breasts heaving as I moved back and forth between her thighs. It looked so hot. I was fucking her; I was fucking this hot glam-bitch with an enormous strap-on cock. My sex was on fire with arousal, the threat of another climax trembling right down into my hardworking thighs.

"Oh, Kim, I like you lots!" she cried out, gasps of pleasure and laughter escaping her. Her neck arched up, her eyelids lowering. She was so close.

"I like you lots too," I replied, grinning, loving her foreign tongue, and thrust hard. She reached down to the juncture of our bodies, rubbing her clit. The fingers of her free hand fastened over my nipple, pinching me while she bucked up. The pinch shot through my body, wiring itself into the heat between my thighs, and I had to fight the urge to shout my pleasure aloud. I looked down at the bucking woman beneath me and grabbed the base of the cock, crushing my clit hard against it and sending us both right over the edge.

Non, je ne regrette rien. I hummed the old Edith Piaf number as I drove my Land Rover into its bay in the underground car park at HQ and stepped out, grabbing my portfolio.

"Hey, Kim, how did it go?" Jack waved to me as he threw his briefcase into his Merc. I had caught him just before he left for the board meeting. What a bonus.

"Success. They went for the whole campaign, Web slots and all." It was a massive contract for the company, my best work to date.

"Excellent. I knew you'd pull it off. That pay raise of yours is secure."

He saluted as he climbed into the car, then stuck his head out of the window. "And you be sure you take yourself a good lunch break. You deserve it!"

I smiled to myself as I headed for the lift. *Too right, honey.* I had just enjoyed the best lunch break I'd ever had, and with a pay raise in the offing, I could afford to visit Kilpatrick's for lunch more often, just as Martine had suggested I should. Now, how was that for staff motivation?

Bingo, Baby
Radclyffe

"Honey, let's go in drag tonight."

I looked up from the newspaper and tried to suppress a grin. Shelby is a femme. Not ultra-ultra-femme—no super-long nails or heavy-duty make-up, but she doesn't leave the house without eyeliner, either. Plus, she's small. Okay, *petite.* Her head comes to my chest. But she's perfectly built—every part of her—from her pert, high breasts to her nicely rounded, squeezable ass. But no one, nohow, would take her for a guy. Not even with a twelve-inch dick. "Sure, baby, but we only brought one dick."

It's tough packing toys when you travel, and the security people at the airport in Provincetown check *everything.* But then I guess they've *seen* everything, too, and there's no way I was going on vacation without my equipment. Still, I couldn't bring a complete complement either, so we both wouldn't be able to dress in full gear.

Shel's lush pink lips parted, her tongue peeked out as she ran it lightly over the velvet surface, and my mind turned to oatmeal. "We only *need* one. For me."

I got hold of myself and dragged my thoughts away from what she could do with that tongue. "Huh? What am *I* going to wear, then?"

"This," she replied sweetly as she held up a tiny swatch of leather.

I paled. "That's a skirt."

"Uh-huh."

"It's yours."

"Uh-huh."

"I can't wear *that.*" I started to sweat. I started to look for the exit. I was in boxers and nothing else. I couldn't run.

"You might be taller, but your hips aren't that much bigger than mine. It will just be a little short."

"A *little?*" God help me, I actually squeaked. Just the thought of the skirt was making my clit shrink. "That won't even cover my crotch!"

"This will."

She held up a black satin thong, and my clit fell clean off.

"Oh no—no fucking way."

"Please, honey?"

Not fair. Not fair, not fair, not fair.

"Then we'll *both* be in drag," Shel pointed out, twirling the thong around her index finger. "It *is* drag bingo, after all."

Ordinarily, Shelby within twenty feet of a thong makes me want to start at her toes and lick my way to the top of her head, but today all I could think about was how much that tiny triangle *didn't* cover. Especially on me.

"We don't have any drag clothes that will fit you. My jackets are all too big." I tried a different tack. Shel was very particular about her clothes.

"Don't worry about me. I'll manage something." She leaned over the sofa, cupped my crotch, and resurrected my clit as she squeezed. "Didn't fall off, now, did it?"

"Ha ha," I muttered as she stuck her warm tongue in my mouth. It was a few minutes before I thought about much of anything except how clever her fingers were. When she stopped doing that wonderful up and down, round and round thing she was doing with her thumb, I groaned in protest. "Hey—what—?"

"Later, honey." She gave me another little tug and kissed the tip of my nose. My clit gave a little jump right back. "I have to get dressed. And so do you."

That effectively killed my healthy, happy hard-on once and for all.

I dawdled. I balked. I downright stonewalled. Okay, okay—I mostly sulked. I showered but then I refused to get dressed. Shelby ignored me as I sat on the foot of the bed staring at the floor, naked, immobile—a pathetic rendition of the Thinker facing a firing squad.

"What do you think?" Shel asked softly.

I turned my head and found myself eye to eye with a pair of black silk boxers that tented out suggestively over the gently bobbing dick inside. Now I have to tell you, I think wearing a dick is about the sexiest feeling I've ever had—except, of course, fucking Shelby with one.

But I've never particularly been interested in being on the receiving end. Fortunately, Shelby has never complained. So I'd never seen her strapped before. I couldn't take my eyes off her smooth, tanned belly encircled by the broad waistband of the boxers and the jutting prominence below. She is such a girl in every way, and I wouldn't have believed how hot she'd look with all that girl power dancing inches from my face.

"Jesus," I breathed in awe.

She made a little sound like a contented purr. And then she reached down and wrapped her dainty fist around the silk-sheathed cock and gave it a little shake. My mouth dropped open and my clit stood at attention.

"Does it always make you horny right away when you put it on?" she asked a little dreamily.

"Usually, yeah," I muttered, watching her hand action speed up a little bit. "Baby?"

"Hmm?"

"If you want to jerk off with that, come a little closer and I'll help."

"Oh no." She laughed knowingly, giving the dick one final tug before letting go. "You just want to distract me so we miss bingo."

"That was the furthest thing from my mind," I protested. It was true, too. In that moment, all I could think about was holding on to her ass and putting her dick in my mouth. *In my mouth? Jesus Christ. What's happening to me?*

"Come on, honey. Stand up. Let me dress you."

My brain was still a bit addled, and without thinking, I complied. The next thing I knew, I was wearing a sleeveless mesh top that was so tight my nipples nearly protruded through the tiny holes, the black satin thong that barely kept my clit covered, and the leather skirt that hit right at the bottom of my butt cheeks. I don't know why she bothered to put me into clothes at all. I took one look in the mirror and almost fainted.

"I can't go out like this."

"Sure you can. I promise your butch credentials will not be revoked."

I turned, ready to take a stand, and got a good look at her as she buckled a thin black belt around her waist. She'd gone for the simple *GQ* look, and it worked perfectly on her. She wore an open-collared black silk shirt tucked into tailored black trousers with dress shoes and the belt. She'd slicked back her short blond hair and wore no make-up. She resembled an androgynous Calvin Klein model, the ones that I always feel a little bit guilty about staring at. I glanced down. She looked like a handsome young man with a very substantial hard-on. *Oh baby.*

"You gonna walk around town like that?" I felt myself getting wet. This was so confusing.

"Why not?" She gave her hips a tiny bump. "You do."

"Well, yeah, but that's different."

She stepped closer, cupped my jaw, and stood on her tiptoes to kiss me. When she leaned against me, I felt the firm press of her dick against my thigh. Now I was wet *and* hard. I put my hands on her waist and moved to turn her toward the bed. To my astonishment, she pushed me gently away.

"Uh-uh. No touching."

"Oh, come on, baby. Let's just stay home."

"Nope." She slid a slim leather wallet into her back pocket and buttoned it. Then she held out her hand and gave me that smile that I've never been able to resist. "Come on, honey. Time to go to drag bingo."

We stood in line along with half the population of Provincetown to get through the white picket fence and onto the grass-covered front lawn of the Unitarian Universalist Church where dozens of metal folding tables had been set up for one of the highlights of Carnival week. Drag bingo. The space was crowded with tourists and townspeople, drag queens, and here and there, a drag king. It was a party atmosphere, and everyone was taking pictures of everyone else. We wended our way toward a free table, carrying our fat color markers and our stack of bingo cards.

I would have felt self-conscious in my less-than-flattering outfit, except no one was paying any attention to me. The drag queens were so flamboyant, so outrageously wonderful, that all eyes were on them. Except for the dykes who were unabashedly eyeing my girlfriend. I had a wholly unfamiliar urge to start scratching eyes out. *Scratching eyes out? Who the hell am I?*

"Can't you strap that thing down?" I said in an irritated whisper after the third time I spied some sexy femme staring at Shelby's crotch.

"It's as down as it's going to get," she said with a grin. "You ought to know."

"Well, *I* never get cruised the way you are when I'm packing it."

She gave me a fiery look. "Oh yes, you do. You just don't know how to stake out your territory. It's a girl thing."

"Then sit down," I hissed, indicating one of the few free seats left, "and hide that before I have to hurt someone."

"I was wondering," she whispered, leaning close as I took the seat next to her, "if it always makes you want to come in your pants really bad, too."

I groaned. I would have banged my head on the table, but they were starting to call out the first of the bingo numbers, and everyone around me was in a frenzy to mark their cards. You didn't interfere with some of these people at bingo, not and keep your body parts.

It's not easy to sit very long in a skirt, I discovered. I tried crossing my legs, but my feet went numb. If I didn't cross my legs, I forgot to keep my knees together, and although I welcomed the breeze, I was afraid that I'd be advertising to all and sundry exactly the state I was in. Which, considering the fact that every few minutes, Shelby would run her fingers up the inside of my thigh underneath the table, was one of terminal arousal bordering on coming in my seat. When she casually picked up my left hand, moved it under the table and into her lap, and pressed it against the bulge in her trousers, I almost did.

"You're driving me crazy," I growled into her ear. "I'm going to the bathroom to stick my head under the cold-water faucet."

She laughed as I walked away.

I passed by the long lines for the Porta-Johns outside the church and walked around to the side entrance. Having been to more than one show in the church auditorium, I knew there was another small bathroom just inside. Fortunately, not many other people thought of it, and the line was short. Two of the three stalls were occupied, and as I stepped into the third—the farthest from the door—I felt a hand against my back and another person crowded in behind me.

"Shh," Shelby whispered before I could say anything.

I couldn't even turn around, we were pressed so close together, her behind me and my knees nearly up against the toilet. When she gave my shoulders a gentle shove, I reflexively reached out with both hands and braced myself against the wall in front of me. It's a good thing I did, because a second later she slipped her hand under the back of my skirt and between my legs, and my knees nearly gave out. For the first time, I appreciated the ingenious nature of a thong. With a practiced flick of her thumb, she swept the material aside and slid her fingertips between my labia.

I heard her groan as I drenched her hand, and I had to bite my lip to hold back a cry of my own. I think I mentioned how good she is with her hands, and I was already pushing my hips back and forth in an attempt to rub my clitoris against her fingers. I'd been so turned on for so long, I knew I'd come in seconds. To my surprise, she pulled away before I could get there. Then I heard it, and my heart stopped.

The unmistakable sound of a zipper slowly sliding open.

When I moved to turn around, she cupped the back of my neck in her hand to stop me with a whisper. "No."

Off balance, still braced against the wall, I had no room to do anything but wait. I felt as if my whole body was waiting, waiting to be touched, waiting to be filled, waiting to be taken. It was wholly unfamiliar and completely natural. With the first brush of the smooth, cool length of her dick between my legs, my clit jerked and I tightened inside and all I wanted was for her to make me come. I pushed back again, this time against the fat, firm head, and felt it slip inside. I moaned. I couldn't help it.

"Feels good, doesn't it, honey?" she murmured in my ear, her breath hot and ragged.

I knew what she was feeling, the pressure against her clit from the base of the cock, the sweet power of being inside her woman, the need to give and take at the same time. I could only whimper and nod my head. I wanted more, but I was afraid. Afraid to be other than I have always thought myself to be; afraid to be not less, but more. She knew, and she helped me.

She moved her hand from my neck around the front of my body and underneath the edge of the tiny skirt. She held my clitoris gently between her fingers and began to slide it back and forth the way she knows always makes me come. As soon as she started, I pushed back onto her dick and she slid deeper inside. As I stretched in body and mind to take her, the pressure surged into my clit, and I knew I was going to come.

She stroked me, I rocked against her, she pushed deeper. Once, twice, and then I felt it—the slow, rolling contractions in the core of me that in another minute would burst shooting from my clit.

"I'm coming," I cried softly. I felt her weight against my back, her body trembling as she worked herself inside me. I heard the quick, high-pitched sound she makes when she's nearing orgasm. Just as I crashed over the edge and lost all sense of anything but her, I heard her triumphant voice in my ear.

"Bingo, baby. Bingo."

AFLAME
GUN BROOKE

"May I have an extra blanket, please?"

The cognac voice from across the aisle caught Corazon Perez's attention as she unbuckled her seat belt. By force of habit, she had closed her eyes hard during takeoff and not paid any attention to anything except her own breathing. *Afraid of flying* was a phrase that didn't cover how bad it really was. She was so terrified of takeoffs and landings she had to fight medicating herself into oblivion.

Corazon looked furtively toward the passenger occupying the window seat. A striking woman who looked to be in her early forties rubbed her arms, which she had wrapped around her chest, as if to warm them. She wore a tight off-white suede skirt that reached just below her knees and a short blue suede jacket over a blue satin shirt. Golden brown tresses, several shades darker than chestnut, had escaped a loose twist and framed a slightly angular, thin face that boasted a determined chin. She wasn't beautiful in the classical sense, but she was definitely attractive. Letting her gaze slide down the other woman's body, Corazon felt her nipples stand at attention.

Suddenly, light green eyes under dark eyebrows locked onto Corazon's, startling her with their shimmering intensity. Almost fluorescent, they shone before warming up as she smiled. "If I didn't know the windows were sealed tight, I'd say there's a draft."

"Must be the ventilation," Corazon offered, a little annoyed at how tense her voice sounded. "A blanket ought to do it. Or…" She leaned back, flashing the other woman a slow smile. "Or you could ask the flight attendant if you can move over here. I don't get a draft."

It was true. She was comfortable in the second of the four seats in the center of the Airbus 330 even without her suit jacket. Reaching across the empty seat next to her, she extended a hand. "I'm Corazon." *Say yes.*

"My name's Blaise. Blaise Donovan." Brightening up, the woman scooted over to the aisle seat, taking Corazon's proffered hand. "Nice to meet you, Corazon. Sure you don't mind?"

God, no, I don't mind. The thought of the gorgeous woman across the aisle sitting next to her made Corazon's heart flutter and roused a familiar tension between her legs. Stunned at the immediate response, she felt her cheeks color. "No, of course not. Why don't I move to the next seat, and you can take mine. That way we'll both be in the middle, away from the aisle."

"Oh, that'd be great." Blaise smiled. "I hate it when someone elbows you in the head when you're trying to sleep or read." She laughed huskily. "Or whatever."

Or whatever? If you only knew. Like hot, strong liqueur, the sound of Blaise's voice trickled down Corazon's spine, tingling along her nerve endings, making her shiver. "Why don't you change seats right now? The flight attendant's on her way back with your extra blanket." *Did that sound as urgent as I feel?* She hoped to God it didn't.

A minute later, Blaise sat in Corazon's old seat, looking content. "Mmm, nice and warm." She spread the two blankets over herself, sighing in obvious pleasure. "Ah. Wonderful."

The blanket lay halfway across Corazon's legs, partially covering her above-the-knee, black tailored skirt and black silk, thigh-high stockings. She had kicked off her three-inch-heel pumps as soon as she sat down.

Blaise shifted and her scent, dark and flowery, wafted toward Corazon. Then she tugged several hairpins from her golden hair, letting it fall in deliciously tousled locks around her face to where it grazed her collarbones.

Eyes roaming, Corazon noticed several buttons of Blaise's shirt were open, revealing pale, creamy skin, and she found herself wondering how her own olive-colored skin would look against such abundant white. Willing herself to lean back into her seat, she inhaled deeply, trying to stay calm. *Out of sight, out of mind? You've got to be kidding. She's the most attractive woman I've seen in years. The perfume. What is it? Like dark, dark chocolate...* In her line of work as an in-demand, high-profile portrait photographer, she had seen many women, through the lens and out of it, but no one had taken her breath away instantly like Blaise.

She reached for her own blanket, unfolded it, and tucked it around herself. Only then did she realize she had also tucked Blaise's blankets more closely around them both.

"Mmm, cozy for both of us." Blaise sighed. "Would you mind turning out the lights? That way, the flight attendants won't bother us with drinks and food. Unless you want some, of course?" She reclined her seat back, ending up with her head closer to Corazon's.

"No, I'm ready for a break. It's been a crazy weekend."

"Really? A crazy weekend in Paris?" Blaise smiled broadly. "Anything you can share?"

Corazon had to laugh. "No, I meant work-wise. This was strictly a business trip."

"What do you do?"

"I'm a photographer. And you?"

"I own a gallery in Miami. Fascination—mainly local artists."

"I can't believe it!" Corazon leaned on her elbow, edging closer to Blaise. "My studio's just a few blocks from you. Perez Portrait Studio."

As they laughed at the twist of fate, Blaise placed a hand on Corazon's naked arm beneath the blankets. "Destiny at work here, you think?"

Destiny? Corazon found it hard to swallow past the lump in her throat. The touch of Blaise's hand, her soft scent, all contributed to Corazon's rapidly climbing arousal. She was disappointed when the other woman removed her hand, settling with her head only an inch from Corazon's shoulder.

Corazon reached for the button on her armrest and switched off the lights. Behind and in front of them, other passengers had done the same, creating a soothingly dark circle of quiet in the middle of the plane. The flight attendants carried out their duties, handing out drinks and something to nibble on, but Corazon declined and leaned back into her seat. Eventually the other passengers settled, most of them, like her and Blaise, curled up with pillows and blankets.

Closing her eyes, Corazon again inhaled the alluring scent of her travel companion, allowing it to fill her senses and flow through her veins. Eventually, she heard Blaise's breathing grow even, and the golden brown head slid closer, finally resting fully against her. Afraid to move, she sat perfectly still, her shoulder burning where Blaise's head rested.

With every minute adding to her excitement, Corazon looked down at the tousled locks, desperately fighting the urge to press her lips against them. Blaise's nearness pulled her in, made her stir restlessly beneath the blanket. She raised a hand to stroke the silky, golden hair but caught herself just in time, pulling back abruptly. *God!*

"You okay?" Blaise peeked up through the strands of hair. "You moaned?"

I did? Oh no, please don't say that. "Ah…I'm fine. Thank you." *And you sound like an idiot, Perez.*

"Good Lord, I'm sorry. I seem to have ended up on your shoulder. Your poor arm." Blaise sat up but, to Corazon's surprise, edged closer. "Here, let me help." Stroking Corazon's arm in long, slow movements, she gave a bright smile. "There. Better?"

"Better." Corazon almost choked when Blaise's fingertips brushed against the side of her breast. Wearing only a whisper-thin lace bra beneath her blouse, she felt the touch as unmistakably as if she'd been naked. Her breath caught in her throat, and she struggled not to betray how her legs pressed together at the touch. Furtively leaning harder against her seat, Corazon tried to move away from the fingers. *More of that, baby, and we'll both be in trouble.*

Blaise seemed oblivious to Corazon's arousal even when the back of one hand slid across the entire side of Corazon's breast. "You're so tense." Looking genuinely concerned, Blaise leaned forward, gazing into Corazon's eyes. "You should've woken me up."

"I didn't mind. Honest." *If you touch me like that again…* Corazon's body went rigid when the slender hands moved inside the short sleeve of the shirt. When they slid up and down as far as they could reach, Corazon broke into a sweat. "Blaise…" *How the hell do I say this?*

"Yes?" The voice was innocent, caring, but now there was a devilish sparkle in the green eyes. One hand moved down to Corazon's stocking-clad right knee, seemingly for support, while the other kept stroking and massaging her arm.

"You don't have to. Really, I'm fine."

Blaise's lips appeared impossibly luscious as she ran the tip of her tongue across them. "I know. You're very fine."

There was no more oxygen on the plane. Corazon opened her mouth to inhale deeply, but nothing happened. Blaise's smile filled her vision, pink lips approaching hers as the hand on her knee began a dangerous exploration. In slow circles, it moved up her leg and slipped under her skirt before Corazon had a chance to object. When the fingers stopped just on the border between the stocking and the warm skin of her thigh, Corazon found new air to breathe. She gasped.

"Am I mistaken?" Blaise whispered.

Hell, no. Corazon wanted to pull her closer, crush their breasts together. Looking around, she couldn't tell if anyone was paying any attention to them in their darkened little island. *Still in plain view, for heaven's sake!*

Blaise frowned, a look of uncertainty on her face. Drawing a trembling breath, Corazon realized she hadn't answered out loud. "No, no. You're not mistaken. About anything." Her words were barely audible, even to herself, but Blaise's eyes flared. Curling up in her seat, she tucked the blanket more firmly around them. Corazon was intensely aware of Blaise never taking her left hand away from between her thighs.

"I saw you were uncomfortable at takeoff," Blaise said and pushed the armrest between them up and out of her way. "Dislike flying?"

"Hate it. Scares me to death every time."

Sliding her other hand farther up, Blaise stroked the damp skin on the inside of Corazon's thighs. She coaxed Corazon to part her legs as much as was possible in her skirt. Her smile faded, replaced with a look of unmasked desire.

"That's right. Spread your legs for me…Corazon."

The sound of her name on Blaise's lips sent another rush of wetness between Corazon's legs.

"I'll show you a very, very good way to relieve the stress of flying."

Knowing how clear her arousal would become if Blaise moved any higher, Corazon turned her head, intending to hide her face against the other woman's hair. Quickly Blaise dipped her head, captured Corazon's lips, and pressed hard against her. She slipped her tongue inside, ravaging Corazon's mouth. Unable to do anything but surrender, Corazon whimpered, almost, but not quite inaudibly.

"Good," Blaise whispered against her mouth, the sweetness of her breath warm against Corazon's skin. "You have to be quiet. Very quiet. All right?" Her hand slipped higher and she ran her blunt nails along the silky skin of Corazon's thigh.

"Yes."

"And you also have to sit very still." Blaise's voice was a mere breath. "Or our neighbors will notice us. Promise?"

"Promise." *I promise, I promise...Touch me! Please!*

"And I want you to whisper very, very quietly to me how you feel...when I do this."

Corazon trembled as Blaise's nimble fingers pushed the drenched silk aside, exposing slick, slippery folds.

"Oh God."

The curious fingertips avoided the rock-hard, protruding clitoris, and still it jerked, over and over, as if begging for attention. Corazon couldn't believe this could be happening, how this beautiful stranger now had access to the most intimate part of her body. *I haven't had sex in months and look what happens.*

"How does this feel?" Blaise whispered.

"So—damn—good," Corazon muttered in a staccato voice and shifted in the seat, managing to spread her legs farther and still be covered by the blanket. "You burn me."

Blaise's fingers played in the wetness, still avoiding the aching ridge, instead circling Corazon's entrance. "Damn good, huh?" Her lips touched Corazon's earlobe as she whispered. "You're incredible. I haven't felt anything like this...ever. So sensitive, so...responsive."

"It's fire. More..." It was agony not to be able to buck against Blaise's hand. She would have given anything to have those inquisitive fingers plunge into her. "I'm soaked." Husky and dark, she hardly recognized her own voice. "You make me too wet."

"There ain't no such thing," Blaise drawled and proved her statement by dabbing two fingers in Corazon's juices. She painted wet traces on the inside of Corazon's thighs before returning to her engorged sex. Cupping it, she took a handful. Corazon pressed her tongue against the roof of her mouth, forcing herself to remain quiet. She needed to be vocal, to moan out loud and acknowledge the roaring fire inside, but willed herself to breathe evenly.

"So, you shave. Nice. Smooth," Blaise purred. Another tug. "I don't, but I trim."

A movement under the blanket to her right caught Corazon's attention. It seemed that Blaise's right arm was occupied, doing something else, something that made her eyes sparkle, casting enticing highlights in the darkness.

"Yes," Blaise whispered. "I'm touching myself, like I touch you. Everything I do to you, I do to myself. You've made me so hot."

Trembling hard, Corazon would have given away her best Hasselblad camera for the chance to pull the blankets off Blaise. She wanted to see what Blaise was doing, to get down between those slender legs and watch those fingers work. And then help her. *Oh yeah, I'd help her.* The image of herself between Blaise's thighs, licking in between busy fingers, was almost enough to send Corazon over the edge. *No, not yet. No, no, no.*

"You make me wet too. I'm positively drenched." Blaise's eyes grew wide and she pushed her fingers between Corazon's legs, harder, pressing just below the clitoris. At the same time, her other hand moved and she shivered and bit her lower lip.

She's as turned on as I am. Corazon turned her head, pressing her lips against Blaise's ear. "You want to touch that clit of yours so bad, don't you?" Corazon mouthed almost inaudibly, her eyes fastened on the jagged movements under the blanket. "Go ahead. I want to come…I need to, so badly."

"Not yet. Not just yet." Blaise leaned against her, her hand never resting. Almost entering her, she pressed hard against Corazon. "You're going to do something for me now. It might drive us over the edge too soon, but I want you to do as I say."

Corazon only nodded, knowing for certain that if she spoke, it would come out as a cry of lust.

"Unbutton your blouse."

Her eyes closing at the suggestive, throaty voice, Corazon reached up, fumbling with the tiny buttons.

"Push your bra up."

Corazon reached inside her shirt, not needing any more encouragement. She pushed her lace bra up and found her nipples rock hard and aching. Applying just the right pressure, she tweaked them mercilessly, opening her mouth in a soundless cry as equal parts of pleasure and pain stabbed through her breasts.

Blaise caught her silent cry with her lips, freeing her right arm for a moment to raise the blanket enough to hide them from anyone who might pass in the aisle. As they kissed, tongues tasting and teasing, Corazon felt inquisitive fingertips slip into her wet center and Blaise's thumb briefly flick over her clitoris. Her hips jerked involuntarily as she sought more of the agonizing pleasure. Glancing down at Blaise, she saw her chew her lower lip and the other hand work furiously under the blanket.

"God. So hungry. So hot," Blaise murmured and leaned closer, her mouth against Corazon's lips. "So...ready."

"Yes." It was a low growl, hushed but urgent. Corazon tugged at her own nipples and rolled them relentlessly into firmly pebbled peaks. Flicking them madly with her nails, she was squirming in her seat. *I need more. Much more.* Rasping the now-aching nipples with her nails, she came closer to what she needed, but not close enough. *Oh God, Blaise, I'm dying here. Take me.*

Blaise firmly clasped the hood over Corazon's swollen clit, forcing the head out with gentle pressure, and ran her index finger repeatedly across the engorged ridge.

"Are you doing this...to yourself?" Corazon managed, the pure bliss striking hard, urging her on. "Are you inside?"

"Deep inside." Blaise's voice was low, but the emphasis on *deep* was enough for Corazon to shudder repeatedly. The small hairs on her arms rose and she shivered as Blaise added a third finger and went impossibly deeper.

Corazon's hot oil drenched Blaise's hand. *So close. It's fire. Damn it, it's pain!* Her hips began the inevitable undulation, and she turned her head into Blaise's neck, pressing hard against fragrant, moist skin. *It won't take much now. I won't hold.* "Blaise..."

"Yes, baby. I know. I know." The repetitive words accompanied the steady movement of Blaise's hands. "You want more, don't you?"

Oh God, yes. "Do you? Can you take more?" Corazon tossed out the challenge in a throaty whisper.

"I'm glad you asked." The fingers pulled out, then returned after an agonizing delay, four of them filling her to the brim. Corazon's sex stretched to accommodate the insistent hand, and she leaned back farther into the seat, needing to see Blaise's face. "You're taking me." Corazon heard the wonder in her own voice.

"Hell, yes." A sublime look of lust and joy spread over Blaise's features as she surreptitiously rocked against her own hand. "It's...too much. I'm going to come."

"Me too." Corazon's head was spinning. Suddenly she was teetering at the edge of the precipice, not sure how she'd ended up there. It was damn near impossible to speak through the red haze that surrounded her. "I'm so close. I can't take it any longer." She wasn't sure the other woman had heard her. Blaise kept up the maddening caress until Corazon was ready to scream. Suddenly the hand almost withdrew, only to alter direction immediately, plunging four fingers deep inside. Blaise pressed the base of her palm against Corazon's clit again, rubbing it mercilessly as the fingers curled up within her, connecting with those special nerve endings she rarely could find herself. *It can't be happening. She can't be pushing me over the edge so fast. I normally have to wait so long, forever, almost. What's going on? What...*

"You feel so good. So hot...so ready." Blaise went rigid against her own hand. "It's as if you're the one taking me. You're...fucking me, aren't you? In your mind?"

"Oh, yes." And she was. In her mind, Corazon spread Blaise's legs with her shoulders, thrust eager fingers inside, and latched onto her inflamed clit with her tongue. "You have no idea how much I want you."

"I think I do." Blaise tipped her head to the left and bit down on Corazon's neck. Feeling the teeth dig into her skin, Corazon lost what little shred of self-control she had left. The orgasm hit with shattering force, turbulence in her pelvis that struck arrows of tormented bliss up her abdomen and down her thighs. She closed her eyes and rode the orgasm toward oblivion, vaguely aware of Blaise's jerking hips next to her. The sharp teeth turned into soft lips and a tongue, soothing the bite. "I'm going to come, Corazon..."

"Yes, that's it. Give it to me." Corazon moved one hand from her breasts and pushed it stealthily toward Blaise, under the blanket. She found a bunched-up skirt; naked, damp thighs; and a furiously working hand.

When Corazon's fingers reached Blaise's hand, Blaise pulled her own fingers out, whispering hotly, "Do it! Go inside!"

Corazon slid home without effort, the copious wetness making it easy. Curling her fingers, she pushed in and out at a steady pace.

"You're going to kill me. Faster." Her voice a mere whimper, Blaise still tried to dictate Corazon's actions.

"Not quite so fast." Her thumb found Blaise's clitoris, impossibly large and wet. When she began to circle it, occasionally flattening it in the midst of all the wetness, Corazon knew Blaise wouldn't last much longer. She placed a series of tiny kisses on her damp forehead. "I've got you. Come!"

The feel of Blaise's fingers still immersed inside her sent new shivers through Corazon. "You're going to make me come again," she whispered against Blaise's delicate ear.

"Oh, Corazon." Blaise pressed her legs together, trapping Corazon's hand. "Now!"

Contractions, bordering on convulsions, clasped Corazon's fingers. Small flutters grew to wing-beats, escalated to a single, hard wave of pleasure. Strange, distant drums, vaguely recognizable as her own heartbeat, echoed inside her head as her body tossed in orgasm. After the storm, they slowly separated. Corazon made sure the three blankets covered them neatly and hugged the somnolent woman in her arms. "You're beautiful. Absolutely gorgeous."

Resting on Corazon's shoulder, Blaise looked up, her eyes not quite focused. "Did it help?"

"What?" Overwhelming fatigue settled on Corazon like yet another blanket. "Did what help?"

"This." There was a brief pause before Blaise gave a husky laugh. "Did it take your mind off your fear of flying?"

"Funny. But yes, it did, come to think of it. It took my mind off that and pretty much everything else."

"Everything?"

"Well, *almost* everything." Corazon kissed her lightly.

"Mmm, I know." Blaise gave a warm smile, tenderness replacing lust. "Everything but you."

PUNCH-DRUNK
RM PRYOR

She was stalking me in the bar where I worked. She was stalking me for a week before she met some friends in there and I became a bet. I was a bet for a week before I knew about it. She sat in my bar long after her friends were gone. She sat in my bar until closing time and the big Samoan security guard took her beer away and threw it down the sink. She was drunk and concerned about the wasted beer. I was sober and worried about trying to get this chick out of my bar without arousing security's aggression, handing her the note with my number written on it without the bar staff seeing, and hoping to hell no one knew what was going on.

She rang me in the morning. She apologized for whatever it was she might or might not have done in her drunken state; she sounded foggy and hopeful and my stomach had tied itself into knots a sailor wouldn't understand. We arranged to meet for a beer the next day and I think my stomach was trying to strangle me. I put down the phone and ripped my wardrobe apart trying to find that perfect something with just the right amount of casual cool to wow her. An hour later I discovered I didn't possess any amount of cool, casual or not, and I started hoping to hell she would ring and cancel so I could go shopping. I spent the next half hour cursing myself for tempting karma and praying to every god I knew the name of that she didn't ring to cancel. I went to bed exhausted but I still couldn't sleep.

I woke up bouncing. The hours dragged by until I couldn't take it any longer and went to the pub an hour and a half early. I bought a beer and read *Catch-22* until she got there. We drank beer and I talked. I talked this nervous talk that is mostly just dribbling shit and trying a little too hard to be funny and interesting and cool and like someone you'd really want to hang out with if you just got to know…

I must have sounded like a raving lunatic. I think I condensed my life story into comic book form and told it to her complete with actions. To this day I wonder why she answered any of my calls after that.

I felt naughty. I felt like a confused, horny teenaged boy trying his mom's panties on. I'd been in a heterosexual relationship and we'd broken up—well, I'd broken up and he was still in the house. I snuck around for a few weeks, trying in some twisted way to save him the pain of knowledge, but then I got mad. Four years I'd tried the right way. Four years I hated myself, and now I was free and I still had this dead thing from a past life haunting my house. I was over it. I was over being nice and considerate and trying to save tears. I wanted to be evil, mean, and dirty. I shaved my head. I hurt him for my wasted years and I didn't feel bad one bit. I got another tattoo. The truth is a valid excuse… I just told him I met a girl that got me all wet to think about her. Found me a girl who's soft and beautiful. Found me a girl… What boy can argue with that? He knew when he met me what my tendencies were. Freedom is a beautiful thing. I hadn't even kissed her yet.

We didn't kiss for weeks. I wanted to kiss her so bad… I'd see her and it was all I could do not to pull her into the closest room and kiss those lips. Fascinated with her lips. She'd talk and all I could do was focus on how her mouth moved to form the words, how her tongue darted out quickly to wet her lips, how her lips pushed the breath out, twitched, smiled. How her teeth pulled at her bottom lip when she was deep in thought, searching for a loose bit of skin to fasten on and worry, pull at until a small drop of blood would well and her soft pink tongue would dart out again to taste the salty red. Exquisite torture. Fuck, I wanted to kiss her, make her mine.

We went to the pub to watch the boxing. She was the first girl I ever met who liked it too. I was falling for this girl and I started to look for a flaw, a blemish, a trait that would drive me mad, but I found none.

I'd been king-hit. This love had blindsided me, left me with no balance, no direction. No legs to stand on or tongue to talk with. This love had hit me square on the chin. My brains crawled down my spine and out my ass. I'm…punch-drunk…cunt-struck. I'm in the red corner (red for passion, red for the color of my swollen clit, red for my heart and the blood that beats through it). I'm in the red corner and they're telling me to throw in the towel. I know she knocks me out and I want it. I'm in the red corner and I'm losing the fight. I'm in the red corner and I'm fighting to lose.

I invited her to a picnic in the park with the ulterior motive of letting my few friends check her out, a last unconscious attempt at finding someone to spot a major fault in this girl before the last traces of reason had left my brain and I fell madly for someone I've never even kissed. No luck, everyone thinks she's great and my heart is a lead balloon.

I sat in the park alone. Everyone had packed up and gone home. I sat alone untangling silence, trying to figure out the thoughts I didn't have. The universe was crammed into my skull. She made the blood pound drum solos in my bones. We watched movies that night at her place and she kissed me and I melted. She kissed me and her mouth was cold from the ice cream we were eating; she tasted like chocolate and felt like velvet. I was nervous and excited and hot. She made me smolder; I wanted to start that same fire deep in her belly. She said I gave her tingles. I left when the credits rolled, we kissed at the front door and my feet didn't hit the ground the whole walk home. I giggled like a fool and fell asleep with a smile on my face.

I was horny. I couldn't concentrate. I was supposed to be working, studying, cleaning, exercising, eating, anything but sitting in my room thinking about her. It was different this time. I won't say that I wasn't thinking of fucking her—I was. I was a twenty-five-year-old chronic masturbator. It's the way I was thinking that was different. I was thinking of her smile close up, just before we kiss. I thought about the kiss, not how it made me feel but how she felt to me. I thought of her body, but not her tits and ass. I thought of her back just above her ass where her hips curved in and that smooth indent that traces the line of her spine. I was thinking poetry not porn.

I didn't close my eyes when we kissed; I didn't need to. Her skin failed to take on the aspects of an alien landscape this close... She was still beautiful to look at. It was so different to the boys I'd kissed, faces growing grotesque and monstrous as they got closer. If I didn't close my eyes by the time they got to my lips I didn't want their kisses. I was happy for the first time in ages. I couldn't stop smiling. I was crazy like a monkey, like a fox in love.

She'd had a fight with her flatmates. She rang me and asked me to meet her after work. I felt like I was going into battle. My hair spray was my helmet; I armed myself with heels and camouflaged with powders and perfumes. I went into battle with my pink jeans on. We walked to a bar and I met one of her friends. I got drunk and ended up playing barroom footy with two boys I know. We all ended up in a heap on the floor. We were out on the street after that—barroom footy wasn't endorsed by the management. The night was over, we were in the kitchen talking soft so I didn't wake the girls I lived with. It was past my bedtime and I offered her the lounge or my bed, casually as I could manage with my heart beating purple and swollen on my sleeve. She took the bed and took my hand. I led her up the hall and into my bedroom. The battle was won. It was so natural, so real. There was nothing uncomfortable in the way she undressed. I didn't feel self-conscious when I couldn't get my foot out of my jeans and my hair caught in her necklace. I didn't feel the need to turn off the light, I wanted to see her. We fell into bed and she covered my face with kisses. I looked at her and I wanted to eat her up. It was sexual but so much more than that. If it were a purely physical attraction it'd almost be perverted. It was so strong, obsessive even. Her smell was in my cells. She electroshocked my DNA. My hair follicles wanted to feel her.

My hands were everywhere and nowhere resisted, we fit together perfectly. She is slick and it's easy for us to fall into a tidal rhythm, a lunar sway. We're made of water and taste like the sea. My tongue found the hard pearl of her clit. She's a thing of sea foam and dreams. She is an orchid that blooms once in a lifetime.

I wanted to say "I love you" but the words seemed like oversized dress-up clothes…sloppy and unreal, used too many times for meaningless bullshit. I love her but I wish I didn't have to use that word. What we have is more pure than that. "Love" has been used and abused and misused too many times. "I love you" is lip service. I need to create a new word just for us. A word made out of salt meat and peach fuzz, of sweat and saliva. A word made from the crystallized feelings I have for her, shining like the sun with a million rainbows. A word no one else in any language ever can pronounce…A word just for us. Our word, our world.

Love-drunk.

OVERDUE
KIM BALDWIN

The clock on the wall of the Meriwether Community Library refused to budge. Emily Fairfield stared at it the way she had the ones in grade school when it was nearly time for recess. She felt now, as she had then, impatient to have her fun.

And sex with Lindsey Carter certainly was fun. *More* than fun. It had become almost an obsession. Emily still couldn't quite believe it. The best sex of her life—by a long shot, she would add—had happened to her at age forty-two. *And with a woman! Who'd have thought?*

Emily had been all raging hormones and full-speed-ahead libido in the six months she'd been seeing the TV reporter, and thank goodness the feeling was mutual.

One or the other made the hour-long trip between their homes every day or two. They always ended up in bed. Sometimes they started there. Lindsey had been celibate a long time too. They couldn't get enough of each other.

But then Lindsey had been sent downstate for a week to shoot a series of reports on small-town harvest festivals, and they'd been reduced to nightly telephone conversations.

Their talks inevitably included vivid descriptions of what they were going to do to each other when they were reunited, the promises getting hotter and more explicit as each day passed.

Emily was simmering on a low boil.

She'd had to fight not to touch herself the night before, while Lindsey described in a seductive purr some of the body parts she planned to explore with her tongue and mouth and hands. And then, just before they hung up, Lindsey had teased her with the promise of a *nice surprise* when she got back to town.

Emily was never disappointed when Lindsey came over with *nice surprises*. The last one had been chocolate body paint.

In her rooms above the library, Emily had set the stage for the perfect reunion. The dining-room table was festooned with her best china and candles, and she'd sprung for some incredibly soft new sheets for her queen-sized bed. Dinner would be takeout from the Slice of Heaven café down the street, because Emily knew that neither of them would want to take time for cooking.

Now she just had to wait. But waiting was impossible. She tried to busy herself putting books away and straightening shelves. But it seemed as though every title that passed through her hands only served to further fuel her imagination. *Between Lovers, The Touch of Fire, Simply Sensual, If You Come Softly, Kiss the Girls.*

Emily's heartbeat picked up as soon as she heard the familiar roar coming up Main Street. It doubled when the sound abruptly died in front of the library. *She's early!* She went to the front window.

Damn, woman, you look fine, Emily thought as Lindsey got off her Shadow and took off her sunglasses and helmet.

Lindsey Carter had on black leather pants, which hugged her tight ass and long legs like a second skin. Her motorcycle jacket was open, and Emily could see the reporter's firm round breasts strain against the plain white T-shirt beneath.

Lindsey ran her hand through her dark hair and glanced up toward the library. She smiled and waved when she spotted Emily.

Emily waved back. She glanced at the clock on the wall. Three p.m. The library didn't close until six. *Oh Jesus, I'll never make it another three hours.*

Emily took a quick run up and down the aisles as Lindsey mounted the front steps, to make certain they were alone. *At least it's usually real slow this time of day.*

She was returning from the back stacks when the buzzer on the front door sounded. "Coming!" she hollered as she rounded the corner of the biographies rack.

Lindsey nearly ran into her coming from the other way. The reporter's eyes were dark, the pupils huge. She looked ready to devour Emily. "Are we alone?" she breathed in a husky whisper that sent chills over Emily's oversensitive skin.

Emily nodded.

They looked at each other only a millisecond before Lindsey leaned down to claim Emily's lips in a hungry kiss that turned up the librarian's burners from simmer to boiling in a flash.

"I don't think you're quite coming *yet*, Emily," Lindsey whispered in her ear. "But I want to remedy that *real* soon."

Lindsey took her by the arm without further ado and led Emily unresisting toward the very rear of the library, into a small alcove that housed the archived periodicals.

There was an oversized easy chair there, and Lindsey pushed Emily down into it.

That was fine with Emily, who was beginning to feel a little weak in the knees.

Lindsey stood before her in her tight black leather, and for the first time, Emily spotted the prominent bulge at Lindsey's crotch.

"Oh my," Emily sighed aloud, staring. She could feel a pool of moisture building between her legs. Her mouth went dry.

"So you've noticed my new toy." Lindsey brought one hand down and brushed it lightly over the bulge. "Let's just say its clever design, especially when combined with the vibrations from the bike, have made me incredibly horny."

Emily swallowed hard as Lindsey leaned down over her, one hand on each of the chair's ample armrests, until their faces were inches apart.

"I need you, Emily, and I can't wait. Can you?"

In answer, Emily reached up and put one hand around Lindsey's neck to pull her close. She nipped at Lindsey's lower lip before opening her mouth and enticing Lindsey's tongue with her own. When Lindsey eagerly complied, thrusting her tongue into Emily's mouth, Emily sucked hard on it as she brought one hand up to brush against the bulge in Lindsey's pants.

Lindsey moaned.

Emily did it again—another teasing brush against the bulge.

Lindsey broke the kiss and leaned in to straddle Emily in the big chair, one knee on either side of her, pressing her groin into Emily's stomach, the cock stimulating her own clit until she was close to losing control.

Emily put her arms around Lindsey and pulled her even nearer, her hands caressing Lindsey's ass through the buttery soft leather. "God, I've missed you, Lindsey."

"Me too," Lindsey grunted. "I've been dreaming about being inside you."

Lindsey's lips found Emily's again as her hands found Emily's breasts. She massaged them roughly through the soft cotton blouse, her fingers pinching the nipples until they became hard as pebbles.

"Clothes off," Emily whispered in a shaky voice, reaching for the zipper of the leather pants.

The front door buzzer sounded and both women froze.

"Be right there!" Emily hollered, her voice a little breathless.

Lindsey jumped off her on shaky legs, but Emily had not yet had time to regain her feet before a voice answered from the front of the library.

"No need, Emily. Just dropping off the paper."

"Thanks, Timmy!" Emily hollered back.

The two women remained frozen as they were for another few seconds until the buzzer sounded again, telling them the paperboy had departed the way he had come in.

Emily got halfway out of her seat—just far enough to reach the light switch on the wall, which turned off the small light in the alcove. Then she leaned forward and hooked two fingers into Lindsey's belt loop and pulled her back to the chair.

"We'd better hurry," she said, running her hand over the bulge. She opened her legs and pulled Lindsey to her, Lindsey's crotch just below eye level. Her hands firmly caressed the leather pants and the body beneath, running up Lindsey's thighs, back to her ass, then around to the front.

Lindsey tried to will Emily's fingers toward the snap and zipper that would set her free.

But instead, Emily pulled Lindsey's T-shirt out of her pants and reached beneath it. Her fingers traced a light path up Lindsey's stomach to the bottom swell of her breast. She was wearing no bra, and when Emily discovered this and groaned—a sexy, low growl—Lindsey felt the sound as a warm hum between her legs.

Emily pushed up the T-shirt and pulled Lindsey's right breast to her mouth. Her lips and teeth sucked and teased the nipple while her hand provided similar stimulation to its twin.

"Oh please, Emily," Lindsey panted, looking down at her. "You're making me crazy."

Emily smiled as she reached for the clasp on the leather pants. Her lips were swollen, her face flushed. "That makes two of us," she said, lowering the zipper. Her mouth resumed its oral adoration of Lindsey's breast while her hand reached into the leather pants and closed around the cock, pulling it free of its confinement.

Lindsey shuddered as the harness sent a delicious friction along the length of her wet folds. "God, I'm so close already," she gasped.

Emily's lips left Lindsey's breast, but she kept her hand on the phallus, stroking it lightly, provocatively, knowing Lindsey was watching her in the semidarkness. "Not yet, Lindsey. I want you to come when you're deep inside me. Do you know how wet I am for you?"

"How wet?" Lindsey barely recognized her voice. She struggled to remain upright. Emily's light touch on the cock was keeping her arousal at an almost painfully heightened pitch. It was excruciating. And wonderful.

"You tell me." Emily's hands left the phallus just long enough to unhook her jeans and pull down the zipper.

Lindsey needed no further encouragement. Her hand slid down Emily's abdomen and inside her jeans.

"Oh yeah!" Emily cried out as Lindsey's fingers found the wet folds and began stroking them lightly, then danced over the hard, throbbing clit. She arched up from the chair into Lindsey's touch, and Lindsey used the opportunity to peel down Emily's jeans and underwear.

It wasn't smart. They both knew it. Anyone could come in.

And they couldn't stop.

They were both breathing hard; the heady scent of their mutual desire clung in the air. They were past the point of no return, and neither cared. They watched each other, Emily in the chair, Lindsey two feet away, standing above her, as the rest of their clothes came off.

Lindsey peeled off her jacket, then shirt, and finally the black leather pants while Emily shed her top and bra.

As Lindsey approached the chair, Emily leaned back in it and opened her legs in invitation. She moistened her lips as Lindsey leaned down to kiss her.

Lindsey slowly lowered herself over Emily, her arms braced again on the armrests, supporting her weight. She claimed her in a kiss that began as a surprisingly gentle touch, then grew quickly more heated when Emily's hands rose up to feel the harness.

Her hands firmly caressed the leather where it crossed over Lindsey's tautly muscled thighs. When the exploration moved to the strap that ran between them, those thighs began to shake slightly, and Lindsey's breathing accelerated.

As Emily's hand found the cock and tugged on it, she sucked hard again on Lindsey's tongue, and Lindsey lowered herself the rest of the way to meet her.

The tip of the cock rubbed up against Emily's clit, and she arched her body up to meet it, seeking greater contact. It entered her—an inch, then two, and she groaned in satisfaction, but just as quickly the sensation was gone as Lindsey withdrew.

Emily started to protest, but the words never left her mouth. The feeling of loss was replaced by the unbelievable sensation of the cock sliding along the lengths of her soaked silky folds, from her heated center to her rigid clit, as Lindsey began a slow, rocking motion above her. Each time, the tip of the cock would tease her opening, but then withdraw, to return a second or two later to penetrate only fractionally deeper.

She felt the pressure building between her legs, the surge of sensations incredible as she began to thrust her hips upward, opening herself up in a way she had never fully surrendered before.

"I'm so close, Em," Lindsey said in a strained voice, her whole body beginning to tremble.

"*Now*, Lindsey," Emily encouraged as she hugged her tighter with her arms, her legs, pulling her in. "*Please*, baby! *Please!*"

Lindsey gave it all to her then, sinking the cock full in, in one hard thrust of her hips—a motion that made them both gasp.

Then they were rocking against each other—faster, faster—Lindsey pumping in and out of Emily, sweat popping out on her forehead as she plunged. The library was silent except for their short, ragged gasps for air and the slapping sound of flesh meeting flesh.

"*Ungh!*" Lindsey groaned and went rigid, the force of her orgasm shooting through her as she thrust into Emily with long, powerful strokes.

Emily was so close behind her that the last one sent her careening over the edge as well, her body throbbing around the cock, waves of aftershocks making her tremble. Unaware of time, they remained joined, breathing hard, the phallus still embedded within Emily, until a ringing telephone brought them back to reality.

Lindsey started to gently pull out of Emily, but Emily grasped her hips, holding her inside. "Let it ring," she whispered, before capturing Lindsey's lips in a brief, sweet kiss.

The phone stopped after a few more rings, and Emily sighed, a soft mewl of contentment. "Well, I hope no one else needs a book today," she declared, a smile spreading across her face. "Because the library is closing early."

"Is it now?" Lindsey replied, smiling back at her, starting a slow, easy roll with her hips.

"Mmm-hmm." Emily tugged at the harness again as her hips began to match Lindsey's motion. "The librarian will be busy...filling special requests."

EXAMINING ALLYN
LYNN AMES

She rose, stripped out of the skimpy, midriff-baring muscle-T and silk panties she'd worn to bed, and sashayed into the shower stall. The hot spray pelted her body and breasts, tiny pinpricks penetrating her skin. A favorite song came on the radio—Allyn began to sway rhythmically, hips and breasts undulating to the beat of the music.

Soapy fingers caressed sensitive flesh, each touch innervating her. Unconsciously, she brushed her palm over the fine hairs at the base of her belly, her fingers seeking pleasure points too long neglected. She gasped as her thumb and forefinger found her clitoris. Gently, she squeezed the tip, moaning as she felt the wetness instantly coat her hand. With her other hand braced against the wall, she stroked herself, stopping just short of delivering the release her body craved. Instead, she reached up and unhooked the shower massage from its cradle, lowering the head and adjusting the spray to concentrate on her throbbing center. Fingers and shower spray combined in a glorious symphony, her climax the crescendo, aftershocks the denouement.

For several moments she stood, legs shaking, heart pounding, head bent forward, the showerhead held loosely in her hand. It had been so very long since she'd felt that physically alive. So very long.

"You made it through, Allyn. From now on, we live in the moment."

She regarded herself in the mirror, wondering what others would see in her. Cancer victim? Survivor? Desirable young woman? Damaged goods? She no longer felt qualified to judge.

❖

The waiting room was abuzz with voices—some old, some young—all impatient to get on with their lives. Allyn selected a seat by a window, as far away from the television as possible. Still, she found it hard to escape the drone of the CNN anchor. Just this once, she didn't care about any news except that which pertained specifically to her.

"Ms. Robson? Allyn Robson?"

Allyn rose and wiped suddenly damp palms on her faded jeans.

"Right this way. How are you feeling?"

"Fine. I feel fine."

"That's good to hear. Today's a big day for you, huh?"

"First day of the rest of my life."

The nurse regarded her thoughtfully. "I suppose it is."

Allyn divested herself of her cell phone, sneakers, and wallet before she stepped up on the scale.

"Good. You've gained a little bit of weight back. The doctor will be glad to see that. Have a seat over here, please."

Allyn squeezed past a very attractive woman in bright blue scrubs and sat in the chair the nurse had indicated.

"Blood pressure's good. Pulse is normal." The nurse looked around. "I'm sorry. I thought we had a room ready; it looks like they're all full."

"Gloria? Room five is available."

"Oh. Thanks, Trystan. I couldn't see it from here."

"No problem."

Allyn thought the voice matched the exotic looks. Was she imagining it, or was the woman smiling at her? Not just smiling at her, but flirting with her? Trystan brushed against Allyn as she passed, headed in the opposite direction.

"Excuse me. Narrow space."

"No problem." Allyn was surprised she could find her voice. "Get a grip, Al," she mumbled to herself, shaking her head as she followed the nurse to the end of the corridor. "Hormones must still be raging from this morning."

Still, she enjoyed the feelings of arousal flowing through her body. The chemotherapy had robbed her of energy and desire for so long.

She stripped out of her jeans, T-shirt, and bra and donned the standard-issue hospital gown just as the door opened.

"Allyn, it's good to see you."

"It's good to see you, too, Dr. Weiss."

"Let me start by saying the bloods we drew last week look excellent. You are officially in remission. There's no sign of the cancer anywhere. And now that the chemo is over, your blood cell counts are back within the normal range."

"Thank God," Allyn breathed around the lump in her throat.

"Lie down, then, and let me have a look at you…"

After fifteen minutes of being poked and prodded, she was allowed to sit up.

"I'm very pleased, Allyn. At this point, I think it's safe to go three months before your next battery of tests."

"Are there any limitations as to what I can do?"

"Not a one." The doctor patted her arm. "Just listen to your body—it will tell you what it can handle."

"Thank you, Dr. Weiss. You've been wonderful through all this. Thanks for making an unbearable situation bearable."

He smiled at her. "Allyn, you're a very special young woman. You remind me of my daughter—never lets anything keep her down."

"I'll take that as a compliment."

"As it was meant. Okay, you know the drill. Flip this switch over here," he indicated a red light switch on the wall near the door, "when you're ready to leave so the nurses will know the room's free. They're forever on my case for forgetting to tell patients to do that."

Allyn smiled. "Don't worry, I promise to protect you from the big, bad nurses."

"As if. See you in three months."

When he was gone, Allyn reached behind her to untie the knot at the back of her neck. She started when the door opened.

"I could help you with that."

Trystan stepped into the room and closed the door decisively behind her.

Unconsciously, Allyn backed up a step and licked her suddenly dry lips.

Trystan moved toward her, her eyes watching intently.

Allyn stumbled slightly as the backs of her legs bumped into the examining table.

Trystan laughed and continued relentlessly toward her quarry.

"Um, I—I've got it," Allyn stuttered.

"I can see that, but I'd still like to help." Trystan was within touching distance now. "Will you let me?"

Allyn's eyes flicked to the red switch. It was still in the "on" position.

Seemingly reading her thoughts, Trystan purred, "As long as that switch is on, the light outside will stay lit and no one will bother us."

"If—if it stays on too long, won't people be suspicious?"

Trystan brushed a stray lock of hair from Allyn's face. "Do you always worry so much?"

"Can't say that I've ever been in a position to worry about something quite like this before."

"No? That's a shame—a beautiful, desirable woman like you. I would have thought you'd have dozens of women begging you to take them."

Allyn blushed and looked down. "Sorry to disappoint you."

"On the contrary. I'm happy to have you to myself." She moved so that their bodies were touching lightly. With her fingers, she lifted Allyn's face to hers.

It was the eyes that were Allyn's undoing—dark brown and teeming with lustful intent. When Trystan's lips glided across hers, she felt herself melting.

"You have such soft lips. Very sexy." Trystan framed Allyn's face with her hands and kissed her a second time. As Allyn's lips parted to admit her tongue, Trystan moaned her delight.

Allyn felt the deft fingers release the remaining knot holding the back of the gown closed and knew a moment's panic. "Don't…"

"Shh. It's okay."

"I have a scar."

Trystan stilled her hands momentarily. "In my culture, scars are considered part of the body's beauty. They are reminders of the body's journey and its remarkable ability to heal." As carefully as if she were handling a frightened doe, Trystan lifted the gown from Allyn's shoulders, letting it fall to the floor.

Reverently, she cupped Allyn's breasts in her hands, rubbing her fingertips over the hardening nipples. Slowly, she lowered her head and brushed her lips over the vivid red line around the side of the left breast.

Allyn shuddered.

"Is this all right?"

"Mmm-hmm." Allyn was unable to formulate words. A single tear trickled down her cheek.

Trystan pulled back to look into eyes clouded with doubt, uncertainty, and fear. Understanding, she said, "I want you. Right here, right now." Her gaze roamed hotly over Allyn's slim, but fit, form. "You are perfect."

"I—"

Allyn's words were silenced by a soul-scorching kiss.

"I'm going to show you just how I feel about your body."

Trystan lifted Allyn effortlessly and laid her gently on the examining table. She leaned forward and pressed her mouth hard against the thin cotton that covered Allyn's mound.

Allyn closed her eyes, gasping as wetness soaked the material. Her body pushed forward, quite without her permission, seeking more.

Trystan stepped back and waited for Allyn's eyes to open. When they did, she moved her hands seductively to the drawstring of her scrubs, untied the knot, and let the pants drop soundlessly. Top and bra followed, leaving her standing in her silk panties. Without shifting her eyes from Allyn's, she ran strong fingers down her own body, dipping them into her center.

Allyn was mesmerized.

Trystan removed her fingers, brought them to her lips, and sucked them inside, her eyes still riveted on Allyn. "You make me so wet."

"I do?"

"Oh, yes." She stepped deliberately out of her panties and touched herself again, this time offering a moist finger for Allyn to sample. "See what looking at your body does to me?"

"Mmm." Allyn savored the taste on her tongue. Before she could pull Trystan to her, she was out of reach.

"Not yet. I have too many things I want to do to you first."

When Allyn felt cool air caress her triangle and an insistent tongue stroke her clitoris, she was lost. The first orgasm flowed over her like a warm summer rain. She had little time to savor the moment, however, as the feeling of tongue and teeth scraping across her nipples brought her body instantly to attention once again.

Trystan was above her now, one thigh pressing unrelentingly into her center. Their mouths fused together, bound by the heat of desire.

Any self-consciousness Allyn felt was washed away on the wave of the second orgasm. She wrapped her legs around Trystan's waist, pushing her throbbing center against abdominal muscles slick with sweat. "I want to please you."

"And I want you to, so that works out nicely."

"I want to touch you everywhere. I want you to feel the way I do."

Allyn sat up, forcing Trystan to rise up on her knees. Spent though she was, Allyn was ravenous for her. She cupped Trystan's mound with her palm, adjusting so that her fingers played fleetingly over a swollen clit.

"God. Please." Trystan's head lolled onto Allyn's shoulder.

Allyn smoothed a hand over Trystan's back, continuing down until her fingers played at the puckered opening. She reached down farther, gathered moisture from Trystan's center, and returned to the opening, pushing lightly in a gentle plea for admittance.

"Yes, baby. Oh, yes." Trystan rose higher, inviting Allyn to go deeper.

Strong muscles tensed around her fingers as Allyn explored Trystan's depths. She used her thumb to stroke Trystan from clit to center. Her mouth nipped at a supple neck and throat. Her other hand pinched a nipple made achingly tight with want.

The power of the explosion, when it came seconds later, rocked them both, leaving them breathless. They clung together, their pulsing bodies searching for equilibrium in a world turned upside down by passion.

When she could talk, Trystan asked, "Are you okay?"

Allyn, newly confident, pulled back to look into Trystan's eyes. She smiled. "Now this is what I call a full-service doctor's office."

The laugh was rich and full. "We do try to please."

"Oh, better give me the satisfaction survey now, then, before I forget the details."

"I'm forgettable, am I?"

Allyn ran her fingers along Trystan's jaw line. "No, somehow I don't think so."

"Good," Trystan said, "because I know I'll never forget you." She rose, kissed Allyn sweetly on the tip of her nose, and dressed.

As Trystan was about to leave, Allyn restrained her with a hand on her arm. "Thank you—for helping me reclaim myself and my sexuality."

"Believe me, it wasn't exactly a hardship. I meant what I said—you are a very beautiful woman." Trystan leaned forward for one more kiss on the mouth.

Halfway out the door, she added, "Oh, and don't forget to flip the switch on your way out. The nurses hate it when patients forget that." The sound of joyous laughter followed her as she made her way down the hall.

THE NEWEST WRANGLER
CLIO JONES

I was the newest wrangler on the Lazy J ranch. I'm not sure why I thought I could do this work. As a girl, I'd ridden horses and I'd loved the power horses had. It was more powerful than anything I knew, until some ten years later I discovered the power women had over me. Femmes in particular, and then Lisa, who'd been my partner until a rather rude awakening a couple of months ago. After Lisa left me, I just about became a one-woman museum to the past of our happy relationship. My friends put up with me for so long, and then they got tough. What I needed, they said, was to get out of town. They didn't really care where. Or how. Or who I met there, as long as she was sexy and took my mind off one certain femme.

The Lazy J was one of the only ranches to use queer-friendly language. I figured enough dykes had cowboy fetishes that some queer ladies would pass through here on a summer trip. I'd made sure to find someplace that would take a lesbian wrangler. Now I just needed to find someone who would fuck one, before I got back to Chicago and my wondering friends.

The ranch was amazing, though. The Wyoming countryside was gorgeous. If you wanted something breathtaking, I could take you on one of the many trails that wound through thick pine forests up the hillside, lush with midsummer flowers. Columbines, yarrow, and buckwheat nestled together in clumps. I'd learned to identify them quickly, because the guests always asked to enhance their wildlife experience. Nameless streams slid around the trails, from snow runoff and the mountain lakes that lay tucked away like little turquoise and hematite gems the tourist shops sold. On a warm day, I'd nap in the sun when we got a break and fantasize about the time Lisa and I made love in a meadow. We'd almost gotten caught, but it had been worth it. Lisa. Shit.

A new batch of tourists and horses was coming the next day. We often traded stock with some of the other ranches. Every time we got a new load in, all the wranglers would be busy fitting the saddles and watching the new riders to make sure we didn't have any major accidents waiting to happen. For me, this usually meant a lot of mucking out stalls, getting up early to feed the horses, and staying late to clean up at the end of the day. In a few more weeks, if all went well, I'd be leading rides and leaving the dirty work to one of the fourteen-year-old local boys who hung out at the ranch.

First thing in the morning I met Kim, a perky blond wrangler with a California accent who looked like she'd been airlifted in from a boardwalk in L.A. Serious actress type. I knew she was going to be trouble when the first thing she said was, "Welcome. You've been here a while, I guess, but I haven't had the pleasure of meeting you. Look forward to working with you." I prefer the cowboys. Usually, they just grunt hello and leave me well enough alone, and if I have a question they don't make me feel like an idiot.

"I'm sure you won't see me much," I said to Kim, then turned back to organizing the tack room.

"You're going to be my shadow for the week," she said. "Coming on all my rides. Dan said so."

"I doubt it," I said. Dan was the head wrangler, and he hadn't told me anything about this girl.

"Helen, right?" she said, stepping in close. Her eyes were gray, with a little flash of brown near the pupil. Real interesting eyes. She was wearing a little tank top with a men's flannel, unbuttoned, over it. Probably her boyfriend's shirt. I could see a thin tan line where a necklace used to be, but the rest of her was golden and freckled. I let my eyes take in the rest of her—strong, wide legs, nice hips, and a little bit of cleavage showing. "You are Helen, right?" she said, giving a big smile that showed her perfect teeth.

"Yes," I said, a little ashamed to have been caught staring. I held out a hand, but she had turned away.

"Great," she said, looking back at me with a playful smirk on her face. "Then you can give me a hand with the horses so I can hit the Jacuzzi before dinner." I followed her, shaking my head. For a minute, I thought she was teasing me, but she clearly had her mind on something else. I'd have to find Dan before dinner and see if he could have me changed to one of the guys. I didn't want to make small talk with Kim halfway up the side of a mountain while yuppies from Seattle talked about the rustic ranch environment. Not at all.

The guests arrived in time for dinner, and my mood only worsened from there. So far, the guests had been decent, and some very sweet. But now we had the weepy recent divorcée and her embarrassed teenage son, two retired couples from Nevada, a family of five from Maine, and two gay men from Miami who looked somewhat shell-shocked. I was pretty sure none of these people would have anything to say on the trail, which might make them ask me why I was here. Or leave me open for more really fun talk with Kim about her perky, perfect life. I mumbled something about an early start and slunk off after Dan, who was nowhere to be found.

"Do you take it black?" Kim asked the next morning. "I thought you would. I brought us coffee."

"I bet you don't even need coffee in the morning," I grumbled. Then I relented. "That's sweet of you. Where are you planning on taking them for your first ride?"

"Our first ride," she said. "We're in this together." I bit my tongue on the sassy remarks and followed her out of the barn. She'd made a chart of which horses to saddle up. She pointed to a blue sliver on the map: Prairie Star. It was a short, woody trail, with a nice meadow and a couple of scenic waterfalls. One of my favorites, actually.

"I'm impressed," I said.

"Good. Drink up, though, cause we're going to have to spark some life into this little group." Then she smacked my ass with a crop as she strode into the barn and began leading out the horses. I nearly spit my coffee out. This girl—I just couldn't get a handle on her. She was so cocky. So sure of what I wanted, which was the weird part.

The Prairie Star trail ride was better than we thought it would be. The gay couple got talking to the retirees about Miami RV parks, and the Maine mom went after the divorcée to plan a shopping trip for western wear. I let Kim talk, figuring she'd lose interest in me if we got this part over with. When we got to the meadow, Kim and I tied up the horses. The dudes trickled off to eat their picnic lunches. I figured I'd have about an hour for a nap, which was good. My body ached.

"Come here," Kim said. "There's something I want to show you." She took my hand in hers and strode off across the meadow. She was wearing men's jeans, a striped shirt with the sleeves rolled up, and a black felt cowboy hat. The hat cast shadows across her face, so I couldn't read her. The field was quiet until I heard the rush of water growing steadily louder. I hadn't seen any streams near here.

"No one knows about this," Kim said. "I like to keep it that way, but you looked so sore and tired."

"No worse than usual," I said.

"Don't try to hide it. Keep hiding everything from me, Helen, and we're never going to be friends."

"We're not—" I began, but shut my mouth when we disappeared into the trees to see water rushing down a rock face, crashing to the ground several hundred feet below. I hadn't noticed the trail went up so high. "It's lovely," I said.

"Just like you," she said, coming up behind me. Now her hat cast shadows on me. When her hands circled my hips, my body stiffened. "I know what you think of me. It's not true, though, you'll see."

"What do I think?" I asked, trying not to gasp as her hands moved up to finger my nipples. She pulled lightly on them, rubbing with her fingers against the thick cloth of my shirt.

"You think I'm some ditz," Kim said. She bit me on the back of the neck, a warning. Light. Playful. "You think I'm the friendliest, dumbest wrangler yet. You don't think I'm strong enough—" Another bite, this time falling on my shoulder and sinking deeper. A shock of pain rippled through my already sore muscle. I tried not to wince. Simultaneously, her hands tugged harder at my breasts, kneading the skin sharply. "But I can hurt you. Much more than she did—whoever it was, the little bitch that broke your heart."

"Lisa," I said.

"Fuck 'em," she said. "How's this for the surprise of a lifetime?"

I meant to yell. I meant to ask her who she was for coming up on me like this, and that we could get fired for this. I surprised myself altogether by saying, instead, "Let me."

"Let you what?" Kim laughed. "Always the gentleman, huh, feel like you have to reciprocate? This is just a tease, cowboy. I want you to spend the rest of the afternoon thinking about me. Riding in your saddle, rocking back and forth, thinking about my body hiding under all these clothes. I want you to be so wet you're trembling and you can't wait for dinner to be over so you can find me in the cabin. Or the hot tub. Or the pasture. We can fuck in all three places, I don't mind." With that, Kim was gone.

True to her words, I did suffer on the long ride back from Prairie Star. I forced myself to ride at the end of the line, so far behind Kim that I could not even hear the chipper twang of her vowels. I struck up a conversation with the Miami men about the scene in Florida. Yet I still felt a light, ghostly touch of her hands on my breasts, and my lips, dry and chapped, twitched to kiss her sweetly while I unfastened her belt and let the Wyoming wind tickle her bare ass as my hands busied themselves in her wet cunt.

I would have to take her by surprise. She was waiting for me, I would bet on it, and so I'd have to one-up her. When we got back to the ring, I hurried through my work. Kim lingered, taking questions about the week's routine and scheduling private lessons. A good wrangler could make at least a grand extra per week giving lessons. I was sure Kim normally earned at least that. I grinned and made myself work faster, sore muscles and all. Kim was right: I could really use a soak in the Jacuzzi. But first I had a lesson of my own to teach her.

I was waiting behind the door of the tack room when she walked in with her saddle. It was a dank, dark room with cobwebs and a boarded-up window. The saddles and bridles hung on the wall in neat rows. I had made sure to put everything away well. In the corner opposite me, a model was set up of saddle, blankets, and gear bags in case any of the new wranglers needed a refresher. Kim stood studying the wall of pegs, searching for a space for her saddle. I'd hidden the free slot on the bottom, making sure she'd linger in front of me for several seconds.

Kim placed her saddle in the slot I'd left. I readied myself, old blanket in hand. As she straightened, I sprang forward, throwing the blanket over her head and pulling the extra fabric taut. I shut the door, certain no one would return to the barn until after lunch. An hour would be more than enough time to return the favor Kim had done me on the morning ride. Kim's body had tensed. I wasn't sure if she was playing along or if the nervousness was real. "Keep quiet," I said, making my voice low. "I don't want any screams or foolishness. You yap, I cut your hair lock by perfect lock. Or worse." That was a bluff—no knives in here, only the riding crop I had placed by the demo saddle in case I wanted to use it. I led her toward the saddle now.

She was light. I hoisted her up onto the saddle, letting the blanket fall as I did so. I used the cord from one of the saddlebag sets to tie her hands behind her back to the pommel. Thank goddess for western saddles. She watched me, a nervous smile of anticipation playing out across her lips. "You were right. I couldn't think about anything but you the whole ride back. I'm really fucking wet, but I figure there's a chance you might be even wetter." She nodded slightly. I stepped up and unbuttoned her shirt, raining little kisses on her neck and face as I did so. Her mouth strained for mine. "Not yet," I said, stepping back. I looked her over—hands tied tightly, not going anywhere, breasts spilling out of the lacy bra she wore, legs spread-eagled. I ran one finger over the crotch of her jeans; Kim lifted her hips up. Sighed.

"No. Fucking. Noise," I said. My fingers plunged underneath her bra as my mouth gave her what she wanted. Her nipples were candy hard. I twisted them and pulled them and she leaned into me, bucking at the restraints. Breathless, flushed, and getting wetter by the second, I tore myself away from Kim's lips to take her sweet, hard nipples into my mouth. I licked at them as though they really were candy. She shook. She really was being a good girl. I could tell she wanted to scream, talk back, or direct me. I also knew she was scared I might stop. Worst of all, I could take off for the dining hall and leave her there.

My hand returned to her crotch and stroked it lightly as she twisted up to meet the pressure of my fingers. She was making small moans now as I sucked at her breasts, and her hips rose to meet my fingers. I had to feel her, dripping wet, bucking like a rodeo rider, entirely at my mercy. My fingers stopped their stroking and roughly pulled her belt open. I watched her as I undid her pants and pulled them down. Yellow lacy underwear matched her bra. I smiled. She smiled back, straining to kiss me again. I slid a finger inside the waistband of her underwear. Lower, lower. We groaned together when I made contact.

"Hurry," she said. "It's getting late." She was right. We needed to have this mess cleaned up before the dudes returned. Now that I had my finger on her clit, I couldn't wait any longer.

I slid one finger inside her, and then another. I wanted to feel my fist twisted up inside her but this wasn't the place. She squirmed around on top of my fingers. "All right," I said. "I get the message." I fingered her clit as I climbed on the saddle, facing her, taking her lower lip between my teeth. My other hand reached for her breasts again. She groaned, louder this time. I didn't care. I worked away at her cunt, fingering her clit and her nipple in quick rhythmic jerks. Our tongues rolled playfully around. She came too quickly, bucking and jerking closer to my hand. I kept going, lightly at first, willing her to come again because I wasn't done touching her. When she finished, spent, I pulled my sticky fingers out of her pants and licked them off. "Got to clean up the evidence," I told her.

She smiled. "Untie me, cowboy."

"I'm not so sure I should. We've got work to do this afternoon. I think I'm afraid of what you might do right now if I untie your hands."

"I'll wait till tonight," Kim pleaded. "I know what you and those muscles need."

"All right," I said, giving her one more kiss as I reached for the ties. "I think we've both got something to look forward to tonight. This ride's barely begun."

SALES CALL
GEORGIA BEERS

It's been the day from hell. *If I have to deal with one more demanding client or one more accounting problem, I may have to kill somebody.* The thought slices through my mind with a vengeance. My phone rings. I growl at it, hoping my ferocity will frighten it into silence, but it rings again. I swear and snatch it up.

"Good afternoon," I say in the most pleasant voice I can muster, considering the foul mood I'm in. "This is Jamie."

"Jamester! How're you doing, you hot, sexy thing?"

I can't help but smile. The exuberance in Carrie's voice reaches in and hunts down what little joy I have available today, pulling it out into the light against its will. She's my best friend and I need her positive energy like I need food or water. "I'm just reminding you about dinner," she says. "You're still meeting us, right?"

Crap. I completely forgot. "Um…" The sigh escapes my lips before I can catch it.

"Oh, don't you do that," Carrie warns.

"Uh…"

"Jamie. Don't you dare."

"I…"

"Don't."

The edge in her voice makes it very clear that I've blown my friends off too many times now and there's no way I'll be allowed to do it again. There will be dire consequences. I think quickly and shoot for the next best thing. "I'm going to be late?" My voice is hopeful.

Carrie makes a strangled sound. "How late?"

"I have a sales call at six thirty."

"Six thirty? Jesus Christ, Jamie. That's an hour and a half after normal people have stopped working for the night, do you realize that? How long will you be?"

"Not long. Half an hour. I'll head right to the restaurant from my client's office. I promise."

"All right," she says grudgingly, then interrupts herself. "Wait." A mischievous tone creeps into her voice and I know what's coming. "Is this sales call with a new client?"

I suppress a wince. "No." Damn it. She can read me like a book even when she can't see me.

"It's The Babe, isn't it?"

I can practically hear the capital letters and I make a face, irritated that she's busted me. "It might be."

"Aha! *That's* why you agreed to such a late call. You can't say no to The Babe. She says, 'Jump,' you say, 'How high?' She's too hot to turn down."

"How would you know? You've never seen her."

"I don't have to see her. You talk about her often enough. I could probably pick her out of a lineup."

"She spends a lot of money with me, Care." It's a feeble attempt to justify myself, and Carrie's absolutely not falling for it.

"Don't forget the part about her being hot."

"She's been a client for a long time."

"And she's hot."

I sigh, conceding defeat. "And she's hot."

"Did you wear a suit today?"

"Maybe."

"You hussy." She laughs again. "I hope it's the green one. Make sure you unfasten an extra button. And show some leg. You'll sell more that way."

By now, I'm laughing too. And blushing. "Yes, ma'am."

"We'll look for you around seven thirty. Try not to be any later than that."

"Yes, ma'am."

"Hussy."

"Shut up."

Michelle Adams was one of my very first clients, and I think I developed a crush on the woman the first time I laid eyes on her. It's never gone away. On the surface, we don't really have much in common, and we don't know much about each other on a personal level. She knows I've got a dog named Ralph, that I live alone, and that I love to read. I know that she's divorced with two daughters and a new boyfriend, that she prefers red wine over white, and that she's addicted to *Law and Order*. And Carrie's right: Michelle Adams is nothing if not hot. Her boyfriend is a lucky, lucky man and her ex-husband must be out of his mind.

The sun is dropping toward the horizon as I pull my Acura into the parking lot of Michelle's building. It's empty, save for my car and a black SUV I assume is hers. I grin as I think of her behind the wheel, sunglasses on, music blasting.

I give myself a quick once-over using my reflection in my car's window to ensure that I'm presentable. My deep green suit is simple but classy and it's the perfect color to highlight my eyes. It also complements my auburn hair nicely—not an easy feat. My hair is twisted back into a French braid and is actually still in pretty good condition despite the fact I've been running for ten hours straight today. I capture a stray lock and tuck it behind my ear. The cream-colored camisole under my jacket is brand new. I tuck it more securely into my skirt, thereby pulling the neckline down a smidge, then grin at the result, thinking how Carrie would nod in approval over the wink of cleavage. The hem of my skirt falls just above my knees, a length I'm not entirely comfortable with, but one Carrie insisted upon. *Whatever works*, Carrie always says. I smooth a finger over each eyebrow, take a breath, and head toward the building, my briefcase in hand.

There's a note taped to the glass of the front door; the door's stopper is down and it's propped open a couple of inches. I pull the note and read,

> *J-*
> *Come in and shut the door behind you. It locks automatically*
> *at 6. I'm in my office.*
> *-M*

I kick the stopper up and shut the door behind me.

Standing in the reception area, I marvel at the quiet. There's a slight eeriness in the lack of activity and the dimness of the lights. I'm not used to it and I feel goose bumps break out along my arms. It's usually such a busy place…phones ringing, conversations filling the air, deliveries being made. At this hour, however, it is absolutely silent. The goose bumps intensify and I pick up the pace, my black pumps sounding uncomfortably loud on the tile floor.

Light is spilling out of the fifth door down and as I approach, I hear the gentle tapping of the keys on a computer keyboard. I also catch the subtle presence of Michelle's musky perfume hanging in the air like a secret, and I breathe deeply. I rap on the door frame and Michelle looks up from her monitor. I'm sure her face brightens a little when she sees me. Or it could be my wishful thinking.

"Hey, Jamie." She stands and crosses the office with her hand outstretched. She's a couple inches taller than I am, but her sheer presence makes her seem even bigger. "It's great to see you; you look great; that's a terrific suit. I'm sorry for dragging you out this late."

I take the offered hand, too distracted by her warm, firm grip to dwell on the fact she just complimented my outfit. Carrie always teases me about what she calls my "hand fetish." Hands are one of the first things I look at on a person and Michelle's are perfect: large, strong, and feminine. I try hard not to imagine them on me, but as usual, it's difficult. Her nails are manicured and her skin is creamy smooth. And did I mention warm?

"No problem," I reply, reluctantly letting her go. "I was working late anyway."

"Let me just finish up this e-mail, okay? Have a seat."

"Take your time." I smile, knowing the more she's focused on something else, the more I can stare at her. I sit in one of the two chairs in front of her desk and I pull my notepad and pen from my briefcase. I jot unnecessary notes in order to look busy.

The office is good sized and well appointed. Michelle's desk is huge and it's made out of the same deep cherrywood as the nearby credenza and armoire. The mauve carpeting is thick, deep, and expensive. The floor-to-ceiling windows on both walls have wooden vertical blinds, and I'm surprised to note that the blinds are all closed tonight. I don't remember ever seeing them like this.

Michelle herself is a little harder to study without being obvious, but I find that if I tilt my head down like I'm writing on my notepad, I can look up at her through my eyelashes without giving myself away. I hope. Her hair is loose today, a fact that makes my heart speed up a bit. It's dark and naturally wavy, the kind every woman wishes she had—

except for the women who actually have it and constantly complain about how unruly it is. The ends fall just past her shoulders and I feel that old, familiar urge to dig my fingers into it and grab a handful. Today's outfit consists of a mouthwatering black pantsuit with a red shell underneath. I immediately wonder if the shell is a tank top. Last summer the air-conditioning crapped out in this building in the middle of an August heat wave on a day I had an appointment. Everybody was cranky and sweating. The receptionist had walked me to Michelle's office and my voice had stuck in my throat when I got my first glimpse of her. She was wearing a navy skirt and a white silk tank, her suit jacket tossed over a chair. The sudden urge I'd had to suck on her bare, glistening shoulder was almost overwhelming.

"There." Michelle hits one final button on her keyboard, then pushes it away. "Done. Sorry about that."

"Not a problem."

She props her elbow on the massive desk and sets her chin in her hand and studies me for several long seconds. "Nothing's ever a problem for you, is it?" There's something different about her today. I can't put my finger on it, but I can feel it in the air.

I shrug. "Nope. I aim to please."

"I'll bet you do."

Is she flirting with me? The little voice in my head poses the question and stuns me speechless. *Is she?* Michelle's direct eye contact is *so* direct that it's making me want to squirm in my chair. My heart picks up the pace and I feel an embarrassing surge of damp between my legs. God, this woman has *power*. I find myself wondering if she knows it. How could she not?

Her deep gray eyes hold on to mine for much longer than necessary, until I finally have to break away. I swallow hard and look down at the nonexistent notes in my lap, wondering what in the world is going on here. I clear my throat, feeling way more jumpy than I usually do around her, the sensation confusing me. "So." I manage to keep my voice steady and light, much to my own surprise. "What can I do for you, Ms. Adams?"

Michelle pokes at the inside of her cheek with her tongue and studies me, as if contemplating how to answer. Then she arches one eyebrow and smiles, a look so brazenly sexy that I feel my skin flush with heat and pray to God she can't see it. She can, of course. I'm about the color of a tomato, I just know it. And my pen is shaking, which is pissing me off. I try my hardest to steady my hand as Michelle crosses the office and shuts the door. My brows furrow when I hear what I'm almost certain is the click of the lock.

Michelle takes a seat in the chair next to me. She's done this from our very first meeting, as opposed to talking at me from across her desk; I've always found it oddly respectful. This time, as she pulls her chair closer and our knees bump, I feel my heart hammering in my chest and I'm afraid I might leap clear out of my skin. I can't believe how nervous she's making me and I'm a little irritated at myself. I'm thirty-four, not sixteen, for crying out loud.

My hands are still trembling and I can't seem to get them under control. I grip my pen so hard I'm afraid my fingers might cramp up. Clearing my throat again, I manage to find my voice and try to keep the tone casual. "What do you need from me today?" Much to my dismay, I find myself unable to pull my eyes from her full bottom lip while she's talking. The gloss on it looks very fresh and I feel myself salivate as I think about licking it off.

"Why don't you show me what you've got and then I can take what I need?"

At this, my eyes *do* jerk up to hers. I practically swallow my tongue while managing to squeak out an "Okay." I feel like I'm the prey and she's the sleek, black cat that's about to pounce on me. Still trying to disguise the uncharacteristic shaking of my hand, I grasp the pen with the other hand as well, gripping both ends, totally impairing my ability to write anything at all. Making a feeble attempt to cover, I pretend I'm just playing with it, clicking the plunger and spinning it between my fingers. Of course, only three seconds go by before the pen flies out of my grip and skitters across Michelle's mammoth desk, stopping at the edge near her keyboard. I close my eyes, unable to believe I can actually be this much of an idiot.

"Oops," I mutter, looking away from the perceptive glimmer in her eyes and tucking a stray lock of hair back behind my ear. Deciding to use this moment to try and pull my shit together, I take my time standing, step toward her desk, and reach across for my pen. I practically have to press my chest against the cherry surface to reach it. Seriously, who needs a desk this big? There's barely anything on it as it is. I manage to close my fingers around the pen, but when I stand back up, I gasp and drop it again.

Michelle is pressed up against my back. Her hands come to rest on the desk at either side of me, effectively trapping me between the desk and her body. Her warm, taller-and-stronger-than-mine body. Her lips are dangerously close to my ear; I can hear her gentle breathing and wonder why she's so calm and I'm such a disaster.

"You seem nervous, Jamie," she says, and the vibration of her voice against my ear—saying my name so intimately—sends shock waves straight to my groin. I bite my bottom lip to keep from whimpering like a puppy. "Are you nervous?"

I swallow and nod slowly, not trusting my own voice. She's moved forward ever so slightly and her forearms are tight against my sides. I am *so* her prisoner right now.

"Am *I* making you nervous?" Her voice is nearly a whisper.

I nod again. "Yes," I manage to rasp.

I feel her hands moving. As she rests them on my hips, she murmurs, "Your cheeks are so red. It *is* pretty hot in here." She sounds so innocent, like we could be sitting in a diner having lunch while she's talking. Her hands move around to the front of my jacket and unfasten its one button. "Maybe you should take this off."

This time, a small whimper does escape my lips as the fabric of the top half of my suit is moved over my shoulders and down my arms. I hear it hit one of the chairs behind us and I feel so exposed I might as well be naked. It's at that moment that it all becomes clear: she's ambushed me. The late call, the empty office, the closed blinds, the locked door. She planned this. The understanding does nothing but push my arousal higher. I plant my hands on the desk in front of me in an attempt to maintain my balance. My knees are weak and I can feel the damp palm prints I'll leave to mar the surface—if and when I ever move again. She rakes her fingernails slowly up and down my arms and rests her chin on my right shoulder. I feel the gooseflesh break out across my entire body and I feel like a teenage boy, ready to explode at any moment.

Her hands slide up to my shoulders as she says, "You know, I really, really like your hair like this. But..." She unfastens the clip and I can feel her fingers softly unraveling the braid. Her voice is so matter-of-fact, yet so, so sexy—a combination that one would think is impossible. Her fingers are gentle and in a minute, my hair skims my shoulders, adding to the tactile sensations threatening to overload my brain. She presses her face into my hair, whispering, "There. That's better. God, I love the color."

My breathing has become embarrassingly ragged and I'm sure that if I weren't balanced on my hands, I'd collapse to the floor, nothing but a puddle of quivering goo. She begins massaging my shoulders. Her grip is gentle and firm at the same time and it occurs to me that she is the perfect dichotomy. Strong yet gentle. Soft yet firm. Giving yet demanding. I feel her pelvis push into my backside again and I try to stifle a small gasp. I'm sure she hears it because I can feel her smile against my hair. Her right hand snakes up my throat and firmly grips my chin. Before I even comprehend the movement, she's turned my entire body and I'm facing her, my chin in her hand. I'm surprised to see her breathing almost as rapidly as I am. The edge of the desk is pressing into the small of my back; she's got two or three inches on me, and the sensation of being trapped by her is both frightening and exhilarating. She surrounds me. The tip of her tongue runs over her bottom lip and I feel my eyes glaze over at the sheer sexiness of the act. She smiles wickedly before covering my mouth with her own.

I hear myself groan into her mouth and I automatically bring my hands up to rest on her waist. Heat pours off her body. The woman can kiss like there's no tomorrow. My mind flashes back to the "giving yet demanding" description I thought of earlier. Her kiss is giving; it's glaringly obvious that she wants me to enjoy what she's doing. At the same time, she's definitely the one in control, her tongue demanding that I surrender whatever it is she wants from me. And I have no doubt that I will. Michelle Adams has me so completely turned on, so aroused, that it's almost ridiculous to realize I'm still fully clothed and all she's really done is kiss me.

As if hearing my thoughts, her hands begin exploring. They scorch me through the silk of my camisole and it wouldn't surprise me at all if the garment fell to the floor in flames. She pulls the hem of it out of my skirt and wrenches her mouth from mine long enough to pull it over my head. A quick, approving glance at my lace-covered breasts and she's feasting on my lips again. This time when her hands come to me, it's skin on skin and she's the one who moans. She wraps her arms around my torso and squeezes me to her, pushing her tongue more deeply into my mouth.

My hands are on her back and it suddenly occurs to me that she's way overdressed. I pull my mouth away from hers long enough to focus on the buttons of her suit jacket. Her eyes clear momentarily and she stops my hands with hers. "Hey," she says and her voice is an octave or two lower than usual. "I'm not done with you." Her tone carries a hint of a threat that sends a wave of excitement up my spine.

"At least the jacket?" I ask, and my voice cracks. I clear my throat. "Please?"

She holds my gaze, then spreads her arms out to the sides in surrender. I hastily unbutton her black jacket and slide it off her arms. I praise heaven above when the red silk tank is revealed. "Oh, God," I mutter, earning a satisfied grin from her as I toss the garment aside. She closes the gap between us, but before she can kiss me again, I fulfill my longtime fantasy and latch my mouth onto her shoulder. I'm sure to leave a mark.

This time, she's the one who whimpers. It's very soft, almost inaudible, but it's there and I hear it and savor it. I taste every bit of the bronzed and perfect skin of her shoulder, working my way to the junction of her shoulder and neck where the scent of the perfume I adore is strongest. Much to my delight, Michelle lets her head fall back and gives me open access to her throat. I take full advantage. Her fingers work their way into my hair as I bathe her neck and throat in kisses, but before I can move southward, I feel her hand close in a firm fist and pull my face back up to meet her lips.

And just like that, I've lost the upper hand. Again. Not that I mind.

She pulls me close, exploring the depths of my mouth, filling me like molten lava or whatever else there is that's hot and liquid. The hand she uses to cup my left breast startles me and I jump, my gasp of surprise changing easily to a moan of pleasure as she causes first one, then the other nipple to stand at attention, visible even through the fabric of my bra. I push into her hand and try to give as much as I can. She's made me so very wet I find it hard to believe I haven't floated completely out of the room yet. I feel her fingers slide down and around and fumble with the zipper at the back of my skirt.

"Off," she demands, pulling back and watching as my skirt falls to the floor in a heap around my pumps. I watch her face as my state of undress registers and a broad grin breaks across it. "My, my, Ms. Carmichael. No panties under the hose. Who would have suspected you to be such a naughty girl?"

"It's the only way to be sure there are no panty lines," I stutter in my own defense. My voice is barely recognizable. I swallow hard as I stand before her and she scrutinizes me.

"I have to say, that new gym membership was a very smart purchase. You look…amazing. Strong. Firm. Sexy."

I look down at my attire. I'm wearing only my bra, my pantyhose, and my black pumps. Michelle thinks I look amazing. I think I'm dressed just right for a porn flick. I smile anyway, because a compliment is a compliment and I *have* been working hard at the gym and *Michelle just told me I'm sexy*. My face splits into a grin. "Thank you."

"Can I see the rest?" she asks as she comes closer.

Reaching behind me, she unclasps my bra without any further discussion. She wings it over her shoulder with a twinkle in her eye, then runs the outsides of her forefingers over my nipples once, twice, the third time making my breath audibly catch in my throat. Her eyes cloud a bit and I realize she likes the sounds she's causing me to make. She slides her fingers beneath the waistband of my hose and pulls them down around my knees. Our height difference is to her advantage here, because she grasps the backs of my thighs, lifts, and sits me on her desk. She pulls off my pumps and hose in one swift movement and I chuckle to myself at how smooth she is. Because I am now completely at her mercy with my legs spread apart while she stands between them. She's got a hand on each of my knees and she stares into my eyes with intensity as she gently pushes out, opening me further. I think my heart may beat right up and out my open mouth at this point; I seriously wonder if I might have a heart attack. I'm not sure how long I can keep up with her, and it's a distinct possibility that she just might be the death of me, that I might keel over dead, right here on her desk in all my naked glory.

As if sensing my worry, she smiles a tender, knowing smile. "You're just as beautiful as I imagined you'd be." There are tiny laugh lines around her eyes and she's never looked sexier to me. She closes what little space there is between us, hooking the back of my neck with one hand as she kisses me and sliding the fingers of the other into the wetness between my legs.

Her fingers probe me as she moves her lips to my ear and whispers, "I've got you now. You're mine."

I feel myself melting right there in her arms, and she kisses me again. Swallowing my groan, she pushes forward until I'm flat on my back on her enormous desk, my legs dangling uselessly over the edge. Her mouth works its way down and she begins sucking at my breasts—first one, then the other, giving each equal time and doing something with her tongue that I can't visualize, but I can certainly feel. I'm positive I'm leaving a giant pool on her desk. I feel like shapeless putty in her hands. I was right on the money when I said the woman has *power*.

She works her way lower, in no hurry at all. Soon, I'm clamping one hand on the edge of the desk above my head and the other over my mouth to stifle my groans and cries. If anybody had told me two hours ago that I'd be sprawled naked on my back across Michelle Adams's desk with her head tucked between my legs and her mouth doing terribly sexy things to me, I'd have laughed them right off the planet. Yet here I am. Chills run up my body as she hits a particularly sensitive spot. I inhale with a sharp gasp and grab her hair. She takes this action for what it is, pushing herself into me, grasping my hips and pulling me closer. My legs are draped over her shoulders now, and I couldn't escape even if I wanted to. Which, of course, I don't. I've never allowed a woman to have such complete control over me, sexually or otherwise, and I find the combination of the unfamiliarity and the decided unease to be more arousing than I care to admit.

I feel Michelle's hands tighten on my hips, then one of them snakes up to fondle my neglected breasts and I realize my orgasm is speeding toward me. My breath catches in my throat and all of a sudden, I'm hyperconscious of where we are. Is there a cleaning crew? Might some poor, unsuspecting custodian find him or herself on the receiving end of my embarrassing shouts of pleasure? Before I can worry any further, it envelops me and I clamp my teeth together, allowing only small grunts and whimpers to escape as Michelle makes me come in her mouth. Every muscle in my body tenses. My back arches. My head tilts back and I squeeze my eyes shut as the pleasure rips through me. Michelle rides it out with me, slowing her pace in relation to the sounds I'm making (or trying not to make). Once I feel like I've returned to earth and my body begins to relax, I inhale deeply and exhale slowly. She brings her eyes up to meet mine. Our gazes hold for several seconds before she smiles and I chuckle softly. She shakes her head with a grin, her face still only inches from my soaked and throbbing center.

"Not quiet in bed, huh?" she teases.

"Not by a long shot." I use both hands to brush the hair from her face. "Come up here," I say.

Her hands play with mine as if she's debating my request. Then her eyes twinkle with mischief. At the very moment I realize she's captured both my wrists, she whispers, "Again."

"Oh my God." It's the only coherent thing I can manage to say before she plunges back into me, pushing her tongue deep inside and holding tightly to my wrists so I'm completely and totally her prisoner. She owns me. The thought sends a new rush of arousal coursing through me and it's only a matter of a few short minutes before she has me riding the crest of a second, more powerful climax. I feel like my body is on fire...that any minute, I'll just spontaneously combust and Michelle will have to call in that poor custodian to sweep the ash residue off her desk so she can finish working. This time, there's no noise at all coming from me. It's all too pure, too intense for sound. There's only feeling. My body under hers, hers on top of mine, her hands holding me captive, my muscles taut like the string of an archery bow.

I come down more slowly this time, trying to get my breathing under control before I hyperventilate. The second I feel her grip slacken, I reclaim my hands. Pushing her gently away, trying to alter my position using what little energy I have left, I pant, "No. No more. No more. Please. You're going to kill me."

She laughs, but relents. As she stands up, her eyes linger on my naked body and she wipes her mouth. "God," she says with simple amazement. I can feel every inch of my skin flush a deep red and I grin like a schoolgirl. She winks at me, then hands me some of my discarded clothing.

I get dressed, trying not to feel uncomfortable in the silence. As is normal behavior for me, I attempt to fill it. "So," I say with a grin. "Thank you for a lovely evening, Michelle. Are you this good to all your vendors?"

"Only the sexy ones."

She's sitting in one of the chairs, her legs crossed, watching me dress, and I actually feel like her gaze is slowing me down. I feel like I'm trying to get dressed and she's undressing me with her eyes and therefore, I'm stuck in some kind of limbo. If she told me right now to take my clothes back off and spread my legs for her, I would. In a heartbeat. "How do you do that?" I blurt the question out before I can stop myself.

"Do what?"

"Make me feel like I'm completely powerless." I have my back to her now and I'm afraid to look at her face, afraid I'm pushing, afraid of making her regret ever touching me. In the next instant she's standing behind me, much as we were when this whole thing started. Only this time, she fastens the clasp of my bra instead of opening it. She pulls the zipper to my skirt up rather than down.

"I don't know how to answer that," she says softly. "We just seem to have chemistry."

"You think?" I ask derisively and she laughs.

"I've had a thing for you for a very long time, Jamie."

"You have?" I stammer.

"Mmm-hmm. And I've seen the way you look at me."

"You *have*?" I'm horrified at this prospect; I pride myself on my subtlety! Her arms slide around my waist and she hugs me from behind. I feel her nod against my hair.

"It turns me on every time…that look you get in your eyes."

She flicks her tongue against my ear and my body turns to Jell-o as I lean my head back onto her shoulder and groan. The idea of her knowing what was going on in my mind all those times and finding it arousing is just so sexy. I'm shocked to feel myself becoming wet all over again.

"Michelle." I shake my head in disbelief. "My God. You're going to give me a heart attack. I swear."

"Maybe. But not tonight." Michelle squeezes me, then lets me go. "What does your schedule look like next Tuesday?"

When I turn to face her, she's in front of her laptop and apparently looking at her online planner. "Tuesday?"

"Yeah. I have a trade show coming up and I'm going to need some stuff."

"Oh." I'm jarred by the sudden leap right back into business, but I manage to find my briefcase and pull out my Day Runner. Trying not to let my hurt show, I say, "I've got a lunch appointment and a one thirty, but otherwise I'm open. What time are you thinking?"

"Around six thirty?"

My head snaps up and her eyes are twinkling again. My center tingles at the prospect of another go-around with Michelle Adams and I nod, catching my bottom lip between my teeth. I'm already planning a sneak attack. A quick image of *her* on her back on the desk shoots through my head and I shudder with erotic anticipation. The subject of next Tuesday's meeting? Role reversal. I toss her a knowing grin.

"Six thirty sounds perfect."

TOUR GUIDE
SYLVIE AVANTE

An entertainment reporter for a rival newspaper caught sight of Allison as she slipped through the door. "Grant! Sinking down to our level now? Who did you piss off?"

"Only here to observe the animals, Mitch." She smiled at him, but her grin was tight.

Interview the star, my ass. She couldn't care less about the latest Hollywood movie being shot in Toronto. Like the majority of people who lived there, she had gotten used to the city being a popular destination for movie producers wanting their movies shot on the cheap. Toronto had been used as a stand-in for New York, Boston, and Chicago in countless productions. She was bored by it. *I'm a crime reporter, for crying out loud.*

"I'm here for the press junket," Allison said to the thin woman who brandished a clipboard like it was a weapon.

The woman eyed Allison. "Got your press credentials?" Allison pulled the card from her back pocket. The woman barely glanced at it before looking back at her clipboard. "We're running a bit behind. Have a seat, and we'll call you." She wrote a number on a yellow Post-it note and gave it to Allison. "You're number forty-six."

"A number?" Dumbfounded, Allison stared at the tiny square of paper. "I'm a bloody number?"

But the woman had walked away.

Instead of trying to find a vacant spot, Allison marched out of the room. *I could be halfway to Greece right now, ready to talk a pretty girl into rubbing oil on my breasts. But no, my editor has me doing a fluff piece with some airbrained actress.* She waited for the elevator, intent now on finding a decent cup of coffee. She slipped inside as soon as the doors opened.

"Hold the door, please."

Allison automatically reached out to prevent the doors from closing, and the woman who had called out stepped in beside her.

"Thanks."

Allison nodded and pressed the button marked Lobby.

"I'm playing hooky," the woman finally said.

Allison shifted to look at her. She was wearing a baseball cap pulled low over her forehead, her long blond ponytail threaded through the opening in the back. All Allison could see was her profile, but that was smooth, and her voice was like slow-moving molasses. Allison found herself wanting to see her face.

"Hooky, huh?" Allison said. "Me too."

"Where to?"

"First, coffee. After that, who knows?"

The woman turned to her then, and Allison suddenly knew what it was to be struck speechless by a woman's looks. *Jesus, she is stunning.*

"I would love a good cup of coffee. I've only just arrived in the city, so I haven't found my way around yet. Mind if I tag along?"

Mind? I would beg you to tag along. "Sure."

The woman smiled. The smile started with her mouth and then moved all the way to her eyes. "I'm Tara."

Allison blinked as she felt the effect of that smile down to her toes. "Uh. Allie. Allison." *Smooth, Grant. Real smooth.*

Tara smiled again and this time her eyes lingered on Allison's face, just a hint longer than necessary. Allison felt the wetness pool between her legs. *Jesus.*

Allison didn't have a clue how she managed to coherently order coffee at the shop on the corner without making a complete fool of herself. If she made conversation, she couldn't remember it. As they stepped outside, she smiled at Tara. "Decent enough for you?"

"Perfect."

From the way the word slipped off Tara's tongue, Allison had a feeling she was talking about more than the coffee. *Now what?*

Almost as if she could read her mind, Tara turned to Allison. "Would you show me the city?"

"I'm a lousy tour guide."

"Still, I'd like to see the city through your eyes."

Their gazes met and Allison took a deep breath, trying to clear her head. It seemed that all of her decisions were being dictated by the incessant pounding between her legs. She couldn't remember ever having been this affected by someone she didn't even know. "Okay."

They spent the next few hours exploring the funky little shops of Queen Street West and walking through Chinatown before ending along the shores of Lake Ontario. Through it all, Allison was conscious of Tara's scent drifting to her now and then and of her frequent looks lingering on her skin. Allison was certain that she had never been so hard so fast without ever being touched.

"Thank you," Tara said.

"My pleasure." The constant hum of arousal was there, vibrating under Allison's skin, and she grinned. She felt so very alive. She studied Tara's profile. *Can you tell how much I would like to feel your skin? How much I want to know what your mouth would taste like?*

Allison looked out toward the lake so Tara wouldn't see her need. And then she saw the sky. "Better take shelter—a storm is coming. Fast."

She pointed to a small abandoned shed, and they hurried to it. Allison shoved at the rusted-out door until it gave way with a moan.

"Afternoon thunderstorms frequently cross the lake during the summer. Sometimes they pass over in an hour or less, sometimes they linger through the night. You can never tell," Allison said.

Overhead, the first raindrops struck the roof with fat-sounding slaps. Tara inhaled deeply. "You can smell the rain."

"Smells good, doesn't it?"

"Sounds wonderful too."

The rain didn't cool the air much, but it had a definite effect on the atmosphere. It became denser, closer. Allison was aware of it, and sensed that Tara was too.

When Tara's eyes moved away from watching the rain though the doorway and found Allison's, they stared at each other through the deepening gloom. Oddly, it wasn't an uncomfortable exchange. Allison would have called it expectant, as it combined curiosity with caution, wonderment with undertones of wariness. She felt Tara's gaze like a tug, drawing her closer, and knew she was looking at Tara with the same intensity.

"What do you want to do now?" Tara asked.

"What I want might scare you," Allison finally whispered.

"Try me."

Allison stepped closer. "I want to feel how soft your skin is. I want to know what your mouth feels like against mine. And God help me, most of all I want to feel if you're as wet as I am."

Tara's mouth had parted at her words. "I've been wet since you introduced yourself."

"I could pretend that I'm going to be able to go slow. But what's the point. I'm dying to see your face when I make you come."

"Hurry, then."

Allison's mouth curved as her lips met Tara's. Then they softened, and opened, and gave. Allison felt herself slide into her. The kiss heated even before Allison slipped her hands under Tara's shirt, ran them up her back, then down again, nails scraping slightly. With a growl, Allison pulled and ripped at the shirt until it was off. Her eyes settled on Tara's breasts and she breathed out once. "You're perfect."

She lowered her lips to savor and taste the tender skin just above Tara's breasts. With her mouth, she learned the flavor and softness of Tara's skin. Her teeth nipped and tugged as they inched toward hard nipples. She felt, rather than heard, the moan that tore through Tara.

"Don't make me wait," Tara implored. "I don't want you to be gentle."

Tara's plea had Allison's clit hardening to the point of pain. She lifted hazy eyes to meet Tara's and fought the urge to shove her against the wall. "You're making me nuts."

"Good. Please put your hands on me. Feel how wet you've made me." Tara rocked her hips, urging Allison to find her.

Allison felt herself slip dangerously out of control. She shoved Tara against the wall and pushed aside the thin layer of cotton. She rested her fingers just above the base of Tara's clit, pressing down ever so slightly. She could feel the heat under her fingertips, the wetness coating them. "You feel so good." She slipped one, then two fingers inside as her thumb circled the lengthening shaft.

Tara let out a low moan and her hands dug into Allison's shoulders, pulling her close. "Yes, that's it. God, you have the greatest hands. Fuck me, please," she whispered against Allison's ear.

At her words, Allison's eyes almost rolled back in her head. With a groan, she dropped to her knees and sank her mouth into Tara's wetness, taking her scent and her taste with one slow sweep of her tongue.

"Oh my God!" Tara groaned. The erotic shock of it had her shoving her hands through Allison's hair to press her closer.

Allison started at the tip of the shaft and slowly, with increasing pressure, licked downward while her fingers continued to stroke within.

"That feels so unbelievable. Oh God...you're making me come," Tara whispered, completely undone by the moment.

Allison's mouth closed on the hard ball of her clit and started to suck it, and Tara erupted with a loud cry. "Yes...oh God." Her movements became frantic as she pushed with a sob against Allison's mouth. Finally Allison relented and gently moved her mouth away from the still-pulsing clit. She was about to withdraw her fingers, but Tara groaned and pressed her hand against them. "Please, don't leave."

Allison continued to gently stroke her until the spasms around her fingers slowed, then carefully removed her hand. She placed a tender kiss on the soft skin of Tara's abdomen and stood up. Tara wrapped her arms around Allison, and their mouths met in a long, slow kiss.

"Can I come now too?" she whispered. When she felt Tara nod against her shoulder, Allison lowered the zipper of her jeans and slipped her hand between her legs. "Oh God."

She closed her eyes as she felt how hard and wet she was. She was so ready that she knew it would only take a couple of strokes to get off. Her fingers slid against her clit, and she groaned. Then her eyes flew open to lock with Tara's when Tara's hand joined hers and their fingers intertwined. Allison couldn't tell where her touch ended and Tara's began as Tara matched her ever-quickening strokes. All she could feel was the exquisite pressure building as she fought to prolong the pleasure. Unable to wait any longer, hips moving in sync, she pushed against their hands, too lost in the pleasure to maintain control.

"I'm coming...I'm com—" Allison threw her head back and shouted as the climax roared through her. Still shuddering, she sank against Tara. "God, that was...I don't know...what the hell was that?"

Tara gave a smile as she pulled their still-intertwined hands to her mouth and slowly licked off Allison's wetness. "*That* was a great tour of the city."

"Well, part of it." The feel of Tara's lips against her skin made Allison's clitoris twitch. "It's a big city."

Tara smiled. "I know."

AN ELEMENT OF POETRY
EEVIE KEYS

I'm nervous. I've never done anything like this before."
I held my violin up for close inspection, willing my hands
to stop shaking. I had just tuned her, and the music wasn't perfect—I
wasn't steady enough. With a deliberate sigh, I tried again, plucking
the E string to hear its high-pitched whine. It was just a *little* bit off-
key—and that was just *slightly* driving me nuts.

You sat demurely on the love seat, hands folded. It had surprised
us both that such a drab dressing room might have a love seat. It was
antique looking and well worn, little claw feet pressing into the dirty
boards that passed for a floor behind the stage. But behind the *curtain*?
Oh, that was another world—well-polished oak and maple, worthy of a
master artist's feet. Music, dance—it was all art.

You had once told me that music was art. You, the artist, the
painter who could shape worlds with your hands. You told me that what
I most treasured was art. I remember feeling different—after you told
me. Like I was somehow *making* a difference.

When I first met you, I thought you immortal. What you chose to
do with your fingers and soul would forever be regarded by the world.
I knew that your bright strokes and dancing curves would make any
woman fall to her knees—your art was your spirit, unashamedly bare
for all the world to see—there, upon the canvas. You could have won
anyone, with your art, you know. You could have charmed the angels
with it.

But you did not charm angels. You charmed *me*.

"You really don't have to do this, you know," you said, for the
fiftieth time in as many seconds, it seemed. Your sentence drew me
back to reality as I plucked the string again. It was as close to perfect as
it could possibly get, and—with a sigh—I tried the next.

"My name is in the program book. People bought tickets with my name on it. My name is above the little box office window. I sort of have to." That string was just fine...What about the next?

I was paying no attention to you, in reality, I admit. And I'm sorry to admit it. There was half an hour before that tapestry of a curtain would rise and my violin would have to speak in tongues. Brow furrowed, I plucked another string. I was thinking of the crowd. I was thinking of those tickets—my name spelled in blocky text. I was thinking of us, of my memories of us. My memories of those fingers. I was thinking of everything and nothing. I was thinking of nothing.

I hadn't noticed you rise, just like a curtain. I hadn't noticed you walking toward me—until your hand touched mine, dulling the sharp yelp of the string into a silence the room had not yet embraced.

"I can always relax you," you said. And your grin had fire behind it.

"You've got to be kidding me." I smiled tightly with frustration. "Please tell me you're kidding."

With gentle fingers, you pried the violin from my grasp and set it quietly on my stool. My tenseness melted as you embraced me. I felt like I wanted to cry, but that lasted only a heartbeat—until your kiss.

The concert hall seated two thousand. I had never played at such a big venue. For a week, I had had that number drawn in crayon posted on my refrigerator. It was sobering. It made me lose my appetite. It had made me lose my lunch, occasionally. Chagrined, I felt those self-same fingers that had scribbled the number in crayon tracing up my back. You were more excited than I was when you heard. You had laughed and danced and made love to me in celebration—because all my dreams were coming true.

I hadn't told you they already had. I was too shy to say it.

Now, you pushed me against the wall—against a wall that had stood for one hundred years, supporting other lovers and other loves, enclosing the passions of artists who would dance and sing and play their way into an audience's heart. Just like you played your way into mine.

You wanted me. I knew that as you broke from me and left a trail of hot kisses down my neck, down to the gentle dip in my blouse. I knew you wanted me as you lifted my skirt, turning my hose into a waterfall of heat as I lifted a leg and hooked it around your hips. The hose were black—they matched my skirt, the barrette nestled within my golden mane. You'd called it that—you, a poet. You'd called me your poetry, each and every night—after you made me scream.

Now, I would not be able to raise my voice in honor of your touch. I whimpered and shut my eyes, digging long fingers into your shoulders as you dug long fingers into my panties—pressing against them— encouraged by the wetness you found, shining through the satin.

It drove you on, harder and faster, making you lift my blouse, wrestle with my bra—cursing it as I breathed out, waiting impatiently, pouting while you undid the closures and found a nipple with your lips. You bit it. You only bite when you want me badly.

You pushed me against the wall, my garter belt stretching against the angle of my thighs as you lifted my leg higher and higher— stretching me wider and wider—spreading my legs until all I could do was whimper your name and clutch your tousled head to my breast.

You bit me and you licked me, hardening me as my aching legs begged to be wider, spread harder... As my wetness grew, you stopped touching me there—there, where I wanted it most. I licked my lips and begged, breathing your name as you scratched my thighs with moist fingers.

You sank to your knees, then, and pushed up my skirt. My thigh-highs were shaming, black without a trace of lace... I bit my lip as you nibbled where the hose stopped and my skin began. You licked up, tasting my skin as I so wished to taste you. Then, you were at my panties again—but this time, betraying fingers cupped my ass as your mouth went forward, tasting me through the satin, prolonging the moment of my desire until I could not bear it. You pushed me to you—you buried your lips into my crotch, and I ground my teeth, pressing myself harder and harder against you, breathing and panting like something wild you had not been able to tame. I wanted it. And I wanted it now.

You chuckled, then, a hot little chuckle that raced through me, feathering this passion you had inspired. I was halfway angry at you for making me spread against a dressing-room wall. For wanting when my violin needed. But you pulled back those accursed panties—at least *they* had lace!—and ran your tongue across what was throbbing...and all thoughts of violins shattered.

You licked me and you teased me, using teeth and tongue to spread me gently, then harshly, taking me in and sucking me until I was too weak for it all. You were Business as you buried your mouth against me, and I clutched your head—your long, thick braid of red—as I willed the weakness out of my knees, asking for a reprieve, wanting to stand until paradise became found.

You took me then. You pulled me from that wall and pushed me against the floor. You were on top of me, between my legs, your hips against my hips, your jeans grinding against my satin-covered pussy... I moaned—a quiet, low moan—as you took my arms and held them against the floor above my head, kissing me fiercely with a mouth that tasted of sex.

Then, you were in me again—this time, fingers—questing, seeking, as I spread myself as wide as I could for you, whimpering as a thumb followed, deeper inside me, becoming as wet as I was.

You came into me—and out—as often as I breathed, and my breath came quickly, a pant I could not control as wave after wave of it all covered me. Again, your mouth found my breast—my right breast—the one you had bitten, and you bit it again, rolling my nipple with your tongue as you bit it harder and harder, using your other hand to pinch my rump, making me grind my hips against yours again—thrusting myself against you, wanting you...

You came down on me once more, forcing my legs up with your shoulders, pressing them back as you spread me wider, filling your face with my wetness, your mouth with my heat. I shuddered as you stuck your tongue inside me—tasting me—tracing it up and up to my throbbing clit. You took it between your teeth and sucked on it mercilessly as I clutched your head, crying out.

I came, then, washing waves of bliss covering us both as I bucked my hips against your head, pressing your face against me as I went and went—six, seven times—a pulse much more beautiful than a heartbeat. I breathed out, and you allowed my legs down as I twined your hair about my fingers, pulling you up now gently to kiss me. I was so delicate—too delicate, too sensitive. You ground your hips against me and I cried out as the last wave covered and held me. You smiled, then, as you did the same. All I had strength to do was breathe.

You smelled wet—I loved it. I breathed you, willing my heart to stop pounding, willing my entire body to stop throbbing. You held me until I had strength to rise, and then you helped me up, straightening my hose and panties, skirt and blouse—once more, all business. But now, Miss Business had a twinkle in her eyes—and a cat-who-ate-the-canary smile. All I could do was grin, a little chagrined, and hope to high heaven that I didn't smell like sex.

There was no help for my hair—once grandly pulled back in a stunning formation, now having to settle for a quick braid. I deftly pulled it back and tied it as you crossed your arms and looked at me, smiling. I laughed—a little—then gathered my violin and bow, glancing at the clock. It was five minutes to.

"You're on in five," a bodiless voice called from the shut door. That was good—that was nice. I plucked each string in turn, remembering to breathe—*having* to breathe—I was so out of breath. And you—just standing there, smiling.

"Aren't you going to say anything?" I finally asked, holding my violin beneath an arm, brandishing the bow like a sword. Your eyes were sparkling, and I was still flushed—blushing, I realized.

"Yeah." You were grinning now. "You're relaxed, aren't you?"

"That's not the point. It was beautiful—it was poetry…just like you said." I paused, hand on door, ready to go out and face the masses with a painted smile on my face. You'd painted it. You had, actually, painted me. I felt like your masterpiece…

"No…" You shrugged, breaking the moment with an evil grin. "*You're* poetry. *That* was stress relief. I think I'm going to become a doctor." You came up, then, and placed your hand over mine on the door. Damn you, anyway! You—the artist—turning poetry to comedy… and everything back again. It was your gift.

You kissed me. You tasted so good, pressing your mouth against mine—reaching inside me to hold my heart, like you had done so many countless times before.

"That was funny," I finally said when you broke away, grinning like a Cheshire cat. Like a sex-obsessed adolescent.

"No. That was sex," you reminded me, and opened the door.

I must admit—I *was* pretty relaxed.

(And… my violin was jealous.)

COVET THY NEIGHBOR
RENÉE STRIDER

Morgan had been lusting after her neighbor ever since Morgan's lover left her and the house they'd shared for five years. It wasn't a bitter breakup, more a culmination of weariness. Though she'd become a bit of a player after the separation, she reserved her real lust for her neighbor, Isabel. Who unfortunately was straight. Yes, she knew better, but she couldn't help it. Isabel had a mouth to die for—full lips, naturally red and almost blurry, as if she'd just been making love for hours. And Isabel's hands were large, with long, elegant fingers. It was so easy to imagine them stroking her.

Isabel was as tall as Morgan, and she wasn't used to that. She fantasized about pushing Isabel up against a wall without having to bend down, her mouth on Isabel's throat, her thigh between Isabel's thighs, her hands pulling Isabel's hips into hers. This was her favorite fantasy.

Part of what fueled the fantasies was that Isabel seemed to be fascinated with Morgan. She frequently complimented Morgan, mostly on her body—what good shape she was in, how defined her muscles were—sometimes to the point of embarrassment. Morgan and her lover would joke about it.

On one occasion, when they were both out by the pool, Isabel joined them as she often did. It was hot and still and muggy, the kind of afternoon when the sound of one cicada can be heard for blocks. Morgan was lying on her stomach on a wooden lounger in her bathing suit. She was still dripping and panting slightly from a vigorous swim, eyes closed, head on her arms, drying off in the searing sun.

Suddenly she heard her neighbor's voice and at the same time felt a hand moving up and down the back of her leg, then up to her shoulder, caressing her. It was Isabel saying what a fine body she had, and such great shoulders. Morgan looked up at her lover, who winked at her and rolled her eyes.

"I work out," she mumbled, blushing to the roots of her damp black curls.

Now peculiar as that incident might have seemed, even startling, it made some sense since Isabel was a registered physiotherapist. So bodies—and their condition—were her profession. Checking out Morgan's was for her a natural thing to do. Probably. But still…

During the year after the breakup, Morgan's recently discovered lust for Isabel waxed and waned. Seeing her at a distance getting out of her car or pruning her roses, both women waving a friendly hello, barely made an impact. Then Isabel would invite her for dinner or a film. One time, in the darkness of the theater, Morgan had leaned over very close to Isabel to whisper a reply. She had smelled her fragrance, felt her heat, and she had almost touched her mouth to the dark auburn tendril lying on the curve of her neck. As Morgan had drawn away, she'd imagined Isabel's head thrown back, exposing herself to Morgan's lips and tongue. She'd been aroused for days afterward, and at home, in bed at night, she would touch herself, imagining her neighbor's face and mouth and hands until the orgasm crashed through her.

This is slowly killing me, Morgan thought more than once. But she could not give up Isabel's company.

In late February, when a blizzard hit the area, Morgan bundled up and shoveled, making two new hills beside her driveway where it met the road.

This was work. These snowflakes had fallen fat and filled with moisture, and the loads she shoveled were heavy. By the time Morgan finished clearing the driveway, she was red in the face and sweating. Scarf, tuque, and mitts had been tossed in a snowbank, and her down jacket hung open. Dark, damp curls, even more springy than usual, hung in her eyes. But she had enjoyed herself. The exertion felt good after being confined to the house during the snowstorm the day before.

She wasn't ready to stop yet and looked over at Isabel's driveway. No cars and no tire tracks in the snow. She decided to shovel the snowbank that blocked it. By the time she had pushed and lifted and thrown enough to make two more huge mounds of snow at the end of the cleared driveway, her coat had joined the other discarded clothes, and she was breathing hard.

It was now midafternoon, but the light hadn't changed much except to become softer still under the gray-white sky.

Morgan arched her aching back and stretched.

She was just putting the snow shovel on her shoulder and gathering up the tossed clothing to go home when Isabel pulled up, stopped, and rolled down the window. Morgan felt a flutter in her belly as they smiled at each other.

"Hi. You've been away," she said. *Oh, very cool. Some opening.*

"Visiting Sandy. I meant to come home yesterday but got snowed in. The roads are pretty clear now." Isabel looked at the driveway, her face lighting up. "Morgan, this is terrific! Thanks! I thought I'd be parked on the road for a while."

"No problem. I really needed the exercise."

Isabel's hazel eyes focused on Morgan, who stood there disheveled and still red-faced, hair and clothing damp from perspiration. She grinned as she looked Morgan up and down.

"You look as if you're about to collapse. Let's go in and I'll make a fire and some hot chocolate and you can recover."

"Okay, great." Morgan followed the car up the driveway to the big, gray limestone house, trying to ignore the faint erotic buzz in her guts.

The light from the table lamp by the door threw out an amber glow. Morgan leaned an elbow against the fireplace mantel and looked at Isabel as she moved around the room. She was dressed in soft black wool trousers and a dark green v-neck pullover that exposed the nape of her long neck, her throat, and her delicate collarbones. Morgan's eyes were drawn to the smooth skin, pale gold in the lamplight. *So beautiful and graceful. Like a dancer.*

Suddenly she shivered, but it wasn't a shiver of arousal, at least not altogether.

"I'm cold," she said, her jaw tense, teeth almost chattering.

Isabel's eyebrows rose in question as she ran her hands over Morgan's shoulders and down her arms, then behind and over her back. "No wonder. Your clothes are still damp. First you get extremely overheated, and now both your skin and your sweaty clothes are evaporating and getting cold. Take them off right now."

"Wha—I, uh…"

"Just take your clothes off." Isabel smiled at her fondly and squeezed her shoulders. "We'll hang them on this chair by the fireplace and I'll get you a nice fuzzy robe. And that hot chocolate I promised. You'll be warm in no time and feel much better."

"Thanks, good idea," Morgan called after Isabel as she left the room. *I'll do anything you say.*

The erotic buzz in her belly escalated and she felt a quick jab of arousal even lower down. The shivers continued, now in counterpoint to her quickened heartbeat. *All right, calm down. Just think about getting warm. That's what this is about.*

While Isabel was making kitchen sounds in pursuit of hot chocolate, Morgan stripped quickly and hung her damp clothes on the chair near the fireplace. Then she snuggled into the soft warmth of the robe Isabel had provided and faced the stove. She sighed with satisfaction as the heat penetrated and soon had to move away because the heat had become too intense.

"That's better," Isabel said cheerfully as she entered carrying a tray. "You look very cozy. When you're completely warm, come over here."

She'd changed into loose olive green drawstring trousers and a snug-fitting beige T-shirt, through which Morgan could see the shadowed protrusions of her nipples. Her chestnut hair hung almost to her shoulders, red highlights shining in the light from the stove and the table lamp nearby. Morgan's breath caught in her throat and her eyes blurred. *So lovely. Jesus, I want her.*

It took only a moment for Morgan to recover and she sat down beside Isabel. "This smells *so* good." She lifted the steaming mug of cocoa and brought it to her nose. "And coconut cookies, great."

They sipped the fragrant hot drinks and munched on the cookies in companionable silence until their eyes met and held. Morgan realized she was holding her breath as a new surge of arousal shot from her stomach to her groin. *Oh God, I can't be this close to her. Don't look at her mouth. Or her nipples.*

Isabel smiled kindly, her hazel eyes crinkling. Long fingers curled gently around Morgan's arm. She slid her hand over and above the elbow, clasping a solid bicep.

"Still in terrific shape, I see. My God, I'm impressed." She squeezed again. "You must lift weights."

Morgan's heart raced and she hoped fervently that her neighbor wouldn't see the pulse beating in her throat. *This is nuts. How can she not see what's happening to me? Must be the light in here.*

Morgan was becoming desperate. Slowly and nonchalantly, she hoped, she pulled away from Isabel and sat back against the couch again.

"Yeah, I lift weights. I go to the gym on campus three times a week."

She willed her voice to remain steady, but now she found it impossible to relax. The antique couch wasn't very comfortable, anyway. That, combined with sexual tension and hours of snow shoveling, had made her neck and shoulders ache. She sat up, grimacing, and moved her neck from side to side, then rolled her shoulders. "I guess I overdid it today, though. I'm a bit sore."

Isabel's eyes lit up with keen—professional—interest and she grasped the back of Morgan's neck, kneading firmly. "Pretty tense. You know what you need, don't you?"

Morgan looked at her dumbly, dark eyebrows raised, mouth curved in a half smile, wondering if she should tell her.

"Well, what do I do for a living?" Isabel's eyes, guileless and innocent, fixed on Morgan's. "I can fix the pain. That's what I do. I can't believe I've never given you a massage. It's the least I can do for the driveway. And after that I'll make us some dinner."

Morgan's heart stopped, yet she still felt her pulse beating wildly in her throat. Her mouth went dry, but between her thighs she could feel herself getting wetter.

"We can use the guest room," Isabel continued enthusiastically, pointing at a second door. "The bed's perfect in there, very firm, and the room's nice and warm. Come on."

Morgan followed Isabel in and watched as she placed two firm pillows on top of the covers.

"You can kind of put your head between these so you can breathe," she said. "Just lie down on your tummy."

"Okay," Morgan said weakly as she focused on the queen-size bed covered with a duvet in abstract pastels. She untied and removed the belt from her robe, tossed it aside, and lay down on her front. Then she lifted her arms, bent them around the pillows, and rested her forehead between them on her clasped hands.

"Yes, that's good," Isabel said as she got up on the bed and straddled Morgan's hips, her knees resting against Morgan's sides.

Morgan could feel the heat even through the fuzzy robe. *Oh God, I'm dying. I'll never survive this.*

"Do you always give massages like this?" she croaked, face between the pillows.

Isabel laughed, completely relaxed as she tugged on Morgan's arms to bring them down again so she could pull the blue robe off, exposing the smoothly muscled, bare back down to the waist.

"Hardly. I do have various massage boards, but this is so much more comfortable. You'll probably fall asleep."

Morgan groaned silently to herself. *As if.*

She felt Isabel's warm hands grasping the rigid muscles at the nape of her neck and moving outward along her shoulders, then returning, the fingers pushing and squeezing the tightness from neck to elbows, down both sides of her back, then in toward her spine. With the heels of her hands Isabel pressed from shoulder to waist. Slowly and surely Morgan's body relaxed and her heart rate slowed down, her mind filled only with the rhythm of Isabel's strong hands on her.

She drifted for a long while as the soothing massage continued. She had almost dozed off when something changed. Isabel's soft, regular breathing had changed. It was still soft but it had become uncertain, slightly ragged.

All of Morgan's senses were suddenly on full alert as she forced her body to remain limp. Now Isabel's breathing seemed to quicken a little, and Morgan's heart pounded in reflex. She almost swooned when Isabel grazed the sides of her buttocks lightly with the insides of her thighs. And then again, until Isabel wasn't just straddling Morgan anymore, but lightly brushing her inner thighs and center along the top of Morgan's muscled cheeks, forward and back, as she continued to manipulate Morgan's back and shoulders with her hands.

"Morgan…I…" Isabel's voice shook. "Oh God…" The massaging stopped as she leaned forward, her hands resting on Morgan's shoulders. In this position the apex of her thighs rested on Morgan's buttocks, and Isabel squirmed slightly, pushing down. Her breathing had become even more erratic. Morgan imagined the other woman's breasts heaving above her.

"Take your clothes off," Morgan said hoarsely. She turned her head sideways to look up at Isabel. Hazel eyes met blue, both pairs darkened by desire in the dim, golden light of the lamp.

"Yes." Isabel's voice was a whisper. She lifted one leg over Morgan and moved away enough to struggle out of her loose trousers, satin underpants, and T-shirt while still on the bed. Then she bent over Morgan and removed the robe.

"So lovely," Isabel said, her voice trembling as she caressed Morgan's smooth, firm buttocks. Again she straddled Morgan and lowered herself slowly to sit, leaning forward with her hands resting on the bed beside Morgan's shoulders. She moaned softly.

"No, put your hands on my shoulders." Morgan's voice was husky as she raised her bent arms again and rested the side of her head on her clasped hands. Her body was once more rigid and tense with arousal.

Isabel clutched Morgan's shoulders and began to slide forward and back on Morgan's buttocks, her thighs spread wide. She was so very wet that Morgan's buttocks were soon slippery with moisture.

Morgan pushed her face into the bed between the two pillows and groaned loudly as she felt the heat and the friction and the slickness from the other woman against her sensitive skin. When she heard Isabel moaning, she groaned again and, gritting her teeth, tried to hold back the orgasm that was about to take her over the edge.

She knew the other woman was close too. Isabel gripped Morgan's shoulders harder. She was gasping. Suddenly she brought one knee to rest between Morgan's thighs and then she was riding just one muscled buttock. She thrust her engorged clit against it hard—once, twice— then her hands came away from Morgan's shoulders as she arched her back and climaxed with a loud wail. Whimpering, she collapsed on Morgan.

Morgan was panting, frantic. She grabbed Isabel's hand where it lay beside her, pulled it between her body and the mattress, and pushed it down against her dripping sex. One touch and she came hard into Isabel's palm, then convulsed again, sobbing in ecstasy.

They lay there, Morgan's heart pounding into the mattress, Isabel's heart pounding into Morgan's back.

"What the hell was that all about? Oh God, what an orgasm." Isabel's voice was a moan in the hollow at the nape of Morgan's neck.

Morgan turned her head so that Isabel's mouth was against her cheek and her silky hair hung over their faces, blocking the light. The memory of her own climax made her guts contract involuntarily. Slowly their breathing returned to normal but they did not move, still enjoying the hot, damp sensuality of their bodies pressed together.

Suddenly Morgan had to know.

"Have you ever thought about us this way before?" she asked.

Isabel moved her head slightly, nuzzling Morgan's face. Morgan could feel the eyelashes flutter delicately against her cheekbone.

"No, never," Isabel breathed. "But I'm sure I will from now on."

"Have you ever had sex with a woman before?"

"No, never. But I'm sure I will from now on."

There was a short pause. Suddenly both women erupted into giggles.

"That was funny," Morgan said finally, still chuckling.

"Yes, but I meant it. That was incredible." Isabel finally rolled off Morgan's warm body and lay on her side, smiling.

Morgan turned onto her side too, head propped up on an elbow as she gazed at Isabel's face and the red lips she had wanted to kiss for so long and still hadn't.

"You're so beautiful, Mor. I've always thought so," Isabel whispered, as the tips of her fingers brushed Morgan's cheek.

Morgan closed her eyes and touched her lips softly to Isabel's. A faint quiver began again in her stomach and moved swiftly down to her belly. She slid the tip of her tongue along Isabel's full bottom lip, then along her top lip, and then gently pushed her way inside. Isabel moaned softly as her tongue met Morgan's, gliding along and around its length. Soon they were both breathing hard again, probing and sucking, claiming each other's mouths. And their hands caressed wherever they could reach—breasts and nipples and hips, and thighs that ended in silky, wet folds.

"Isabel. Let me taste you. Please, will you let me taste you? I need…" Morgan could hardly get the words out.

"Yes. Yes, baby. I want you to." Isabel was panting slightly as she moved to lie on her back, her hands going to Morgan's head in anticipation of guiding it down.

"No, come and sit here." Now Morgan lay on her back, motioning Isabel to straddle her again, but this time to sit on her stomach.

Isabel did, thighs pressed against Morgan's sides. First she sat very lightly, partly resting on her knees, but when she felt the firmness and strength of the abdominal muscles beneath her, she settled more heavily. Both women moaned softly as Isabel's hot, wet center pressed into Morgan.

Morgan gazed up at Isabel, at eyes dark with passion, mouth swollen from kisses, and full breasts bathed in the glow of the bedside lamp. She cupped Isabel's breasts, tugging gently on the dark pink nipples with her thumbs and forefingers.

Isabel arched her neck and pushed down on Morgan's stomach, groaning. "Stop, you're going to make me come."

Morgan stopped, and they looked at each other through a haze of desire. Morgan caressed Isabel's hips, then pulled them forward.

"Come up here. Come up to my mouth so I can taste you."

Isabel moved up Morgan's body and gripped the headboard for balance. She was trembling slightly. Before she could lower herself to Morgan's mouth, Morgan's hands were on her hips, holding her in place.

"Wait, I want to look at you. I need to see you, " Morgan murmured shakily. She looked up at Isabel's center and her breath caught as she saw the rosy tips of Isabel's labia not quite hidden by the soft, down-covered flesh protecting her vulva. With two fingers of each hand she parted the silky-soft inner labia and spread them open.

"The Japanese call this 'butterfly,'" she whispered. Her eyes teared at the beauty she saw there: delicate, glistening flesh almost scarlet in the lamplight, and the tip of the clitoris like a tiny red pearl where the folds joined.

Now she let Isabel lower herself slowly to her mouth, and she licked gently all along the slick, satiny length of her, drunk with the taste and fragrance. Isabel cried out softly as Morgan gently impaled her with her stiffened tongue. In and out Morgan thrust while rubbing her face along the length of Isabel's clitoris. Isabel's sharp cries of ecstasy as she came brought Morgan to climax instantaneously, her hips arching up from the bed. Once again Isabel collapsed on Morgan, sobbing her release, and Morgan held her tightly.

When the aftershocks had abated, Isabel mumbled, "I can't take this anymore. If I have another orgasm like that, I won't survive." Her face was still hidden against Morgan's throat.

Morgan grinned. "Yeah, I'm pretty tired."

"I was going to make you dinner," Isabel sighed as she rose up on her elbows and looked down at Morgan.

"I know, but it's too late now." Morgan lifted her head up and touched her lips to Isabel's throat, barely brushing the delicate pulse she saw there. "I need to get my clothes. I can shower at home."

"Well, while you get your clothes on I'll have a really quick shower. Don't leave till I've finished, okay?"

Morgan admired Isabel's long bare legs, smooth back, and full buttocks as she disappeared into the bathroom. Seeing her like that was all it took. Morgan sighed, enjoying the faint tickle of arousal in her belly and waiting for it to pass. Then she remembered something. A minute later, she opened the door to the steamy room and her stomach clenched at the sight of Isabel through the glass door. It was an erotic pose, head thrown back, eyes closed under the pulsing water.

Morgan opened the shower door and stepped under the warm cascade. Water poured down on them both, and instantly Morgan's black curls were plastered down on her head. For a moment their eyes locked. Then Morgan pushed Isabel up against the wall of the cubicle. Their wet bodies slid against each other. Lust shuddered through Morgan as her mouth found Isabel's throat. Her thigh pushed up between Isabel's thighs and her hands pulled Isabel's hips hard into her. Isabel moaned loudly as Morgan sucked and licked her exposed throat while her thigh thrust back and forth along Isabel's clit. Isabel's hands clutched wildly at Morgan's shoulders. Release was sudden as she cried out and came violently, jerking against Morgan's slippery thigh.

Isabel's weakened legs buckled and Morgan let her slip slowly through her arms till she was on her knees clutching Morgan's legs, her forehead pressed against the hollow between hip and thigh. Morgan turned the full force of the showerhead away from her, then stooped down, offering her arms to help Isabel up.

But Isabel didn't get up. Still breathing hard, she looked up at Morgan through the steam, rivulets of water coursing down her beautiful face.

"I haven't tasted you yet and I'm in the perfect position to. I'm going to drink from you and suck your clit very hard until you beg me to stop."

Morgan swallowed convulsively, the rapidly increasing moisture from her throbbing center mingling with the water from the shower. Her favorite fantasy was turning out to be so much more than she could ever have imagined.

THE DEFENSE RESTS
RADCLYFFE

On the ride up to her exclusive condo on the twentieth floor of a high-rise overlooking Washington Square, Trey Pelosi considered the fact that it was getting harder and harder to find acceptable bed companions. It was a bad idea to sleep with women connected with work, but when work was 90 percent of her life, exactly *how* was she supposed to find someone somewhere else? *Socializing* with any of the women she might meet in the course of business was impossible—neither clients nor colleagues were acceptable dating material, especially given her particular proclivities in that regard. Besides, on her rare free evening, she wasn't looking for candlelit dinners and slow walks by the riverside. She was looking for someone to take her beyond the confines and constraints of her too-busy, too-pressured, too-high-powered life. She was looking for someone to make her forget reason and rationalization and gamesmanship. She was *looking* for someone to reach inside her and make her scream with the simple pleasure of not thinking at all.

Tonight was one of those nights.

Trey let herself in and deposited her Coach briefcase on the marble-topped walnut pedestal table just inside the door. She shrugged out of her tailored Jil Sander silk suit jacket and was about to kick off her Prada heels when the phone rang.

"No. No, no, no. Not tonight."

She'd just finished one of the toughest cases of her career—defending a corporate executive charged with multiple crimes arising from alleged fraud. She'd negotiated a settlement for him with the SEC for securities fraud violations, and he'd repaid twelve million dollars. But after the SEC action was settled, the Justice Department filed criminal charges. The SEC might have been satisfied with money, but the DOJ wanted blood.

The trial had lasted six months. Forty-seven witnesses were called by the prosecution. There were seven *hundred* prosecution exhibits, including photographs taken at her client's three-million-dollar New Year's party the previous year, which just *happened* to have been written off against the corporate expense account.

Crossing the room to check the caller ID display, Trey smiled to herself, remembering the thrill of triumph when she made *that* particular little peccadillo disappear into the miasma of accounting errors and budget shuffling endemic to all huge conglomerates—none of which, *of course,* had been her client's fault. After she'd finished laying it out for the jury, they'd been as confused as her poor client by the labyrinthine details, and if *they* couldn't understand, how was he supposed to have been able to?

Parker, McKay, and Mitchell
800-757-3224

"Shit." She scooped up the receiver. "Pelosi."

"Congratulations. I hear you brought them to their knees."

"Thanks, Reg." Trey laughed, recognizing the familiar baritone of Reginald Parker, the firm's senior partner and her mentor. "Not a clean kill, but almost."

"These things never are, but with Not Guiltys on most of the charges, the prosecution won't get the ten to fifteen they *thought* they had all sewn up."

"No," Trey agreed with a note of triumph, "and I bet I can get him a year in a federal penitentiary close to home. One year, and he'll be out with his Cayman bank account intact, sipping piña coladas in Cancun."

"So everybody wins."

"Yes, but we win more." She was satisfied with the outcome, having no delusions that her clients were always good guys. That was just the nature of corporate law. It was a dog-eat-dog world, and no one was truly innocent. Her clients needed representation, they had the money to pay her fees, and even though she'd made partner, at the end of the day she still had to earn her keep.

"True," Parker concurred. "Plus I'm delighted to know that the blood, sweat, and marriages of your support staff haven't been sacrificed in vain while helping you to prepare the case."

"We'll make it up to them come bonus time."

"Excellent suggestion."

He paused, and the silence on the line had Trey narrowing her eyes. "Reg—I'm not two hours out of court and—"

"I know, I know," he said hastily, "but that telecommunications discrimination suit is starting to heat up, and I don't think Jones can handle it. Now that you're free—"

"I'm not exactly free," she growled, thinking of all the open cases she was juggling. But even as she protested, she knew it was an empty gesture. Because this was what she did—she was the designated hitter, the one the firm called in to take on the tough cases, the swinging dick the *other* swinging dicks called for a rescue. She thrived on the adrenaline rush of trial and the ensuing victory, playing the game with the best and winning. While a trial was in progress, she lived it and breathed it, often sleeping at the office to micromanage the preparations. She was always *in control*—had to be, lest her opponents smell weakness. One misstep and it could be *her* blood in the water, not theirs.

"You can reassign some of your—"

"The hell I will," she cut him off. "Listen, I'll be in at six tomorrow and look over the file."

"Perfect," Parker replied smoothly. "Let me know what you decide."

They both knew she'd take the case, because that was what she did.

Trey fingered the business card she'd received two weeks earlier tucked into a cream-colored note card from a woman with whom she'd once had a brief but intense affair. The flowing script was concise and to the point.

> *Trey, darling, you'll find what you're looking for here. Trust me—you won't be disappointed.*
> *Love, J.*

"Will I? And how would you know?" Trey murmured, as she dropped the card onto the table next to her briefcase and walked out the door.

Less than ten minutes later, she studied a simple brass plaque next to the stairwell leading down to the garden level of an elegant brownstone in Society Hill. *Aurora*. From the sidewalk, she could just make out a heavy, ornately carved wooden door with a small peephole.

After receiving the note from J., she'd made some discreet inquiries. Word of mouth had it that this club was members only— exclusive, elite, and catering to those with *eclectic* tastes. Fortunately, J. had also provided her a reference. They'd ended on good terms even though Trey had been forced to tell her that monogamy was not in her nature, nor was a serious relationship. She just didn't have time. Tonight, though, she had all the time in the world.

She pressed the buzzer set into the carved wooden frame and put on her best cool-as-ice courtroom face. As she waited, unblinking, staring at the small hole in the door, she wondered what the eye on the other side gleaned from her appearance. Her butter-soft, midthigh, black leather skirt and three-inch heels wouldn't be apparent through the aperture, although her nearly sheer black satin blouse might be. Shoulder-length dark hair, subtly cut to hold its casual style no matter the wind or weather. Light make-up, clear, pale complexion, hazel eyes gleaming even in the dim light. Piercing eyes—hard, unreadable eyes most of the time. Once in a while emotion surfaced—when the woman in her arms touched her heart as well as her body, fleetingly, unexpectedly. Rarely. When the stress of a particularly grueling case wore her down; when she was weary. But not tonight—tonight she was high on success; tonight she was in control. All she wanted was a diversion before the battle was joined again—a few moments when all that mattered was the pleasure.

The door opened, she made the necessary responses, and the immaculately tailored guardian of the gate allowed her entrance. She walked down the long, shadowed corridor toward the even darker room at the rear, feeling the rhythm of the music through the floor, aware of the answering beat of her heart. Her blood surged, stirring with the excitement of the unknown. What, or who, awaited her in the arena where titles and names and histories had no meaning? Where only the moment was real, and the reality you chose to create was all that existed. You were anyone you chose to be for as long as the spell lasted. All that was required was the right partner to join in the game.

After securing a drink and a place along the highly polished bar, Trey surveyed the room. Muted recessed lights, a requisite space for dancing, and some intriguing alcoves along the perimeter suggested this was not the type of club designed for simple socializing. *Good choice, J. You* do *know me well. I'll have to thank you properly one of these days.*

A fleeting thought of just *how* she would do that fled as her eyes adjusted to the dim lighting and she found something of more immediate interest. Blond, built, and at the moment encased in black leather pants and a black silk shirt open far enough to expose one small, firm breast nearly to the nipple. Trey's senses rippled at the thought of how good that body would feel under her.

Sipping her drink, she took her time, letting the anticipation build. She watched the blonde watch the crowd, a lioness hunting. The first time their eyes met, there was only a momentary hesitation, a slight flicker of appreciation, before the insouciant gaze glided away. But the second time the blonde's attention focused on Trey, it lingered, sweeping over her from head to toe, caressing her with almost tangible intensity. She felt herself swell, grow damp, throb. Oh yes—that sweet mindless panacea for loneliness and rage. So welcome—sensation replacing thought, desire replacing longing, lust replacing...

Trey set her glass down carefully and slipped into the crowd. She'd had enough. She was ready.

A moment later, Trey moved out of shadow to stand quite close to the austere blonde with, she could now see, the brilliant blue eyes. When their gazes met, the flare of desire was reciprocal. Trey smiled, then looked down to appreciate the expanse of skin laid bare by the partially open shirt, the trim fit of hips, the... Trey caught her breath, sucking her lower lip between her teeth to stifle the gasp as she focused on the leather-clad crotch. Casually, she lifted her eyes to search the handsome face and caught the faint grin before it was quickly extinguished. *God, she's an insolent thing, and so fucking hot. And she knows it. We'll have to take care of that right now.*

Not to be outdone, Trey angled her body to mask her movements and cupped the bulge so obvious now under the fly of the tight black pants. She squeezed the cock lightly in her palm, then rocked it once, twice; on the third time, the other woman gasped.

"I hope this isn't just for show," Trey whispered, stepping closer still. Her breasts pressed against the woman's arm, and her skirt rode up high on her thighs as she loosely straddled one long, tight leg.

"Oh," the woman murmured, covering the hand in her crotch with her own and pumping into it, "it works just fine."

"We'll see, won't we?" Trey studied the sharp planes of the woman's face, caught the glint of arousal and something else—amusement?—in her eyes. "What's your name?"

"Les."

"Mmm, that's nice. Neat and to the point." Trey continued to thrust her hips gently as she slowly manipulated the cock beneath the hot leather. She knew damn well every movement was rubbing its base over Les's clit, and she hoped to hell it was making Les as hot as she was getting from rocking on her leg.

"Careful," Les warned softly, her breath a hot breeze in Trey's ear, "you'll make me come in my pants."

"Mmm, no you don't," Trey murmured, easing off on her hand motion, but not letting go. "Too easy. I want to make this last."

"What's *this,* exactly?" Les moved her mouth over Trey's neck in a series of slow kisses. Toying with Trey's earlobe with her teeth, she slid her fingers beneath the edge of Trey's skirt and smoothed her palm up the inside of her thigh. Her breath caught at the first touch of bare, silky skin but before she could reach the hot vee between Trey's thighs, Trey grabbed her wrist to stop her explorations. "Off limits?"

"Not necessarily," Trey replied, moving her hand from between Les's legs and replacing it with her thigh. "Just my rules. Can you handle that?"

Les slipped her arms around Trey's waist and brushed her lips against Trey's cheek, nibbling at the corner of her mouth. "What if I say no?" She moaned in surprise as Trey pushed hard against her crotch, driving the cock firmly down onto her clit. "Oh fuck...that's good."

"Is that a yes?" Trey ran her tongue over Les's upper lip, then eased inside her mouth to stroke and explore. She caught Les's tongue and sucked on it rhythmically, mirroring the motion with her thrusting hips until Les moaned again. "I'm sorry. Did I hear a yes?"

"Christ," Les panted. *"Yes."*

"I'm just a few blocks away," Trey said, trying desperately to keep her voice steady. The firm pressure of the phallus in Les's pants rubbing against her clitoris through the thin layers of leather was almost too good to bear. She was hot and hard and wet. She wanted those fingers to move up her thigh to the heat between her legs, to stroke through the swollen folds, to slide into the wet, aching... She caught back a moan of her own. "Can you walk that far without this cock making you come?"

Les smiled, that half-smile of impudence and challenge. "I'll manage if you stop jerking it off."

Trey frowned. "Well—for a minute or two."

"Then let's not waste any more time." Les took her hand. "I'm not made of stone."

"Oh baby, I know," Trey whispered as she led her into the night.

Silently, Trey drew Les across the darkened living room to her bedroom. A night-light glowed faintly in the adjoining bath, casting shadows in long fingers across the walls and illuminating the bed.

"Take your shirt off and lie down," Trey said quietly, reaching beneath the coverlet to the drawer built into the platform bed. The soft clink of metal sounded in the air.

Les hesitated for one second. *Her rules, remember.* Then, a decision made, she released the few remaining buttons on her shirt and stripped it off. The muscles in her chest and arms were tight with anticipation.

"On your back," Trey added, not looking at her.

Wordlessly, Les complied, not resisting as the soft leather cuffs closed around her ankles and wrists. Even when her arms and legs were spread almost to the point of discomfort, she did not speak. To speak would break the spell and shatter the acknowledgment of her willingness to be taken. Incongruously, her cock thrust up against the restraint of her leather pants, an impotent sign of her power reduced to servitude. Her clit pounded beneath it, stimulated both by its presence and her inability to use it.

Trey stood beside the bed, slowly disrobing. "Are you hard for me yet?"

"You know the answer," Les rasped.

"Mmm. I like to hear you tell me." She watched in fascination as Les twisted subtly against the restraints—not from pain, but from insistent desire. Les was breathing faster now—a thin mist of sweat glistened on her breasts and belly, and her hips thrust upward, the bulge of constrained phallus clearly evident. Trey climbed onto the bed, naked, the first trickle of arousal sheening her thighs. "Are you?"

"Like a stone." Les's eyes followed the sway of Trey's full breasts and her throat tightened with want. "Jesus, you're beautiful."

Trey straddled Les's slim hips, hovering just above the leather-covered cock. "How bad do you want to fuck me?"

"Bad—so fucking bad," Les moaned, trying to push her hips up into Trey's wetness.

"I'll bet you do." Trey leaned forward and settled onto Les's stomach, arching her back as her clitoris encountered hot skin for the first time. *Oh God. Careful. Careful.* Gritting her teeth against the instant surge of pleasure, she dangled her breasts just out of reach of Les's searching lips. Les's swift intake of breath, an almost hungry, desperate sound, made her clitoris twitch, and again, she fought back a warning twinge of arousal. *I will not come. Not until...oh yes, that's so nice...not until I'm ready.*

Trey lowered her head to take one tight, hard nipple into her mouth. As she bit down, she settled firmly onto the ridge of leather over Les's cock, sliding slowly along its length. Her moan melted into Les's, their bodies jerking as one.

"Oh man," Les gasped. "That'll make me come." The muscles in her neck stood out beneath satin skin as she arched higher, trying to get more of her breast into Trey's mouth. "Please," she cried sharply as Trey pulled on her nipple with her teeth, then abruptly released it to the cool night air.

"Not yet," Trey directed thickly, struggling to ignore the urgent tingling in her clitoris where it dragged over the prominence in Les's pants. "I'll...tell you when."

"Soon," Les implored. The pressure on and in her clit was approaching the boiling point as Trey kept up the steady slide. "I won't last."

Pinching Les's nipple with one hand, Trey lifted her hips, reached down with her other hand, and worked Les's zipper down. "*Now* how much do you want to fuck me?"

"More than I want to breathe." Les was close to weeping. "Please take it out. Please touch it. Please let me fuck you. Oh God...*please*."

Trey slipped her fingers inside Les's fly and grasped the pliable cock, warm with Les's body heat. She pulled it free until it projected upward between the spread folds of Les's fly. Gripping the shaft, she rubbed the head between her own soaked lips.

Les watched Trey fist her cock and whimpered.

"Ah—yes, baby," Trey groaned as she slid the smooth head over and around the exposed tip of her clitoris. Her eyes closed against her will as she began to thrust rhythmically against it. She wanted to come badly, had wanted to from the first moment she'd seen the outline of the cock nestled against Les's belly. She wanted to ride Les until they were both coming, uncertain—uncaring—of who fucked whom. "Oh yes."

Les panted in the near darkness, a prisoner of the relentless motion mercilessly working her clit to the bursting point. "I'm...gonna...come you'remakingmecome..."

"*Don't.*" Trey forced her eyes open and bent her head to watch as she slowly slid the long cock into herself. As she took it in, swallowed it deep inside, the intense pressure filled her pelvis and her muscles spasmed rapidly around it. "Oh yeah, oh yeah, that's so nice, baby."

Trey leaned forward, lacing her fingers through Les's above the cuffs, one nipple level with Les's lips. "Suck it," she gasped as she rocked her hips up and down the shaft, pushing and pulling her clit along its length. She was very close to coming already, but oh, how she wanted it to last. She hadn't counted on Les being able to move.

"Oh—sweet God!" Trey cried in surprise as Les jerked her hips, burying the cock just a little deeper. "Don't... Wait—"

"Can't," Les grunted, increasing the tempo of her thrusts. "Gotta come...now."

No, not until I say. Not until I... Oh yes. There. There... Just like that. Trey was lost, the swirling ribbons of release escaping her control as her hips flailed, her body erupting. The orgasm raced down her legs, streaked through her spine, and burst into a rainbow of color behind her eyes. "Oh noooo..."

"Oh *yeah*." Les surrendered with a deep groan of her own, and for a moment all was motion and sound as they fought their way to peace.

Sighing, Trey collapsed onto Les's chest, her face pressed to Les's neck, her body trembling around the cock inside her. She managed to raise one hand and release the snaps on the arm restraints. "You pack quite a punch," she whispered in Les's ear, feeling herself contract around the cock in a small series of aftershocks.

"Yeah." Les stroked Trey's back, holding her close. "And *you* fuck like a girl."

"*Perfectly,*" they said in unison.

RIDE
J.C. CHEN

There's a bar on the outskirts of town that I like to frequent. If this were Texas you'd call it a saloon, but here in Jersey—a land with no quaintness or jargon—a bar is a bar is a bar. Hell, a 7-Eleven could pass for a bar if you happen to be driving through Secaucus on a Saturday night.

It's not a big place. There's a jukebox next to the entrance that plays Springsteen, Bon Jovi, and other assorted Jersey classics. It's playing "Born to Run" when I walk in and it will play "Born to Run" at least a half dozen more times before I leave. The bar itself is a circular wooden island in the middle of the room. The bartenders are nice to look at but impossible to get the attention of. They serve two beers on tap: lukewarm Miller Lite and some overpriced local swill that passes for lager. They do have about fifty different bottled beers on the menu, including some impressive Belgian lambics, but when you look around the room, most of the women have Coors longnecks in their hands.

I like to hang out at the back of the bar, near the ratty pool table where the butches like to posture with their pool sticks while overdone femmes fawn and hang all over them. Nobody actually plays pool, since the felt's all torn up and the even-numbered balls have been missing since the early nineties. But those butches sure look extra butchy twirling those cues like some dyke Tom Cruise out of *The Color of Money*. It's a predominantly bridge-and-tunnel clientele, but the kind of B&T that can't quite get their acts together to actually make it over the bridges or through the tunnels to Manhattan, where the real action lies.

On good days, this place is packed with fine women who don't take no for an answer. On bad days, like today, the place is teeming with floozies who don't *give* no as an answer.

In short, good day or bad, this is the best place to get laid this side of the Hudson.

I'm just about to call it a night when I see her standing across the room, her eyes telegraphing an invitation and a threat. There's an empty stool next to her and already I can see the floozies circling. Silly girls. Don't they realize what they're courting? Surely they must know that to be taken into her space, to be enveloped by the energy that is rippling outward from her like tremors from a fault line, is to surrender to danger wrapped in a cloak of sexual electricity. And even as my mind fumbles around that thought, my body draws ever closer to her.

I'm not sure exactly when it happens—probably soon after we make eye contact—but there's a distinctive sensation, like a tightening in my chest, when I know I'm doomed. She inclines her head slightly and I drop eagerly, wordlessly, into the seat next to her. Most of the other girls begin to disperse at this point. Although a few of them stay around, whether out of curiosity or spite, I'm not sure.

She lets me buy her a fancy German beer although I sense that she is more amused than flattered by my gallantry. I love the way she holds her bottle: so dangerously loose that it might drop and shatter, yet elegantly indifferent, as if that would be someone else's problem. Her fingers are long and slender, her skin tanned and smooth. She's taller than I am with the long, lean frame of a distance runner. Her shoulder-length hair is an unremarkable shade of brown but her eyes— a mercurial hazel that shades continuously from dark amber to vivid green—more than compensate as her most arresting feature.

I talk extensively about nothing of consequence and our bodies draw closer with each drink. She doesn't say much but I can tell she's listening. Or rather, she's absorbing my words and measuring them like she's biding her time or waiting for a signal. I must have babbled the right thing because her hand, which started intimately on my knee, is now resting possessively on my inner thigh. There's a molten heat radiating from the spot where her hand meets my leg that, paradoxically, causes me to shiver. She leans in and asks me if I want to leave. Hastily, I throw a few crumpled bills onto the bar.

I pause at the threshold to look around the room at the women I'm leaving behind, little Lolita-girls in their skintight skirts and fuck-me pumps. I look over at my companion, deadly in threadbare denim and Doc Martens boots. More fuck you than fuck me. I entertain for a moment the notion that there might be a decision I should be considering at this point or a caution I should be heeding. But one look in her eyes, now a shade of green that you only find in rare emeralds or poisonous snakes, and I can't for the life of me figure out what I should be careful about. I follow her out the door.

She leads me to the back of the parking lot, where it's dark and private, to what looks like a light-colored Honda Accord under the guttering lamplight.

"This your car?" Arousal and a twinge of nervousness make my voice high and tight.

All thoughts of the absurdity in this situation are immediately abandoned as she forces me backward onto the car and presses her body along the length of mine. I feel the hood buckle slightly beneath my back as she leans in. Her face is close to mine, close enough for me to see the dark hunger in her eyes.

"Something wrong with that?"

I hesitate, not wanting to insult her, and I choke back the moan that is threatening to erupt from my chest from the feel of her—all muscle and sinew—pressing up against me. She laughs and brings her lips a whisper away from mine.

"Never…" Her voice is soft and deadly.

"…ever…" She licks her lips and the moan escapes.

"…mock the ride." Her mouth descends on mine and if I had a reply, it's lost in a melee of dueling tongues and bruised lips. She has a tongue ring, a metal barbell with a smooth ball on top, which she strokes with practiced skill along the length of my tongue.

I'm not sure whose hands start wandering first. But I'm brought sharply out of my lust-filled haze by the sensation of strong hands on my breasts, only to find that my own have unbuckled her belt and are working their way down the buttons of her jeans. My task is hindered when her hips begin to grind against me. And it is altogether forgotten as her errant fingers start to pinch and pull my nipples through my shirt in time with her thrusts. She is warm against my thigh and I feel a rush of wetness between my legs in response.

There is no grace. Only raw, carnal desire as her hips pick up an erratic pace. Her fingers have stopped moving, my breasts forgotten. I hear her ragged breathing and the rhythmic creaking of the shocks as her car absorbs the brunt of her need. My clit is pounding in sympathy and I want to thrust back against her, relieve some of the pressure that is building excruciatingly in me. Instead, I lean back and let it happen. And when she comes, I am transfixed by her beauty: the flush in her cheeks, the swell of her lips, the thin-corded muscle in her neck twitching with each wave of her orgasm.

She rests against me for only a minute before looking up and into my eyes. I have to remind myself to breathe as she crawls up the length of my body, once again bringing her face so close to mine.

"Your turn."

Her lips find mine again and her tongue claims my mouth. Her tongue-ring slides against the roof of my mouth and I melt with pleasure. I swallow a cry of surprise as her hand slips under the waistband of my trousers. Without breaking the kiss, she positions herself between my legs and, using her knees, eases them apart. She slides her hands down farther and pauses, pulling her face away from mine. Moments pass before I open my eyes to the sight of her looking down on me with passion, pleasure, and triumph. And then she is pushing into me, her hips driving her fingers even deeper, her body rocking against mine.

I try to hold back, prolonging the inevitable for as long as possible while she pounds into me with the force of her weight. But the pressure is too great—and the pain too sweet—such that when she grinds the heel of her palm into my clit, I orgasm immediately. Hard.

I realize as she backs away from me, buttoning her jeans and buckling her belt, that she hadn't removed one article of my clothing during the entire encounter. I slide off the hood of her car, wincing slightly at the dent we leave behind.

"Sorry about that," I mumble.

"Not a problem." She pulls me into a long, slow, thorough kiss. My eyes close involuntarily, blissfully. She pulls away but I can still feel the ghost of her against me, inside of me.

By the time I open my eyes again, she is halfway across the lot.

"That's not my car," she calls back over her shoulder as she disappears into the night.

PUMP
KENYA DEVOREAUX

The waning day tentatively offers its pale light through the window behind me, warming my bare shoulder with a soft caress. I am really growing bored with this job, stacking books every single day—albeit for only five hours, but for five long hours I must straighten and restraighten. Arrange—stack—lift—place. I don't know how much longer I can keep this up. *The Politics of Sex*. Gee, now where is call number 155.3? I lift the book with my right hand from its place on the pile atop the trolley and with my left I widen the space between *The Pocket Book of Sexual Positions* and *Popping the Cherry: A Guide to Your First Time* and fill the vacant spot with *The Politics of Sex*. I step to my left slowly. Once, then again. I scan the shelves from the one at eye level, up one, then, rounding my back, lean over to check the shelf closest to the floor.

A woman clears her throat deliberately behind me. I stand up quickly and turn.

"Hi, do you work here?" She is a pretty young woman with radiant white skin and a slight rose to her cheeks.

I glance down at the book in my hand, then at the trolley, then look into her eyes. "No. I'm dyslexic. I thought I'd stand in the middle of a room full of books and torture myself."

"Oh. Okay. I'm trying to find a book called *Pheremones: The Molecules of Desire*."

"That's on this side." I point to the case next to us. She nods and smiles and busies herself with searching the bookcase.

"Would you like some help? You can give me some authors to look for if you like."

She faces me. A wavy, auburn lock has fallen in front of her right eye. She tucks it behind her ear and blinks, long eyelashes thickened with mascara. Her navy blue tank top is overwhelmed by large, round breasts. *I* am overwhelmed. The nipples are visible through the material. They are soft. And they are small. And I wonder what they would feel like beneath my fingertips, in the center of my palm as I circle them, caress them, and hold them firmly. Her skin is pale, void of even a freckle, and as smooth as youth. If ever the opportunity arose to press my face into her ample cleavage, while just rubbing myself…

I glance to the side and down at a piece of dust on the carpet, my arousal interrupted by a sting of guilt. I shudder. This girl is innocent and sweet and too young for my ravishing gazes. Those curious green eyes don't even know they are looking at me. The real me. This forty-one-year-old body that has surrendered over and over to men it didn't love, being used rather than cherished, and that now has the opportunity for something it's needed forever.

And I. Can't. Move.

I want to grab her by the shoulder and snatch her to me. Her big breasts mashed against my smaller ones. Her pelvis pressed against mine. Instead, my eyes drop and I stare. Such large, lovely breasts. She adjusts her neckline, as if trying to cover herself. I keep staring. She mumbles something and then rushes away.

At night I touch myself again. Tingling with the fantasy of the young woman in the library. She is at the foot of my bed, a large, cream-colored dildo jutting from between her thighs while I, in a silk gown, growing expectant, await her approach. She walks toward me…

I am rubbing myself quickly. One hand kneads my breast while the other kneads my cunt. I can't do this…I can't do this…I can't do this! I stop. Throbbing and frustrated beyond bearing, I must stop. I can't fantasize about having some barely-out-of-her-teens stranger I met in the library fuck me with a strap-on dildo. I am so desperate. I need a *woman's* body now. I don't want a man, and now I can admit I never did. I need soft hands caressing me…

In the morning, I stare at the phone and finally dial the number of the personals section of a lesbian magazine. A woman answers. She has a deep, husky voice.

"Hello, lesbian lovers dot com."

"I would like to place a personals ad, please?"

"Oh, you do that over the Web."

"But the only computer I have access to is at the library."

"Well, I guess you'll be spending a lot of time at the library, now won't you?"

The bus is so cramped. Everyone is smooshed together like chickens in a coop. Everyone's body bumps into the body next to it as we jerk along the jagged street. Some grumble an apology, while others ignore the disturbance. I stare into the pinstriped lap of the woman next to me. Is her vulva shaved? She has thick, red hair, red eyebrows, and red eyelashes. She probably has a thick red bush with a few blond strands. The woman standing in front of me—smart peach-colored pantsuit and silk blouse—with one hand holding the pole and the other holding a book...she's very neatly put together. She probably has a closely trimmed strip of hair that ends right over her clitoris. If I could be with her, I know just what I'd do to her. Though I have never made love to a woman, I know by instinct how I would do it. I've read and reread the sex tips in *Lesbian Lovers* magazine. I know every position possible in the bedroom. I am familiar with everything one can do with one's mouth, down to every possible flick of the tongue. I know where every erogenous zone is located, down to the precise point at the back of the knee. I know how to make love to breasts, suck toes, bring a woman to orgasm by playing in her ear with my tongue. But everything I know has only been realized in my frequent wet dreams and fantasies. It is time to do what I know I need to do. Time to feed my spirit with the body of a woman and cease its forty-one-year blight. Time to feel what it's like to move in rhythm with someone else, smoothly—like waves on an ocean. Time to cry my partner's name out of love and appreciation, not obligation. I am going to place an ad.

The Web site comes up. There is a garden with two women standing, one in beige slacks and a navy blue blouse, the other in a pink, flowing dress. A "Welcome" button flashes at the bottom of the screen. I click the button labeled "New User." It asks me for a username. I search around the room for any object I could choose for a cute username. I scratch my head and tousle my hair a bit. It is so wild. I like it that way. It makes me feel sexy. And that is very much how I've been feeling lately, since I've come out to myself. That's it! Wild! No. WildLovely! My stomach does flip-flops.

The next screen asks for my profile. Now what shall I write? What am I looking for? What's my type? I enter:

```
MY GREAT DESIRE
Longing looks, sweaty 'nights. Wanting
every beautiful woman who comes close
enough. I can't wait for this anymore.
I am looking for a dyke, age and race
unimportant, to show me for the first time,
but definitely not the last, how good this
can really be.
```

I read over what I have just written. I smile to myself and press Return.

Several hours later I rush to my neighbor's apartment, trying in my haste to knock as politely as possible. "Hi," I say as she opens the door. She is holding a drink. "Listen, could I use your computer for a second? I need to check something on a Web site."

"Sure. Come on in."

Her apartment is a one-bedroom. The carpet is lush, the furniture opulent. The room is a sultry backdrop to her exotic looks.

"Would you like some wine?"

"Yes, thank you."

She opens the liquor bar by the window. I sit at her computer. Her Siamese cat jumps onto the sofa beside me and begins to lick its paws. I turn the computer on, click a few icons, and make my way through each portal. She places the wine beside my hand, holds my shoulder for a moment.

"I'll give you some privacy," she says and then walks into the other room.

I suck on the lip of the wineglass as I tilt the liquid toward my mouth. I take in just enough to wet the inside of my mouth, then set the glass down and click my in-box. I'm smiling now. I have two messages—one from someone who calls herself Rock and another from CherryFemme. I decide to open this one first.

> You wrote a beautiful ad, WildLovely.
> I understand your yearning for womanly
> companionship. I've felt it too, for a
> long time. Your ad was surprisingly tame
> for a woman called WildLovely—lol—but I
> guess you said it all without saying it.
> I know what you must want to do to a woman
> and what you must want to have her do to
> you. I think I could make you feel all
> you've asked for in your note, and more.
> Please write back.

She seems sweet. We'll see.
I click on the response from Rock.

> I really liked your ad. You, WildLovely,
> are definitely ready to feel passion
> with a woman. I could read between the
> lines exactly HOW much you want this. I
> would like to share an evening with you.
> Dinner, maybe a little shopping first. And
> then I'd like to give you whatever you
> want—whatever you need—to fill you beyond
> anything you could ever conceive. I hope
> to hear from you, WildLovely.
> Cass

I gulp and put my palm to my throat. There is a little square photo at the corner of the screen. Just to see what will happen, I click on it. It triples in size. Her long, aristocratic nose is accented by dark, rich eyebrows arched like a forties-era movie star's. A head full of short, black hair the texture of an unusual type of silk. Icy blue eyes that stare sharply into the camera. She wears an amethyst pendant. The stone is a rich purple and is solid against her chest.

I press the Reply button.

❖

In the morning, my phone rings. The machine will pick it up.

"Hello. This is Cass speaking. I have a message for WildLovely…"

I rush to the phone, almost falling in my haste. "Hello? H-hello, Cass?"

"Yes. WildLovely? You gave this number…I thought—"

"That's okay, Cass. That's okay."

"Would you like to meet tonight?"

"Where?"

"There's a store on Fifty-eighth and Third called Sweet Pleasures. Five thirty?"

"Yes."

"What will you be wearing?"

"A light blue short-sleeved dress."

"Sounds beautiful. See you then."

The phone clicks before I have a chance to ask Cass what she'll be wearing, but it doesn't matter. I'll know her. I tuck my hair behind my ear and walk quickly back to the kitchen, humming.

That afternoon I take extra care dressing, having spent all day in an onanistic frenzy, engaging every oblong object I could wrap my grip around. I stand before my mirror and sigh, then choose the lotion with the lavender scent. I flip open the top and squeeze the air from the bottle, taking in the scent with two quick inhalations. I squeeze a little onto the pads of my fingers and press them against my breast, squeezing my nipple as I caress myself. In my dream right now it is Cass's hand upon mine, guiding me over the hot, charged plane of my body. She knows exactly where I like to touch myself, precisely where I must go to make myself wet. Together we squeeze my vulva and she whispers something sweet into my ear—

I open my eyes and stare at myself. My fantasy will come true soon, I know it will. I want to wipe the wetness from my labia, but if I get too close I won't be able to take my hand away. The throbbing is so deep inside me, its reverberations causing a tickling sensation within the walls of my vagina, and the swollen lips throb at the same rate as my anxious heart.

❖

I am walking up Third Avenue toward Fifty-eighth Street, searching for the store. Nothing. I turn to my right and wander down another block, which is heavily shaded by trees. The brownstone before me is red with a gold door. A little sign hanging on the handrail says Sweet Pleasures. I sigh with relief. Someone taps me on the shoulder.

Before I can turn around, someone takes my hand gently and squeezes it. It is Cass. She leads me up the stairs. With one hand in her pocket, she turns to me and smiles. Her perfectly placed teeth glisten. She rings the buzzer and an elderly woman pulls open the door, greets us, and ushers us in. My mouth drops open just slightly as a flood of throbbing heat teases my vagina. We walk across the threshold. Wall to wall dildoes. Of every size, shape, and color imaginable. Cass slides her hand from mine and grips my waist.

"Look around, dear," the elderly saleswoman chimes as she squeezes my arm. "Everything you want is here."

I turn to Cass. She is much taller than I and lanky in her loose-fitting denim jacket. Her dangling earrings, which are in the shape of a string of stars, bounce against her cheeks. "What are you thinking about?" she asks.

I look up and she kisses me on the lips.

"I know just what you two would like." The saleswoman smiles beatifically as she reaches beneath the counter. "A new item that was just made for you!"

Cass and I blink, the moment broken.

"It's beautiful, isn't it?" She opens a box and presents an iridescent white, double-headed phallus, fifteen inches long, thick and pliable.

Cass takes it, strokes it during her examination. "I think my girlfriend and I would prefer a strap-on…just for me."

I gulp and swallow my own saliva. No one notices how tense my body has just become, how my knees are beginning to tremble. I shift from leg to leg, every sensitive area twitching. I fight the impulse to orgasm right here in the store.

"The leather harness is more secure. You can really move around with it. The velvet is soft but you can't be too rough with it—"

"Oh, so when I want to make her scream I'll wear the leather. But if I just want to make her pant a little bit, I'll wear the velvet."

Cass and the saleswoman laugh. I take a shallow breath, my arms stiff at my sides. I—the one who wants to fuck like a madwoman and scream at the top of her lungs how much she loves women, how much she loves tits and pussy and smooth, fleshy asses, the one who thinks so frequently about having a cock of her own to enjoy, of being *in* a woman, of sliding up into the welcoming wetness, with her tightness around my rock-hard cock—I stand like a soldier, jaw squared shut, ass muscles tightly clenched. I imagine Cass on top of me in her bedroom as I lie under her on my stomach. I say stiffly, "Get that one, Cass."

I meander toward the other end of the case, then point. "What's this?"

The saleswoman reaches under the glass before me and hands me a fleshy, fat beige dildo. "Rub your thumb on it."

It feels like a slightly overripe peach.

Cass laces the fingers of her right hand through mine. The saleswoman pats Cass's left hand and smiles. She walks away.

Cass takes the dildo and beats it lightly against my thigh. "If I were to stand you up and take the head of this and press it against your clitoris, and say…dip into you just a little and pull out…and then rub your clitoris with this covered in your come just under the head…and let you feel your own wetness… How would that feel to you?"

Before I answer, she strokes my lips with her fingertip and kisses me, wetting my mouth fully with her tongue before thoroughly filling me. She withdraws from between my lips. "Ma'am?" she calls to the saleswoman. "We'll take the leather harness and this velvet cock."

Cass and I stroll down the street, her arm wrapped tightly around my waist, my arm wrapped around hers. I am filled with a searing desire that has threatened my quiet life with destruction. Those fantasies have brought me here. Unknowingly, every beautiful woman I've ever met has brought me to this moment. I am a lesbian now. And I'm ready for a new life…with wild and lovely possibilities.

APPALACHIAN CANTICLE
SAGGIO AMANTE

Sex is easy. Love is hard. At least that's what I used to think. So, when love walked out the door after four years, three months, and two days, I made a decision: *sex*. Lots of it, with no attachment. What I hadn't counted on was how empty, and ultimately unsexy, a life lived without attachment could be. That's when I chose celibacy. I packed up my easel, brushes, and paints, and headed for the farthest hills, which in this case meant an A-frame deep in the woods in the Appalachian Mountains.

I established a ritual. Each morning I rose a little before dawn, made a cup of tea, and took it out to the porch. I sat and watched the sun rise in postcard-perfect splendor over the mountaintops and listened to nature's wakeup calls. The sounds and smells of the forest in the early morning were like nothing I had ever known. Here, coves of hardwood mingled with tall fir, and blankets of rhododendron crept into small trails that wound in and out among the trees.

Down below, I could see the river meandering through ancient rocks, flowing over them in small waterfalls into a pristine pond large enough for swimming. This property had been handed down through our family for generations. The land was posted and people seldom came here except by invitation, which I sometimes grudgingly gave. But mostly, when I came here, I stayed alone and basked in the serenity and sense of renewal that this place visited on my soul. It had always been a place of refuge for me. I'd been here for three months now, and I was beginning to feel almost human again.

I had no radio, no television, got no newspaper, and seldom even plugged in my phone. My laptop sat in the corner gathering dust. I did check my e-mail now and then, and I stayed in touch with my agent and a few close friends on a semiregular basis. As for family, I have none, which can be both a blessing and a curse. Now, it was a blessing because there was no one to infringe on my privacy or make demands on my time.

Well, there was no one until I saw Rêve. The day I first saw her was extraordinarily clear and bright. The normal morning fog didn't appear, and the sun seemed to have warmed the earth much earlier than usual. I decided to bring my easel out onto the porch and try to capture the beauty of the mountain morning.

I had just begun to put a splash of color on the canvas when I heard the snort of a horse carried on the forest air. I watched with surprise as a large, beautiful chestnut mare walked slowly out of the woods and stopped at the edge of the mountain pool. Even more beautiful was the woman who slung her leg over and slid with practiced ease down the side of the horse and onto the grass. She was tall and slender, and her long, auburn hair was a perfect match to that of her mount. She wore black riding boots and black breeches that fit her like a second skin. She put her arms around the horse's neck and pulled the reins over its head, letting them dangle on the ground, and then she turned to grab a saddlebag as the horse stood there grazing.

Under normal circumstances I would have yelled down to the offending person that she was trespassing and to please leave, but this time I had no voice. I could only stare in breathless awe as she pulled a blanket from the saddlebag and stretched it carefully out on the ground. Next, I watched her disrobe slowly, piece by piece, dropping each article on the blanket as she welcomed the touch of the morning air against her skin. When she was through, she stretched her body languorously, arched her back, and dove into the cold water.

She stayed for almost two hours, floating in the water and then lying on the blanket to dry. I watched as she lay there without moving, one arm behind her head, a knee bent. I sketched furiously, afraid she would leave before I could get the scene down on paper. She seemed as oblivious to me as I was aware of her.

I had almost completed the drawing when I saw her move her hand out from behind her head and reach down to touch her breast. She took her nipple between the fingers of one hand as the other hand moved between her legs and she began to stroke herself. I felt each stroke between my own legs, felt the heat rising in my loins. I was swollen, and wet, and hot.

I tried to continue sketching, but the sight below me was too mesmerizing. Without conscious thought, I laid the pencil and pad onto the table and stared with glazed eyes as she pleasured herself. My breath came in short gasps as she tightened her legs around her hand, and I could feel myself responding as though she were touching me. I continued watching until she rose and slowly dressed. She placed her foot in one stirrup and smoothly pulled herself up into the saddle. She rode away at a canter without looking back, and as I saw her figure fading in the distance, I prayed that I would see her again.

The next morning I bounced out of bed and hurried to the porch in my robe, hoping to get another glimpse of the beautiful woman with the chestnut hair. She didn't disappoint me, but this time instead of undressing and diving directly into the water, she disrobed and began a series of yoga movements and stretches, beautiful rhythmic poses that I couldn't get down on paper quickly enough. It was as though she were putting herself on display for me.

I watched as she stood facing the sun, her hands palm to palm at her heart. Slowly, she arched her back, lifting her breasts to the sky. Her movements were lovely and fluid. I wanted to go to her, run my hands along the beautiful lines of her body as she moved and stretched in the morning sun. Instead, I remained the voyeur, touching myself and imagining it was her hands I felt.

I became addicted to the mornings. My creativity was soaring along with my libido. On the fifth day, I sat on the railing of the porch, sketching her, and when I looked up, I saw her looking back at me. She was standing on the blanket, her clothes at her feet. My hand froze over the sketchpad and then I raised it, waving tentatively at her. I held my breath, not knowing what her reaction would be, and exhaled with relief when she waved back at me. She wasn't embarrassed by her nudity or my presence, and I wondered if she had known all along that I was watching her.

Now we had a new ritual. She would do as she always did; I would watch her and sketch. When she left, she would look up at me and wave. I began to translate my sketches to oils but couldn't get them exactly right. They were good, but there was just something missing. *Tomorrow*, I thought, *tomorrow I will ask her to pose for me.*

During the day, when she was gone, her image filled my mind; during the night, her image filled my dreams. More than once, I woke up midorgasm, my hand between my legs, caressing my wetness. Celibacy was not as easy as it sounded, though I told myself masturbation didn't count as a broken vow.

I woke up on Tuesday with a sense of anticipation and sat on the porch waiting for her...and waiting...and waiting. Over an hour passed since her normal arrival time, and she still did not appear. *You idiot*, I thought, *why did you wait so long to talk to her?*

I could hardly contain my sense of disappointment when suddenly, there she was. She was riding an Appaloosa instead of the chestnut. She looked up at me and waved, hello this time instead of good-bye. Although she was a good distance away, I thought I could detect a faint smile on her face.

"Come visit after your swim," I shouted down to her.

She started to dismount and then sat back down in the saddle, guiding her horse into a slow trot up the hill toward my house. "Perhaps I'll skip the swim today," she said as she brought the horse to a halt at the bottom of the steps. "I think it's time we met, don't you?"

I was surprised to hear a touch of a French accent. Her voice was deep and breathy, just as I had imagined it, and her eyes twinkled with amusement as she looked at me. She had no guile at all, no sense of shyness. She was more comfortable in her own skin than anyone I had ever met. Her look was direct and confident, and her eyes were greener than I could ever have imagined them. She slung her leg over the saddle and dropped to the ground, then tied the reins to the railing.

I held my breath as she strode up the stairs on legs that seemed to go on forever. At five feet nine inches, I've always considered myself tall, but she was two or three inches taller than I. My hair is blond and cropped rather short; her chestnut hair fanned out in flames around her face. From a distance, she looked beautiful; up close and personal, she was breathtaking. There was something familiar about her, but I couldn't put my finger on just what it was.

She stuck out her hand. "Rêve Lémarique."

Rêve, her name is Rêve. My mind scrambled to translate the name. Rêve—*dream*—it finally came to me. *What a perfect name; what an absolutely perfect name.*

At the sound of her voice, the hairs stood up on the back of my neck and the blood moved quickly south. I stood staring at her, ignoring her outstretched hand.

"Are you all right?" she finally asked, jarring me out of my reverie.

"What? I...oh," I stuttered. "I'm sorry. Logan Blair." I grasped her hand and felt the sensation of our touch in every nerve in my body.

Her fingers were long and tapered, like I would imagine a pianist's hands to be. And then I remembered. Of course! This vision, this woman who had occupied my thoughts twenty-four hours a day for the past two weeks was *the* Rêve Lémarique, the composer.

"I enjoy your works very much," I managed to say, hoping I didn't sound as foolish as I felt.

"And I have enjoyed yours as well, Ms. Blair. Perhaps you will show me your latest work, no?"

I reached for my sketchpad and handed it to her. I sat in an Adirondack chair while she sat on the top stair with her back against the baluster. She turned the pages slowly, contemplating each sketch intensely. Finally, she looked up at me. "These are wonderful."

"Thank you." I was filled with gratitude that she liked them.

"But they are not finished." She said it as a statement, not a question. The artist in her had recognized that an element was missing.

"No."

"Will you translate them to oil?"

"Yes. When I can get them right."

"I see." She looked at me, one artist to another. "What can I do to help?"

I inhaled deeply. "Will you pose for me?" The question did not even hang in the air.

"Of course," she answered immediately. "These must be finished."

Relief washed over me. "Would you like some tea?" I asked, hoping that I didn't sound too giddy.

"That would be lovely."

I stood, and she followed me inside. While I brewed the tea, she looked at the paintings I had stacked around the room. She didn't say anything; she just walked from painting to painting, lifting one up now and then to view it in a better light.

I watched her move about the room. Her body was long and firm; her breasts pushed against the silk of the blouse that she was wearing, and I could see the hardness of her nipples. I wanted to paint her; I wanted to touch her. *Get a grip, Blair*, I thought. *Don't scare her away.* Even as those thoughts crossed my mind, I knew that there probably was not much that would scare this glorious woman.

"Your work is very good." Her voice was warm and sincere.

"Here," I said, handing her the cup of tea.

She took it and sipped slowly, her thumb and forefinger holding the ear of the cup, her pinky slightly crooked. Each time her lips touched the cup, I fantasized her mouth on mine.

"So, when shall we start?" she asked.

"What?" I was so lost in fantasy that I didn't hear her words.

"When shall we start? When would you like me to pose for you?"

"Would today be too soon?"

"Not at all. Today would be fine. What would you like me to do?"

"I, uh…would you mind…" Somehow, I just couldn't get the words out. I wanted her naked, but I didn't know how to tell her. I had been sketching her naked for days, yet I couldn't find the words to ask her to get naked here, in my house.

"You need me to be nude, yes?"

I looked at her, stunned. Nudity seemed as natural to her as breathing, and naked models were nothing new to me. But the thought of her this close, modeling nude for me was almost more than I could take.

"Yes, I need you to be nude." This time I matched her directness.

"Of course." Her smile lit the room.

"I'll set up in here. You can change in the bathroom if you'd like. There's a terry robe behind the door." I hoped I sounded more professional than I felt.

She walked away from me toward the bathroom, and I turned my back to busy myself with setting the scene in front of the large glass window that ran from floor to eave at the front of the house. I pulled an air mattress from the closet and inflated it. It was a handy thing to have on hand for company, and I was glad to have it now. I placed the mattress in front of the window and covered it with an emerald green satin sheet, knowing that it would bring out the color in her eyes. Then I put large pillows here and there atop the mattress and grabbed a matching emerald sheet to drape her form.

She padded from the bathroom in bare feet, wearing the white terry robe that was just a little too large for me but fit her perfectly. She looked at me questioningly. "What do you want me to do?"

Let me touch you, I thought, swallowing my words. I held the sheet out to her. "Lie down there." I pointed to the mattress. "On your side, and drape this sheet over you loosely." I turned away from her and held my hand out so that she could pass me the robe.

In a moment, she asked, "Is this what you want?"

I stepped back and turned. She was on her side, the green sheet draped across her hip, barely covering her breasts. She had propped her head in her hand and her long auburn hair hung down to the side. Her eyes were lidded and her lips slightly parted. She had captured a perfect look, midway between desire and satisfaction, and I knew I had to get it down. I grabbed a brush and began to paint. The background had been painted days ago. The waterfalls, the pool, and the horse were fine, but it was the woman on the blanket in the picture that wasn't quite right. Now, looking at her so close to me, I was possessed. The image flew effortlessly from my fingers through the brush and onto the canvas. Never had a painting come so easily.

And so, a new ritual began. Each morning at precisely 10:00 a.m., Rêve would arrive at my door. We would have tea and talk a while; then she would disrobe, and I would get to work. I began to get more and more familiar with her body. I became used to touching her, rearranging her pose. She acted like the consummate professional model, I like the consummate professional artist. I couldn't let her know the passions that were seething underneath the surface. I couldn't tell her how I touched myself in the night and whispered her name as I came against my own hand. I treasured the time we spent together and was in awe of the work that was happening. I vowed I would do nothing to ruin either.

I knew the series of paintings was coming to an end. There was just one more left to do, an idea that had been percolating in my mind. I wasn't sure how to approach Rêve about the concept, but my inner self told me to be honest and direct. All she could say was no, which would be a disappointment but certainly not a catastrophe.

I was nervous as I opened the door that last day. Rêve seemed amused at my nervousness, but she never said a word.

"We're almost through," I said, handing her a cup of tea.

"Yes. Perhaps you will let me see them now?"

"I'd like to do the last painting, and then you can see them all."

She put her teacup down and started for the bathroom to change.

"Wait," I said. She looked at me quizzically as I continued. "I want to paint you naked...on the horse."

She seemed to hesitate and then replied softly, "I trust your artist's eye, Logan. I trust you." And then she began to undress, without the formality of the bathroom or the terry robe.

"Stay here a moment," I told her. "I'll come back to get you."

I took the paint supplies out onto the porch, then went down the steps and unsaddled the Appaloosa. The horse looked at me curiously as I draped a small, fresh blanket over her back, then went back to grazing as I walked into the house to get Rêve. I led her out of the house and down the steps. She was naked, yet she walked out into the day with the dignity of a queen. If I hadn't fallen in love with her before, I fell in love with her then.

"What do you want me to do?" she asked.

"I want you to lie on your back. Let your legs and arms drape down on each side. Turn your head toward me and close your eyes."

She grabbed the horse's mane and mounted it; then she lay back, her head toward the horse's rear. She relaxed into the pose, and I was delighted at the picture in front of me. She had effortlessly captured what I wanted, as though she could see the picture in my mind. Luckily, the horse did her part, standing and grazing as if nothing were different. Still, there was something wrong with the picture, and it didn't take me long to realize what it was.

"Do you mind if I touch you?" I asked as I always did before rearranging her pose. "This isn't quite right."

Her eyes were laughing as she answered. "You are the artist, Logan. Come. Do what you must."

I rearranged her hair so it fell like a blanket across the horse's rear. I opened her legs just a little wider, and then I took her arm and laid it across her stomach until the long fingers of her hand rested against her pubic hair.

"I need your nipples hard," I told her as I ran my hands over her breasts, lingering just a little too long.

She moaned slightly as I touched her.

"I'm sorry," I said. "I...I didn't mean to...It's just..."

Her emerald eyes darkened in what I thought was longing, but I wasn't really certain. I hesitated, worried that I had offended her. She broke the silence first. "It's all right," she said. "I want you to get this right."

I painted in a frenzy, each stroke bringing Rêve to life on the canvas. When I was done, I took the painting into the house and placed it in order among the finished paintings. Then I removed the covers that draped the others and went out to get Rêve.

I was surprised to see that her eyes were still closed. I stood watching the rise and fall of her perfect breasts. How I longed to reach out and cover them with my mouth! Instead, I shook myself from my thoughts and touched her hand. She opened her eyes, using one hand to shield them from the sun as she looked at me.

"Are we done?"

"Yes. Here, let me help you." I moved to help her from the horse and was surprised when she took my hand and placed it on her breast.

"Don't be shy, Logan," she purred. "Touch me. Stroke me."

I stood on the ground next to the horse. She was of average size for an Appaloosa, little more than fourteen hands—about fifty-eight inches high at the withers. For once I was thankful for my height, which put my mouth and hands at just the right level to reach Rêve's body without effort. I began to stroke her, running my hands down her body and across her breasts. I could feel the tremor in her muscles as my hands moved on her skin. I walked around the horse, looking at Rêve as I went, touching her firmly as though I were examining prime horseflesh. She lay there so beautiful and exposed, so trusting.

"Touch me, Logan," she said again, guiding my hand between my legs.

I opened her lips and looked at the pink flower covered with pearly wetness. I slid my fingers into her and laid my thumb against the swell of her desire. Her breath came in short gasps as I moved slowly in and out, up and down. She let her legs relax, opening them wider, inviting me deeper. Almost imperceptibly, she seemed to stop breathing and I knew she was going down into the orgasm, focusing on the feeling that was building between her legs. She tightened around my fingers and then she came against my hand, her juices running out over my fingers. I placed a soft kiss on her stomach and laid my head on it as I waited for her body to calm.

She moaned as I slipped my fingers from her. I lifted my head off her abdomen and looked deeply into her eyes as she sat up and slid off the horse into my arms. Her body burned against mine as I gently lowered her to the ground. We stood for a moment, barely touching, and I fought the desire to cover her mouth with mine.

"Logan," she whispered, stroking my cheek with her fingers.

I grabbed her hand and brought it to my lips. "I know," I whispered back.

"Do you?"

I nodded as I took her hand and led her into the house. The first painting she saw as we entered was of her standing at the edge of the pool, her back arched, ready to dive into the cold water. She walked slowly from painting to painting, and I watched as one small tear rolled down her cheek. I held my breath when she stopped in front of the picture of her by the side of the pond, her long fingers tangled in the auburn hair between her legs, a look of ecstasy on her face.

"These are extraordinary," she said as she turned to face me.

"You are extraordinary," I replied solemnly.

She stepped into my arms as easily as she had ridden into my life. I sank my fingers into her hair and pulled her mouth against mine, drinking in the sweetness of her lips. She answered my kiss with her own, and somewhere in the distance, I heard myself moan as her tongue danced hot and demanding against mine.

"I'm going to take you, Logan," she said huskily, pulling me toward the mattress in front of the window.

She tore at my blouse as we fell onto the pillows, and I felt the buttons pop, then heard them clicking against the wooden floor. All the desire I had kept locked up burst in waves of burning heat as my breasts touched hers.

"Oh God, Rêve," I groaned as I pulled back and struggled to get rid of the rest of my clothing.

She lifted her mouth from mine and nibbled her way down my body until her mouth reached the essence of my desire. Her fingers opened me and slid up and down in firm, circular motions. I lay under her, atop the green satin sheet, and her chestnut mane feathered against my thighs as she placed her mouth on me. Her tongue was firm and insistent and her mouth was soft but demanding as she pulled me into it. I pushed hard against her, moving my hips to let her know that she was reaching just the right spot.

I wanted this to last; I wanted the moment of our coming to be perfect—not the hurried passion born of frustration, but the deep waves of an orgasm born of love and desire. I knew I was about to come, but it was too soon…too soon, and so I stopped her.

She moved up and lay against me, breathing heavily. "Mon Dieu, why did you do that?" she complained as she rolled over on her back.

"Shh. Shh. Just let me love you, Rêve. Just let me love you." Her skin was soft and smooth under my fingertips as I drew ever-widening circles against her thighs. She arched up against me, grabbing my wrist and pushing my hand between her legs.

"Not yet, Rêve," I whispered against her mouth, then placed my hand just above the curve of her buttocks and slid her closer to me.

I touched her cheek and kissed her reverently, with small, soft kisses that trailed a path down her throat to her breasts. Her breasts were so beautiful, firm mounds of silky flesh that fit perfectly in my hands. I lifted first one, then the other, into my mouth. I sucked them, then took the hardened nipples gently between my teeth. I could feel her body react with each movement I made, and my body responded with equal fervor.

"Oh, Logan," she cried, her voice thick with desire.

I kissed and touched every inch of her skin, delighting in her desire, until I lay between her legs, my cheek against her thigh. I slid my fingers between her lips, opening them gently. She was swollen and hard; small drops of her juices glistened like diamonds in the chestnut hair between her legs, and it excited me to know that I had done that to her.

I leaned into her then, opening her hood with my tongue just enough to touch the hard bud beneath before pulling her into my mouth. I slipped my fingers into her and curved them ever so slightly until I found the small rough button that lay just inside. I massaged and tapped it gently, letting her movements lead the way until she arched against my mouth and trapped my fingers inside with the pulsating waves of her orgasms. I stayed in her until I felt her body relax against the pillows, and then slowly moved up to hold her in my arms.

She didn't say a word, but the wetness on her cheeks told me all I needed to know. She stretched against me as though she could not get enough contact and then slid her hand down to touch me. Her hand covered me and her long, slender fingers slid between my folds. No piano concerto she ever wrote could be as beautiful to me as the feel of her fingers playing against my skin.

"I want you, Logan," she said, slipping her long fingers inside me, filling me with her touch. "I want you to come for me, now."

Her words, her touch, were all it took. I couldn't hold back a second longer. The dam burst, and I rocked with wave after wave of ecstasy. Her fingers were magic, and I was alive again.

We lay sated in each other's arms, lost in our own thoughts, until I heard Rêve sigh. "I don't want this to end, Logan."

"It doesn't have to end. We have all the time in the world, Rêve." I kissed the top of her head softly and ran my hand down her side, bringing it to rest gently against the curve of her hip.

"Do we?" she whispered.

I lay awake until dawn, holding Rêve in my arms as she slept, listening to the soft puffs of her breath caress the silence of the night.

"I love you, Rêve," I whispered into her hair as the morning light started to move slowly into the room. Then I began to stroke Rêve gently, waiting for her desire to reawaken as mine already had.

Even in the twilight of her sleep, Rêve responded to my touch. She stretched against me and slipped her hands between my legs as she began to wake. "I heard that," she mumbled sleepily as she nuzzled my breast.

"I'm sorry. I thought you were asleep." I was suddenly shy and unsure.

She sat up, her legs stretched out in front of her, and looked down at me. "Logan?"

"What?"

"Come here."

"Come where?"

"Here," she said as she pulled me to a sitting position and motioned across her lap.

I straddled her, sliding close enough for our pubic bones to touch, and put my arms around her neck. She nibbled on my upper lip and I was surprised when I felt sparks of electricity between my legs each time she did that. I sucked on her lower lip and she pressed harder against me. I started to grind my pelvis against her as our kisses deepened, but she put her hands on my hips and stopped my movements.

"Just the kiss, Logan. Feel it."

And I did feel it. I felt her breath moving into me, stimulating the nerve endings from my mouth to my clitoris. I felt myself becoming engorged and wet again. I began to breathe in sync with her. I let her lead me deeper and deeper into ecstasy until we both came with achingly beautiful orgasms born of a lover's kiss in the early morning hours of an Appalachian dawn.

In Pursuit of Love
Lesley Davis

Detective Dana Silvester tentatively twisted the doorknob and sighed under her breath as the door opened. "Careless," she muttered and drew her gun before taking another step. Silently, she entered the house. As a precaution, she flipped the lock on the door so that whoever had gotten in would not be getting out so easily. She listened carefully, trying to pinpoint where the intruder was in the house. She crept along the wall toward the living room, where she could hear muffled noises. Her ears pricked at the sound of a clock's chime being played. Its merry tune sounded loud in the otherwise silent home. The living-room door was ajar and Dana cautiously stuck her head through it, searching for the figure she knew to be inside. There she was, dressed in a black bodysuit that clung to every curve of her slender form, standing at the mantelpiece, the clock chiming in her hands as she placed it in its rightful place. Dana's eyes swept from the jet-black hair down to the shoes designed for speed rather than fashion. Gun drawn and trained on the intruder, she entered the room.

"You left the door unlocked," Dana said softly.

"That wasn't very smart of me, now, was it?" The woman started but didn't turn around, reaching out instead to silence the chimes. "After all, it just invites anyone in here to follow me."

"You just can't keep your fingers off the timepieces, can you?" Dana said, stepping farther into the room and trying not to gasp when the woman turned around and fixed her with beautiful blue eyes.

"I admire things of beauty and precision, is that a crime?"

"Stealing them is," Dana countered.

The woman spread her hands out before her. "I haven't stolen anything yet. I was just admiring this one's charms." She grinned at Dana. "You can put your gun down, Detective. You know I'm never armed."

"I feel like every call-out I get, it's to find you taking clocks. I always arrive after the fact. Tonight, though…" Dana paused. "Tonight you're waiting for me. I'm curious as to why."

"I wanted to see the intrepid detective who keeps chasing after me. I've been waiting for the right time to introduce myself. I felt tonight was the night."

"Who are you?" Dana lowered her weapon and holstered it, never taking her eyes off the striking woman before her.

"You can call me Carrie." The woman moved toward Dana with the grace of a cat. She reached out to touch the detective's hair. "I wondered what your hair would feel like. It's so very blond. You cut it short; it's like fine bristles. Fascinating." She continued to run her fingers like a caress over Dana's hair.

Dana had to resist the urge to close her eyes against the seductive touch. She grabbed Carrie's hand. "You're awfully cool for someone caught in the act of stealing."

Carrie shrugged. "But I haven't taken anything. The clock is on the mantelpiece." She gestured over her shoulder nonchalantly. "Tell me, Dana, are you always this dedicated to getting your woman?"

Dana frowned. "How do you know my name?"

Carrie laughed sweetly. "I made it my business to find out who was on my trail. I liked what I saw, but you're even more beautiful close up."

Dana swallowed hard against the lump that appeared in her throat. "I need to arrest you," she said finally, trying to break the staring match that seemed to have started between them.

Carrie reached out to trace the wrinkles firmly etched on Dana's forehead. "Tell me, Detective, do you ever smile? Does anything ever make you laugh and chase these lines away? Or do they only go in the throes of passion?"

Dana stared at her. "I smile," she replied, watching as a look flirted its way across Carrie's face at the blush that obviously had covered Dana's.

Carrie pulled her hand from Dana's grasp. "I could make these nasty lines go away for a moment." She gently rubbed her fingertips over Dana's brow.

"Could you now?" Dana asked, feeling the warmth from Carrie's touch easing away the tension.

"I could make you feel so good," Carrie all but purred.

"I'm on duty," Dana muttered, trying hard to keep her feet firmly fixed in reality.

"Don't all you officer types get doughnut breaks?" Carrie teased, brushing her fingers through the short hairs on Dana's neck.

"I have to report in, tell them there was something suspicious going on in this house."

"There's nothing suspicious going on here. My motives are very clear where you're concerned, Dana!" She pressed close to Dana's chest, snuggling into her. "Hmm, you're shorter than I am, but more solid. I like that!" She pressed in closer, her hands still in Dana's hair. She gently tilted Dana's head up a fraction. "You have the right to remain silent."

With that, Carrie pressed her lips to Dana's. She kissed her gently, softly. Only when Dana let out a soft moan did she turn up the heat. Kisses rained over Dana's cheeks, then over the lines on her brow with such tenderness that Dana felt her knees begin to buckle.

Carrie nibbled on Dana's earlobe. "Anything you say will be used against you."

"Like what?" Dana asked, lost in the feel of Carrie in her arms.

"Like how much you could love me," Carrie replied.

"I hardly know you," Dana retorted, trying to move her head back to reach Carrie's questing mouth.

"Oh, you know me. You've been following me for months now, and I've been watching you. I know all about you, Dana. I want to know more. I want to show you how easy you are to fall in love with."

Dana pulled back from Carrie's hold. "If you truly have been finding out about me, then you know I have a lousy track record with women!"

Carrie smiled widely. "That's because none of them are adventurous enough for you. You crave excitement, a touch of danger; you yearn for the unexpected. I am all those things in one." Carrie pulled Dana toward her. "I'm going to steal your heart."

Dana groaned. "You're too much of a complication that I just don't need right now."

"I am exactly what you need right now," Carrie countered and ran her hands up Dana's front to push aside her jacket and reach for her breasts. She began to chafe the nipples that responded even through the material of Dana's shirt and bra.

Dana's hips bucked when Carrie deftly unfastened her trousers and tugged them down enough to reach under the boxer shorts to rest against Dana's soft fur.

"What I have in mind for you is surely illegal! Would you arrest me for breaking and entering?" Carrie rubbed her fingers across Dana's sex.

"You won't break anything, you have very delicate hands," Dana replied, her hand moving to push Carrie's where she needed her the most. "I've witnessed that in the scenes you leave behind."

Carrie fondled the soft folds beneath her fingers. "You're very wet," she moaned, pulling her hand free to suck at the juices coating her fingers.

Dana let out a groan at the loss. "You made me that way," she said, watching the sensual display before her.

"So it's all my fault, eh?" Carrie teased, slipping her hand back in and swiftly entering Dana's waiting flesh.

Dana moaned aloud and then felt the cushions of the settee behind her as she was pushed down onto its edge. The movement drove Carrie's fingers more tightly inside her and Dana closed her eyes at the exquisite feeling of fullness. "I'll take some of the blame," she gasped as Carrie's fingers pulled out once more and teased at her entrance.

"Oh, you're guilty all right." Carrie leaned up to kiss waiting lips once again. "I've spent my time watching you, waiting for you, stealing clocks to get your attention—to draw you after me, bring you to me."

"Couldn't you have just asked me for a date?" Dana asked, her whole body quivering under Carrie's masterful touch.

"I wouldn't have caught your attention as surely." She ran her tongue over Dana's open mouth, licking the shape of Dana's lips. While teasing her with her tongue she entered Dana once more and allowed the welcoming rush of moisture to guide her in deeper. Dana opened up further inside and Carrie took advantage by adding another finger. Carrie's thumb rubbed on Dana's hardened clit, and Dana's rocking quickened, her breath ragged and panting. She felt Carrie press on the sweet spot inside and she cried out Carrie's name as she was rocked into an intense orgasm. For a long moment after, all Dana could do was try to catch her breath and regain her sight from all the lights she could still see flashing.

"How am I supposed to take you in now, after that?" she grumbled, watching as Carrie removed her fingers.

Carrie ran her thumb over the sticky remnants that coated her digits. "I'd say I have all the evidence against you, Dana, right here in my hand!"

Dana tried to regulate her breathing and ignore the fact she was sitting with her trousers around her knees in front of a known cat burglar.

"You could just let me go." Carrie reached into her tight jacket and pulled out a pair of black gloves and a handkerchief. She wiped off the excesses that were clinging damply to her hand, then she put on her gloves.

"You know I can't do that."

"I didn't take anything—nothing that wasn't freely given, anyway." Carrie smirked at Dana's blushing features. She smoothly got to her feet as Dana scrambled to get up and pull her trousers back on.

"You're still the main suspect in a series of robberies," Dana said, trying hard to be professional when all she wanted was to peel down the zip of the tight jacket that hid Carrie's body from her view.

Carrie saw where the detective's eyes rested, and smiled. "I think we need to talk about this some more, say, maybe…when you're off duty?"

"I'm off duty in an hour."

"Then come see me and we'll discuss my life of crime versus being the girlfriend of a respected detective."

Dana's eyes lit up suspiciously. "You'd give up stealing?"

"You'd have to make it worth my while," Carrie replied sensuously. "There's quite a thrill in being chased across the town by a young blond officer of the law!"

"I'll put some thought into it," Dana promised. "Where can I find you?"

Carrie unzipped her jacket and revealed a tantalising glimpse of her chest to a dazed Dana. She drew out a white card. "Here, come visit me when you've hung up your handcuffs for the evening." She paused, then gave Dana a lecherous smile. "Or you could just bring them along with you."

Dana finally chuckled.

"Ah, so you can smile!" Carrie looked enchanted. "But I have to say I could become addicted to the sight of you coming in my hand."

Dana gulped at the fire in those blue eyes. She accepted the card and read it. "You live above a clock repair shop?" she asked in surprise.

"How else do you think I knew which timepieces are housed where?"

"You'll have to return those you have 'borrowed,'" Dana said seriously.

"Sure." Carrie headed toward the window and gently pried the frame open. "Maybe you can follow me from house to house while I return them all to their rightful owners. After all, that's what I was doing tonight."

Dana stared at the clock on the mantelpiece. "You were bringing it back?"

"You never caught me stealing. How ironic you finally catch me when I'm returning things!" Carrie sat on the window ledge, her long legs dangling out through the opening. "Catch you later!" She waved and leapt from the ledge.

By the time Dana got to the window, the enigmatic young woman was nowhere in sight.

"Too late," Dana said softly into the night air. "I think I'm already caught!"

THE BLUE LINE
KI THOMPSON

I see her almost every day on the Metro. I'm uncertain as to where she gets on in the morning, but she gets off at the Smithsonian stop. I imagine that she is an archaeologist, working on some obscure, extinct species in a back room that even the Smithsonian, with its massive collections, has forgotten. During sabbatical, I envision her traipsing about some tropical rain forest, wearing tight khaki shorts and a pith helmet. Her blouse would be open to the heat with the sleeves rolled up in earnest to her elbows.

My reverie is interrupted as the train glides to a stop at the Smithsonian station. As usual, she gets on the last car, something I discovered early on in the commute. She either arrives at the last minute to board, or for some odd quirk, she likes riding in the final car. It's my lucky day, because she finds an empty seat across from me on the opposite side of the doors. I am sitting in a seat facing the rear of the compartment, she in one facing the front. She looks at me and smiles. Perhaps there is the faint recognition on her part that she has seen me before. Whatever the reason, I smile back. I would love to hold the eye contact, but she glances down at her watch, and in reaction, I check mine. It is 5:37, a little early for both of us to be getting home from work, but somehow fate has decided to bring us together again.

After a few minutes of riding, I am astonished to see her get up to stand in front of the doors; she is going to disembark at the next stop. This is not part of her normal routine and arouses my curiosity. She turns her head to look in my direction, but it can't be me, so I search over my shoulder, wondering what lucky individual has attracted her attention. When I turn back around, she is still gazing at me and I see what appears to be an invitation in her eyes. I must be hallucinating, but as I stand up, she smiles more seductively, an encouraging sign.

The train comes to a complete halt and the doors hiss open. She steps off and I follow.

Aboveground she heads up Twelfth Street, her brief case swinging from one shoulder with a newspaper shoved haphazardly inside. Her gait is purposeful but unhurried and I wonder where she is leading me. At E Street she turns left, and as we pass by the National Theatre, I don't even glance to see what's showing. After crossing Fourteenth Street, she turns and enters the Willard Hotel. I follow her down a short hallway off the lobby to the bar, where she sits at a table near a window. Hesitating, I take a place at the bar next to two bureaucrats drinking bourbon and debating the last election. She orders a white wine while I order a Manhattan.

I sit and watch her drink. Occasionally she glances out the window at the passersby but I can tell she isn't really seeing them. Her neck, like a prima ballerina's, is impossibly long and her hair is gathered up in a French twist, although a few wisps dangle loosely about her face. I want to reach out and brush them away and fantasize that I'll have the opportunity to do just that. She finishes her drink and leaves cash on the table. When she begins to rise, I throw some bills on the bar as well and follow her out.

I lose sight of her for a moment when she rounds a corner, but somehow I know she is heading to the hotel elevators. Sure enough, I catch up just as she enters one and I walk in after her. The doors quietly close and we begin the ascent. She doesn't speak to me, nor does she even look in my direction. Surely she knows I am following her, or have I misinterpreted her intentions? When the car eventually comes to a halt, she steps out and I once more obediently follow.

She stops in front of a room, where she pulls out her hotel card. As she inserts it into the slot, the newspaper in her bag falls to the floor. I see this as my opening and gallantly step forward.

"Oh, thank you," she says as I pick it up and hand it to her. "Won't you come in, then?"

"I would love to." I swallow hard, knowing the game has been leading up to this moment.

When the door closes, she drops her bag on the floor and grabs my wrist, spinning me around. I find myself pinned with my back to the door, trapped beneath the weight of her body and the firm grip she has on both of my wrists. She forces her knee between my legs, pushing them apart, and then presses her mouth to mine. She bites my lower lip, not hard, but not gently either. I wince from the pain but then feel her tongue reach out to soothe it away. Just when I begin to enjoy this delicious attention to my lip, she forces her tongue inside and assaults my mouth. When she finally allows me a gasp of air, she lets go of one hand to reach into her pocket.

"Don't move," she commands.

I stand there, intimidated by this abrupt and unsuspected change in her behavior. It is so out of character for her, or rather what I had envisioned her to be like, that I begin to tremble; partly out of fear, and partly out of fascination of the unknown. I am already wet.

I feel cold steel encircle my wrists and realize she is cuffing me, a realization not entirely unwelcome.

"Being a cop comes in handy sometimes, don't you agree?" She laughs throatily as I hear the click of the handcuffs locking in place.

She pulls me by my wrists to the bed, where she yanks the sheets and blankets down. After pushing me back onto the pillows, she quickly removes her shoes and stockings and is on top of me before the last stocking hits the floor. She tears at my clothes in her haste to remove them, all the while humping my right thigh. In short order, she has my shirt completely unbuttoned and my trousers and briefs pushed down around my ankles. My shirt won't come off with the handcuffs on, but apparently she doesn't care about that. She takes my manacled wrists and extends them over my head, then she attaches them to the headboard with the scarf from around her neck. My hands are immobilized, and with my pants around my ankles, she has effectively subdued me. She stands on the bed in triumph and strips quickly, then crawls up to my head.

"I need your mouth now," she says urgently as she straddles my face.

She is hot and ready and just the smell of her arousal makes me hard. I begin by teasing everywhere but where she wants it, but she is too far gone for foreplay.

"No, suck it now," she insists and takes hold of my head to keep it where her need is greatest.

I acquiesce willingly and take her fully into my mouth. She rocks against my face, coating my nose, cheeks, and chin with her essence.

"Yes, keep doing it like that, yes, that's got it."

Within minutes a low rumble emanates from deep within her chest and I listen as it ascends to the top of her head. Needing an outlet, it erupts into one long volcanic groan as her body jerks spasmodically over my face. Afterward, she slides down my stomach and collapses on top of me. Breathing hard from her efforts and still moaning softly, she manages to grind her hips against me, working a thigh between my legs. I raise my hips in an effort to relieve the pressure and she presses down harder.

"Please, I can't wait any longer," I beg. The pressure feels good, but I need something more direct. She responds by tugging on my nipple with her teeth.

She descends to a point between my legs where her face can rest on my inner thigh. I feel her blow gently against my clit and the pain is exquisite. Without thinking, I try to reach for her, but the tug on my wrists reminds me of my incapacity. The ache below increases and I need her to make me come.

"Please." I hear myself whine, but the agony is too great to be embarrassed.

She understands the urgency in my plea and, without warning, plunges three fingers deep inside. Shocked, I come instantly. Behind closed lids, bright molecules dance erratically across an endless void before erupting into fireworks at the periphery of my vision.

I awake to the sound of water running. Within seconds, it shuts off. She steps out from the bathroom, one towel wrapped around her body and another around her head, turban-style.

"Hi, honey." She smiles warmly at me.

"Hi, baby." I smile back. "I missed you so much."

She laughs. "I couldn't tell." She leans down and kisses me slowly. "I missed you too, baby. The next time they send me to Peru, you're going with me."

"Okay by me," I say emphatically. "But will the museum agree to cover my expenses?"

She shrugs. "Sure, I'll just categorize them under 'Meals and Entertainment.' Speaking of which"—she eyes me hungrily—"I'm ready for dessert."

BETWEEN THE STACKS
JEAN STEWART

The ancient grandfather clock by the wide wooden staircase thumped and whirred, then sounded out the three o'clock hour in a slow, deep cadence. Martha echoed each strike with her index finger, tapping the smooth page of *Orlando* while her eyes lingered on what she thought might be the longest, most lyrically written sentence in history.

Sighing, she lifted her bookmark from her lap and slid it in place. It was an odd bookmark, she supposed, but it continued to find its way into each volume she read. The woman in the photograph grinned up at her, windblown dark hair half in her eyes. The cleanly scissored edges of the photo, originally in the campus newspaper, had started to fray before she thought of laminating it, and now, years later, it was a touchstone.

The photograph had been taken the day the university field hockey team had won its division, and the woman in the photo had been carried off the field on her teammates' shoulders. Martha had seen the game. She still remembered the cold November wind slicing through her. She was shrieking encouragement from the sidelines when Eleanor the Great ran by, a thunder of long legs and gasps for air as she cut off an opponent's pass. The dark eyes had lifted, just for a few seconds, making contact with Martha's. It was as if a door deep within Martha had shuddered open and yawned wide, exposing her awakening soul. Then Eleanor had looked down, gathered up the white ball, and sent it to a teammate with a crisp, hard crack of her stick. In a blur of strides she was gone. And Martha had been left with a question.

How can she make me feel so much just by looking at me?

Martha had been a lowly freshman, then, and Eleanor Watson had been a senior. Martha was a library major, a bookworm, and though she could hold her own in many recreational games, she was no school athlete. Her ripples in the pond that was campus life never lapped over into the waves surrounding Eleanor. Never had a crush been more unattainable.

Five years had passed since then. Martha shook her head at herself. The photograph was more than a bookmark. It was in reality a torch whose embers would not die.

Warm late-September sunlight was pouring through the tall window behind her like butterscotch, pooling across her jeans-and-sweatshirt-clad body like syrup on a sundae. She was comfortably ensconced in a plush but battered brown leather armchair, with her legs hanging over the armrest, close enough to the scarred information desk to look as if she were on duty. Martha had decided several years back that she would only endure the desk stool while under direct supervision. When faced with the choice of spending a six-hour shift luxuriating in a 1950s stuffed-to-the-max armchair or perched on a hard-as-hell Shaker stool, there was really no contest. Thank heaven her boss Charles had decided he valued her willingness to take extra shifts enough to look the other way on the few occasions when he'd caught her enjoying her luxurious leather throne.

The separate 1970s glass-and-steel architectural monstrosity that was the main library was located behind this graceful little building. Constructed of green-hued serpentine stone, with white marble columns rising above a flight of wide entrance steps, the century-and-a-half-old library was set aside for specialty information. Hundreds of legal and medical texts were housed downstairs, under the supervision of Charles and two other library aides. Up here, where she was, were the rarer archives and century-old books. This was where the college and local counties histories were kept, where all the secrets lay.

In the locked rooms at the rear of the second floor, Martha had seen the original, handwritten parchments detailing the Continental Army's retreat at Brandywine, had read the passionate account of the wounding of Lafayette as told by the doctor who had treated him beneath a tree that still lived in a park not ten miles from here. She had examined the letters of local farmers who had been part of the underground railroad, helping runaway slaves make it to the port city of Philadelphia. She had scoured the confessional letters of women who had met with Elizabeth Cady Stanton and Susan B. Anthony when their husbands had told them not to, giving pin money and brainstorms in the cause of women's suffrage, risking their marriages and financial security for a right some modern-day women failed to exercise.

The second floor of the small F. H. Green Graduate Library was an isolated, mahogany-paneled, oak-shelved mausoleum for most of the library aides in the university's student staffing program. Martha looked around, smiling faintly, then closed her eyes and inhaled the scent of waxed wooden floors and hundreds and hundreds of hardbound books. To Martha it was a little slice of heaven.

No one came here except the graduate students. And they were another breed altogether: quiet, orderly, businesslike in their approach to research. By the time you became a graduate student, you knew how to use the computers, the microfiche, and even the wonderfully musty card catalogues for the really old texts. They came in with their laptops and legal pads and briefcases, and set themselves up at long tables like they were making camp. Then they prowled from one row of shelves to the next, searching the stacks for something they had illegibly scribbled on a sticky note, pulling out tomes, leafing through them, and then lugging the massive volumes to the copier. Rarely did they trouble her for information.

Which, Martha knew, was sad, in a way. A grad student herself, and only a thesis away from a Master of Library Science degree, Martha knew in incredible detail the contents of the second-floor grad library. She knew the relationships of each area of knowledge to the others. And she knew where the unexpectedly rich little nuggets of intellectual gold lay. However, rarely did anyone ask her for help, and so she never got to exercise what she thought was her greatest talent: her limitless retention of minutiae.

Eyes still closed, she was so lost in her musing that when a woman said, "Hey," Martha nearly levitated from the chair. *Orlando* abruptly flew off her lap, bounced on the leather seat cushion, and somersaulted over the edge. The woman lurched forward and dropped to her knees, catching the book with the adroitness of a center fielder.

For a moment, Martha simply stared at her.

Big, dark brown eyes, curious and half-mooned with laughter. An open, even-featured face with freckles sprinkled over the nose. Silky-looking, dark brown hair that fell forward over her shoulders. And she wore a faded light blue denim shirt tucked into stone-colored chinos.

Shit, Martha thought. *Eleanor Watson!*

"I need help finding a book," Eleanor said, gesturing toward the rear of the second floor.

She was, of course, still beautiful.

Martha's heart went from zero to sixty in the approximately ten seconds it took Eleanor to speak. Stunned, Martha simply gazed at a slightly older rendering of the face so inadequately captured in her bookmark before reminding herself that this was the real woman and she shouldn't be staring at her like a complete idiot. In a rush, she levered herself awkwardly over the armrest and scurried toward the desk.

All long limbs and athletic grace, the other woman got to her feet, looking at something in her hand and then glancing sharply at Martha. Lanced by the curious gaze, Martha tucked *Orlando* into the small shelf under the desktop and hopped onto the tall stool. She concentrated on reorganizing the placement of the pencil holder and the mouse pad as Eleanor pulled a backpack up over one shoulder and came to the other side of the desk.

"W-what's the t-title and the author's name?" Martha asked, feeling her face heat up and cursing herself for stuttering.

Eleanor replied in a soft, clear voice, sliding a three-by-five index card across the desk to Martha. Martha fixed her eyes on the card, her heart still booming in her ears. She could barely hear the specifics as Eleanor went on speaking. Martha kept her attention riveted on the screen as she ran a series of complex searches. It took her four minutes and an improvised respelling of the author's last name, but she found the book.

"It's in the library archive," Martha said, wonder entering her voice.

"Oh."

"You need a permission note to get in there."

Eleanor looked down, then adroitly slipped whatever it was she was still holding in her right hand into a back pocket. Smiling at Martha, she reached into her front pocket. "My sponsor gave me this." She handed over a folded piece of paper.

Martha opened the note and found the signature of the head of the psychology department at the bottom of a neatly typed letter explaining that Eleanor Watson was pursuing her doctorate in behavioral sciences and gathering data for her dissertation. The letter requested the assistance and cooperation of all computer and library study officials in helping Eleanor access whatever she needed.

"Doctorate," Martha murmured. "Huh."

Eleanor shifted from one foot to the other, looking a little nervous.

"Okay, you're in," Martha pronounced.

She placed the "Desk Closed" sign on the desktop, then opened the desk drawer and got the keys.

"Please follow me," she told Eleanor, managing to briefly make eye contact. Trying to muster a pretense at dignity, Martha marched out from behind the long counter, leading the way to the back of the library. Now that she was in official business mode, she thought she could handle the fact that the most incredible woman she had ever laid eyes on, the source of her sexual fantasies and her romantic enthrallment, was walking a few steps behind her, looking like an advertisement for the Olympic Games.

When they got to the door to the archives, Martha's hand barely shook as she pushed the key into the lock. The second lock was a little trickier. As Martha tried to get the special "pull the knob and twist the lock" combination that was required, Eleanor stepped up behind her, asking, "Need some help?" It was spoken near Martha's ear and she couldn't stop the trembling flush that coursed over her body.

"No." It came out in a small voice.

The lock turned, and Martha pushed the big metal fire door open. She turned on the lights and then they stepped into the chamber where the climate control features of the facility began. Dutifully, Martha closed and locked that door behind them and moved ahead to the next door. This was the original oak-and-glass fixture that the university founders had installed, just after the Civil War. Martha inserted the fork-end key in the cartoon-shape hole above the doorknob, then used the 1930s improvement in the second lock higher up on the wood. This was where a lot of people made jokes about entering Fort Knox.

"Jeez," Eleanor muttered. "With the historic worth of some of the documents in there, you'd think they could afford a little better security!"

Points! Martha's mind crowed as Eleanor echoed her thoughts on the matter. Then realization struck. *Oh my God! She's a scholar!*

Anyone who understood the finer nuances of archive maintenance—like security measures—was, in Martha's book, a scholar.

The door opened and Martha pushed through, thinking hard. "And here all this time, I thought you were Big Jock On Campus."

She stopped dead, her hand still on the doorknob, shocked to realize she had spoken the thought aloud. Eleanor went by her, turning and laughing.

"Ah, now at last we get to it."

Her face felt hot again. "W-what?"

"I know you from somewhere. I recognized you as soon as I saw you."

Martha busied herself with closing and locking the door. "Nah. You're probably thinking of someone else."

"Then how did you know I was a jock?" Eleanor placed her backpack on the rectangular table, her brown eyes moving over Martha in a casual nonchalance that did little to hide how intense the regard really was.

She's cruising me! For a moment, Martha was so astounded she missed the question. Then, in quick succession, her brain fired off a barrage of damning reactions: *My hair is a mess! I'm five pounds overweight! I'm wearing the jeans with the holes in them and a sweatshirt, for cripes' sake!*

Smiling, tilting her head as if mildly perplexed, Eleanor watched her.

Suddenly aware that the silence had gone on too long, Martha's mind finally shuffled Eleanor's question to the top of the heap. "Uh, I was on the sidelines the day your team won the division championship."

Eyebrows rose. "Oh." Now it was Eleanor who was blushing.

Taking a deep breath to settle herself, Martha walked forward, passing the rows of nineteenth-century first editions and the precious parchments locked away in metal cabinets. It was chillier here due to the climate-control features meant to preserve the ancient paper all around them. Martha shivered a little, glad of her sweatshirt. She couldn't hear Eleanor's steps, but she sensed the woman was right behind her.

They turned down the row that housed the behavioral sciences, and as she slowed, searching for the code that would mark the spine of the book, Martha became aware of the titles. *Sex, sex, and more sex,* Martha thought, and could not suppress a giggle at how preposterous the afternoon was turning out to be. *Trapped in the archives, hunting down an obscure sex book with Eleanor the Great!* She would get months of imaginary scenes out of this encounter, she was sure.

"What's so funny?" Eleanor asked.

Her voice made the muscles beneath Martha's shoulder blades wiggle and melt. *Oh God, I've got to get out of here.* Then her eyes fell on the title. *"Sexual Inversion* by Dr. Charlotte Fellers. Here it is."

As Martha plucked the book from the shelf, she turned and found Eleanor less than a foot away, sliding behind her. She glanced down at the book, then asked again, "What's so funny?"

Mouth dry, Martha found her gaze caught and held by the vulnerable dark eyes above her. She swallowed and involuntarily found the truth coming out of her. "You, me, in the sex shelves behind two locked doors." She tried to rally with a flirtatious little laugh, but it came out as a cough.

"Oh," Eleanor said, and made a bemused face, as if recovering from a misinterpretation of some kind.

"Why did you think I laughed?"

She shrugged as if it didn't matter, but her eyes told Martha that it mattered very much. "You called me Big Jock On Campus. And now I'm making you go to so much trouble, and all, to get this book for my dissertation..."

A clue abruptly arrived. "You thought I was laughing at *you*?"

"You wouldn't be the first," Eleanor mumbled.

"I would never laugh at you," Martha said, her voice hushed but insistent. "I think you're—" Aghast at what she had been about to say, Martha stopped speaking and stood there, momentarily tongue-tied.

Those soft, dark eyes were moving over Martha's face again, curious and strangely tender. "You think I'm...what?"

They were so close to one another that Martha could feel Eleanor's body heat. With gentle hands, Eleanor took the book from her and slid it onto the tops of some others on another shelf. "First things first," Eleanor murmured.

Martha felt the hair stand up on the back of her neck. Mesmerized, she watched Eleanor slowly edge closer. There was no mistaking what was about to occur. Eleanor was giving her plenty of time to withdraw if that was what she wanted to do. Instead of withdrawing, Martha leaned toward her, trembling. A hand slid behind Martha's neck and goose bumps erupted. Martha closed her eyes.

Yes, yes, yes...

It was a sweet kiss, expressing courtliness as well as desire, as if to let her know that the woman kissing her was chivalrous. All the same, Martha found herself breathing harder, erotic anticipation roaring through her. The kiss was so good that when it stopped, Martha swayed like wheat in the caress of a zephyr.

Within seconds, the sweet lips were back, giving small kisses, until Martha realized that she was being asked a series of questions. *How much do you want? When should I stop? Where are the boundaries?* Those soft, questioning lips kept leading her on, and she had to follow, answering more and more boldly. *I want more. Don't stop, there are no boundaries—not when it's you.*

She was being gathered in, held by strong arms in soft blue-jeans cloth, fitted into a leaner, larger body. Her own arms were around Eleanor, and she was giving herself over. She was reveling in the way she felt, unabashedly chasing the mouth that interrogated her, the dialogue between them being paced with gasps for breath.

Eleanor's hands went beneath her sweatshirt, sweeping over her back and her ribs, and Martha thought she would shoot out of her skin. She writhed against the taller woman, her voice choking loose in a high cry of need. Giving a low grunt, Eleanor brushed a hand near Martha's breast, and through the sweatshirt, Martha grasped the hand and directed it where she knew it wanted to go. Almost as if possessed by a sudden surge of ownership, Eleanor lifted her and pressed her against the stacks. Martha shuddered, and her head fell back and bumped into the soft leather spines of the large texts there. Within seconds Eleanor's fingers were teasing a nipple. Bending her head, Eleanor delicately licked the edge of her ear. A thigh pressed lightly against Martha's center, thoroughly igniting her, and then easing away. Martha could barely stifle a cry, and her hips jerked forward of their own accord, trying to reconnect.

There was a whisper at her ear, and after straining to focus, Martha realized the voice was appealing to reason. "This is crazy. We don't even know one another. We're in the library!"

"Don't you dare stop!" Martha ordered. "Library be damned! I've been waiting...so long...I can't wait anymore!"

She laced her fingers through Eleanor's dark, wavy hair, then used her palms on either side of Eleanor's beautiful face to direct that lovely mouth back to her own. Kissing her fervently, Martha pleaded with her tongue and lips for the salvation she had unwittingly prayed for each time she held her bookmark. For so long now, she had used the laminated photograph of this woman to mark the pages of what she read, and now she found she had marked her own soul. One more day, one more week, one more month without Eleanor the Great. Until today, nothing she had ever felt was as electric as that incredible exchange of gazes on the hockey field. This seduction among the archival media could not end in frustration.

Eleanor's thigh nestled in again, pushing between her legs. Martha had to break their kiss to breathe. "Yes! Yes!" she urged. Martha was pressed into the bookshelves at hip and shoulder level; it was an easy and instinctive act to hike one leg up and wrap it around Eleanor's thigh. In one primal move she betrayed the depth of her need, her womanhood offered in open invitation.

Eyeing her with an almost savage fierceness, Eleanor eased away. "Now, isn't this something," she said. With a deliberately teasing stroke, Eleanor caressed her abdomen, watching Martha twitch helplessly. "Right here, then?" Beyond words now, Martha could only nod, gasping as the hand roved over her. Slowly, Eleanor unbuttoned Martha's jeans, and fascinated, Martha watched her.

"Let's find out what you like," Eleanor coaxed, sliding her hand into Martha's panties, tickling the hairs a friendly hello and then moving steadily down lower. Two fingers slid on either side of Martha's clitoris. Martha moaned. "That's it," Eleanor said. "Almost ready."

The strokes began, slow and long. Martha's entire body arched and went rigid, more susceptible than she could have imagined to this touch. *Eleanor is doing this!* Her insides squeezed tight, and her breath couldn't come fast enough. Head flung back, feeling the nips traveling along her neck and hearing the quiet voice telling her how good she felt, Martha braced herself against the bookshelves. Her hands clenched Eleanor's broad shoulders while her hips surged back and forth. It was a wild, salacious dance, utterly outrageous and glorious all at once. She was riding Eleanor's hand, desperate for release. For several minutes Eleanor played her, obviously learning what made her crazy-excited and whispering her name when she quivered and cried aloud.

In the far recesses of Martha's mind, it occurred to her that she was not being fucked; she was being adored.

Then Eleanor's fingertip swirled around the edge of her darkness and Martha forgot everything. This was sex—sweltering, powerful, soul-shattering sex—and she wanted to come so badly she would scream if it didn't happen right now.

Martha's hips trapped Eleanor's hand between her body and that maddening thigh, mounting the finger in a rush of wet heat. Then Eleanor was lifting her, swirling another finger in, and Martha was suddenly in the grip of blistering, white sensation. Every nerve ending was going off like Chinese firecrackers, blasting along each appendage and up and down her spine. Her own voice was ringing in her ears, hoarse from the rapture, and it all felt so blindingly good.

She went limp at some point, but her pelvis was still grinding hungrily against Eleanor, begging for more. When Martha embraced her, feeling overcome, Eleanor cradled her in her arms and lowered her tenderly to the floor. For the next little while, Eleanor cuddled her and soothed her, and before Martha's befuddled senses figured out what was happening they were kissing again and her clothes were mostly off and she was completely on fire. One part of her mind was shouting, "Whoa!" while another part was chortling with glee.

Eleanor leaned over her, telling her, "I've got you. Everything's all right," while those hands moved over Martha like a master cellist, drawing sounds from Martha that she had never heard herself make. Eleanor was relentless, but this time, as Martha was driven crazy, she took Eleanor with her. She managed to ease sideways and crawl on top, and from there it got easier to control the action. She was half aware of the brush burns that the hard wooden floorboards were giving to her elbows and knees, but for the most part her awareness was dominated by the thrill and spectacle of making Eleanor the Great come undone. Passionate, and abandoned, she loved Eleanor with five years' worth of pent-up longing, and Eleanor came with a mighty exaltation, yelling "Oh God!" twice, and then quaking like a birch tree on a blustery autumn day.

They actually fell asleep for a short time, but then the cold woke them both up. With a start, Martha sat up, her face fiery with embarrassment. She felt too good to be truly ashamed, however, and after Eleanor gave her a lingering kiss, it all seemed perfectly natural. She was turned on just looking at the woman, but a kiss, well, that made everything undeniably clear. Eleanor the Great could not be resisted.

Her next concerns were the books on the stacks where they had been going at it, and she leapt to her feet. Carefully, Martha examined each book on the shelves, amazed that she had risked harming them. "Holy mackerel," she uttered. "Thank heaven I didn't wreck anything."

From her lethargic position on the floor, Eleanor laughed.

They dressed slowly, kissing and hugging one another, exclaiming about how they had never done anything so absolutely insane or divine. Martha took the Charlotte Fellers book from its place on the shelf, handed it to Eleanor, and joined her in the walk to the copying machine. They chatted about going out for coffee while Eleanor found and copied the material she wanted to reference. Then they returned the book to its niche in the behavioral sciences shelves.

Roughly an hour and a half after they had gone into the archives, they were on the outer side of the last door. Martha locked up, and grinning happily at each other, they walked to the information desk.

After they had exchanged phone numbers and addresses, Eleanor reached behind her and pulled something from her back pocket. Looking a little shy, she extended her hand. "I think this is yours."

Martha's breath caught in her throat. Eleanor held the laminated bookmark with the photo of herself. "How did you—?"

"It fell on the floor when I startled you—when you dropped your book."

Martha opened her mouth to speak, then closed it and crossed her arms over her chest. *Oh God, no! She thinks I'm a stalker!*

Eleanor moved closer, laying her hand on Martha's cheek. "I know where I met you," she said firmly. "I saw you that day. In the middle of the game, while I was chasing a ball, I ran up to the sideline and you were yelling 'Go, Eleanor the Great!' And when I looked into your eyes, I felt like I'd been hit by lightning."

For a moment, Martha couldn't speak. "Me too," she sighed.

"I looked for you after the game, you know. I looked for you the whole of that year—in the cafeterias, on campus—every time I walked to or from class."

Almost afraid to believe her, Martha felt the tears edge into her eyes.

"And now here you are. My lightning." Eleanor leaned forward and kissed her.

Martha nodded. "I can't believe it."

"So," Eleanor asked, "why were you calling me Eleanor the Great?"

Because I love you, Martha wanted to say. But no, she wouldn't say that yet. That could wait a bit. Maybe a few months. "It suits you," Martha replied.

A finger pressed on Martha's nose. "Oh no. Inspiring as it may be, that nickname has got to go."

Martha grabbed the finger and laughed. "We'll see." She brought the hand to her mouth and kissed the palm that had loved her. "We'll see, Eleanor."

TWO AFTER MIDNIGHT
MEGHAN O'BRIEN

Jamie cornered me as I hurried out of the kitchen on another errand for Natasha, the bride-to-be. She grabbed me by the arm and tugged me into the bathroom, closing the door behind us. I could see familiar desperation in her eyes as she pushed me against the wall.

"It's been a week," she growled into my ear. I shivered when her hot breath tickled my neck. She pressed her lean body—clad in a tuxedo for Maria and Natasha's wedding—against mine and ground our hips together. "A goddamn week, darling, and you look so good today and I want you so bad."

My stomach flip-flopped at the pure need in her voice. Her hand crept under my skirt and brushed the soft skin of my inner thigh. She looked amazing, decked out in black, and I'd been watching her across the room all day.

"I want you too," I whispered, and touched the side of her face. I'd wanted her all week long, but somehow we just hadn't managed to find the time. And now, after hours spent helping to make sure Maria and Natasha's big day would go smoothly, my need had reached a fever pitch and there was no relief in sight.

"God, sweetheart," Jamie groaned. Her fingers found the heat between my legs, skimming over the crotch of my panties. "Five minutes?"

It was difficult, but I managed to shake my head. "Natasha asked me to run upstairs and get her necklace. I don't have five minutes, baby. The guests are about to start arriving." Then, despite my protest, I leaned in and kissed her hard.

Jamie whimpered and pushed her fingertip beneath the elastic leg of my panties, tickling the short hairs she found beneath. I broke apart from our kiss with a gasp and planted my hand on her chest.

"No."

Jamie gave me a petulant frown. "But you kissed me."

It was so hard to resist the desire in her brown eyes, but I was determined to be strong. "I'm sorry, baby. It's the tux. You look so fucking hot, I can hardly stand it. But we don't have time now."

Growling, Jamie left me with one last searing kiss. "Later," she said, then slipped out the door.

❖

After the ceremony, there was dancing. Jamie claimed me quickly, dragging me over to a spot in the corner of the floor. She pulled me against her body and bent her head for a quick kiss. I looped my arms around her waist, feeling my nipples harden just from that simple reconnection.

Needing to breathe, I pulled away with a dazed grin. "I haven't stopped looking at you all day," I murmured as I recovered from her shattering kiss. "When Natasha was saying her vows, I realized just how hot and wet I was. You're torturing me."

Jamie pulled me closer and chuckled. "You love it."

"I never said I didn't." I ran my hands up and down her strong back, wishing for the pressure of a firm thigh between my legs. "But I'm dying, I want you so bad."

In the middle of the crowded dance floor, Jamie leaned in and licked my earlobe. "I've been hard for you all day too, sweetheart." She pressed her hand against the small of my back, holding me tight against her body. "Tell me how you want me."

Blushing, I looked around at the dancing couples who surrounded us. I met Natasha's knowing eyes and then, when the newlyweds turned in a slow circle, Maria's cocky grin. They looked so happy in each other's arms, and seeing their joy only served to make me want Jamie more. Six years together, and my wife still made me burn.

I whispered into Jamie's ear. "I want you inside me. Your fingers at first, then your cock. I want you on top of me and inside me, making me feel so good."

Jamie pulled me closer and touched the back of my thigh with a warm, heavy hand. "I want to be in you so bad right now. I've been thinking about fucking you all day long. All fucking day."

"We could sneak away—"

Jamie nipped at my neck, stopping my words with a delicious shiver. "You want me to fuck you, sweetheart? You want me to take you in the bedroom with all these people out here, and—"

She stopped talking and turned her head. Entranced by her words, I didn't realize for a moment that Maria had tapped her on the back. Our friend, handsome in a tuxedo that matched Jamie's, gave us both an apologetic grin.

"How's the groom doing?" Jamie said with an easy grin, and slapped Maria on the back. In an instant, she went from seductive lover to butch buddy, and I watched the transition with a fond, if frustrated, smile.

Maria beamed, then sobered. "I'm really good. Perfect, actually. Except—"

"Except what?" Jamie asked, and gave me a subtle glance that telegraphed her deep need.

"Except Natasha's sister. She's wasted, and so is her husband, and I'm not sure what to do with them. They drove three hours to be here, and I'm not sure how they planned to get home…"

I saw the comprehension in Jamie's eyes even as I felt a wave of disappointment roll through me. "You want them to stay with us?" Jamie offered. "I know you two want to be alone on your wedding night."

Maria gave her a guilty look. "I don't want to impose."

I shook my head and touched Maria's arm. "Not at all. This is your wedding night. You don't want someone in the next room while you're showing your wife how much you love her. We totally understand."

"Well, if it's really okay—"

"It's okay," Jamie said. She gave me a lingering, apologetic look. "We really do understand."

After everyone but our houseguests had gone home, I escaped into our bedroom and closed the door behind me with a weary sigh. "I put Nicole and Ethan in the guest bedroom." Natasha's sister and her husband were very drunk, and very amorous. I had just been resenting the hell out of them as they groped each other while stumbling toward our guest bed.

Maria and Natasha owed us big time.

"What about Carrie?" Jamie asked. She was sitting up in bed, arms folded over her bare chest.

I sighed again. "On the pullout bed. She kept apologizing over and over again for needing to sleep over. She's so embarrassed she got drunk."

Jamie managed a tired smile. "She's earned it, I guess. I know she's been hurting since the breakup."

"Yeah." My arousal, which hadn't left me throughout all the bustle of the day, was suddenly overwhelmed by a deep exhaustion. "Shit."

Jamie's eyes shone with sympathy. "I know, sweetheart."

With a pained groan, I trudged over to the bed and tugged off my skirt. "This isn't gonna work, is it?"

"I don't think so."

When I finished undressing, I dropped onto the mattress next to my wife. "But I've been wanting you all day." Worn out, I felt tears threatening at the corners of my eyes. "This isn't fair."

Jamie encouraged me over onto my side so she could spoon me. Curling an arm around my stomach, she pulled me tight against her body and dropped a gentle kiss on the back of my shoulder. "I know, sweetheart," she said again.

I was too exhausted to do anything about it, but my bone-deep need just wouldn't die. "I want you to fuck me," I complained in a whisper. I pressed my bottom backward, feeling a tired delight at the sensation of wiry curls brushing against my bare skin.

Exhaling against the back of my neck, Jamie leaned up and planted a kiss on my cheek. "I will," she murmured into my ear. "But sleep now."

When I woke up, she was inside of me.

"Oh—" I gasped, but then her hand was pressed over my mouth, silencing my cry. I moaned into her palm and arched my back as she fucked me with the fingers of her other hand.

She leaned down until her lips brushed against my earlobe. "Quiet." Her voice was rough with sleep, her breath warm against my neck. Her hand never stopped moving between my thighs.

I could hear the sound of my own wetness as she thrust in and out of my pussy. When had I gotten so wet? One minute ago, I had been dreaming.

"I need to fuck you." She withdrew her fingers, dragged the tips up over my labia, then milked my clit for a frantic heartbeat. "I'm going to put my cock inside you and fuck you until you come."

Even if I'd been able to speak, I wouldn't have known what to say. I never would have expected this from Jamie. For her to enter me while I was sleeping, to hold her hand over my mouth, to pin me to the bed with her heavy bulk. Never mind that we'd been wanting one another so desperately for a week; I couldn't have predicted this.

I spread my legs slightly and stared up at her as she pulled back, though I wasn't sure she could see the desperation in my eyes in the darkness of our bedroom. I wondered what time it was and if everyone else in the house was asleep. I wondered how long she had been touching me.

I mouthed her name into the warm skin against my lips. Her fingers slipped back inside my pussy, and she pounded into me, long, deliberate strokes. I was soaking wet, ready and open, and I wasn't sure I was even completely awake yet.

Jamie lay down on top of my body and pulled out of me again. Her hand moved between her own legs, and I felt her shifting into position above me. She rested her forehead on the pillow, grunting a little as she guided the head of what I thought felt like my favorite dildo to press against my opening.

"I'm sorry, I woke up and I just needed to fuck you so bad—"

She was pushing into me as she spoke, and her quiet words cut off when I groaned out loud at the penetration. I recognized my favorite cock, the silky firmness of the cyberskin, the maddening ridges that teased at my walls as she slid it home. I was wet, but it was a big cock. Just this side of too big. Exactly how I liked it.

"Does it feel good, baby?" She eased her hips back, then pushed it in again. Slow, firm, unyielding. I wrapped my legs around her waist and closed my eyes as I adjusted to her length.

It felt good, but I knew she wasn't really expecting me to answer.

"Spread your legs for me," she mumbled into my ear. "Let me in, baby. That's my pussy, isn't it? Let me fuck it."

I nodded and spread my legs, letting my thighs rest against the mattress. She continued to move inside me, deep, rhythmic thrusts. Her chest was damp against mine, and when I brought my arm up to curl around her shoulder, it was covered in sweat.

She removed her hand from my mouth and planted her palms on either side of my head. Holding her torso inches from mine, she started rocking her hips in earnest. As her speed picked up, so did the strength of her strokes, and soon she was moving the bed beneath us with the intensity of her fucking.

I wondered if we'd woken anyone up yet. I didn't care enough to stop Jamie's frantic motion.

Taking her earlier command seriously, I didn't speak. I moaned, because I knew how much she loved to hear what she did to me with her cock. I gasped, because she was taking my breath away. I whimpered, because somehow Jamie had tapped into one of my favorite fantasies and I'd never seen it coming.

"I couldn't believe you didn't wake up when I start fingering your pussy," Jamie growled close to my face. "You got so wet, but you barely even stirred."

I brought my other hand up to her shoulder, intent on hugging her, but she lowered her body onto me and wrenched my hands above my head. Lacing her fingers in mine, she held my hands as she continued to fuck me.

For the first time since I'd woken up, she took my mouth in a deep kiss. I cried out into the joining of our lips and at the electric shock of her hard nipples brushing against mine. My pussy tightened around her cock, increasing the friction of her unrelenting thrusts.

Jamie broke our kiss. "I love you, honey."

I turned my head to the side and bit my lip as she settled into a driving rhythm that hit me in the most perfect spot. A deep, burning pressure began to form low in my belly, and I released a keening moan to let her know not to stop what she was doing.

She bent her head and bit my earlobe gently. "You like being woken up and taken, don't you?"

I whimpered, then gasped as my pussy contracted around her cock.

"Tell me." She never stopped moving inside me.

"Yes," I hissed, desperate to stay quiet. I didn't want to wake anyone else in the house. "I love it."

She slammed her pelvis into mine, then ground her hips in a slow circle, mashing into my swollen clit until my toes curled in ecstasy. When her thrusts started again, they were shorter, harder, faster. It didn't take much before I clamped down on her cock, gritted my teeth, and came with a hoarse cry of pleasure.

Jamie collapsed onto my body, breathing hard. Her skin was slick and hot, and damp tendrils of short hair brushed against my temple as she rested her head on my shoulder. She shivered and released my hands, and I brought them down to press against the firmness of her muscled back.

"I couldn't sleep," Jamie mumbled. "I just needed you so bad—"

I tugged on her shoulders until she lifted her face and I could drop a gentle kiss on her mouth. "You surprised me," I said.

"I've just missed you so bad." She planted her hands beside my head again and started kissing her way down my neck, over my chest, across my nipples. "I'm sorry I just took you—"

Threading my fingers through her sweat-soaked hair, I pressed her face to my breast and exhaled as she sucked a nipple into her mouth. "Make it up to me." My tone made it clear that there was nothing for me to forgive.

She took my nipple between her teeth with a little growl, shaking her head back and forth in a gentle show of aggression. I was surprised to feel the new flood of wetness between my already slick thighs. I arched my back, offering my breasts to her.

Moving to chew on my other nipple, she brought her hand up to squeeze the breast she couldn't lick, pinching and tugging on the erect peak until I released a noise of pure want. Then, as if she knew exactly what I needed, she kissed her way down over my belly to the damp thatch of hairs that covered my sex.

I spread my legs and tangled my fingers in her short hair. Forcing her face close, I said, "Lick me, baby. Show me how much you missed me."

She lapped at me hungrily, slow at first, drawing it out, then faster, like she couldn't hold back. I kept my legs open and held her to me with a firm hand on the back of her head. My hips started thrusting without thought and I ground my pussy against her, delighting in the feel of her nose bumping my clit, pushing between my labia. I rode her whole face, using her like she had used me.

Her muffled groans and the sight of her hips pumping against the mattress let me know that she was enjoying being used as much as I had.

"Jamie," I whispered, then dug my heels into the mattress and raised my bottom, overcome with waves of delicious sensation. Her hands gripped my buttocks and held me tight against her mouth, which covered my clit. She licked in fast circles with the tip of her tongue, drawing every last bit of pleasure from me until I relaxed, boneless, and whimpered for her to stop.

She crawled up the length of my body and kissed me. I pulled back after a moment and cleaned her face with my tongue, enjoying the decadence of tasting myself on her skin. She reciprocated with gentle licks to my lips and chin, and when we were done, she collapsed onto the mattress at my side.

"Think you can sleep now?" I asked.

Jamie reached out and snagged me with a strong arm, pulling my naked body close. "I'm sure of it."

ACHE
RONICA BLACK

Loneliness plagues me, spreading through me like cancer, eating away my insides, filling me with darkness. She's been gone for weeks now, and I'm unable to shake her from my thoughts. She's with me every aching second of my existence, no matter how hard I try to push her away. My hand trembles as I reach up to rub at my watering, exhausted eyes. Beyond me, her picture comes into focus through my blurry vision. She's smiling at me from within an expensive oak frame upon my desk, luring me with her hypnotic eyes. My poor heart leaps at the sight of her, still greatly affected by all that she is, all that we shared. Looking away, I shudder, feeling the pain rock through me in devastating waves. I know I should remove the picture, or at the very least turn it face down, but I can't yet bring myself to touch it; my mind still is not ready to accept her absence.

I glance out the window and study the rhythm of the blowing trees and wonder for the millionth time whether or not I will survive her leaving. Expecting the weather to coincide with my dreary mood, I'm surprised to find the day to be crisp, bright, and breezy. A beautiful mild December day in the desert Southwest, the high sure to top out in the mid to high sixties.

My office is busy, my heart broken, and my coffee cold. Sighing, I run a frustrated hand through my short dark hair and yawn with fatigue. Grimacing at my Starbucks cup, I suddenly feel alive with purpose and walk briskly out of my office, winding my way to the countertop nestled in the busy hallway. Much to my dismay, I realize the coffeepot in front of me is empty and my secretary nowhere to be found. Around me, I hear my patients clutter and cough in my waiting room while my staff scurries about answering phones, taking blood pressures, charting the course of human existence.

Damn it. I'm so tired from weeks of little to no sleep, so strung out from the dull ache in my gut from all those lonely nights. All I want is a fresh cup of coffee, liquid life to help see me through yet another dark day.

I turn and face the small walkway of my private practice, shoving my hand down into my chinos. I sip the cold coffee and cringe, thankful it's finally Friday. Maybe the weekend will grant me the graces of sleep, or at least a numbing of some of my pain.

"What are you doing?" A loud voice startles me from my depressed trance. "You've been behind all morning!" My busty, middle-aged secretary appears from around the corner, smacking me on the arm as she hurries by. Patti is plump and hyper, her face shiny and alive with an abundance of liquid make-up.

Swallowing against my tight throat, I force myself to sound human. "I'm caught up now. And hey, there's no coffee!" I call after her, holding up my cup, a painful smile cracking my heavy-feeling face.

"Tough titties. Now get a move on." She turns midstride and gives me a wink, fingering her oversized turquoise necklace as she makes her way back out to the front desk. Sighing once again, I toss the cup from my dawn trip to the local coffeehouse and approach an examining-room door. I pull down the chart and flip through it, going through the motions of my everyday routine, trying desperately not to think about life, about love, about her. With a little relief, I relax, recognizing the patient as one of my snowbirds. The winter months bring me hundreds of senior citizens, all of them desperate to escape the cold, brutal weather of their home states.

I open the door with a smile, determined to do my job the best I know how.

"Frank, good to see you." I cross the small room and take his hand warmly in mine, noting its roughness from years of hard labor outdoors.

"So how's Bangor?"

"That's Bang-or," he corrects as I approach. "Not Bang-er. If you say it like that, people will know you're from away."

"Away?"

"Yeah, you know. Not a Mainer."

"Oh." I smile and fold my arms over my chest. "Well, when I visit you one of these summers, I'll keep that in mind." My smile slowly

ACHE

fades as I think of vacationing alone. Again the dark loneliness spreads through me, chilling me. As if Frank can feel the cold deadness seeping from within me, he squirms a little on the examining table, crinkling the stiff white paper underneath him. He studies me in silence, his face ashen, his hands nervous. Not wanting him to remain uncomfortable, I speak, my voice heavy and thick with strain. "So tell me, Frank, what can I do for you?"

He clears his throat apprehensively and looks at the thick, weathered skin of his hands. "I, uh…well, it's hard to put into words, Doc." He speaks softly and slowly, his voice lacking confidence. I stand very still, shoving my hands down in my pockets as I nod my head, encouraging him to continue. He does so tentatively. "I'm a very private person, as you know. And…it's just, well, I've been having some trouble in the, you know, bedroom." The last word is merely a whisper and he glances up at me and then looks away again quickly.

Sensing his embarrassment and feeling great empathy for his situation, I stand and make a quick note in his chart. Then, with a warm smile, I turn and give him a friendly pat on the knee with his file. "Relax. I understand." He looks up at me through the heavy lenses of his eyeglasses.

"You do?"

"Sure. With all the patients I see, don't you think I've heard it all before?" I continue to smile at him while I run through the pertinent medical history and examine him for any physical causes that might affect his performance. Satisfied that his overall health is good, I reach in my back pocket and pull out my prescription pad.

"The Mrs. said you would understand." He rubs the back of his neck nervously. "She told me not to be afraid to ask you."

Scribbling quickly, I look up at him and tear off the small page, wishing that I too could mend my troubled intimate life with the pop of a pill. Feeling the weight of sadness bear down on me once again, I hand him the prescription, needing to keep moving to keep my mind clear. He takes it slowly, his brown eyes scanning the paper carefully.

"Give Doris my best." As I watch the elderly man disappear around the corner, I smile and shake my head. Another Viagra success story.

With my heart still heavy but refusing to stop pounding, I glance at my watch. It's almost lunchtime, but I have no appetite. I have to keep going, have to keep moving. Otherwise the pain and loneliness are worse, leaving me no other choice than to pine away for the one woman I cherish most in this world.

I approach the next room and stare at the empty shelf on the door. No chart. Huh. I sigh and turn the doorknob, thinking my medical assistant must have it to add more notes. The door creaks softly as I push it and walk in.

"Hi, Doc," she says to me from the high examination table. I sway instantly at the sound of her throaty voice, my eyes flying up to search her familiar face. I close the door quickly behind me and stand stiff as a board, completely baffled. My throat tightens, along with the muscles in my arms, as a rush of heat washes through me, pounding into my head. Katie stares at me with her wicked green-gold eyes, her luscious lips curving into a devilish grin. Already she recognizes the effect she has on me.

"Hi," I manage, a little breathless. She crosses her long legs under the white lab coat as she continues to watch me. I study her carefully, completely bewildered.

"That's my lab coat," I whisper, clueless with surprise. And yet I can't tear my eyes away from the soft, shiny flesh of her firm legs, and I wonder what else she is wearing.

"I know. I hope you don't mind, but I got a little chilly." She reaches up and lightly runs her hand across her neck, softly stroking just inside the collar of the coat. Her dark hair is pulled back from the strong angles of her face, and I feel my face flush as I realize how long it's been. Almost four weeks. Four weeks of darkness and despair, of unrelenting pain and unbearable loneliness. I'm unable to stop my gaze from traveling slowly up and down her incredible legs, and the heat of her presence reaches down to the tips of my fingers, which tingle with involuntary anticipation.

"I wasn't aware we had an appointment." I move over to lean on the counter, trying to sound cool and unaffected. I do not know why she is here, and I'm not about to act happy to see her. The pain has been too great, too devastating to my life. But she knows me well, and I watch her eyes take in the heated flesh of my cheeks.

"We didn't." Her eyes flash at me in a familiar flame of desire. "But I was feeling a little under the weather."

I fold my arms confidently over my chest, very much aware of the heavy pounding of my heart behind my breast. Katie is here in front of me after weeks of my tossing and turning alone in my bed, aching for her presence, crying out into the midnight blue of the cold night. I blink, focusing on her tall, lanky form, and I am overwhelmed at just how much I've missed her.

"You don't look well." Her eyes travel across my face, focusing on the dark circles under my eyes. "You look tired, and thin," she whispers, emotion crawling up her throat.

"I've missed you." My voice breaks, my soul crying out to her.

Her green eyes lock with mine. "I've missed you too. More than you know." We stare at each other in silence a moment as our words play out.

"So what brings you in?"

Her gaze leaves my eyes and travels down to my arms. She studies the slight bulge of my biceps under my polo shirt as she chews on her lip. She's always had a fondness for my physical strength, and I sway a little under her stare.

"As you know," she says, looking me completely up and down. "I've been away." As she speaks to me, she continues to stroke her own skin, slowly and deliberately, playing herself like an erotic instrument. I swallow hard and remain standing, my body stirred by her deep, sensual purrs. "And the whole time I've been gone, I've had this ache." Her fingers glide down the front of the lab coat, unfastening the buttons one at a time. "I was hoping you could help me with it." Slowly, she opens the white coat, teasing me with winks of the tanned flesh hidden just beneath it.

I clear my tightening throat and step away from the counter. Hot blood surges through me and I know why she is here. It's been weeks since I've seen her, since I've held her, since I've taken her. My heart hammers in my ears and the cluster of flesh between my legs fills with hungry blood. The rush of arousal is so great it nearly chokes me as I try to breathe. I've longed for her, ached for her, died for her, and no matter what I tell myself, I know there will be no stopping me from having her once again. Walking over to the door, I push in the lock, then approach her slowly. Her hand is inside the coat, circling the deep rose of her puckering nipple.

"Tell me," I say, standing before her, leaning in to inhale the sweet, alluring scent of her body lotion, "where is this ache?" A surge of white light rushes through me as her familiar scent invades me like the powerful stroke of an invisible, knowing hand. She laughs a little as she watches my eyes dilate and my body shudder with desire.

"Right here," she breathes huskily, opening the lab coat all the way, exposing her nude and gloriously beautiful body. She spreads her long legs and fingers the dark pink shaft of her core. I lick my lips and feel my eyes grow liquid and hazy as I watch her pull at herself. She's wet and slick and glistening and I can already imagine her warmth and heavy sweetness.

"It's so full, so ready. I need to come," she whispers, her green eyes glinting with mischievous shades of gold. "So bad." She sucks in a quick burst of air as her fingers delight in her folds, awakening her hunger.

"I think I can help you with that," I say, my eyes locked with hers. Sex has always been our strong suit, and she knows it would be impossible for me to say no, no matter what the circumstances. She was the greatest fuck of my life, and nothing will ever change that. Absence has only caused me to want her more.

"Can you, Doc?" she says breathlessly, her body tensing in response to her knowing fingers.

"Oh yes, I'm sure I can." Carefully I ease down in front of her, positioning myself on my knees. Her wet heat is directly in front of me and I inhale her deeply, my mouth watering at the anticipation of tasting her thick, rich honey. I push her hand away and she jerks involuntarily as my hot breath caresses her. Her hands find my hair, kneading and knotting, pulling me to her.

"I've missed you," she says, arousal thick on her voice.

My mouth finds her hot and juicy, engorged and ready for me. I moan deeply as I envelop her silky meat, pulling it firmly into my mouth, massaging it knowingly with my tongue. She arches her back as the lightning from my tongue branches up into her body. A strangled cry crawls from her throat, and she holds my head tight, thrusting herself deeper into me. "Take me," she rasps. "Fucking take all of me."

I groan at her words and suck her harder, holding her stiff clit firmly with my teeth. She jerks with gratitude and pulls my hair. My eyes water with the sweet pain of her pleasure, and I know she's desperately close to climax already. I look up at her as she roughly tugs my head away from her.

Her bottom lip is full and marked from her teeth, her cheeks flushed with wild desire.

"I want to come all over your face." The words are spoken deeply and demandingly, the pupils of her eyes wide and alive; she is determined to take what she needs. She pushes me away and climbs down off the table. I lick my numb lips and taste the slightest hint of blood. I've sucked her so hard, I'm not sure if it's mine or hers, but it stirs something deep and primal within me. She walks toward me like a hungry tigress, eyes flashing madly with want. She strips off the lab coat and throws it against the door, allowing me to take in her gorgeous lean body, so ready for the sensual assault that I know is about to ensue.

"Lie down," she demands, shoving me onto the table, forcing me to lie back. I comply readily and she crawls on top of me gracefully, moving slowly up my body. Her hot tongue finds my neck and licks long and slow up my chin to my lips, where she plunges deep inside me. She groans and claims me ravenously, sucking and biting my lower lip. My hands find her smooth, soft back and I run my nails up and down it, clawing and claiming. She groans again and pulls away, her eyes intense and hungry, ready to devour me.

"I can taste my come." She leans down and licks my chin again, tracing my lips with her agile tongue. "It tastes so good on your lips."

She moves again, this time bringing her warm body all the way up mine, straddling my face. She braces herself with her hands against the wall and eases her wet, meaty flesh down onto me. Her come is cool on her folds and I grab the tight spheres of her ass and warm her once again with my tongue. She twitches and dances atop me, riding my face with long, slow gyrations, coupled with quick, tense movements as the warm pleasure electrifies her. My hands move up to her hips as my tongue extends, slowly entering into her wet, tight walls. She cries out, her throat tight with strain, her eyes clenched shut.

"God, yes, baby, fuck me. Fuck me with your tongue." I plunge into her long and deep, shoving my knowing tongue as far up in her as I can. I feel her tensing around me, holding me tight within her. Her warm, silk honey flows all around me, running onto my chin. I moan and swallow her down, feeling her flow warm and smooth through me. She tastes so good, like water to a dry, parched mouth that is dying of thirst. I nearly cry as I take in her silk, relishing all that is her. I've missed her so much and I know now that I never want to let her go. I want her with me always, want her flowing down into my mouth every night, filling me with her warmth, her essence. I reach up and run my fingers lightly over her soft, damp skin, awakening her small breasts, raisining her nipples.

I watch her move rhythmically on me, her hands finding mine, leading them to her nipples. I take them roughly between my fingers, and the tight muscles of her abdomen tense and ripple in response. She sucks in more air and opens her eyes to look down on me. Her jaw is clenched as she moves, shoving herself harder upon me. She grunts as she watches me, her eyes ablaze with sheer arousal.

"I'm going to come now," she declares, her voice like rough sand. "I'm going to come all over you. All over your mouth." Her words are deep and strangled and deadly serious. She reaches out and braces herself on the wall. My tongue continues to plunge, while my lips suck the rest of her wet flesh. I moan my delight into her, making love to her with my mouth, creating the beautiful dance of her above me. She clenches her eyes and jerks hard, once, then twice. She groans heavily, gyrating herself harder, faster, deeper onto me. Her body tenses and shudders as the orgasm rocks through her, shattering her from the inside out. Her voice goes hoarse as her body slowly stills. She breathes deep and quick, her eyes slowly opening. Her soft body goes limp in my hands and she smiles weakly down at me, crawling carefully down my body where she rests on her belly on top of me. She runs a finger across my lips, taking me in with her lazy eyes.

"You, Doctor, have one incredibly talented mouth." I take her finger and lightly suck it, still hungry for her. She laughs and leans up to me, her lips a mere breath away. "Do you do that for all your patients?"

I lick my pleasantly bruised lips and smile weakly. "Only those that break my heart." She smiles in reflective silence and I sit up, needing to kiss her.

"Well I'll have to do that more often, then." She crawls from me and stands, and I gently trace the beautiful angle of her jaw as she steps into me. My mouth finds hers, warm, soft, welcoming. We kiss slowly, gently, our desire only slightly doused, still burning deep within. She pulls away from me with a sigh, her face relaxed, her cheeks brushed with color.

"You have to go, don't you?" she asks, referring to my other patients. Her hand fingers my cheek, tickling me with promise.

"Yes," I answer reluctantly. The darkness within is quickly vanishing, replaced by bright and warm light, awakening my spirit. I lick my lips and taste her come, letting it fuel me, feeding me with a desire for life.

She blinks slowly at me, her gaze wandering down to the crotch of my pants. Her hand presses into me, stroking me through the soft fabric of my chinos.

"You're hard."

"Mmm," I moan, my hips immediately thrusting against her hand. She unbuttons my pants and slips her hand in, maneuvering beneath my underwear to finger my slick center.

"And so wet." She bites her lip and inches closer to me, sliding her fingers up deep within me. The burning from her strokes spreads up through my belly, and I buck up against her, wanting her harder and deeper, needing her in my life so desperately. I close my eyes, so close to climax, her fingers curling up in me, pumping me like only she can.

"Yes," she purrs. "Ride my fingers." A knock sounds at the door and I convulse, choking out a sob as I clutch her wrist to me and come hard and quick.

"Doctor!" my secretary sounds.

"Give me a minute!" I manage to rasp out, my temples throbbing along with my clit. The room spins as Katie eases herself out of me with a soft chuckle.

"Mmm, at least I got a little taste of you." She opens her mouth and sucks me off her slick fingers. I shiver as the aftershocks of my orgasm wash through me. I lean in and kiss her once again, this time my taste fresh on her lips.

Lazily, I tuck in my shirt and button my pants, rubbing my face as I smile. I bend down and pick up my lab coat, the taste of her still potent and fresh on my mouth and chin.

"Don't take that," she says, walking over to me in worn jeans and a tight-fitting blouse. She grins impishly and takes the coat from my hands. "I want a follow-up appointment sometime and, well, I might want to wear it again."

I nod, my throat too tight to speak. She moves by me, brushing my cheek with her hand as she goes. With a slight smile, she opens the door and walks back out of my life. And as I try my best to gather my thoughts, my hand trembles once again as I massage my lips, desperate to feel her there all over again. I step back into the hallway where her scent lingers, and I wonder if I'll ever see her again. I move on to the next room and swallow hard, still feeling the warm silk of her sliding down into me. The cold darkness that had been eating away at me is momentarily stifled and I smile a little, knowing it was her doing, her choice. I grab the next chart and leaf through it as I think of her. Whether she's with me or not, one thing is for certain. There is no cure for the ache of wanting her. The ache will always be there.

STANDING ROOM ONLY
RADCLYFFE

Riding a train for twenty hours is not something I would ordinarily choose to do. In fact, my idea of traveling is a first-class seat on a nonstop flight with an Airfone and power source at every seat. Then, while a flight attendant silently and efficiently brings me endless cups of coffee and occasional sustenance, I can work on my computer. With my headphones on and a selection of instrumentals on my iPod creating a false but comforting sense of isolation, I can lose myself for hours.

That had been my intention until ten hours ago, when the arrival of an unexpected and decidedly unseasonable blizzard in the Ohio Valley grounded every flight going in and out of anywhere for five hundred miles in every direction. To make matters worse, it was already late on Friday afternoon of the holiday weekend when the word came that all flights were canceled, and I couldn't get another one for at least forty-eight hours. By then, the holiday would have passed.

So there I was, along with a hundred other people, sandwiched into an Amtrak coach car designed to hold two-thirds that number. It was hot, everyone was cranky, and worst of all, I couldn't use my computer because I didn't have a seat. Hell is a day without Internet access. God only knew what decisions were being made in my absence, what critical discussions going on without benefit of my experience, what formative plans being instituted without my input. I smiled at my own sense of self-importance, knowing that my silence undoubtedly echoed loudest in my own ears.

"If you can find something to smile about today," a molasses-thick voice drawled, "you simply must share."

I looked down upon a visage worthy of El Greco—eyes dark as midnight, skin the color of sun-bleached desert sand, vermilion lips full and moist. Her face as she looked up at me was level with the buttons on my 501s. And about two inches away. I had the instant urge to take a step back, but I couldn't. Someone's elbow was firmly planted in the middle of my back, and from the feel of the people leaning into me on either side, I was providing a convenient resting post for more than one. I actually heard a soft snore just behind my left ear.

"Laugh or cry," I said, trying for a shrug but barely managing a twitch. "And right now, *my* day is looking a whole lot better."

She smiled, a knowing smile, and shook her head as if to say my lack of subtlety was more amusing than offensive. I was glad for that, because the movement made her shoulder-length, wavy black hair swing across my thighs, and I imagined I felt the subtle brush of silk on skin even through the coarse denim. For just an instant, I saw us naked on flawless white sheets, sunlight filtering through gauzy curtains, the air, heavy and still, shifting about us on a sultry breeze. Mediterranean heat, cerulean sky, sweat-slicked skin...

"What?" she asked.

"What?" I echoed inanely, the sensation of her fingertips trailing down my abdomen so acute I shuddered.

"You said something."

I started to deny it, but she went on, "It sounded like you said *beautiful*."

In that instant, the conductor turned the lights down in the train car, low enough for the comfort of those who could manage to sleep, but still providing enough illumination so those who needed to move around could do so without stepping on unsuspecting fellow travelers.

It made no difference that her face flickered in and out of the shadows cast by the moonlight or that the spotty illumination from occasional buildings as we streaked past gave me only glimpses of her eyes, shining brighter than the dim lighting allowed. The image of us together was crystal clear. I could feel her naked limbs, lithe and supple, twining around me. Her dusk-tipped breasts, high and firm, just kissed mine as she curved above me, thighs straddling my waist. A tiny rivulet of clean sweet sweat trickled down the center of her abdomen to disappear into the secrets hidden between her thighs. I shook my head.

"If I said *beautiful*, it was an understatement."

With a self-deprecating laugh, she disagreed. "I can't imagine what you see that makes you say that."

"If I told you, you'd think me forward."

"I doubt that. You seem quite appropriate to me."

I couldn't prevent my voice from deepening, because my throat had suddenly gone thick and dry. "Then I know you're not reading my mind."

A blush does wondrous things to skin the color of hers. It glows, more than darkens, and invites a touch. My right hand was less than an inch from her cheek. As the train rounded a curve with the screech of metal on metal, my hip caught the edge of her seat, and I stumbled. As I struggled to maintain my footing in the unforgiving space, further unbalancing myself, I reached out automatically for an anchor. I felt first heat, then incredible softness, then the whisper of wings fluttering across my skin. Was that the brush of lips across my palm? My hand landed on her seat back, just behind her head.

"Careful," she murmured, placing her hand on the center of my thigh to steady me.

Long fingers, slender but strong. Like her. She fanned her hand slowly back and forth across my leg, slow small strokes that might have been only the movement of the train transmitted through her body. I could feel each fingertip, round firm points of pleasure. The heat seared my skin, and I shivered. How could fire burn like ice?

"Why don't we switch places?" she said from far away, her voice barely penetrating the roaring in my head. "You can't stand for the next ten hours."

"I'm okay," I croaked, sounding anything but. The muscles in my leg quivered uncontrollably, and she rubbed her hand in a small circle in response.

"What makes you think a girl like me wouldn't want to be chivalrous?" She smiled as she chided me, and her words sent the shiver coursing along my spine. This time it wasn't cool, but scorching.

Her hand remained on my leg, her eyes on mine. Her lips, still curved in gentle reprimand, were parted ever so slightly, and moisture glistened on their velvet surface.

"What makes you think a girl like me wouldn't want to be rescued?" I hoped I sounded steadier than I felt.

Her gaze took me in from head to toe, and I saw myself as she must. Brown hair just long enough not to be thought short, tousled from too many frustrated hand-thrusts throughout the course of an endless day; rumpled white shirt; frayed jeans; a black leather coat that swung at midthigh; and scuffed, heavy-soled black boots. Not exactly your picture of a damsel in distress.

She arched one elegant brow, silently mocking. I laughed, and so did she.

"All right. Point taken," I conceded.

Then, in a move that caught me completely off guard, she abruptly stood in the narrow space between her seat and the one in front of it. She angled to face me as she came upright, and her breasts brushed over my stomach and then nestled quite naturally against mine. Her mouth was kissing close as she steadied herself with a hand against my shoulder.

"We can both stand," she murmured, "or you can sit down for a while."

Without thinking, I braced my right hand on the top of the seat she had just vacated and slid my left beneath her silk blazer to rest on the curve of her hip. Her pelvis rocked gently against mine, and we swayed body-to-body in time with the motion of the train as it glided along the tracks into the night. Those who surrounded us paid no attention, lulled by the rhythm of the rails and dulled by the fatigue and frustration of the day.

"I'd rather stand all night," I whispered, my breath lifting the strands of hair that clung to her cheek, "than give up being this close to you."

"What I'm planning won't take all night."

She hooked her fingers inside the waistband of my jeans, nudging my shirt aside until the backs of her fingers brushed my skin. The muscles in my stomach jumped, and she made a sound in her throat that reminded me of purring. In a move so subtle it barely registered at first, she flicked the top button of my fly open with her thumb. It wasn't until the second was loosed that I realized what she'd done. The shock was followed by an instant flood of desire, and I knew that if she reached the third she would feel the evidence of my arousal on her fingers.

"What are you doing?" I groaned softly, my lips against her ear.

She turned her head and pressed a kiss along my jaw. "*You* know."

"What about...?" Helplessly I tilted my head toward the dark forms around us.

"We're safe," she whispered. "I'm watching."

She turned her palm to cup me and dipped her fingers inside my jeans. I lurched forward with the sudden jolt of pleasure, but she braced herself and stopped my fall. I clutched the seat in front of us with my left hand, both arms stiff and trembling as she slowly, carefully, explored. My thighs fused to hers, rigid columns threatening to crack under the strain of my arousal. Her fingertips found the stiff core of my need and she deftly strummed my straining clitoris to the point of explosion. The coiling tension rose and fell in the pit of my stomach with each stroke of her hand, my orgasm gathering with each pulse of the engines pulling us through the dark.

The surface of my skin tingled and my vision wavered. I mouthed the words but no sound escaped.

You're going to make me come.

Her eyes were fierce, riveted to mine, and I saw my pleasure reflected in her face. The corner of her mouth lifted into a satisfied smile when I tilted my hips to take her further inside, muscles clenching spasmodically with each wave of sensation—one following upon the other, coming fast, faster. The clatter of steel on steel, the rush of flesh to flesh, the thunder of machine and magic in my blood drove me over. I don't know when I stopped breathing, or when I uttered the first helpless cry, but she curled the long fingers of her free hand around my neck and drew my face against her shoulder, muffling the paean of my release.

Other than turning my face to her shoulder, I had not moved, despite the bone-melting force of my climax. We were as alone as any two lovers in that instant of consummation, and she was all I knew.

My breath returned as the pulsations gently ebbed and she withdrew on a sigh. I was shaking, my legs too weak to hold me. Gracefully, she pivoted, sliding an arm around my waist and guiding me down into the seat she had vacated. With her arm outstretched along the headrest, she leaned down and spoke so that only I could hear.

"This is one time I really don't mind standing. When you catch your breath, I'll be waiting."

She straightened, and I rested my cheek against her thigh, eternally grateful for the unexpected snow, the last train from Baltimore, and standing room only.

THE CONTROL ROOM
SHERRY MICHAELS

We walk for what seems like hours through a maze of tunnels, the sunlight left farther behind with each corridor that leads us deeper into the cavernous building. Door after door requires a card-key or passcode for entry.

"Are you sure I'm supposed to be here with you?" you ask nervously, as if thinking this must surely be a top-secret location.

Laughing, I respond, "Don't worry, Jay. It's all right. I've got the weekend graveyard shift, and no one will be here. Even if someone shows up, it'll take at least forty-five minutes to get down to where we're going."

I take your hand and lead you through one more door, this time using an old-fashioned handle to gain entry. A rush of cool air brushes our skin as the heavy steel door swings open, revealing its hidden treasures. You stand in awe as you take in the scene—row after row of monitors light up the darkness, tiny LEDs blinking here and there, and a quiet hum of energy pulses throughout the room. An eerie green glow casts its shadow on the walls. As our eyes adjust to the light, a couple of desks, filing cabinets, and two beds over in the corner come into focus.

"This is amazing! I can't believe…"

Finally grasping the situation, you turn to me with a glint in your eye. "So, Missy," you ask, flashing that lopsided grin I know so well, "are you sure we're alone down here?"

"Yes, darlin', we are very alone. There is nobody on this floor, and once this room is occupied, nobody else can enter without a confirm code from the person or persons inside, which happens to be me."

I know your mischievous mind and I see it begin to work as you grin even bigger.

"You mean, we're alone alone?"

"Yes, totally."

You sit on one of the bunks, gazing around the room, then sliding a sly look at me. "Are the beds comfortable, Miss?"

"Try it yourself."

You sit on the bed across from me, bouncing a bit, as though testing a mattress in a sleep-center showroom. I know full well what you're thinking. "Go ahead, lie down and get comfortable."

When you do, I move over to the bed across from you.

You ask, "Won't we get in trouble?"

"No," I tell you with a smile. "I'm the one in control of the room tonight, and as long as we straighten up the beds, no one will ever be the wiser if we…um…chat a bit—you on your bed, me on mine."

I sit on my bed, looking at you lying there on a bed in an underground, cold war–era bunker now housing state-of-the-art security systems, and think, *Nobody in the world could get in here unless I let them in.* "I have a meeting tonight at seven, so we have about three hours free."

You smile that devilish grin of yours and innocently say, "Hmm… I wonder how we shall spend it? What exactly do you have to…uh…*do* tonight, my dear?"

My heart twists. You are so beautiful, so vibrant, that look in your eye intensifying, yet softening at the same time. I've come to know that look so well, and yet each time it fills me with unquenchable desire.

With your smoldering gaze fixed on me, I realize my hand has strayed to the top of my shirt, slipping it open. Oblivious to our surroundings, I slowly unbutton my shirt and pull it from my skirt, letting it fall to the floor. Your eyes take in my body as I stand there in just my skirt and a bra. My hands find their way to the waistband. I undo the button inside and let the skirt fall to the floor. You swallow hard as you take in my small frame and generous breasts, covered only by my baby blue bra and matching panties. I love to watch you watch me, and teasingly, I place a hand on my breast and run my fingers over the smooth material of my bra. My nipple comes to life, making a very noticeable bump in the shiny fabric. Your eyes are dreamy, and I smile as I see your hand drift slowly to your lap. I know what my teasing is doing to you and it inflames my desire further.

Passing my hand over my breast again and tugging the nipple through the material, I move my other hand across my stomach, caressing as I go. Slowly stroking down to the panty line, fingernails dipping under the waistband, watching you follow my hand as it disappears ever so slowly into my panties. Your eyes widen, your tongue licks your lips, your hand twitches in your lap as you watch this dance I have started for you. I see your heartbeat in the side of your neck and your body tensing slightly as you watch me standing there before you, next to your bed, in my panties and bra.

I move my hand across my body to the top of my breast, and my fingertips find the lacy edge of my bra, inching ever so slowly inside. I smile as you become more and more flustered, your hand in your lap dipping slightly between your legs now. My hand is inside my panties, wrist disappearing as I reach down and inside, your eyes glancing from my panties to my bra and back again. I draw my hand out of my panties and raise my middle finger, glistening wet. I watch your breasts swell and move as you breathe deeply, so turned on from my obvious desire. With my other hand still caressing my nipple, I raise my fingers to my lips and taste myself with the tip of my tongue. You groan at the sight. I insert my finger into my mouth and pleasure in your body writhing there on the bed. "What's the matter, darlin'? Is there something you need?"

Your answer is in your eyes.

I lick and suck my finger slowly, savoring the saltiness of my desire, knowing exactly what my actions are doing to you. Your hand, between your legs, is groping and pushing; your other hand rubs the nipple under your shirt. Your eyes are glued on my slender, wet middle finger as it moves down my belly again, and when it once again disappears beneath the soft, baby blue material of my panties, I say, "You think I should share…?"

I look at you standing there, wearing nothing but your intimates, as you slide your hand down your panties once again. The throbbing inside me is almost unbearable and I feel the wetness spread—I want you so badly! I watch as your hand begins to move back and forth, subtly stroking, your nipples hardening so they look as if they're going to burst right out of your bra. A red flush begins between your breasts as you stroke, moving up your chest to your neck. I raise my gaze to your eyes, which are lowered, but still looking at me—knowing what you are doing to me—and your lips curl into a deliciously teasing smile.

I simply can't stand it anymore. I unbutton my own shirt as slowly and deliberately as you did, pausing to touch my breasts, stroking my nipples through the lace until they ache for release. I shrug off my shirt, leaving only my black lace bra. Then I start on my pants, unbuttoning and unzipping them, then lowering them enough to reveal matching black lace panties. I see your eyes widen.

"I wore them just for you, baby."

You are so surprised, the sensual stroking rhythm you had going stops, so I reach toward you and say, "Come here, beautiful—let me see if I can help you out a little."

I take your hand, draw you to me, and pull you down to lie next to me on the narrow bed. You grab hold and I feel your body shake—not from fear of falling, but in anticipation of what is to come. I pull you close, saying, "Better hang on, darlin'. I want to take you someplace you've never been before."

Then I take your hand, still wet and glistening from being inside you, and touch it to my lips, kissing each finger, inhaling your scent. Slowly, I envelop your fingers in my mouth, sucking and licking each one, lingering over your middle finger. When I finish, I lean close to you and brush your lips with mine, running my tongue around them, parting them to gently explore your full, luscious mouth. Our tongues meet and you taste yourself on me. And just as quickly as I have given you a taste, I pull back, covering your face with tender little kisses, sliding my lips down your neck, feeling your pulse race as each touch inflames you that much more.

Your hand is still in mine, and I ask you if you want to know what you are doing to me. You nod silently, eyes burning with anticipation. I slide my pants completely off and take your hand, first placing it on my breast, letting you feel the hardness of my nipples. Then I slide your hand down the curves of my body, feeling the heat rise as you touch me. With my hand on top of yours, I slip your hand inside my panties. As it continues in, I move mine over so you can feel the panties slide over the back of your hand, a feeling I know you love. I guide you farther, pressing your fingers up until I feel you touch my wetness. As hard as I try, I can't keep from shaking. My nipples harden even more. I close my eyes to the sensation and unconsciously move my hips back and forth. When I open my eyes, you are quivering, shaking with desire, and I take my hand and slide it into your panties, into your wetness... your most intimate place.

I gently squeeze your clit with my thumb and forefinger, and you gasp, responding with your own squeeze. I moan, feeling the fire in me burning out of control. I stroke you—your wetness all over my fingers, my hand—feeling the racing of your heart even there. You press against me again, willing my hand inside you, and I almost give in. I want you so, but I slow my hand, reaching to stop yours touching me as well.

"Baby, not yet...I have so much I want to do to you first."

With great difficulty, you slow your breathing, but your desire is plain. Still, you say, "As you wish, baby."

I turn toward you, claim your breast. I caress the outside, feeling the nipple under the fabric—but it's not enough. I lean over you, letting my lips suck your nipples through the fabric—but it's not enough. I want to *feel* you. I reach for your bra and with one snap, your breasts break free, nipples hard and beautiful. I lower my face to them, burying myself in your scent and warmth. Your hands are in my hair, stroking my neck, my back, your nails running across my skin until I have nothing but goose bumps standing up everywhere. I take your breast into my mouth, feeling the nipple harden as my wet tongue encircles it. At first, I suck gently, enjoying the feel of you swelling in my mouth. I hear you softly moan, and I know exactly what I am doing to you. As I suck your nipples, my left hand explores your body—moving across your belly, down your thigh, touching your inner thigh, teasing you with a soft stroke of my finger as it slides between your legs, through your wetness. Just as quickly, I move back up, stroking and pinching one breast as I suck the other. You start moving your hips to the rhythm of my sucking and touching, urging me on.

Taking your nipple between my teeth, I graze it, pulling harder with each pass. Your moans turn into gasps. I keep sucking and biting, a little harder each time, stroking you with my hand as I go, knowing I am driving you crazy. Your hand grabs mine and tries to lead it to the heat inside. I give in, sliding my hand between your legs, stroking you, circling your clit with my thumb, feeling your excitement grow as you moan more loudly. Rubbing back and forth in your wetness, I slide one finger inside, moving it in and out, slowly. You gasp. Then I slide it completely out.

When I slide two fingers in with the next motion, you whisper, "God, baby, you feel so good...please don't stop..."

I stroke slowly, feeling your excitement grow. I look at you, your eyelids lowered in passion, beseeching me to love you. "Miss, you are so beautiful...I love how you feel...how my hand feels inside you... how you respond to me...but it's not time..." And I slowly remove my hand. A cry of frustration escapes your lips as you reach toward me, imploring me to continue, but I resist.

"What's wrong, darlin'?" I say, mimicking your earlier words in that sweet Southern accent. "Is there somethin' you need?"

Fiercely, I pull your mouth to mine, filling you with a kiss that makes the fires burn even hotter. You return my kiss with an urgency I've never felt, a passion fueled by the love we started. Lost in our kiss, I don't notice that you have pushed me onto my back and moved on top of me. Our lips part slightly, and you gaze at me with a white-hot fire in your eyes. Cocking your head, you look down at me with a slight grin as you see my surprise at the turn of events.

"I think we've had enough *teasing* for the moment, don't you, darlin'?" Your hips begin to gently rock against me. "In fact, sweetheart, I'd say it's about time you learn exactly who is in control."

You pin my hands above my head, leaning down to kiss me. Our tongues embrace as your hips rock faster. I feel your wetness on my thigh and press my leg into you harder, hearing you gasp at the increased pressure. You release my hands and go straight to my core, sliding your fingers inside me, bringing a cry of pleasure from my lips. I move my hand inside you, furiously stroking your wetness, knowing you are moments from coming. Amidst the frenzy of touching, stroking, kissing, our cries fill the silent room.

"Oh, Jay, God don't stop...I'm almost there..."

"Damn, baby...I'm coming..."

The blaring sound of an alarm fills the air. I jerk my head up, frantically searching for the shutoff. I breathe in a sigh of relief as I hit the control panel and switch it off. Sheepishly, I glance around, realizing that I am still alone at my desk, the security board blinking normal as usual, and the racy pulp novel open to the last page I read... before falling asleep.

SITTING PRETTY
THERESE SZYMANSKI

C'mon, Kirsten," my roommate Julie said one brisk fall afternoon. "Jennifer, Jackie, Jillian, and I are going to the mall!"

I glanced at my watch and frowned. "God, Julie, I hate dissing you like this, but I really need to go to the libe and get this paper done."

She sat down next to me on our little dorm-room couch and put her hand on my thigh. "Oh, c'mon, you're acing all your classes as it is." She squeezed my knee. "'Sides, the new Leonardo DiCaprio flick is out. He is so hot!" She jumped up and looked at herself in the mirror. "Does this lipstick go with my blouse?"

I rolled my eyes. "Julie, you always look perfect." And she did. She was the captain of the cheerleaders in high school—and everything about her was perky and perfect—from her clothes to her makeup to her gestures and body. Everything about her was beautiful and...perfect. Especially her body...

She had incredible, firm breasts that had no need of a Wonderbra. Her legs were tanned and toned—even her thighs! And her tummy was flat without being overdeveloped. Her hair was long, wavy and blond, naturally, and her features were defined without losing their softness. And of course, in keeping with all this perfection, her eyes were green, the deep green of newly cut grass in spring.

"You know, you're never going to meet Mr. Right if you never go out," she said, turning to me.

"Jules, I went to the bar with you Thursday night, I went to the movies with you on Tuesday, I went to the mall and the frat party with you last weekend—I just need to work today, okay?"

"Well, if that's the way you're going to be... Think you'll be up for a slumber party tomorrow night?"

Just then Jennifer, Jackie, and Jillian came to the door.

"See you guys later!" I called cheerfully after them when they left.

❖

"Make yourself at home," Alex said from the kitchen.

I glanced around her studio apartment. Light filtered in through the large windows, casting a dreamlike quality to the simple furnishings, making it all seem even more like a fantasy than it was already.

I took a deep breath and made myself continue looking around the small space. A textbook-and-artbook-laden bookshelf stood against the same wall that held the entry door, with only a closet separating them. The kitchen, really a room in the upper corner of the studio, was hidden from view by swinging doors.

She was behind those doors, just out of my view.

The other side of the room had a couch and chair at one end, with a wooden folding chair between the two and a stand-up screen with a robe tossed over it at the far end of the couch. Several yards down the room was an easel with a canvas on it, situated next to a large table covered with paints, pencils, brushes, chalk, and charcoal, a palette, and various other artist's implements.

I took a deep gulp of air. I couldn't believe I was doing this. I was in a strange woman's apartment, about to take my clothes off.

Maybe I should just leave? Get away from here and not let anything happen. I could meet up with the gang at the mall, sit between gorgeous women drooling over Leonardo.

Well, that option wasn't the most appealing thought that had crossed my mind in the recent past.

I sat on the couch, demurely crossing my legs, and pulled the hem of my miniskirt down, as if it could actually go any lower. I pulled out my compact and ran my fingers back through my mousy brown hair, wishing yet again that I were blond and thinking about bleaching it.

What would be the point? I'd still be plain. I'd still have the same nondescript features and the same okay-but-bland body.

I'd still be me.

Regardless, I'd never have the guts to do it anyway. Granted, it wouldn't be a permanent thing, like a nose job or tattoo or anything, but… I still couldn't do it. I couldn't be anything but what I was.

Maybe that was why I was here—I was simply trying to run away from myself—be someone I wasn't.

But I knew exactly what it would feel like to be naked in front of this ever-so-sexy woman. How it would feel to do a slow striptease for her, shedding each article of my clothing till I was down to just my bra and panties, and then…and then I'd take them off…revealing myself to her. Showing Alex how hard my nipples got for her…

Even the thought made me wet.

Down a bit from where I sat were a number of canvases, but I couldn't help noticing the bed against the far wall, right out in the open. Talk about teasing. How could she have something so significant right out in the open?

I had a quick vision of Alex's mouth and beautiful hands on my naked body.

My knees were weak. My legs could barely withstand my weight…

"Can I get you anything?" Alex asked from the kitchen, all too suddenly, abruptly pulling me back to reality.

"A…A glass of water would be great," I replied, suddenly noticing the dryness in my throat. I turned from the bed to start looking through the canvases against the wall. I couldn't look at her because I knew I was bright red.

I studied the canvases. They were good, very good. And mostly nudes. Both male and female. And I knew I had fallen out of the frying pan and into the fire.

I recognized Alissa among the stack. She was with me when Alex approached me at the coffeehouse about modeling for her.

"Don't worry," Alissa told me when we sat down to enjoy our lattes, "she's really good, makes you feel really comfortable, and doesn't try any funny stuff."

"'Funny stuff'?" I repeated, unable to find any words of my own as I stared across the crowded room at the lean figure debating some point with a mixed group of people I just knew were writers and artists.

"Yeah, you know what I mean," Alissa said, leaning back and sipping her drink. "Some of these so-called art students figure it's a good way to get people to take off their clothes for them. As if I'm gonna have sex with some jerk just because I took my clothes off for him!" Alissa and several of her friends modeled for a wide range of people and classes—because, they said, it was the quickest and easiest way to make money. Almost as good as stripping or topless dancing.

"Well, I know I couldn't model for a guy," I said, feeling a tingling between my legs at the very thought. I knew that just below Alex's too-large clothing was a firm body with nice, soft curves. My eyes trailed over her breasts as she turned away from her group to meet my eyes. I wondered if she was getting as turned on as I.

I could melt into her green eyes, but instead I flushed, wondering if she would follow through on the look she was giving me.

Alissa laughed. "I don't know for sure which way she goes, but I do know both men and women who've posed for her, and nobody's had any problems." She tilted her head to follow my gaze across the room. "I really think she's a dyke, though. Not that it matters to me—to each her own."

After Alissa left, when Alex came over on her way out to reaffirm her invitation to pose for her, I figured it would be the easiest hundred bucks I ever earned, and took her up on her proposal.

After all, sometimes long shots do pay off.

"She was a great model," Alex said, walking up beside me and handing me a glass of water. She had a cup of coffee. She took the painting from me, pulling it out of the stack, as if I looked at naked women every day of the week.

"She has a very nice figure and posed quite naturally, but I didn't quite do justice to her eyes." She put down the canvas and flipped through others till she came across one of a beautifully sculpted, well-hung man. "Now, I got his eyes right, but I had a bit of a problem with the shadows and skin tone." We both studied the painting for a moment. The man had well-defined features, a broad chest covered with a thick mat of curly, black hair, thick legs, dark chocolate skin, and a thick, long penis that would've made any horse proud.

If I had questioned where my interests lay, this should've answered them—the painting did nothing for me.

I don't know if it was Alex's nearness, the musky smell of her skin, or the pictures of naked women so casually displayed in front of me, but I knew I wanted to feel Alex inside of me. I wanted to taste her, and for her to taste me. I wanted everything, I wanted to go all the way for the first time in my life, and I wanted it so badly I wanted her to take me down, right there and then.

She put the painting back down and turned toward me. "We should get started. You can change behind here," she said, indicating the screen, "and put on that robe."

She turned and walked toward her easel with its fresh, clean canvas.

She turned away from me, telling me only that she wanted me to get naked.

I walked nonchalantly behind the screen. Or at least, I tried to walk nonchalantly behind it. At least I didn't trip.

I took off my shoes, unzipped my skirt, stepped out of it, and unbuttoned my green silk blouse and dropped it onto the floor.

I tried to focus on the chill I was suddenly feeling, hoping it would calm me. Distract me.

I reached behind me, undid my bra, and let it drop to the floor. I slowly caressed my breasts, imaging what Alex's touch would feel like. My breath quickened as I squeezed my nipples.

Then I realized that I didn't want her to think I was so turned on, but nonetheless, I couldn't calm myself. I stepped out of my lacy white underwear.

I tried to forget that a gorgeous woman was just beyond the screen and that I was completely naked. I tried to focus on neatly folding my clothes and placing them in a pile on the floor. Everything had to be perfect. I breathed deeply, trying to focus my center, trying to make myself calm down...

"You ready?" Her voice came over the screen like...like the voice-over on a commercial. A used-car commercial.

I reached up, grabbed the robe, put it on, and walked out from behind the screen.

She looked at me. Her thick, black hair fell behind her like a mane, and her white, collarless shirt was open enough to reveal the tops of her luscious breasts. She had the sleeves rolled up, revealing her muscular forearms, and I suddenly realized that she must work out.

The glasses perched on her nose, covering up her expressive green eyes, were the finishing touch on her sweet and innocent look. She looked like an ingenue. Well, she did except for the tight jeans that showed off her nice, firmly rounded ass.

"Good. Very good," she said, giving me a quick once-over. "Now, take off the robe and make yourself comfortable." She indicated the areas in which I could make myself comfortable—the couch, chair, or floor. "You can sit or lie, just realize you'll have to keep the pose for a while."

The black man in the portrait had sat on the overstuffed chair, confidently spreading himself out. I couldn't pose the same way a man had. I also didn't want to have to worry about how self-consciously I could stand.

I also could only think of the more classic nudes I'd seen of late, like Alissa's.

I turned away from Alex, dropped the robe, giving her a nice view of my butt, the only part of me that I really liked, then sat on the couch. I desperately wanted to cover myself up, but still managed to lean slightly back against the pillows, then bring my legs up onto the couch, relaxed, but still somewhat self-conscious. I laid one arm along the back of the couch and the other hand on my thigh.

I was glad I was sitting upright, because then my breasts didn't flatten out against me; instead they appeared somewhat perky.

The air still caressed my private parts, and heat started coursing through me.

"Good, I like that. Except… Can you bring yourself a little more my way?"

I inched my hips forward a bit, looking to her for guidance.

She smiled. "No, move your hips back and open yourself up a bit. Don't be self-conscious. Know how sexy you look."

This direct reference sent energy running through me. Her gaze sent electricity through me. I knew she was watching me.

I wanted to blush, or cover myself, and I hoped she couldn't see how turned on I was getting.

"Just relax," Alex said. I heard the scratch of pencil on paper. "Breathe normally and forget I'm here."

She was trying to calm me, relax me, with her soothing tones, but she did the opposite. Her words proved that she was seeing me, seeing me as a woman, a woman who could be taken advantage of.

I tried to relax and think about other things. I tried to leave my body behind, ignoring all of the electricity that was pulsing through me, but my eyes kept wandering back to her. I studied the length of her fingers, imagining what they would feel like inside of me. I noticed the sure way she moved, comfortable with her body, and then thought about what her skin would feel like against me.

I just knew her body would be muscular, yet soft. That she would have curves my fingers would love, yet she would be sure of herself in bed. She would take what she wanted. I wanted her to take me and make me scream.

I had never even gone all the way with any guy I'd known. I'd let them feel me up occasionally, and kissed more than a few in my day, but it had never felt quite right, I had never been really tempted to let them do what they wanted to with me.

But with Alex, I wanted her to take me out of my mind. I wanted her to do *whatever* she wanted to with me. I wanted her to use and control me.

I didn't notice the passage of time, but I did suddenly realize just how wet I was. I was so ready for her, I'd come if she just touched me. Just the thought of her touching me, stroking me, sucking me, licking me...

I looked over to watch her and the way she would look at me, then move her brush over the canvas. The hours had already ticked away. I hadn't even noticed when she moved from pencil, or whatever, to brush and paint.

I suddenly hoped she could see how wet I was. I opened my legs just a little bit more, hoping she could notice how turned on I was. I felt as if I could come. If she only just touched me I knew I'd have a screaming orgasm.

For hours I had been getting wet and ready, feeling my nakedness throughout me—and she had just been watching. A voyeur beyond belief. She was watching and enjoying it, I was sure.

She'd look up at me, then use her brush on her canvas, occasionally licking her lips. I wanted that tongue on my clit.

I was exposed to her artist's eyes, and she was enjoying it. I opened my thighs up a bit more, under the excuse of stretching. I left myself open, allowing her to see my swollen lips.

I thought about touching myself, about squeezing my nipples, stroking my clit, dipping my fingers inside of myself. I wondered if doing so would drive her into action, would make her come over and take me.

I wondered if she'd like to see me masturbate, see me touch myself intimately.

The thought of touching myself in front of another person made me begin to involuntarily arch. I wasn't sure if she had seen it. But I was so turned on I could feel the ache in my abdomen, I could feel it in my stomach.

I didn't want to come while she watched. Maybe in the future it'd be fun, but not for today. I wanted her to make me come.

Her eyes again lifted to look me over, studying every detail of my naked body. My hips surged upward, ever so slightly, and I knew I would go crazy waiting for her.

I stood and walked over so I was behind her, staring at the canvas.

"You're a very good model," she said. "Very relaxed and natural." Her eyes stayed on the canvas, her fingers around the brush. I wanted those fingers deep inside of me.

I put my hand on her shoulder. "I've never done this before." She continued to move her brush, apparently oblivious to me. Her arm moved like a well-oiled machine, and I could sense the strength in her arms. "It turns me on to have you see me. To have you watching me." My voice was thick in my throat.

"A lot of first timers discover that to be seen by another is sexually enticing," she said nonchalantly. Or apparently nonchalantly.

I moved up behind her, putting my other hand on her other shoulder. My naked body pressed against her back. Her clothes rubbed abrasively, sensuously, against me. Her ass pressed against my cunt.

"No," I corrected. "Having *you* see me is what does it."

Her brush paused. I went for it.

I placed her hand on my hip, rubbing it up and down my naked flesh. I breathed deeply when flesh met flesh. "No. This is for you." I put her fingertips into my wetness.

A tremor went through her body.

I dropped my other hand down to the open collar of her shirt, running it inside over her collarbone, then dropping it further to caress her hardened nipple, unrestrained by a bra.

Her breathing started to match my own. I started unbuttoning her shirt. "It's such a turn-on to be naked while you're still fully clothed."

She yanked off her glasses and quickly turned toward me. "Then let's leave it like that for now."

Before I knew what was happening, the brush was dropping to the floor and her hand was cupping my cunt, sliding through my wetness.

"God, you are *so* wet."

She ran her hands over my naked body, caressing my breasts, squeezing my hardened nipples, then grabbing me tight and pulling me hard against her. Her mouth found my tits, and then her teeth were caressing, sucking, and biting my nipples. I arched against her leg, which was now between mine, and it was as if I was riding her hard thigh.

She dropped to her knees, then grabbed my ass and pulled me into her mouth. Her tongue explored my clit, collecting my wetness and making me even wetter. Her tongue darted up inside of me, and then she flicked it back and forth over the hardened apex that rode over my swollen lips. My hands found the back of her head, guiding her, directing her, holding her tight against me as her tongue worked me over. She moved her hand from my ass to between my legs, gradually penetrating me, first with one finger, then another. She slid into me, and I accepted and urged her on, even as my legs buckled beneath me.

I fell to the floor, but her strong arms caught me, then lowered me the rest of the way, her tongue never stopping its exploration of my most intimate places, places no one else had ever been before.

She was inside of me, and I rode her fingers, arching up and down to guide her, my body knowing exactly what I needed.

She kept on top of me, even as I bucked and twisted and turned...

The world was melting in on itself, and I could feel the orgasm gathering as I reached the brink...it worked its way up my legs and down my torso. I felt it in my stomach and thighs, a creeping fire building within me.

She held on to me, staying with me, her tongue beating its pattern across my clit, her long fingers deep inside of me, touching me everywhere... Then it hit...

...and...

"God, oh God"—her mouth felt so good—"Alex! Oh Alex!" I was exploding...

"Come for me, baby!"

"God..."

Her fingers, her tongue didn't stop. She rode me relentlessly, pushing me on and on…

"God…"

And further still…

"Oh my fucking God!"

I came into her mouth, and she licked up all of my wetness, not wanting one drop to escape, and she kept going, making me come again and again…

I lay, naked, with her, fully clothed, lying between my legs, which were still spread wide, with her head on my thigh, her breath warm on my cunt.

I felt both exposed and powerful. I buried my hands in her thick dark hair, urging her to move up my body, to lie with her head on my breast, holding me.

"Oh, baby, I know you're gonna be ready for more. You gotta be," she coaxed.

I felt myself arching yet again under her soft caress, turning me on yet again. She blew softly on my wetness, and to my sensitized body it was torture, but with her gentle ministrations, it became heaven. I stretched out, wanting her hands on me again. I opened up for her, letting her examine everything. I wanted her to know me, intimately. I wanted her everywhere, touching every part of me.

We kissed. Long and hard. She fucked my mouth with her tongue, hard.

I rolled her over onto her back, wedging my leg between hers, pumping it against her crotch.

I enjoyed the way she arched against me when I held her arms out above her head on the ground.

"You're not gettin' off so easy," I said, using one hand to hold both of hers down. With my other hand I ripped open her shirt, exposing her beautifully full, pert breasts.

"I like silk," I said, caressing the shirt just before I tore it off her body.

I reached down to grab her crotch through the coarse denim of her tight jeans, then pulled down the zipper and reached into her panties to finger her hot, wet cunt.

Her lips were swollen and she was so wet she was practically dripping. My fingers slid in and out of her easily. I wanted to taste her, feel her juices on my face and tongue.

I yanked her jeans and underwear down and off her, leaving no question as to what I wanted. I sat up on my haunches and looked down at her beautiful body, liking the contrast of the dark triangle of hair between her legs with the paleness of her skin.

I reached down and opened her lips, examining her in the light, looking at every inch of her.

She squirmed under my gaze, gradually arching, wanting my touch on her.

I reached to touch her plush breasts, enjoying the softness of them as compared with the hardness of her nipples. Then I began to softly caress her entire body, running my hands over her skin, enjoying her softness and the effect my touch had on her.

I loved making her wiggle and squirm. She had made me do so for far too long.

I reached between her legs and opened her lips, then I lay on my stomach and gently began licking her.

I loved the power of it. I loved the effect my tongue had on her—I loved making her arch up and cry out. I pressed against her, burying my face between her thighs, burying my face against her, in her wetness.

I thought about what I liked, I noticed what she liked, and I kept doing it—first running my tongue up and down her, imagining how it would feel against me, then flicking her hardened clit back and forth, gaining power and confidence as she arched and squirmed.

I brought my fingers up to touch her hole, teasing her, but I wouldn't give her what she wanted. She groaned her protest when I didn't enter her, when I didn't give her what she was aching for.

"Don't worry, I'm gonna fuck your brains out." I shoved three fingers harshly into her, my other hand squeezing her nipples, hard. Pinching them. Pulling at them. While my tongue beat against her and my fingers plunged in and out of her.

Her squirming and moaning told me she was enjoying every moment of it.

As I was.

I loved the control I had over her, and I loved her taste, and silkiness. The smell of our sex danced around us in an erotic swirl as I gained momentum, fucking her hard.

Her hands were in my hair, pulling and tugging at me as she increased momentum, as I took her further and further. She alternated between harshly yanking my hair, then gently smoothing it down, playing with it like silk.

I loved being inside of her, I loved the way she bucked me, the way she began throwing me across the floor—but I held on to her, not wanting to lose a moment of her incredible orgasm.

I was beating her like a plow horse, and I knew I couldn't stand it much longer...but I had to keep it going, had to keep it up, doing her, being inside of her, taking her...

I wanted her to remember me.

"Fuck me, Kirsten!"

And then I fucked her. Hard. I rode her like a bronco, like a new-bred, thrusting in and out, my whole hand sliding up into her, being consumed by her, and then I began pulling it out, pushing it in, all the while feeling her body against mine, feeling myself inside of her, consumed by her. I shoved, pushed and pulled...taking her all the way...

"Kirsten!"

I held on to her while she tossed me across the floor.

When she finally released me, I could think of nothing except that my blond roomie and her friends had no idea what they were missing.

Roll Number Five
Jessica Casavant

W ho do I have this morning?" Cassie asked as she walked into the recording studio.

"Big film from Raincoast Films. Big. I mean one of our biggest."

Having picked up on his nervousness, Cassie gave the studio manager a thoughtful stare. "Daniel, it's not the first film I've ever worked on."

"I know. I know. It's just, well, the producers requested you."

Cassie was only half listening. Producers often requested people they had worked with before. It was all part of building relationships in the industry, so you could work with people you were comfortable with.

"I didn't know until now that the talent was also one of the producers," he added.

That was when Cassie finally started to pay attention to what he was saying. Attention to his body language, to the worried look on his face. She frowned at him, instinctively knowing what had caused his consternation, but not wanting to believe it. Before she could form her questions, before the dread had a chance to rise, the door opened and her past walked in.

Life sure had a way of turning everything on its head. One step, and the woman who had haunted her for years stood in the studio smiling as if their past didn't exist.

"Hello, Cassie."

Cassie's eyes shifted to the attractive blonde who had so devastated her years before, when she'd left abruptly, without explanation, after the shoot for her last film was done. After everything... "Hello, Sarah."

Daniel looked at them both and smiled. "Miss Houston, welcome back to Toronto."

"Miss Houston? Daniel, since when are we so formal? It's Sarah."

"Yes, of course. Sarah." He rubbed his hands together. "Well, I should leave you two to get started." He avoided Cassie's stare and hurried away.

Cassie turned back to Sarah. "It's been a long time." She was pleased that her voice was so calm.

Sarah smiled. "Yes, it has. You're looking good."

"You too." The polite conversation felt absurd. Cassie shifted her weight to look down at the scripts, needing time to clear her head. *Focus on the job at hand.* She fought the urge to either hurt her or kiss her. Over the years she had avoided watching any films that Sarah starred in, not wanting to remember what she looked like, sounded like, felt like. Now, standing so close to her, Cassie felt her senses rip into overdrive. On screen Sarah always came across somewhat cool, remote almost. In person she was infinitely more beautiful, and Cassie remembered only too well the passion that burned under the cool façade.

"I hope this won't be too uncomfortable," Sarah said. "But when we decided to do the postproduction in Toronto, I knew I only wanted you."

Their eyes met and Cassie forced herself not to look for meaning between the lines. She nodded, then turned her attention back to the script. "Let's take a look at what needs to be done." Without another word, she led the way to Studio A at the back of the building. She was aware of Sarah walking behind her. The sheer electricity of her presence had goose bumps rising along her skin. She paused in the doorway of the studio to let her eyes adjust to the dim room. As she reached out to find the light panel, Sarah caught her hand.

"Leave it, please. You know how I like to work in the dark."

Jesus. Cassie swallowed, fighting against remembered images that instantly resurfaced. "Sarah…"

"What?"

Cassie stepped back from the dangerous edge. "Nothing." She flipped through the marked script, reading quickly, getting a feel for how the session should be organized. "Why don't we start with the top of scene four? It's a telephone conversation, so that should ease us into the scene." She looked up and her heart gave a jolt when her eyes met Sarah's. As the look held, Cassie felt the needs building, experienced the now-familiar tug-of-war between intellect and emotion. She felt the wetness pooling between her legs and the pounding in her clit. The battle seemed longer this time, with the result less certain. By the time her reason took control again, she was shaken and weak—just as if Sarah's mouth had been on hers.

Be very careful, Cassie warned herself, wrenching her gaze away. She strode to the console on legs that weren't as steady as she would have liked and pressed down on the intercom.

"Put up roll number five, please. Thanks." She turned and glanced over at Sarah, who was reading her lines. "We'll be ready in about ten minutes. Would you like a glass of water or something?"

Sarah's eyes met hers briefly, but Cassie couldn't read them. Was there a question in them? She wondered. What was she asking her?

Something not quite defined crossed Sarah's face, then she looked back at her script. "No, I'm fine," she replied softly.

Cassie studied the bent head for a moment. In that moment, she remembered why she had been so drawn to her in the first place. That mixture of vulnerability and coolness made Cassie want to peel away at the layers to get to her core.

Instinctively, Cassie placed a hand on Sarah's shoulder. When the muscles there tightened, she increased her grip and gathered Sarah close. Wordlessly, Cassie lowered her head until their lips met. This had nothing to do with the other kisses they had once shared. It might have been the first. Sarah's mouth was so soft. *And careful,* Cassie thought dimly. Careful, as though Sarah wasn't so sure of herself. When Cassie drew away, they stared at each other, each as perplexed as the other.

"What was that for?" Sarah managed after a moment.

Cassie shook her head. "I'm not sure," she murmured. "I'm still angry with you. And yet I look at you and all I want is to feel your skin, hear you come again." Shaken, she took a step back.

Sarah stared at her. "I want to be with you again. I've been thinking about it since leaving L.A."

Jesus. Jesus. Cassie bit back a groan as her clit swelled. "I can't do this again." She didn't realize she had spoken the words out loud until she felt Sarah's hand touch her face.

"What if I promise that it will be different this time? You scared me before. The way you made me feel…" Sarah shrugged, helpless now under the weight of her desire.

"What's so different now?"

"I'm only afraid of *not* feeling like that again."

Cassie felt desire pounding in her, demanding freedom. She shook her head once, as if to deny it, but the need pulsing through her was too great. Surrendering to all the needs raging inside her, she pulled Sarah's mouth back to hers and took what she wanted.

With a groan, she unbuttoned Sarah's shirt with fingers that trembled. Sarah had nothing on under the shirt and her nipples tightened instantly. Cassie watched Sarah's eyes darken with desire. It fed the craving crawling in her stomach. She closed her mouth on Sarah's nipple and felt the muscles of Sarah's stomach jump under her hand.

"Oh God, that feels so good," Sarah moaned, then pushed Cassie away. Holding Cassie's gaze, she opened the top button of her jeans and lowered her zipper. As she pushed her jeans down her hips, Cassie could see the wetness on her thighs. She wasn't wearing anything under her jeans either.

"Jesus, Sarah. I'd forgotten how very beautiful you are," Cassie whispered. Almost reverently she dropped to her knees and breathed in Sarah's arousal. With her index finger, she pulled the folds apart and stared at the glistening, hard clit. Under her touch she saw it lengthen, grow redder. As if synchronized, her own clit jumped and got harder.

"I'm so ready," Sarah whispered. "Go slow."

Cassie gently tongued the shaft as her fingers slid against the slick skin. Sarah's hips jumped and started to pump against her mouth. Following the path of her fingers along the wet, swollen folds, Cassie plunged her tongue into the tight opening, pulling a groan from Sarah. Sarah's fingers tightened on Cassie's head, drawing her mouth closer.

"God, oh God. That's going to make me come."

Cassie's tongue stroked back up to where Sarah's clit stood out, stiff and pulsing. She wrapped her lips around the hard nub and started to suck, still licking along the shaft.

"I'm coming…Cass…I'm coming."

As Sarah's orgasm bore down on her, Cassie slipped her fingers inside and started to stroke her in an ever-quickening pace. With a shout, Sarah doubled forward, pumping hard against Cassie's mouth as Cassie sucked her. "Oh God…oh." Sarah jerked against Cassie's fingers.

Cassie closed her eyes and continued to lick Sarah as she felt her own climax vibrating through her. She tried to fight it off, wanting to keep her attention on Sarah's pleasure. She pressed her free hand against the throbbing heat between her legs, intent on stopping it, but the pressure of her fingers against her swollen clitoris was too much to bear. With her mouth still on Sarah, she cried out and jerked against her hand, coming in a long, rolling wave. She lay gasping against Sarah's wetness, breathing in her scent, as the aftershocks continued to shake her.

The mechanical voice broke through. "Cassie, roll number five is up and ready."

Cassie, still leaning against Sarah, met her eyes. "Time to go to work."

Sarah's hand drifted down to brush at the damp hair on Cassie's forehead. "Will you come back to the hotel with me later?"

"Yes. I want to roll this scene again."

"And I want to taste you."

Jesus, give me strength.

SEASON PASS
LC JORDAN

Heat shimmered above the pavement of the narrow two-lane highway as I drove home in the late afternoon. It was miserably hot and so humid that you could probably wave a bandanna around and wring a pint of water out of it. The greenhouse effect of the sun slanting through my windshield made the air conditioner basically useless.

I slowed as I approached a line of traffic that was turning left off the highway into the old county fairgrounds and instantly knew what to blame for the heat. Every year; it never failed. It could have been the coolest summer on record for a century, but when the fair came to town all bets were off. For that one week in July, the temperature could be counted on to be at least ninety degrees with 70 percent humidity.

Despite that, I could remember going every summer until I went to college. It is ironic that as you age, your world both shrinks and expands. We outgrow things, tuck them away in our minds, and are surprised to find them again one day.

Maybe it was nostalgia or just the ingrained instinct of sheep following one another off a cliff, but I turned on my blinker and headed for the parking lot. At the ticket gate, I rolled down my window and paid the admission fee.

Once parked, I allowed myself to be swept into the small ocean of people as I slowly walked down the midway. The maze of booths and trailers with their colorful lights and streamers provided a distraction from the oppressive heat. The food vendors were lined up first and the tantalizing aromas reminded me that I hadn't eaten yet. After paying a ridiculous amount for a lemon shake-up and a corn dog, I continued my exploration.

The games hadn't changed much in ten years; darts and balloons, numbered yellow rubber ducks with rings, and hand-crank minicranes that were highly addictive to me. The pitches and taunts of the barkers rose above the general din of the crowd. I followed the sound of pulsing music and muffled screams and headed toward the rides.

The big draw seemed to be the Octopus. A group of at least twenty teenagers waiting their turn gathered behind the fence surrounding it. Edging closer, I had no intention of buying a ticket, but I did want to watch the kids try to stand up straight after they exited the ride.

The machine slowed to a halt and the man at the controls brought each compartment down to earth in turn. A woman in a blue tank top and jeans raised the bar on each capsule and freed its occupants, only to fill it again with more excited teens. A Chicago Cubs ball cap was pulled low on her head and mirrored sunglasses hid her eyes. When she had safely locked in the last of the riders, there was still an empty compartment left. She spotted me and crooked a finger in my direction. "Room for more," she called out.

Looking behind myself, I realized she was talking to me. "Oh, no thanks," I yelled above the noise, shaking my head.

The woman grinned and secured the last capsule, waving to the operator to start. As I stood watching the ride pick up speed, I tried to nonchalantly observe the carnival worker. She stood with her arms folded across her chest, the muscles clearly defined by the tight-fitting top. A short dark ponytail peeked out the back of her cap and a pair of gloves hung from the back pocket of her jeans. A two-way radio was clipped to her belt and as I sipped the last of my drink, she reached down and brought it close to her lips, saying something I couldn't hear. Within a minute or so another carnival worker appeared, apparently to take the woman's place.

Before I realized it, she had casually swung over the fence and was walking toward me. I couldn't read any expression on her face and those damn sunglasses didn't help. In four or five long strides she closed the distance and stopped in front of me. Only then did she tip her head to the side and smile.

"You look a little lost." She swept me with a quick gaze, taking in my pleated skirt and silk shirt, which I realized was at the moment plastered to my breasts. "Not exactly dressed to go on any rides."

Hoping she would attribute the rising color in my face to the weather, I nervously explained, "This was an impulse. I just got off work and haven't been home to change."

Her smile widened. "Impulsive women; gotta love 'em," she said, but was cut short by a disembodied voice on her radio. *"Shayne, Carl has some kind of problem at the front gate. Can you get out there and see what's up?"*

Snatching the radio again, she answered impatiently, "Yeah, I'm on it. Give me a couple minutes to get there." She reached into her hip pocket and handed something to me. "Here," she said. "In case you have another impulse."

I automatically accepted the small rectangle of cardboard but before I could comment, she was gone. Reading the print on the card, I had to laugh. "Season Pass: Admission for One." The fair never lasted more than a week, and it was already Thursday.

The next day I was restless at work. I had five depositions to type and two more that needed to be scheduled. The law firm had recently added a new junior partner and I fervently hoped they'd hire another paralegal as well.

The weather matched my mood that afternoon. It had been raining for hours. Not a downpour, but a steady stream that kept my wipers busy on the drive home. I knew the rain would have caused the fair to cancel for the night, but I turned off the highway just the same.

The front gate was closed and the ticket booth empty. There were lights on in a few of the trailers and for just an instant, I thought I saw a figure wearing a blue ball cap dart from one to another. I turned my car around and made my way back home.

Saturday morning I took advantage of my day off and slept in until eight. The sun was out in full force, making up for yesterday. I knew it was the last day of the fair, but I wanted to wait until evening to go. I told myself it would be cooler then, but the real reason was Shayne. I was hoping she worked the same hours as she had on Thursday.

Dressing for comfort, I put on my usual khaki shorts and sleeveless polo. I made the short drive out to the edge of town in record time. Parking was free the final night and I showed my season pass at the ticket gate.

The crowd was large, people not wanting to miss whatever magic was left in this last rite of summer. I traveled down the midway, scanning the rides. After a half hour of searching with no sign of Shayne, I was having a hard time convincing myself I wasn't terribly disappointed.

Not yet ready to leave, I walked up to the nearest booth and laid some money down. Too late, I realized it was a shooting game. I had never held anything besides a Super Soaker and doubted my ability to hit a target.

The man behind the counter picked up an old lever-action Daisy BB rifle. Cocking it once, he handed it to me. The general idea seemed to be to knock over one of the inverted Styrofoam cups and win the prize that matched the number beneath it.

My first shot missed completely and went into the backstop of straw bales. The man took the gun from me, cocked it again, and handed it back. My second attempt winged a cup but it remained upright. As he took the rifle from me again, I began to suspect that the old gun didn't even have enough air pressure to knock the cups over. Taking aim with my last shot, I heard a voice behind me say, "I thought that was you."

Turning around, I couldn't help the smile that spread across my face. There stood Shayne, with her Cubs hat and radio but minus the sunglasses. She wore a black T-shirt with white lettering that spelled "Security" across the front. The corner of her mouth lifted in a crooked grin and I was momentarily stunned by how attractive she was.

"I was hoping that you might come back," she said. "Win anything yet?" She nodded toward the booth.

Finding my voice again, I said, "Hi. No, this isn't really my forte."

"Maybe I can give you a few pointers. I'm Shayne, by the way."

"I know. I mean, I heard," I explained by way of gesturing toward her radio. I extended my hand. "Allison."

"Allison," she repeated, folding my hand in hers. Leaning closer, she whispered, "Let's win something."

"She's playing again," Shayne told the man as she passed a folded bill across the counter and turned her ball cap backward. Taking the BB gun from me, she cocked it four times and gave it back. Positioning herself close behind me but not actually touching me with any part of her body except her hands, she began coaching.

"Snug the butt up against your shoulder and support the barrel with your left hand. Wrap your right hand around here and squeeze—don't pull—the trigger when you're ready."

She put her hands over mine and helped hold the Daisy steady as I tried again. With the added air pressure and the perfect aim, the Styrofoam cup flew off the shelf. I was so excited I let out a totally uncharacteristic scream and Shayne burst out laughing. The man behind the counter didn't look nearly as enthused as we were, but only raised one eyebrow at Shayne and said nothing.

Twice more we blew a cup away and the man handed me two small stuffed animals and a key chain. I was more than satisfied, but Shayne was preoccupied looking at the bigger prizes that hung from the top of the booth.

"Which one of those do you like?" she asked.

"These are fine," I laughed, gathering up my souvenirs.

"How many to trade up for one of those?" she asked.

"Ten," he replied.

Another folded bill passed between them and once again Shayne handed me the Daisy. I wondered just how much she was paying the guy and I started to protest, but she only placed her hands on my waist and gently turned me around. A few people had stopped to watch, making me nervous, and it took fifteen shots to accumulate ten small toys.

"Now, which one do you like?" Shayne asked me again, looking pleased with herself.

Shaking my head, I scanned the animals. "Snoopy," I decided.

"Snoopy it is," Shayne told the man, who was obviously relieved to see us leave.

Checking her watch, Shayne frowned. Thinking maybe I had kept her from her job too long, I suddenly felt foolish. "If you need to get back to work, please don't let me keep you."

"Oh no." She seemed surprised. "I'm not working tonight. I was just seeing if we had time to take in some rides. They're closing early tonight."

"I'm really not much of a ride person."

"Not even the Ferris wheel? If we wait until they start shutting down, I can pretty much guarantee us a spectacular view."

Giving in to the expectant look on her face, I agreed. We walked in companionable silence as the crowd got thinner. The lights up and down the midway blinked off once, twice, signaling the close of the fair. Shayne led the way toward the Ferris wheel and called out to the man I remembered from the other day.

"Hey, Jimmy, can you hold off for one more ride?" Shayne placed her hand on the small of my back, guiding me closer. "We want to see the view from the top."

Casting a curious glance in my direction, he replied, "Sure, just don't stay up there all night, okay?"

"Thanks, Jimmy. We won't. I'll yell when we're ready to come down," she said, tapping her radio. Taking Snoopy and sitting him against the fence, she placed her cap on his head and said, "Don't want him getting sick up there." With that, Shayne motioned me into the swinging compartment and slid in after me.

The wheel slowly turned, lifting us higher until it stopped at the top. As we watched, the lights of the vendors and the other rides winked out one by one. Soon the only glow left was the Ferris wheel, and it was suddenly very quiet.

Shayne leaned back and regarded me with that crooked grin. "Peaceful, isn't it?"

"Yes, it is." I waved my hand in an arc, indicating the grounds. "So how long have you done this?"

"Not long, just this summer. I spent six years in the Air Force and needed something different when I got out." Seeing that I was waiting for more, she teased, "Haven't you ever wanted to run off and join the circus?"

"There have certainly been times I would have liked to, but who really does that?"

"I did," she said simply. "What about you? Born and raised here, I take it?"

"My whole life. Pretty boring, huh?"

"Allison, I wouldn't say anything I've seen about you so far is boring," Shayne said, bumping my shoulder.

"Then you haven't seen anything yet." I suddenly shivered. The air was much cooler now, in stark contrast to the earlier heat.

Shayne noticed and asked, "Cold?"

When I nodded, she turned sideways to lean back against the end of the compartment. Bending her right leg, she placed her boot flat on the wide seat and motioned me over. I hesitated only a moment before I scooted in her direction. Reaching around me, she settled me into the space between her legs, my back resting against her chest. I pulled my knees up and she swung her left leg onto the seat, enclosing me in the shelter of her body. The fabric of her jeans chafed my bare legs in a not unpleasant way as she rocked us back and forth a little.

"Better?"

I could feel her breath ruffle my hair. Since I didn't know what to do with my hands, I just rested them on top of hers.

"Is this okay?" Shayne asked, her voice low.

I was having trouble speaking since my mouth had gone dry.

She tipped me a little to one side and looked down into my face. "Allison, is this okay?"

She was so close I could have counted the dark lashes that framed her eyes. "Okay," was all I managed to say.

She bent her head slowly, giving me every opportunity to pull away. I kept my eyes open until the second I felt her kiss. At least I thought she kissed me. The contact was so fleeting I wasn't certain until I felt the softness return.

Again and again, Shayne's lips brushed over mine, never lingering long enough to satisfy. She seemed in no hurry, content to restrict her exploration to this teasing contact. Warmth spread through my body as desire built, making me impatient. Reaching up with one hand, I curled my fingers around the back of her neck and initiated a searing kiss that got her attention. Immediately her arms tightened around me, hands splaying across my rib cage. I was certain she could feel my heart beating wildly as she gently cupped my breast through the thin material of my shirt, her thumb rubbing back and forth across my hard nipple.

Opening my mouth in an involuntary "Oh," I felt the soft tip of Shayne's tongue glide along the sensitive skin of my inner lips. I granted her full access and met each stroke of her tongue with mine. Desperately needing air, we broke apart for only seconds before I felt Shayne's teeth on my neck. Leaning my head back against her shoulder, I closed my eyes again as she trailed a wet path down my neck to my collarbone.

Needing more, I unconsciously began to squeeze my thighs together, rhythmically rocking my hips to relieve some of the pressure building between my legs. Shayne soon joined me in the sensual dance, tilting her hips forward with each of my backward thrusts, one hand moving in circles on my stomach, inching downward and causing my knees to part automatically. A flick of her wrist and my khakis were unsnapped and the zipper lowered, her palm pressing hard against my mound. My body stiffened and I nearly came right then. Sensing this, Shayne stilled, allowing me time to catch my breath.

"Still okay?" Her voice was rough with the effort at restraint.

"Very much okay," I assured her, covering her hand with mine, encouraging her to continue.

Keeping her lips against my neck, she ran her index finger along the elastic of my bikinis, tracing the edge before slipping inside. I knew I was so wet they had to be soaked. When Shayne discovered that for herself, she groaned and bit down lightly on my neck.

I was already so close and Shayne knew it. Dipping her fingers between my folds, she carefully entered me. I whimpered and wrapped my arms around her upper thighs, dimly wondering if I'd leave bruises there.

After withdrawing briefly, Shayne returned with two fingers, then began a steady rhythm pumping in and out. I didn't realize I was squeezing her legs in time to her thrusting hand until I felt her quads contracting in time as well. In seconds my stomach muscles clenched and an electric current burned down my spine. Adding a third finger, Shayne stroked deeply one more time while reaching down with her other hand to draw a fingernail across my swollen clit. My whole body rocketed off the seat, taking Shayne with me. Beyond the roaring in my head I could hear her saying my name over and over.

"Allison, beautiful Allison."

The only sound in the night was that of our breathing when Shayne finally withdrew her fingers. She pulled me tight against her, not speaking. I was reeling with so many emotions, I was afraid to say anything. All I knew was that I didn't want her to go. Before I could stop, the words fell out of my mouth. "I can't believe you're leaving tomorrow."

I was mortified when I heard my voice. I was sure she'd think I was foolish to even consider asking her to stay. When she didn't answer right away, I knew I'd blown it. I started to sit up, but she wouldn't release me. Clearing her throat, she finally spoke.

"No chance of you joining the circus?" she asked doubtfully.

"I could, if I have to," I answered honestly.

Shayne let out a huge breath, laughing. "Nah, I don't think I want to share you with the general public. Besides, it's my turn to be impulsive, and I have a very strong impulse to stay."

Just then her radio crackled and an annoyed voice came through. "Shayne, are you ever coming down?"

Grabbing it off her belt while hugging me closer, she pressed the button and said, "No, I don't think I am."

TIME TO WAKE UP
CLIODHNA O'BANNION

I can't sleep any longer. Though the movie of yesterday plays, I know there is no going back, and my mind is filled with today, this morning. It is an anniversary, a celebration, a festive adventure, a wonderful anticipation.

There you are, still glowing—at your weekly aerobics class, your friends pounce on your radiance. They quiz you. They want all the details; they get but a few. How many years has it been? You still wear this happiness like a slinky teddy; anyone can see there is so much promise and mystery, but only I am allowed to explore it and discover all that you are. Your shy discretion keeps us cocooned, away from prying and prattle, safe in our secret places where no one else even gets to visit.

Ah, our meeting. We are at a backyard cookout. I am late; you plan to leave early. Our intersection begins with chatter about spiders and visits to urgent care centers, moves to our careers, what we're reading, changes to growing-up tales. You are bold enough to ask for my phone and e-mail. I don't think twice. You overstay your deadline, preferring to be late to your next potluck in order to spend more time with me. We walk to your car, you lower your cool shades, I see your eyes for the first time, and I am smitten.

An exchange of e-mails, quickly made plans, and we are making out like high-schoolers in public. When dark falls fully, we hear ominous rustling in the brush near the water. We race to my house, and I reach for you and for the clothing that is in our way. I stretch to hold you in place when you declare you are nearing the point of no return and that means you must leave. I know with certainty that I have passed that point. Immediately, my thoughts turn to "next time."

"Next time" comes; we do, too. I feel shy and awkward, clumsy and inexperienced. The years gone since my last relationship have taken a huge toll. But I begin to find my way, with your indulgence and patience. I have never been so noisy during sex, but with you I take no measure to restrain myself. You use your fingers and hands and eyes and lips and soft murmurings; you inflame me as no one has. Long-lasting kisses, curious tongue, whispering into my ear about what you want to do, what you're going to do, what I can't stop you from doing, and I can hardly contain my wanting. My desire grows and grows until I am ready to push your fingers into my pussy myself, to show you what I want, where I want it, when I want it.

It is your deliberate pace that is working its timely charms on me. You test the curve of my neck. Yes, your chin fits nicely and that gives you a good view of my lips as you caress them, barely touching them with your fingertips, as your forearm brushes against my breast, and I can only mutter *Oh*. It is almost too languid as you talk about my body, demonstrating with a touch. My temperature is rising, along with my pussy as I raise my hips to offer a better angle, not such a reach, a hint of my urgency. Finally, you take the plunge and give the length of my pussy lips a long swipe and I cannot help but scream my thanks. Then your hands are everywhere, and your mouth joins them at the spring of my wetness, and you are the only thing that is keeping me anchored on the bed. I want, I want, I want, and I want.

There are no words simple enough to say through my heaving breath, but you hear anyway and push two, no, three fingers into me and twist your arm as I shout. Twist and shout. I want to squirm away. I cannot take all this pleasure. I'm not going anywhere. You see to that with your leg covering mine, your mouth covering my clit, your hands holding me down so you can take your pleasure.

This pleasure, this desire, this fulfillment goes on forever and it can't get any better until you begin moving your fingers in and out while you rub my inner lips and zero in on the hood of my clit with your tongue. That sturdy tip, which carries all those words of love, bounces me into another realm. It is all clit and tongue, pussy and fingers, humming and screaming.

I don't lose control; I give it over to you, willingly, gladly. I want you to drive me over the edge. I need you to think for both of us. One thought enters my brain: *How do I keep this going?* Another thought: *I can't take much more.* I shake and shake as your tongue swirls and curls and finds and takes so much pleasure that I am sure I will faint. Is that me? Can that be my voice? I am saying nothing intelligible and that says it all. I am yours. You can take me anytime. And when I pray, I pray that you will…take me…now…later…in between. Fast and furiously without a thought, pushing me against the wall and making my knees buckle; pushing me down on the bed and sucking furiously; taking me from behind so thoroughly that I feel as if I'm in a coma; slowly, lovingly caressing every nerve ending; begging me to sit on your face; twisting so we can both use our tongues for their greatest, highest purpose. It's your choice.

With these orgasms, we cement our pairing. We indulge in sex at my house, at your house; blushing by e-mail; giggling by phone.

We start laughingly calling ourselves the old fuddy-duddies. After all, we are women of a certain age; we enjoy gardening and bird watching, sewing and reading, walking and writing. You read all the relationship and lesbian sex books that you can find at the library and in bookstores. You share your findings, often in the most exquisite of pleasing moments. We both read for work and still take such great pleasure in reading at home, lounging at either end of the couch, you with one leg extended just enough to touch my toes. The cats battle for lap space.

It's great fun to realize we will do things together that we do not wish to do alone. Day trips to watch eagles and see tulip fields in bloom, long weekends to sweet spots in Canada, holidays at the ocean, days off spent at home as if they were holidays. All seems better when the sights can be shared.

There is an assumption at hand—we have all the time we need, all the time we want to perfect the state of being a couple.

You touch me deeply with your hands, mouth, smile, eyes. You work your way into my heart, a place you will always be. One look and anything is possible. Nothing is out of bounds. Experiments abound.

My hands mold themselves to your body, those sinuous curves, those dense muscles. I thirst for your mouth, your ears, the curve of your breasts, your elbows, as I take my agonizingly sweet slow time to reach your pussy, to reach in for your clit, to reach in and pull out all of your moans, sighs, sobs, screams.

We talk of the days when sitting at work will be a reminder of a long time rubbing on my inner lips; when riding a bike will be all about sex memory; when my hand brushing near my mouth will bring with it your tastes and smells that send me into a throbbing reverie.

I am crazy for you, crazed by your look, your touch. I want you more each time. Your lips grazing my ear. Your mouth on mine. Your fingers tracing from my mouth to my breasts. Your hands grasping my breasts. Your teeth nibbling, biting my nipples. Your eyes casting downward, and you following. To find my toes, ankles, bicycle-strong calves and thighs, moving ever higher and ever inward to the one place where you must reach right now. The dark, damp, dripping core of my being. The fire that cannot be extinguished, only banked until your return.

I find myself dozing, not knowing what is the dream and what is the waking. No matter. I am filled with desire. I want you. I look over and wonder—

Are you awake?

I pull back the covers and stare. My fingers glide over your back, just enough to make you stretch and fall back into a light sleep. My hands follow the curve of your hips, reach toward your knees, and you roll over, opening all your possibility to me.

No turning away now. I glide my lips around your breast, my tongue electrifies your nipple, and as I graze it with my teeth, I hear you moan.

Are you awake?

I take both your hands and stretch your arms above your head. You open to me further and I kiss and caress and chant to the pulse points in your temples, at your throat, then follow the fall of your neck to your shoulders, to your collarbone. And you arch, strain to put your nipples in my path. When I bite one, you gasp.

I think you're awake.

Still, your eyes are closed. Your legs fall open. I slip my body between them, and again you moan as I lick your palm, tongue the spaces between your fingers, nuzzle the inside of your elbow, kiss your shoulder, and find your nipples and suck.

You groan, stretch farther. With my hands on your breasts, fingers twisting and pinching, I find your belly ring and tug with my teeth, caress your belly button with my tongue. You bend your knees and bring your feet close and lift. I cup your sweet ass in my palms and you lift again with anticipation.

Surely you're awake.

I sit back on my heels and take your toes into my mouth and suck all sorts of sounds from you. I rub your foot and slide up your calf to the back of your knee, just touching the ends of the hairs that stand and quiver. You start talking to me as my mouth moves up your inner thigh: yesyesyesyesyes...

I push your legs farther apart and admire you. I tell you the gorgeous truth about your pussy and what I will do with it and how I will stamp it as mine. You are already moaning when I reach with my fingers—reach for your core. Ohohohohohohohoh...you give voice to this dance, louder and higher...pleasepleasepleasepleasetouchmetouch metouchmeplease.

I twist my fingers and I find your clit with my tongue and I know your eyes are wide open. You shake and twist and babble. I lick and suck you, and you start to growl. I reach and pinch your nipple, and you scream and buck and I'm right there, and you might fly away but I hold you with my hands and my mouth until you are all shudder and whimper.

And I move up to kiss you hard and long.

Because you are awake.

LAID
KATHRYN WOLF

The conversation had started with…
"For God's sake, Sarah. Will you stop bitching about everything and just go? Do us all a favor; go get yourself laid while you're away. *Please.*"

Five years ago she'd gone back home to take over the running of the family business, and she'd worked solidly until it all started to pile up on her. Her friends were right; she did need to get laid. Badly. The insane weekend she had spent in bed with a Swedish tourist she'd met in a pub seemed now exactly what it was…a very long two years ago.

Now she was holding up the bar at another pub she had not been to in years, and she didn't recognize a soul. None of her old friends were on the scene anymore; everyone had paired up and settled down. In the last week she'd been chatted up twice, but no one caught her fancy; the spark just wasn't there, mostly due to the fact they were baby dykes doing the chatting. However, it did stroke her thirty-six-year-old ego nicely. Tonight, hardly anyone in her immediate vicinity even looked old enough to drink, let alone be out and proud. One of the bleached blondes bopping around behind the bar scooted over to her as she finished her beer and signaled for another. The girl had "Bar Bitch" emblazoned across her breasts and an almost blinding amount of bright steel facial jewelry.

Sarah resigned herself to the fact that now, on her last night before she pulled up stakes and left for home, she was not going to be able to fulfill her promise to her friends. That was, until she looked up from her glass and straight into a pair of green eyes above a lazy smile. The light sheen of sweat on the woman's rich tanned skin suggested she had just come in from the dance floor. The grin broadened slightly when their eyes met and held. The woman picked up her drink and walked around to Sarah's side of the bar. Sarah sat transfixed as she watched her push through the crowd, stomach twisting sharply when the whole of the woman's body came into view. Her tight white tank top stopped halfway down tight abs, and she had poured herself into a pair of black leather pants that rode low on her hips. Sarah felt her body heat as her heart rate picked up. A grin matching the one of the woman walking toward her made its way across her face.

Turning the bar stool around, the dark-haired woman eased her way in to stand between Sarah's knees. Sarah swallowed convulsively as fire shot through her veins and wetness pooled suddenly between her legs.

"I'm Dillon," the woman said as she leaned in. "Come and dance with me."

For a second, when the woman's rich southern American accent rolled over her like a wave, Sarah thought she was going to come on the spot. As Dillon moved to ease her off the seat, she resisted, and Dillon raised an eyebrow in question. Sarah had a sudden burning need to feel soft hot skin not her own. She slid both hands around Dillon's waist, pulling her in tighter between her legs.

"I'm Sarah," she said before slipping off the stool and gliding down the front of Dillon's body. Her move was rewarded by a tight groan from deep in Dillon's throat as she allowed Sarah to pull her through the crowd toward the nightclub.

Dillon could not believe the way her insides jumped the moment her eyes landed on the blonde sitting alone on the other side of the horseshoe-shaped bar. She had been single for the last six months, and since then she'd had the odd fling here and there just to scratch the itch, or out of sheer boredom, but nobody had grabbed her attention like this. When their eyes locked, the twist of desire was so strong, she had almost groaned out loud. The heat spread through her body and focused between her legs as she shifted upright, and then all of a sudden, there she was, standing between the woman's knees and introducing herself. Her mind switched off as she felt warm hands, one still moist from the beer glass, slide over her skin. She barely registered the woman's name before she was pulled through the crowd into the central courtyard of the old building toward the nightclub in the back.

Dillon suddenly pulled back on the hand tugging hers and drew a startled Sarah into a shadowed alcove next to a lush potted tree. Her hot mouth descended on Sarah's, eliciting a deep groan from Sarah as her back connected with the rough brick of the wall. In a very small corner of her mind, Dillon was slightly shocked at her own behavior, and then Sarah lifted a booted foot up onto the edge of a nearby planter, grabbed hold of her hips, and pulled her in tight between her legs. Arousal flooded her body and drowned out all coherent thought as she tore her mouth away and looked into hot blue eyes. Keeping the eye contact, Dillon eased her upper body away from Sarah's and with slow deliberate movements began to undo her shirt buttons.

Dilated pupils and flushed skin betrayed how much Sarah anticipated the touch of Dillon's hands against her naked skin. She gasped when instead of sliding inside her shirt, those hands slid down over her hips, lifting her slightly so Dillon could grind against her center. Sarah emitted a soft cry, and her head fell back against the brick as Dillon kissed down her now-exposed throat to the hollow between her breasts.

"Oh God...ah...I thought we..." The rest of Sarah's sentence was cut short as strong fingers shifted around her body and pressed into her aching sex through her jeans. At the same moment, Dillon bit down gently on a rock-hard nipple through the fabric of her bra, ripping another cry from her throat.

"Have you ever made love in public?" Dillon asked against Sarah's ear before claiming her lips again in a searing kiss. Nipping and biting, the women struggled to find the perfect fit for their lips, their breathing harsh and ragged.

Dillon suddenly let go of her grip on Sarah's center and roughly ripped open the button fly of her jeans, plunging her fingers beneath the soaked denim. Working her way lower, she moaned out loud as her fingers invaded hot wet flesh.

The moment Dillon slipped two fingers up inside her Sarah was lost; at that point she would not have cared if the woman had stripped off her clothes and gone down on her in the middle of the Rugby World Cup grand final pitch. The pleasure was intense as Dillon started up a slow thrusting rhythm, the palm of her hand flat against Sarah's swollen clit; she tore her mouth away and focused on hot green eyes.

"More," Sarah demanded and Dillon growled, thrusting a third finger deep into her. As her slick inner walls began to contract around the questing fingers, Sarah's head dropped to Dillon's shoulder, nails scratching into her strong back muscles. Dillon picked up the pace, thrusting her body against Sarah in time with her fingers. Then Sarah was there, her body convulsing, squeezing down hard on Dillon's fingers as she gave a sharp cry of release.

Dillon could not focus, could not grasp any form of coherent thought. All she could feel were Sarah's slick walls pulsing around her fingers, and her own clit, so hard it was rubbing against her leathers. All she had to do was provide a tiny bit of friction. Sarah stirred as Dillon gently pulled out of her body and ran her hands down Dillon's back to her hips. When Sarah shoved a muscled thigh firmly against her aching sex, Dillon came hard, her head falling back as Sarah pulled her in tighter, teeth gracing the flesh of her exposed throat.

As Dillon came, Sarah suddenly became aware of a sound and was horrified to discover they had drawn an audience, who had begun to applaud. She was even further mortified when she realized the cheering had caught the attention of a rather large bouncer, who currently waited with arms folded and a slight smirk on her face. Sarah swore loudly as she tried to pull away far enough to refasten her clothing. Finally realizing what was going on, Dillon stepped back slightly, giving Sarah room to move but still shielding her body.

"We're about ten seconds from being thrown out," Dillon said softly.

"I figured that." Sarah chuckled ruefully, trying to tamp down her embarrassment.

"It's still early…" Dillon left the statement hanging.

Sarah searched Dillon's eyes and felt a kick run through her system again. *Damn, I haven't felt like this in years.* The decision made, she pulled Dillon into her body.

"Come with me," she breathed against her ear.

The taxi ride and climb to Sarah's hotel room was accomplished with complete silence between them. Sarah unlocked the door, switched on the lights, and motioned for Dillon to precede her, giving herself plenty of time to admire the view of the woman's firm ass and muscled physique.

"Do you want a drink?" she asked, her voice sounding thick.

Dillon turned from where she was looking out over the ocean, giving Sarah a feral smile. "No."

Sarah turned off the lights when Dillon motioned for her to join her at the window. When she was an arm's length away, Dillon said, "Take off your clothes."

It was both a command and a request, and Sarah's heart rate picked up as she focused on Dillon's eyes while unbuttoning her white cotton shirt. Her skin flushed as she watched hot green eyes follow the movement of her hands. When Sarah removed her bra to expose her firm, coral-tipped breasts, Dillon's hands twitched, but she kept them at her sides. Sarah closed her eyes in anticipation as Dillon moved in behind her.

"Walk over to the window," Dillon breathed into her ear, sending a shiver of arousal sweeping down her spine. "I want to see you in the moonlight when you take off the rest."

Sarah shakily complied, standing next to the window and lifting her foot up on to the desk chair to remove her heavy lace-up boots. Her body was screaming to feel those strong tanned hands against her hot skin as she pulled open the buttons of her fly and slowly pushed the denim over her hips.

Dillon was certain she would have collapsed on the floor as Sarah bent slowly from the waist to push her jeans down over her legs if not for the chair she had dragged under herself at the last minute. As she knew from their earlier encounter, the gorgeous woman was not wearing anything under the jeans, and when she bent over, Dillon was presented with a seductive view of her wet swollen sex.

"Oh God," she breathed in almost silent benediction.

By the time Sarah straightened and let down her loose ponytail, she was almost dizzy with arousal, and she cried out in pleasure as strong arms encircled her waist and pulled her in against a hot hard body. She dropped her head back against Dillon's shoulder, her breathing suddenly ragged. One strong hand pinched and chafed at a hard nipple, while the other brushed down to slide between her wet folds. Blindly, she reached for some kind of support as her body convulsed in pleasure. Then Dillon gently walked her forward two steps until her searching hands met the cool glass of the floor-to-ceiling window. When Dillon started a slow circling of her swollen clit, Sarah gasped, "Please…Ah… I need you…inside me…"

Anything else she might have said was choked off as Dillon bent her forward and slid two fingers inside her. Sarah reached down, stilling Dillon's hand, and heard a choked groan of frustration.

"Wait," Sarah panted through clenched teeth. "I need… something…more." Gently but forcefully she pulled Dillon's fingers from inside herself. "In the top drawer of the side table… the wooden box…"

Sarah gasped as cool air reached the hot skin of her suddenly exposed back and she held her breath, praying she would not hear the sound of the door.

"Well…" Dillon chuckled.

She had not been quite sure what to expect when she pulled the wooden box out of the drawer, but it sure as hell hadn't been a brand-new strap-on. A fresh flood of moisture flowed between her legs when she realized she could put it on without removing her leathers, and she had an instant vision of taking the blonde hard against the plate glass of the hotel window. When she had the cock adjusted to where she wanted it, she took it in her hand and stroked, drawing a tight groan from her throat as the base of the shaft rode against her swollen clit.

Sarah heard a muffled groan, then felt Dillon's body against her back, this time with the added sensation of hard nipples rubbing over her back and hard silicone pressed against her behind. Sarah gasped and reached back to pull Dillon harder against her body and groaned when she realized Dillon still wore her leather pants.

"Is this what you want?" Dillon rasped against her ear. "Tell me, Sarah. Do you want me to fuck you?" Dillon slipped both hands down the front of Sarah's hips and slowly leaned over, sliding the silicone shaft between Sarah's legs, chafing against her heat. "Tell me. I want you to say the words. Tell me what you want me to do."

She punctuated her words with a steady thrusting motion, a gentle teasing against Sarah's swollen folds.

"Oh God…please…I want you inside me," Sarah gasped.

Dillon growled low in her throat as she slowly guided the shaft into Sarah's waiting heat. She watched as the shaft disappeared into Sarah's hot flesh, gritting her teeth with the effort to control her movements, wanting nothing more than to thrust hard and fast into the body beneath her. Finally buried to the hilt she stopped, relishing the sensation of the shaft grinding against her clit as Sarah's body spasmed around it. Leaning forward to run the tip of her tongue up along Sarah's spine, she reached down and softly traced an invisible pattern up the inside of the blonde's thighs. Sarah cried out again as Dillon's fingers parted her swollen folds and found her clit while she started a slow thrusting rhythm with the silicone shaft.

Sarah could not think, she could only feel, as soft fingers caressed her hot flesh and the now-warm shaft filled her body. Even with the edge taken from her need, she could feel her orgasm approaching fast and hard, and it took every single shred of control to pull her body away from Dillon once more. She wanted this powerfully, but she wanted it face-to-face. Wanted to be able to watch Dillon as the woman made her come. Placing hasty fingers over lips opened in protest, Sarah guided Dillon backward and down onto the bed. When she took her in, her knees nearly buckled at the sight. Dillon sat slightly slouched against the headboard, her leather pants open and riding low, her eyes hooded and dark with lust as she looked back at Sarah.

"Come here, baby. I got something for you," she said as she grasped the base of the silicone shaft, grinding it against her clit. Sarah's body turned liquid at the sight of Dillon's obvious pleasure from the silicone cock rising up out of her pants, and she climbed onto the bed to straddle Dillon's knees. She gasped as strong hands grabbed her hips and guided her down into Dillon's lap.

Sarah cried out as Dillon pulled her forward and took a hard nipple into her mouth. The shaft, still wet and warm from her body, came to rest once more hard against her clit. Sarah rocked against it convulsively; a mutual cry of pleasure rang through the room as silicone slid into hot wet flesh. For a moment, neither woman moved—two heads thrown back, fingers gripping—and then finally Sarah began a slow grinding movement of her hips.

Dillon managed to pry her eyes open—she simply had to see the moment this beautiful woman blasted over the edge—and was rewarded by the view of the lithe body arched bowstring tight above her. She knew it was only moments before Sarah exploded into orgasm, and a sudden wicked smile crossed her face as she forced a halt to all movement. Sarah's eyes snapped open and silently pleaded with the woman inside her to continue, she was so close. Dillon leaned forward and felt Sarah's body spasm slightly as she spoke close to her ear.

"Wait."

With gentle strength Dillon moved Sarah off her body and laid her on the bed before sliding across and standing up. Never taking her eyes from Sarah's, she removed the last barrier of clothing and moved to the foot of the bed.

"Do you want this?" she asked indicating the silicone appendage. "Or do you want me?"

"Why can't I have both?"

"Absolutely no reason at all."

Dillon reached out and Sarah pulled her onto her body. Dillon groaned as the shaft slid slowly home once more. She rested on her hands above Sarah, and with their eyes locked, resumed the slow grind of hips. Almost instantly, she was rewarded with the most exquisite of sights as bright blue eyes suddenly glazed and darkened. Sarah's legs locked around her hips and Dillon felt the golden body go rigid with the strength of Sarah's orgasm. When a sudden sheen of sweat appeared on fine skin, the sight was enough to finally send Dillon over the edge; her eyes closed and an inarticulate cry ripped from her throat as she came.

Sarah felt dazed, her body almost floating in boneless bliss. She awoke slowly, rolling over and reaching blindly across the bed. The sound of water running in the bathroom cut through her sudden disappointment at finding the empty space beside her. Sliding from between the sheets, she padded quietly to the door of the bathroom and watched as Dillon ran a washcloth over her shoulders and neck. Sarah's body began to ache once again as she watched the ripple of back and shoulder muscles moving under sleek skin.

Dillon gasped when her back met the cool tiles of the bathroom wall and Sarah's warm full lips descended on hers. She groaned again when Sarah closed her lips, then her teeth, over a rock-hard nipple.

"Oh, God, Sarah," Dillon cried out as the soft hands continued their exploration of her heated skin and Sarah's mouth began an agonizingly slow descent down her body. She buried her hands into thick blond hair, her head falling back against the tiled wall as Sarah drew her nails up the backs of her thighs and over her behind. Her breathing echoed harsh around the white tiled walls as her legs began to shake with the effort to keep her body upright.

Kneeling on the floor between spread feet, Sarah laid a soft kiss on each hipbone. When Dillon's legs began to tremble, Sarah wrapped a strong arm around her left hip and drew her right leg over one shoulder, bracing Dillon against the wall. Dillon tried to form a coherent sentence, but it was reduced to a sharp cry as Sarah stole her first taste of sweet, swollen flesh.

Dillon twisted her hands in Sarah's hair, trying to pull her mouth into closer contact. Resisting, Sarah tightened her hold on tawny skin and teased the slick folds.

"God...please...Sarah, now," Dillon pleaded, her voice cracking on the last word.

Sarah looked up, catching Dillon's eyes as she slowly pushed her tongue into direct contact with a very swollen clit. "Is this what you want?" she asked as she pulled away.

"Yes, yes...please."

With excruciating slowness Sarah lowered her mouth to the waiting heat and sucked the aching flesh into her mouth. Dillon's body convulsed with pleasure and Sarah had to readjust her hold as she increased the pressure.

Dillon's head fell back against the tile once again. She could feel the cool slick tile against her back, the thick silk of the kneeling woman's hair wrapped in her hands, and the light caress of fingertips against her abdominal muscles. All of this warred for supremacy with the incredible sensation of Sarah sucking on her swollen clit and as she focused, the sensations flooding her nervous system began a sharp upward spiral.

Sarah tried to absorb every sensation—the silky feel and sweet taste of the flesh under her tongue; the heady aroma of the woman's arousal. With her right hand braced against Dillon's abdomen, she could feel the orgasm building with each ripple of her taut muscles, and her own body began to tighten in return. Then the muscles beneath Sarah's hands went rigid, hips jolted forward, and she held on tight as Dillon called out to a host of deities. With great care, Sarah kept up the pressure, drawing out her orgasm as it peaked, then slowly began to ebb. When it finally abated, Dillon sagged and Sarah helped her sit, a leg on either side of Sarah's hips.

❖

Dillon wrapped her arms around Sarah and buried her face in Sarah's neck, inhaling the sweet scent of her skin.

"Damn. I could get used to this," she said quietly and then stiffened when she realized what she had said. "Come on, let's go back to bed."

Dillon watched Sarah climb into bed and settle against the pillows, her eyes feasting over the gorgeous expanse of flesh.

"You're not tired, I take it," Sarah said with a chuckle.

"Well, you did ask me earlier if you could have both."

Dillon smiled, realizing the hungry look must have been evident on her face, and slid her body over Sarah's, eliciting a groan of pleasure as their legs tangled together. She wasted no time, sensing how ready the woman below her was from the evidence against her thigh. She pulled Sarah's leg over her hip, her own center coming in contact with the other thigh as she ran her free hand over Sarah's body.

"Oh God. Please don't tease me...I'm ready now," Sarah said in a tight voice.

"I know."

Sarah captured the hand responsible for the exquisite torture and placed Dillon's fingers firmly against her sex, leaving her lover with no doubt as to what she thought of her earlier teasing.

"Yes, my lady," Dillon whispered and captured Sarah's lips in a slow, burning kiss.

Sarah was roused from dreamless, sated sleep by a knock on her door. Sitting up, she surveyed the room and sighed with resignation, realizing the only clothing she could see belonged to her.

"Oh, well," she thought. "The memory is worth it."

"Room service, ma'am. Your breakfast."

With a puzzled frown, Sarah pulled on her robe and answered the door. "I didn't order breakfast."

"It's definitely for your room, ma'am. I was also asked to make sure you received this," he said, handing her a cream envelope bearing the hotel's logo. Thanking him, Sarah opened the envelope and drew out a single sheet of thick cream paper and a business card.

"I thought you might need the energy. Dillon."

Sarah smiled as she examined the business card. On the front was "Butler Design, Integrated IT Solutions. Dillon Butler, Software Designer." Handwritten on the back were a mobile phone number and the words, "Only if you want to."

Sarah's smile grew as, breakfast forgotten, she reached for the phone.

ZOOSCAPADE
AUNT FANNY

I was on my way to the sea lion exhibit when she swerved into my path, causing me to pull back suddenly. The pail I was carrying sloshed violently. I accidentally splashed her with half a bucket of fish. She took it well, considering.

It was the evening of the Zooscapade, a late summer fund-raising event during which socialites paid large amounts of money to attend a fancy-dress ball that took place on the zoo grounds. I'd spent weeks scrubbing every nook and cranny, every exhibit and shelter until they gleamed. For the last three days I'd strung lights around the trunk of every palm tree in the zoo, so that once the sun set, the place would twinkle like a virgin's eyes. The orchestra was setting up in the bandstand, and our wealthy patrons were slowly beginning to arrive.

The pretty woman whose pink silk ball gown now reeked of raw fish just stared at me. Now, I'm the first to admit I'm not much to look at, but she took it beyond a casual glance. She absorbed my six-foot frame, beakish nose, dung-brown eyes, and short dark hair on the sweep up; my wide, sensuous lips, boyish shape, and middle-aged, masculine bearing on the way down. Her blue eyes registered the stitched name on the pocket of my zookeeper's uniform. *Bud.* Her eyes lingered on my crotch before she suddenly brought them back up to mine, verifying. Yes, I'm a woman.

As I apologized profusely, I drank her in. She looked to be in her early twenties. Her blond hair was swept up into an intricate twist, tendrils curled delicately against both cheeks. Her long, slender neck was draped in a single strand of expensive pearls, with matching earrings dangling from delicate ears. Porcelain skin blushed rose-petal soft, caressing her eyelashes whenever she blinked. Pouty lips, darkened and lined, pursed as she decided how to respond to her sudden drenching.

"I need to change, Bud."

Surprised, I raised my eyebrows, set my lips, and nodded. Beautiful *and* sensible. My kind of woman. "This way." I waved her before me and smiled to myself as I led her to the zoo office, empty now for the evening. I unlocked the door and showed her to the employees' bathroom, then gave her an old zookeeper jumpsuit and worn-out old tennis shoes, figuring it was the least the zoo could do for her.

"I'll have to leave you here. Can you manage?" I asked, looking at my wristwatch and taking the opportunity to flex my biceps. She noticed. "I have a show to do."

"Sure." She turned around and presented me with her back. I took it as a dismissal and turned to leave. "If, Bud," she tossed over her shoulder, causing me to turn back to her, "you'll help me with my zipper, first?"

I felt heat rise to my face. One step brought me up close to her back, and I grasped the delicate fabric between my thick fingers. The scent of her perfume had gotten lost in the smell of fish, so I bent close to her neck and inhaled deeply of her fragrance while pulling the zipper tab slowly down the back of her dress. She caught the front of the strapless gown before it fell away from her body, but her pink bra caught my eye, its lacy front quickly covered back up. A set of impressive breasts rose and fell with each breath. I felt her interest, and she felt mine.

"Thanks," she said, shutting the door of the bathroom in my face. A glance at the clock on the wall forced me to turn and flee.

For the next thirty minutes I put Sammy through his paces, the same barking, horn-honking, flipper-slapping act I worked out with him two years ago. He's an old pro at entertaining and drew loud applause as we ended the set. Exactly on time, the public address system announced the next scheduled performance at the predator birds display. As the elegantly dressed guests drifted away, I finished feeding Sammy and his mate, Sally. They're a friendly pair of sea lions, and we played catch and toss for a few minutes, unaware anyone was watching.

A lone clapping made me look up, and there she was, standing in my old navy blue uniform, legs and sleeves rolled up neatly, her bare feet thrust into my cast-off tennis shoes, which were clearly too big for her. Her jewelry was gone and her hair had been loosened into a curled ponytail. The uniform hugged her curvaceous body in all the right places. A cool breeze kicked up as the lowering sun began to blaze.

"I'm going to be your assistant tonight," she told me, grinning wickedly. "Whatever you do, I'm going to help you." So she'd decided to dump her own kind and go slumming. Game playing? That could be interesting.

"I'm pleased," I answered, figuring this spoiled little rich girl would disappear back into her crowd in a moment. "Surprised, but pleased. I'm feeding the lions next."

Her eyebrows rose, but she stuck with me as I walked into the big cat exhibit. I drew the line at letting her into the back area where I'd be doing the feeding, and left her happily standing before the large glass display windows in the front. As the back panel opened and I slipped meat inside with a long-handled pan, I saw her watching me with rapt attention.

Showing off a little, but telling myself it was to help with the fund-raising, I entered the area that Larry and the three females shared. Linda, Lisa, and Lilly were in good moods, and the crowd that gathered got a good view of the lionesses playing gently with the ball I gave them. Her eyes never left me.

"Very impressive, Bud," she told me when I rejoined her.

"What do I call you?" She'd piqued my curiosity. The sunset was beginning, and the breeze sent the various scents of wild animals scurrying around us.

Grinning at me she answered, "Just call me Kitty," and nodded back at the lions.

I shrugged, and nodded. "Let's go, pretty Kitty."

Next I thought I'd enjoy watching her do a little of the dirty work that goes into tending a zoo, so I took her with me to sweep out the camel display. I spread out the special food I'd prepared earlier in the manger at the back of the outdoor exhibit. As our three camels ambled to their dinner, I motioned for my new friend to come join me. I handed her a large shovel and a bucket, took another set for myself, and set off to sweep up the camel dung. She just laughed and raced me to the piles. We finished in record time. The wealthy patrons enjoying the evening who saw us must have assumed she was on the zoo payroll.

"You're a good sport."

"It's fun. I think I'd like to have your life," she answered ingenuously.

"You have to work hard to get to my status in life." I laughed and plucked at my zoo blue jumpsuit. "Don't you want to rejoin your friends?"

"Not particularly. When do you go off duty?"

I looked at my wristwatch and grinned. "Actually, an hour ago." I looked at her speculatively. "I don't have to be anywhere for at least another hour."

She grinned at me and looked down at herself ruefully. "I need to clean up again." Her even white teeth gleamed in the glow of the strings of tiny lights winking on all around us. The sun had finally set. "Take me back to the office, will you? I need to pick up my things anyway."

Back in the zoo office I left the lights off, navigating through long practice the dark rooms to the big back office. Opening the door of the private bathroom, I flicked the light on and entered first, then quickly washed my hands. As the hot water ran over my hands, she pooled liquid lather from the porcelain dispenser in her hands and started massaging the soap into mine. Our hands worked together under the streaming water as I looked up and saw her beautiful young face next to my homely, middle-aged one in the mirror. As if to reassure me, she leaned over and kissed my neck.

I turned around just as Miss Kitty stepped back and grabbed the front of her blue jumpsuit and yanked. The dozen snaps popped open to below her crotch. She was naked beneath it, revealing large breasts tipped with dark pink nipples and a thatch of curly blond pubic hair. Involuntarily, I sucked in my breath. She was stunning. The strains of "The Blue Danube" danced through the window in the office behind us, the orchestra sounding fine.

Looking directly in my eyes, she reached past me and shut the bathroom light off. We stumbled back in the darkness as she shrugged her shoulders out of the jumpsuit and let it fall to her ankles. She reached out to steady herself on me, and I took her arm, swiftly wrapping my other one around her waist. Since she was bent over trying to kick her feet free, my hand filled with her full, naked breast. My thumb strummed her nipple. I let go of her as she straightened and stepped out of the crumpled jumpsuit, turning to me. Both of my hands dropped to her hips and around to her bottom. I cupped her cheeks and pulled her naked body against me.

My lips found hers, pulling her tongue into my mouth as I patted, lifted, and caressed her bottom. I lowered one hand to the narrow space between her thighs, then brought it swiftly around to her front. My fingers took control of the moment, twirled and tugged at her blond curls, then pushed her fleshy lips apart, quickly finding and circling her clit. She was already wet, so my first finger slid easily into her, making her gasp into my ear. My other arm still cupped her bottom, ready to hold her up if she went slack.

She found her knees and wrapped her arms around my neck, surrendering to my kisses and touches. Her naked body was cradled against my still-clothed one, which gave me a sense of power. I flexed my arm muscles as I thrust a second finger into her, earning another small cry.

Removing my fingers, I abruptly brought them up to her mouth. She opened her swollen lips and sucked them, tasting herself. Her tongue snaking out and around them caused a tidal wave within me.

I pulled the desk chair over with my foot, seated her in it, and twirled it around so she faced me as I stood in the pale light from the decorated palm trees outside the window. Slowly I started popping the snaps on my own uniform, one at a time. My muscular body emerged inch by inch until I stood before her in boxer briefs and a sports bra. Her eyes skimmed my six-pack, then stopped and fixated on the telltale bulge beneath my briefs.

Instead of addressing her curiosity, I raised my arms, enjoying the cut of my biceps. I loved the appreciation I saw in her eyes. Reaching up and over, I pulled off my bra and tossed it aside, knowing my tiny nipples were tight as raisins. I flexed my chest, glad I'm so flat.

She reached for the waistband of my briefs, but I stopped her. Instead, I swung her chair around and stepped between her and the desk. I propped her legs on the desktop on either side of me and spread them wide. Then I squatted.

Her blond bush was inches from my nose, and I smelled perfume. I love when women do that! My nose inhaled as I nuzzled first her curls, then her swollen lips. The tip of my tongue traced the length of her slit, teasing rather than invading. I stopped just above her clit.

"Tell me what you want, Miss Kitty," I commanded, blowing hot breath down on her bottom.

She squirmed in her chair, moaning. Through the open window I heard the elephants trumpeting as the trainer put them through their paces for our elegant guests, which reminded me that the clock was ticking. I blew hot air against her pussy lips, enjoying the clean, fresh scent of her moisture.

"I want you to tickle me." She surprised me again. Playful.

Knowing just what I wanted, I ducked under her leg and disappeared into the bevy of offices, and returned with a large peacock feather in one hand and a zoo scarf in the other. I held out the feather for her to appreciate, then quickly stepped behind her and blindfolded her. I reached over her shoulder and drew the feather softly up her flat belly and along the curves of her breasts. She shivered. I traced her blond curls and tickled the inside of her exposed thighs. I watched the gooseflesh rise on her skin. Swinging the chair around again, I helped her to her feet, letting her stand still, feeling her naked vulnerability. The feather brushed her knees.

"Spread them."

She shifted the weight on her bare feet until her legs parted. So did her lips as her breath escaped raggedly. Her hands seemed unsure of themselves, so I took them both in one of mine behind her back, giving her an anchor and causing her breasts to swell proudly as I tickled them with the peacock feather. Her nipples lengthened and hardened in the cool night air. A moan escaped her. I rewarded her with a kiss.

I tickled her ribs and slender waist, returning again to the nipples for a flick now and again. The velvety tip of the feather dipped between her breasts, up her long, arched neck, and down across her shoulder blades. I kissed the back of her neck as she leaned into my touches, eager to experience more.

Bending her forward over my left arm, I moved the feather teasingly, slowly along her legs until she quivered. I used the feather to tenderly caress the backs of her knees, as well as her ankles. The higher I tickled, the more she responded, so I spent a long moment tickling her bottom, enjoying the sight of her squirming.

I pushed her gently but firmly down and forward until she was bent across the calendar blotter on the desktop, her head pillowed on her arms, and stood directly behind her. Dropping the feather, I put one hand on either of her hips. She moaned, "Yes."

I slapped her bottom once, then twice, two loud cracks that made her jump and could easily be heard through the open window. The blush of heat rose from her pale flesh into my hand and down to my belly. My hand traced the perfect globes of her ass, teasing the sensitive skin. I drew my fingers up against her slit, found and released the moisture held at bay there. I leaned forward and rubbed the crotch of my briefs up against her; the rough cotton kissed her soft wetness.

"More," she groaned, swaying her bottom against my crotch.

My hand rose and fell for a sweet dozen strokes. I alternated cheeks for the first six, then slapped both together in the final six. Twice I paused long enough to trace my rough fingertips over her reddened skin, which gleamed in what light broke through the window. Her eager moans reinforced my slaps, and after the last one, I thrust two fingers deep inside her, drawing a lower and more intense one. "Now," she commanded.

I reached into my briefs, freeing my cock through the front panel. I hadn't anticipated anyone seeing it today; indeed, only a whim had caused me to wear it at all. Usually it's reserved for special dates, but today for some reason I'd felt formal. It's bright blue, but from her vantage I doubt Miss Kitty appreciated that. What she did appreciate was its length and depth, which I know how to use expertly. I slipped deep into her, taking my time and doing the in-and-out dance of easy penetration. The orchestra was playing again, and I let them set the rhythm.

Once firmly ensconced, I raised her to stand by grabbing her breasts and pulling. Soon her head was thrown back onto my shoulder as I turned us both, then leaned back, perching my butt on the desk for support. My fingers milked her breasts softly, rolling her full flesh through my rough fingers, pulling at her nipples until they stretched as tight as my own, which were pressed firmly into her back. Her belly bowed outward as her hips curved back to accommodate my legs between hers.

She was tiny enough for me to lift, and I did so until her weight was balanced on my muscular thighs. I rocked her forward and back on my cock, enjoying the moans escaping her pale throat, stretched tight. My arms supported her, and she relaxed totally into my control. Soon I set a quickening pace to match her breaths. Outside, the loudspeaker announced cocktails for sale by vendors scattered over the grounds. Gourmet delicacies were also available.

Her strong thighs clamped around mine. Both of her nipples became so tender I took to palming them, then massaging her breasts. My hand slipped down to her hip, then around to her clit. My forefinger found it and began a circular motion that complemented the rhythm of my hips. Her hips rocked back and forth on my lap.

Miss Kitty tossed her head back against my shoulder, and I leaned down to lick her neck. As the soft tip of my tongue touched her skin, she spasmed and cried out, grabbing my hips with her hands. The strength of her orgasm racked her until she finished. I slowed and finally stilled, unwilling to interrupt her pleasure. I lowered my legs until her feet touched the ground. She rose off my cock, turned around, and gave me her body to cradle. I held her closely.

Soon she revived and lifted her face to be kissed. My lips covered hers, then explored her eyelids and cheeks. She lowered her head and fastened her lips around one of my nipples. Her tongue flicked me until I gasped, and then she bit me.

I pulled her hair sharply, snapping her head back. She shook her hair free of my fingers and laughed at me. Then her lips pursed as she closed in on my nipple again, sucking it in and nipping at it gently. This time I allowed it.

One of her elegant hands caressed my hip through the fabric of my briefs, finally finding and circling my cock. She began to stroke it with one hand while the other reached inside the fly and dipped low enough to find my opening. I felt her finger invade my space, stopping just at the door as I tensed. She respected my needs and dipped only so far within, then set up her own shallow pumping.

Her lips devoured mine as she thrust her tongue into my mouth and teased mine. She tasted of wine and rose petals. I felt myself melting into her embrace.

I was still leaning against the desk, so she took advantage of being between my legs and pushed them farther apart. Quickly she knelt in front of me and swallowed my cock. I gulped as I watched her mouth surround it, wishing I could feel her lips. Her fingers reached once more into my briefs, one finger reinserting itself while her thumb circled and stroked my clit. I watched her lipsticked mouth moving up and down on my blue cock and pretended.

My swollen clit strained against her talented thumb as she circled and circled patiently. Not far from the office window, people walked by and conversed, their voices dangerously close. My breath came quickly, making my chest rise and fall. The faster her head bobbed up and down on my cock, the faster her thumb strummed my clit. One knuckle swizzled the lips of my cunt, urging me on. I took her head in my hands, running my fingers through that luscious hair, and felt her motion. My hips flexed to help with the thrusting. A searing heat began to spread from the pit of my belly outward.

"Gawd!" I bawled as my orgasm shook me. One wave after another rocked me as her motion stayed the same. She drew more out of me than I'm used to, and it took me a moment to recover. By that time she was tucking my cock back into my briefs, leaning forward to plant a kiss on my fly. She rose into my arms and hugged me. I swept her up and off her feet, kissing her deeply. From outside I heard the hired announcer begin the scheduled festivities. It was already ten o'clock.

I kissed Miss Kitty on the lips hurriedly, then bolted into the bathroom. I washed myself quickly, making sure to remove any trace of lipstick from my face and neck.

"I've got to go, honey," I growled at my new lover as she stood in the doorway watching me. She leisurely pulled the blue jumpsuit back on, snapping it up until only the line of her cleavage showed. She picked up the bundle of her ruined pink silk dress and folded it to carry.

"What's your hurry?" She leaned against the bathroom door frame as she deftly wound her long hair back into its ponytail. I scrambled past her and fumbled with my sports bra, getting it over my head and tugging it into place. Stepping quickly to the closet door in the corner, I opened it and removed my tuxedo.

"What?" Miss Kitty stared as I thrust my feet one at a time into the trousers, quickly fastened the pearl buttons of the white pleated shirt, and snapped my purple cummerbund into place. I sat in the same chair in which I had her spread before me just moments earlier and yanked on black silk socks before shoving my feet into a pair of black loafers. I rose and donned the black tuxedo jacket, then pulled a purple bow tie from its pocket and snapped it easily in place.

"Come with me," I urged. I swept her before me as I hurried to the bandstand. Leaving her in the crowd, I advanced through the people and climbed the stairs. When I glanced back, I saw her staring dumbfounded as the announcer introduced me.

"And now, here is our Chief Zoologist, Dr. Rose 'Bud' Sayers." He stood back and led the applause as I took my place center stage. I looked down into Miss Kitty's beautiful upturned face.

"I'd like to thank you for coming," I said, looking straight at her. "It's generous contributions like yours that keep our zoo running effectively."

She winked at me.

STOLEN MOMENTS
RADCLYFFE

I was thirty-five minutes early. Thirty-five minutes to sit on the side of the bed—fully clothed, my hands fisted on my thighs—watching the door. There were at least a million reasons why she wouldn't come. Something as simple as a last-minute change in the duty roster could leave me waiting here for hours.

My civilian clothes felt wrong against my skin. It's not as if I never wore them, but I never felt entirely *me* unless I was in uniform. Even the part of me that everyone said didn't *belong* in uniform—part of the very heart of me—felt right at home in dress blues or khakis. And the other piece of my heart wore the uniform too, except for those few hours every other week or so when we took the chance that if we were both away at the same time, no one would notice. Then, we would shed the symbols of our pride and our duty in order to express our love. Even that concession was not enough to protect us, but it was a risk we were willing to take.

The first time I ever saw her was on the parade ground, and she was all spit-and-polish shiny—shoulders back, head high, short, thick, sun-bleached hair barely contained by her cap. One look and I knew. I knew that she, with her cocky grin and her intense dark eyes, was part of my future. I didn't know when, and I didn't know how. I just knew it would be. After that, I waited. She saw me watching her, and I saw her watching me back. Quick glances across the mess hall; the spark of recognition that lit her face when I walked into a room; the smile that lingered just a few seconds longer than it should have when we passed in the hall. Waiting and watching, agony and ecstasy.

When I couldn't manage to lose myself in work, she was all I thought about. I thought about the way she moved, all easy grace and self-assurance; I thought about the way she laughed, an amazingly free and joyous sound; I thought about the way she turned and stood very still, her eyes on mine for the barest of seconds that seemed like a lifetime. I thought about the way her skin would feel beneath my fingertips, against my mouth, on my tongue. I thought about how she'd smell—fresh and clean like early morning rain and then, after we made love, thick and warm and rich, like a summer night at sundown. I thought about her. I thought about her. Until there was no difference between my dreams and my days.

"You have the saddest look in your eyes," she said one afternoon as we stood slightly apart from the others, waiting for a briefing. "What are you thinking about?"

"You," I said before I could take back the word.

"And that makes you sad?"

Her tone was so gentle I wanted to weep. Instead, I smiled and shook my head. "No. That makes me happy."

"Then what is that I just saw in your eyes?"

We only had a minute. A minute before the connection that felt so right would be destroyed. I felt the pressure of something precious slipping away, and I spoke the truth. "Wishing. That was me wishing for you."

Her dark brown eyes grew even darker, but I could not read beyond their shadows. Her lips parted, and a soft sigh danced between us. "You shouldn't."

"I can't help it. I'm sorry."

"I don't want you to be sorry."

She never moved, but I remember to this day the sweet sensation of her fingertips gliding over my cheek. "I want you to tell me what you wish for."

"Don't you know?"

Her eyes danced then, alive with joy. "I do. But I want to hear you tell me."

"When?"

"Soon."

Soon turned out to be weeks later. Weeks filled with glances that now, looking back, I know would have given us away had anyone chanced to notice. Hunger stalked the air between us. I went to bed thirsting for her touch and twisted through the long hot hours of the night, soaking my sheets with the sweat of unrequited lust and desperate, failed attempts at relief. The hollows beneath her eyes matched the aching void within my chest until finally, we did the only thing we could.

"Friday night," she murmured as she passed me a stack of requisition forms. When she transferred the files, she pressed a metal object into my hand. "The Walton. Ten o'clock."

"Are you sure?" My stomach was suddenly queasy as I pocketed the key. What if…what if I turned out to be a disappointment after she risked everything?

"I'm dying for you."

The whispered words nearly brought me to my knees. "Yes. Yes. I'll be there."

Waiting. I remember waiting that night, too. I walked around the block a half dozen times before I mustered the courage to go inside. The hotel lobby seemed to stretch for a hundred miles. I was the only person there except for the desk clerk, whose eyes followed me knowingly on my trek to the elevator. Once in the room, I didn't know what to do. I was too nervous to sit, too unsteady to pace. The sound of a key in the lock brought my heart to a standstill.

And then she was inside with me, and there were no more questions. She smiled and so did I. I met her halfway and put my hands to her face as she brought hers to my shoulders. I kissed her and she kissed me back. And then we stood for a long time, arms around each other, holding so tightly that we didn't even sway. I listened to her breathe, felt the timbre of her heartbeat against my chest, smelled her shampoo—tried to memorize every sensation that was her. Knowing I would need those memories to last, to live on, perhaps forever.

"You're here," she murmured.

"Yes."

As I did all the nights I lay awake aching for her touch, I closed my eyes and watched her face grow fierce with pleasure. I took a breath and smelled her hair. I brushed my thumb over my fingertips and felt the silky smoothness of her skin. Immersed in her, I waited.

The scratch of metal on metal drew me back and I looked around the strange but familiar room. I held my breath, as I always did, until the heavy wooden door swung open and she was inside with me, safe.

"You're here," she said softly, as she always does.

"Yes."

Tonight, she unbuttoned her blouse as she crossed the room. By the time she stood in front of me, she was naked from the waist up. She curved her fingers behind my head and led me to her, pressing my face against her abdomen. I licked her skin as I circled her hips with my arms. She settled both hands in my hair and stroked my neck and shoulders as I caressed her with my mouth.

Finally, I tilted my head back and swept my gaze up her body. Her breasts rose and fell rapidly, counterpoint to the pulse that beat beneath the arched column of her neck. The pink nipples were already swollen and hard with arousal. Her pupils were solid black disks beneath heavy lids.

Watching her watch me, as I had done for so many long, lonely months, I worked the button loose on her waistband and slid down the zipper. Her thumbs dug into the muscles at the angle between my neck and shoulders and her thighs shook. I caught the edges of her panties in my fingers and slid them down along with her slacks. When she stepped free of the garments, she left her shoes behind as well. Nude now, she stood between my parted thighs, swaying slightly. I held her gaze as wordlessly I skimmed both hands up the inside of her legs to frame her sex, crowned by a darker shade of gold than those sun-kissed strands above.

I did not touch her. I did not need to. She was ready for me, rising full and proud, beckoning my mouth. Her lids flickered once as I circled my lips around her clitoris, pulling her in, and she leaned more heavily against me, trembling. Here in this room, time meant nothing. All that mattered was the flush on her neck, and the dew of desire on her skin, and the flood of arousal on my lips. I felt her heart beat inside my mouth as I watched the echo in her throat. She tensed, pushing against me, bruising my lips. Her gaze was fierce as she prepared to come, swelling and pounding against my mouth. Only then did I fill her, letting my hand take some of her weight as she settled down upon my fingers, stretching to take me in.

I pulled at her with my lips, devoured her with my tongue, caressed the tight muscles inside until her lips parted with a high, thin cry. Still, she kept her eyes open, fixed on my face as her orgasm broke over her. I stopped breathing and grew light-headed, but I wanted nothing—not even the sound of my own breath moving in my chest—to dampen her cries of pleasure.

I would live on those sounds for weeks, feasting on the beauty of her passion, filling the hungry places in my soul with the memory of her pleasure. I would have kept my mouth on her, would have made her come again, if she hadn't nearly fallen as the crushing climax released her. When she sagged against me, I rose and held her close, murmuring words of love so inadequate I nearly wept at my impotence. With my mouth on hers, catching the last sighs of her release on my tongue, I eased down onto the bed with her in my arms. Side by side, we lay gently touching.

"You're here," she whispered at last.

I smiled and kissed the wistfulness from her eyes. "Yes."

"They're never enough, these moments."

I pressed my fingers to her lips and then replaced them with my mouth. I had no answer, only my kisses. Those I gave freely, along with my heart, until her sadness turned to desire, and desire to demand. She pushed me over, stripped me bare, and took what was already hers. When she was over me, inside me, there was no time at all. No past, no future, no moments to steal or lose. Only us, joined—one love, one truth.

CONTRIBUTORS

SAGGIO (SAGE) AMANTE is a fun-loving and passionate raconteur who lives, loves, and writes in the deep South. She enjoys work, pleasure, culinary adventures, pleasure, Sapphic fiction, pleasure, Sapphic poetry, and pleasure. One of her favorite quotes is by Margaret Mead: "Always remember that you are absolutely unique. Just like everyone else."

LYNN AMES is the best-selling author of *The Price of Fame* and *The Cost of Commitment* and a contributing author to *Infinite Pleasures: An Anthology of Lesbian Erotica, Telltale Kisses,* and *Call of the Dark.* An award-winning former broadcast journalist, Ms. Ames is a nationally recognized speaker and CEO of her own public relations firm. For additional information, short stories, etc., please visit her Web site at www.lynnames.com or e-mail her at authorlynnames@cox.net.

AUNT FANNY is a professional storyteller, a graduated fellow of the Greater Valley Writing Project, and a former guest speaker for the California Reader's Association at Asilomar. She now lives in St. Paul, Minnesota, with her Beloved, whom she married at San Francisco's City Hall. She's turned her hand to writing and has one novel making the rounds of publishing houses. Another is under way.

SYLVIE AVANTE is a jazz singer who has performed on cruise ships around the world. When she is not performing, she likes to write about her experiences. *Tour Guide* is her first published work.

KIM BALDWIN lives in a cabin in the north woods. She began writing fiction after a twenty-year career in journalism. Romance, nature, and adventure are key themes in her stories. *Overdue* revisits a couple introduced in *A Slice of Heaven,* a short story on her Web site at www.geocities.com/woodsbard. She has two books in print with Bold Strokes Books: *Hunter's Pursuit, Author's Edition* and the new romance *Force of Nature.*

GEORGIA BEERS was born and raised in Rochester, New York, where she still lives with her partner, Bonnie (bless her patient heart,

Bonnie has put up with Georgia for over a decade—nobody knows quite how). She happily divides her time between sales and writing. In addition to several short stories, she has published two novels with Regal Crest Enterprises, *Turning the Page* (2001) and *Thy Neighbor's Wife* (2003). Visit her Web site at www.georgiabeers.com.

RONNIE BLACK lives in the desert Southwest, where she pursues writing as well as many other forms of creativity. Learning, reading, traveling, and playing sports are a few of her other sources of entertainment. She also relishes in being an aunt and thoroughly enjoys the quality time spent with family and friends. Her first novel *In Too Deep* is available from Bold Strokes Books (2005).

GUN BROOKE hails from Sweden, where she resides with her family. Crediting her writing origins to fan fiction, she is the author of *Course of Action* (Bold Strokes Books, 2005). When not busy editing *Supreme Constellation: Book 1—Protector of the Realm*, due December 2005 from Bold Strokes Books, Gun maintains her own Web site, where she posts her stories and computer graphics: www.gbrooke-diction.com.

JESSICA CASAVANT is the author of the Boston Friends series, which includes *Twist of Fate*, *Walking Wounded*, and *Imperfect Past*. She can be reached at cdjc@sympatico.ca.

J.C. CHEN wrote ScullySlash in a previous life under the ridiculous pseudonym Fatladysing. While not the most aesthetically flattering of pen names, that alter ego did manage to produce four Spooky Award–winning stories, including first place in 2001 for "The Sketch." Recently, J.C. quit her Real Job as a management consultant to form a film production company with her two best friends. Their first feature film, *Red Doors*, will be making the film festival circuit in 2005.

LESLEY DAVIS lives in the West Midlands of England with her American partner, Cindy. She is devoted to writing fantasy/romance for lesbians who want heroes. Her published works are available from www.WindstormCreative.com.

KENYA DEVOREAUX is a lover of beauty in all Her forms. She is a femme-oriented femme lesbian who has found the means with which to inspire other lesbians, but still searches for the woman with whom she can share all that is inspiring. The meaning of life for her would be to traipse the landscape of art and politics, sword in one hand and her partner through time in the other.

CLIO JONES is a librarian and smut writer from Cape Cod, Massachusetts. She enjoys good shoes, strong coffee, red wine, and keeping the library quiet. Clio has published online at kinkygurl. com and is making her print debut here. Clio may be reached at cjones@bust.com.

LC JORDAN is a thirty-seven-year-old Midwestern woman who, while new to writing fiction, has had a lifelong passion for reading. Having inherited a love of books and music from both parents, she grew up composing songs and poems as a hobby. Crediting Radclyffe and the online world of fanfic as inspiration, she recently began writing the stories that kept floating just below the surface of her mind. The search for that perfect alchemy of words is still in the Bunsen burner stage.

KARIN KALLMAKER is best known for more than fifteen lesbian romance novels, from *In Every Port* to the award-winning *Maybe Next Time*. She recently plunged into the world of erotica with *All the Wrong Places* and numerous short stories. In addition, she has a half dozen science fiction, fantasy, and supernatural lesbian novels (*Seeds of Fire, Christabel* et al) under the pen name Laura Adams. Karin and her partner will celebrate their twenty-eighth anniversary in 2005, and are Mom and Moogie to two children. She is descended from Lady Godiva, a fact that pleases her and seems to surprise no one.

EEVIE KEYS is an aspiring violinist whose first dream just happened to be writing. This blonde is madly in love with her fiancée and will soon be married to the most beautiful woman in the world, providing college doesn't kill her first. Her poetry has been published in various and sundry magazines and she uses dashes like Emily Dickinson… We promise, it's not a coincidence. See more of her poetic-ness at www.Oceanid.org.

MARIE LYN'S erotica has appeared in cleansheets.com, Desdmona. com and *The Best Women's Erotica of 2005*. She studied English literature and creative writing at the University of Michigan, and her "traditional" fiction has been published in *Xylem* and *The Sarah Lawrence Review*. She currently lives in a lovely apartment in East Harlem, New York, where she enjoys taking long walks and listening to her iPod.

SHERRY MICHAELS is one of those night-owl creatives living in the land of the great Dust Bowl. When not working furiously to feed her two dogs, one cat, and iTunes habit, she often dreams of a house in the country, a couple of horses, and having an intelligent and beautiful girlfriend by her side, not necessarily in that order.

CLIODHNA O'BANNION lives in Seattle, where she works as a journalist and publishes in a variety of forms. She enjoys spending time with her girlfriend and lives comfortably with two cats (and somewhat uncomfortably with a long list of things to do). Her passions include bicycling, watching Euro pro bicycle racing, reading, the night sky, and orca watching.

MEGHAN O'BRIEN is a twenty-six-year-old software developer who lives in Brighton, Michigan. She's happily domesticated with her partner of over six years, Ty, and their many cats. She loves video games, writing, and, of course, women. Her first novel is *Infinite Loop* (2005).

KAREN PERRY lives happily in the shadows of Tennessee's Great Smoky Mountains. When not writing or romping through the woods, she enjoys photography and slaving away in her flower gardens. Life is shared with her partner of eleven years and their two dogs. Professionally, Karen is an advocate for students with learning differences. This is her first published piece.

RM PRYOR was born Rhiannon-Marie Pryor in 1979 in Tamworth, New South Wales, Australia. Currently living in Newcastle, she moved out of home at fifteen to fuck up, flip out, have fun, and find love. She thinks she succeeded.

RADCLYFFE, having practiced surgery for thirty years while writing for pleasure "on the side," established Bold Strokes Books, Inc, a lesbian publishing company, in 2004 and retired from the practice of medicine to write and publish full-time in May 2005. She is the author of numerous short stories and over twenty novels.

JEAN STEWART was born and raised in the suburbs of Philadelphia, Pennsylvania. She loves books, music, dogs, and people who laugh. She earned her living as a teacher and coach in her early years, but left education to pursue a writing career. She lives near Seattle, in the beautiful Pacific NW with her partner Susie, three badly behaved dogs, and a reclusive Maine Coon cat named Emily Dickinson. She has published five Isis books and a stand-alone novel, and has had stories published in numerous anthologies.

RENÉE STRIDER is a researcher, translator, and editor who lives with her partner and their dog on a big honking lake in Canada. Her interests include languages, history, and art history. Occasionally she writes articles about art and lesbian fiction. This is her first lesbian fiction submitted for publication. Write her at reneelf@cogeco.ca.

T. SZYMANSKI is the author of the Motor City Thrillers/Brett Higgins Mysteries, including the Lammy finalist *When Evil Changes Face*. She's also edited *Back to Basics: A Butch/Femme Anthology* and *Call of the Dark: Erotic Lesbian Tales of the Supernatural*. She has shorts in more than a dozen anthologies and has a novella in the notorious *Once Upon a Dyke: New Exploits of Fairy Tale Lesbians*. An award-winning playwright, she's ridiculously proud of using the word *damselling* in her novella *A Butch in Fairy Tale Land*.

KI THOMPSON states, "This is the first time I've ever written fiction, so any and all feedback is appreciated (MyMuses@comcast.net). I never dreamed I could or would write something like this, and the fact that I have done so at all is because of two people. Thank you, Radclyffe, for the encouragement and honesty. And to Kathi, thank you for believing in me."

SASKIA WALKER is a British author who has had short erotic fiction published on both sides of the pond. She has selections in *Seductions: Tales of Erotic Persuasion* (Dutton); *Sugar and Spice, More Wicked Words* and *Wicked Words 5* and *8* (Black Lace); *Naughty Stories from A to Z, 3* and *4* and *Naked Erotica* (Pretty Things Press); *Taboo* and *Three Way* (Cleis Press); and *Sextopia* (Circlet Press). Her first full-length erotic novel, *Along for the Ride*, is due for publication in 2005. www.saskiawalker.co.uk.

KATHRYN WOLF fell into fanfic literally by accident several years ago and, after receiving much encouragement, began to write it. She states, "I have always wanted to write, and this seemed the best way for me to pay my dues, as it were. I have several stories posted to the Net, though time and real life have been against me, so two remain unfinished."

Other Books Available From Bold Strokes Books

Force of Nature by Kim Baldwin. Wind. Fire. Ice. Love. Nothing for Gable McCoy and Erin Richards seems to go smoothly. From the tornado that sets its sights on them to the perils they face as volunteer firefighters, the forces of nature conspire to bring them closer to danger—and closer to each other. (1-933110-23-6)

In Too Deep by Ronica Black. When undercover work requires working under the covers, danger is an uninvited bedfellow. Homicide cop Erin McKenzie embarks on the journey of her life…with love and danger hot on her heels. (1-933110-17-1)

Stolen Moments: Erotic Interludes 2, edited by Stacia Seaman and Radclyffe. Love on the run, in the office, in the shadows…women stealing time from ordinary life to make passion a priority, if only for a moment. Fast, furious, and almost too hot to handle. (1-933110-16-3)

Course of Action by Gun Brooke. Actress Carolyn Black desperately wants the starring role in an upcoming film produced by Annelie Peterson, a wealthy publisher with a mysterious past. How far is Carolyn prepared to go for the dream part of a lifetime? And just how far will Annelie bend her principles in the name of desire? (1-933110-22-8)

Justice Served by Radclyffe. The hunt for an informant in the ranks draws Lieutenant Rebecca Frye, her lover Dr. Catherine Rawlings, and Officer Dellon Mitchell into a deadly game of hide-and-seek with an underworld kingpin who traffics in human souls. (1-933110-15-5)

Rangers at Roadsend by Jane Fletcher. After nine years in the Rangers, dealing with thugs and wild predators, Sergeant Chip Coppelli has learned to spot trouble coming, and that is exactly what she sees in her new recruit, Katryn Nagata. But even so, Chip was not expecting murder. The Celaeno series. (1-933110-28-7)

Distant Shores, Silent Thunder by Radclyffe. Ex-lovers, would-be lovers, and old rivals find their paths unwillingly entwined when Drs. KT O'Bannon and Tory King—and the women who love them—are forced to examine the boundaries of love, friendship, and the ties that transcend time. (1-933110-08-2)

Hunter's Pursuit by Kim Baldwin. A raging blizzard, a remote mountain hideaway, and more than one killer for hire set a scene for disaster—or desire—when reluctant assassin Katarzyna Demetrious rescues a stranger and unwittingly exposes her heart. (1-933110-09-0)

The Walls of Westernfort by Jane Fletcher. All Temple Guard Natasha Ionadis wants is to serve the Goddess, and she volunteers eagerly for a dangerous mission to infiltrate a band of rebels. But once she is away from the temple, the issues are no longer so simple, especially in light of her attraction to one of the rebels. Is it too late to work out what she really wants from life? (1-933110-24-4)

Change Of Pace: *Erotic Interludes* by Radclyffe. Twenty-five hot-wired encounters guaranteed to spark more than just your imagination. Erotica as you've always dreamed of it. (1-933110-07-4)

Fated Love by Radclyffe. Amidst the chaos and drama of a busy emergency room, two women must contend not only with the fragile nature of life, but also with the mysteries of the heart and the irresistible forces of fate. (1-933110-05-8)

Justice in the Shadows by Radclyffe. In a shadow world of secrets, lies, and hidden agendas, Detective Sergeant Rebecca Frye and her lover, Dr. Catherine Rawlings, join forces once again in the elusive search for justice. (1-933110-03-1)

shadowland by Radclyffe. In a world on the far edge of desire, two women are drawn together by power, passion, and dark pleasures. An erotic romance. (1-933110-11-2)

Love's Masquerade by Radclyffe. Plunged into the often indistinguishable realms of fiction, fantasy, and hidden desires, Auden Frost discovers a shifting landscape that will force her to question everything she has believed to be true about herself and the nature of love. (1-933110-14-7)

Beyond the Breakwater by Radclyffe. One Provincetown summer three women learn the true meaning of love, friendship, and family. Second in the Provincetown Tales. (1-933110-06-6)

Tomorrow's Promise by Radclyffe. One timeless summer, two very different women discover the power of passion to heal and the promise of hope that only love can bestow. (1-933110-12-0)

Love's Tender Warriors by Radclyffe. Two women who have accepted loneliness as a way of life learn that love is worth fighting for and a battle they cannot afford to lose. (1-933110-02-3)

Love's Melody Lost by Radclyffe. A secretive artist with a haunted past and a young woman escaping a life that proved to be a lie find their destinies entwined. (1-933110-00-7)

Safe Harbor by Radclyffe. A mysterious newcomer, a reclusive doctor, and a troubled gay teenager learn about love, friendship, and trust during one tumultuous summer in Provincetown. First in the Provincetown Tales. (1-933110-13-9)

Above All, Honor by Radclyffe. The first in the Honor series introduces single-minded Secret Service Agent Cameron Roberts and the woman she is sworn to protect—Blair Powell, the daughter of the president of the United States. First in the Honor series. (1-933110-04-X)

Love & Honor by Radclyffe. The president's daughter and her security chief are faced with difficult choices as they battle a tangled web of Washington intrigue for...love and honor. Third in the Honor series. (1-933110-10-4)

Honor Guards by Radclyffe. In a journey that begins on the streets of Paris's Left Bank and culminates in a wild flight for their lives, the president's daughter and those who are sworn to protect her wage a desperate struggle for survival. Fourth in the Honor series. (1-933110-01-5)